Elusive Echoes

Kay Springsteen

δ

Dingbat Publishing

ELUSIVE ECHOES
Echoes of Orson's Folly, Book 2
Copyright © 2011 by Kay Springsteen
ISBN-10: 1940520207
ISBN-13: 978-1-940520-20-9

First edition 2011 Astraea Press LLC
Second edition 2014 Dingbat Publishing

Published by Dingbat Publishing
Humble, Texas

Back cover photo © 2008 Daniel Norton, user Danorton on
Wikimedia Commons. Image entitled "Bluebonnets in a field
adjacent to the UT Brackenridge apartments on Lake Austin
Blvd in Austin, Texas"

Dedication: First, this is for my Lord and Savior, Jesus Christ, who continues to inspire me to fly even as He shelters me beneath His wings.

Second, to my childhood friend, Jeanne Ledingham Theunissen, not only for her endless hours of patiently proofing my work and brainstorming, but for her steadfast friendship, which has surpassed time and distance and continues to prove that the true love of best friends overcomes both. Though we came from different families, we both understand the meaning of sisterhood with one another.

Third, to Carol Horn, Jeanne's mom, one of the most loving mothers I've ever met and a second mom to me. She took me under her wing the way Christ takes us all to Him, and she never gave up on me. She has been a huge influence in the Christian faith I have today.

Prologue

Twenty-two years earlier

Sean sat on a big gray rock overlooking the camp. For days he'd watched the wranglers round up the cattle and drive the calves into chutes. The poor babies didn't know hot irons waited there, which would brand them with marks that told who they belonged to. Everyone said it didn't really hurt them but they always cried. And one time when he looked at his mom she had tears in her eyes, too. It also stank when the brand was burned into the hide and the smell made him sick at his stomach.

His Aunt Alice told him that was just ranch life and he'd best get used to it because he'd be doing it soon enough. He didn't like Aunt Alice. She was creepy. But his mom wanted him to be polite so he listened when Aunt Alice talked to him and never gave her any backtalk.

He could ride a horse. He'd been riding since before he could remember. But his dad said he had to wait another year, when he would be eight, before he could help round up the cattle. So Sean just sat and watched.

The rounding up and branding had stopped suddenly after lunch the day before, though, with a lot of yelling and scurrying, when his brother, Ryan, had returned to the camp yelling for their dad. Then everyone with a horse had ridden off into the hills really fast.

Everyone except Sean.

They'd all been gone a long time. But Sean had sat on the rock and waited, because that was what his mom had told him to do just before she rode off to find some lost cows. The back of his neck had tickled like ants were crawling there and he hadn't liked that much. But still he sat.

It had been dark when his father came for him. His daddy's face had been very sad as he'd told Sean that his mother wasn't coming home. There had been an accident and the river had taken her away. Sean had asked if she would be back the next day instead, and his dad had hugged him hard and said his mom was in Heaven and couldn't come home ever again.

Later, Ryan had brought him a hotdog and some beans. He'd even cut the hotdog into pieces and mixed it in with the beans the way Mom had always done it. Ryan had sat with Sean for a long time. He hadn't cried, but he was sad. He'd said that their mom was dead, but she'd wanted Sean to know she loved him.

Ry had helped Sean get his sleeping bag ready for the night, and then he'd lain next to him talking about the stars the way their mom always did. Sean hadn't fallen asleep, and he didn't think his brother had, either.

After he ate the oatmeal Ryan made him for breakfast, Sean had climbed back on the big gray rock, because that's where his mom had put him.

The branding was still stopped. The people riding out didn't laugh and joke as they usually did, and when they came back to the camp, they didn't bring any cattle.

"What do you think's happening?" A little girl with hair the color of sunshine climbed onto the rock next to him and sat down, dangling her legs over the edge.

"Ry says they're looking for my mom because she fell in the river." Sean turned and looked at the girl.

He'd seen her around with her father, Mr. Mitchell. Sometimes she sat in front of him on his horse. Her hair was really bright yellow, kind of like Sean's own hair. But his skin was dark and hers was very white, like the sun on a hot day. Her big blue eyes made Sean think of the sky. She was little and delicate like the china doll his mom had on her dresser at home.

Sean couldn't stop looking at her.

"My name's Melanie." She kicked her feet back and forth. "Do you think they'll find your mama soon?"

Sean lifted one shoulder. "I don't know. Ry says she's dead."

"Oh." Melanie looked at him. "When my cat was dead, we put her in a box and buried her in Mama's rose garden."

"I saw a dead calf once." Sean stared out over the prairie. "It was just layin' there. Its nose was blue and it looked kind of flat, like an old balloon. Dad called Mr. Tom and he put it on a truck and took it away."

"Oh." She picked up a stick and threw it off the rock into some prairie grass. "What do you think they'll do with your mama?"

Sean shrugged again. "Dunno. I just wish — wish she could come home again." His chin quivered and his eyes filled with tears, and he clenched his jaw tight. He didn't want to cry in front of Melanie. She'd probably tease him if he did.

But she moved closer to him and put one of her thin arms over his shoulders. They sat like that for a while. Her body was warm and he didn't feel so alone with her there.

"Look!" Melanie pointed excitedly toward a bluff not far away.

A big bay horse stood still as stone, staring at them, head up, ears pricked forward. The only movement came from the light breeze whispering through the dark mane and tail.

Sean thought he'd never seen anything so powerful. As if to agree with him, the horse snorted and tossed his head, then wheeled around and left the bluff.

Melanie's innocent smile lit her pale blue eyes from the inside. "I want to ride a horse like that someday. I bet it'd be fun going real fast on his back."

That was when Sean decided he liked Melanie with the sunshiny hair even more than he liked horses.

Chapter One

Present day

The letter sat next to the register behind the bar. It might as well have been a rattlesnake. It bore a sender's name but no return address, though it was postmarked in Des Moines, Iowa. *Denny DeVayne.* Mel couldn't remember if she'd ever seen her brother's name written out before. She had seen his freakishly neat handwriting, and had recognized that instantly. But he was part of the life she'd walked away from the second she'd turned eighteen. More than a decade had gone by and he'd never once attempted to get in touch.

No, nothing good could be in that letter, and she didn't want to open it. So, treating it like the snake it reminded her of, Mel went out of her way to avoid it. She should just chuck it in the trash and be done with it the way she'd been done with that life.

But something stopped her. So it sat. Later she would take it up to her apartment and put it with the other unopened letters, the ones she'd received since early May.

* * *

With a whistle on his lips, Sean's step was light as he walked the short distance from stable to house. It had been a good day. If he was lucky it would be an even better evening. And as long as he got his sorry tail to Valentine's where Mel was tending bar, all signs pointed to the promise of *very* lucky.

Rounding the corner of the house, he pulled up short at the sight of the gawky redheaded teen leaning against the railing on the back step. He propped his chin in one hand while he used the other to fiddle with an MP3 player. When he saw Sean, he pulled out his earbuds.

Tinny voices and a heavy metallic beat blasted from the tiny speakers, painting the insane image of an all-cockroach rock band. He raised an eyebrow. "Kid, you're gonna go deaf."

"Hi, Sean." Ricky's nervous laugh accompanied a wary glance at the kitchen window. "You sound just like Da— ah, Justin."

Sean suppressed his smile at the kid's near slip of the tongue. Though they weren't related by blood, he'd settled into the role of Ricky's big brother over the past year and a half, and it felt pretty good. The boy's mother wasn't in a position to take care of him, and his grandparents had rejected him. Too bad for them. They didn't know what they were missing. But their loss was the McGee family's gain.

"Get locked out?" asked Sean.

Ricky sent another look up at the window as two deep furrows plowed themselves across his forehead. "They were doing it again. I didn't want to go in."

Sean sighed. He didn't have to ask who "they" were or what they were doing.

Right on cue, the clatter of cookware being slammed together filtered through the glass. Sean shied away from the back of the house in case the sound was followed by something heavy exploding through the window.

"Dang it! I don't need a babysitter!"

He flinched at the angry feminine voice. Sandy, currently the sole feminine touch at the Cross MC ranch, was usually slow to anger. He didn't have to ask who she was yelling at. Only one person ever pissed her off that much.

"I'd just feel better if you weren't out here alone." And there he was — Sean's brother, Ryan, trying to placate with a calm tone.

Sean grimaced and glanced at Ricky. "They been at it long?"

The boy lifted his too-thin shoulders and heaved a huge sigh before he settled into a resigned slouch. "Since before I got home from work about ten minutes ago."

The sound of breaking glass was followed by an angry shriek. "Oh! You are such a bossy *jackass!*"

A new voice entered the fray. "What in Sam Hill are you two doing in here?"

"Great. Now they're on Dad's radar. I don't want to go in there, either." Sean cocked his head and studied Ricky. The kid's face was crowded with a blend of angst and confusion only a teenager could survive. It was probably hard enough being a kid of just seventeen without wondering if his happy home was going to remain that way. Especially when the boy hadn't had anything close to a happy home until he'd been almost sixteen. Sean shot him a conspiratorial grin. "If I show you the alternative entrance, do you promise not to use it for sneaking out at night?"

Relief washed some of the anxiety from Ricky's features as he gave an emphatic nod. He swept his hand along his white Western shirt and black denim jeans, the unofficial uniform for his job as busboy at Valentine's Bar and Grill. "I just want to get out of these geeky clothes so I can chill."

Unable to resist the big-brother-sized temptation to tease, Sean tilted his head the other way. "I don't know…" Then he grinned again, because he really did know. Ricky was a good kid who tended to hang at home rather than go out and get in trouble. Sean himself had raised more Cain as a kid than Ricky ever did.

More clattering came from the kitchen, followed by Sandy's irate voice. "But I'm *fine*."

"Come on." Sean led Ricky to the far side of the house.

The cottonwood tree had been standing since before Sean was born. It now soared close to a hundred feet with an impressive canopy that spread like an umbrella over the southern exposure of the house. That just happened to be the side Sean's bedroom window faced. And one of the tree's branches just happened to be growing right outside that window. Which made it very effective as an alternative to using the door. Several occasions had arisen during Sean's teenaged years when he'd experienced the need to sneak in after curfew.

A burst of nostalgia shot through him as he remembered how it had never done any good. Every time he'd made the climb to his window in the dark, he'd invariably snuck into his room to find his father lounging on his bed waiting for him. And one time in the middle of winter he'd come home to find Justin had nailed his window shut. After that, he'd taken his dad's advice to use the phone when he was going to be late, even if it did make him look uncool.

The memories faded but the pleasure remained. However, they still had a house to get into. They stood beneath the cottonwood, with Ricky sending a dubious look along its trunk toward the second floor. Sean grinned. Time to pass the baton.

Motioning Ricky over, Sean crouched and cupped his hands beneath the lowest branch. "I'll give you a boost."

"Ahh..." Ricky hesitated, sending another glance up. "I've never climbed a tree."

It was always the little things that proved the most telling. The little things that showed this kid hadn't had anything close to a normal childhood. Every time one of those reminders popped to the surface, Sean felt the need to choke the living shit out of someone. Starting with Brody MacKay and his bitch of a wife, Alice.

Not the time. Shoving the images to the black part of his soul, Sean only shrugged. "Time to learn. See that lowest branch there? Grab onto that, wrap your knee around it, and pull yourself up. Then look for the next highest branch and do the same thing."

Ricky placed a foot in Sean's hands and accepted the boost. The kid shimmied to the next branch like a natural.

"Sean, what are you doing out here?" The too-shrill voice of his sister-in-law was out of her normal character and somewhat akin to having shards of glass shoved beneath his fingernails.

The smile that had formed while watching Ricky popped like a balloon. He tried to bring it back, but he wasn't feeling it. Slowly, he turned around. Maybe she wouldn't notice. "Hi, Sandy."

Fixing him with a knowing glare, she folded her arms over her chest and rested them on an enormous belly.

Morbid fascination drew his gaze to the mound. Man, had she gotten bigger since breakfast? And was it... *moving?* Sean's stomach did a little flip of its own and pregnant cow references knocked all the good words from his brain. "Wow! You're looking really great."

She stared at him in stony silence until he looked away. "You didn't answer my question. What are you doing back here?"

"I was just checking on some — things."

"Checking on teaching Ricky how to climb in your window?"

Busted. Sean tried his most engaging smile. When she only glared at him, he gave up and sighed. "Okay, when I came in from the stable, he was just sitting out back because you and Ry were—" Cancel that! Too late; no other words offered themselves as a sacrifice. "—ah, fighting. We're just trying to give you some space."

"We weren't fi—" Sandy blew out a long, slow breath. She rubbed her forehead then ran her hand through her dark hair. "It's okay. I know I've been a witch lately."

"No, not really—"

Her eyes narrowed.

"Okay, maybe a little mean. You've got a lot on your mind."

"And an overprotective husband." She smiled. "I love your brother, Sean, but he's driving me crazy. If he can't be with me, he makes sure someone else is with me. I'm never, *ever* alone. I'm not going to break."

"I can talk to him if you want."

She made a face and shook her head. "He'll just say I went running to the Great Voice of Reason."

Sean chuckled at her use of Ryan's nickname for him.

"It'll be over soon." Sandy caressed her belly. "Then he'll be able to be overprotective of the little one."

More likely his brother would just be doubly protective of the two of them. But Sean didn't voice that thought.

"How's Domingo? Ryan won't let me even go visit him."

Sean's heart softened. He knew Sandy missed her horse. She and Ryan would never agree when it came to keeping the big roan. But everyone thought she was showing good sense to stay out of the stables completely in the last weeks of her pregnancy.

"I give him his daily apple and I swear he looks over my shoulder to see if you're behind me."

"I didn't think I'd ever miss riding so much." Her wistful sigh softened her pinched expression. "Is he getting enough exercise?"

"Every day." Sean frowned and tapped his chin. "But I've been thinking of seeing how he'll take to Ricky. I've got a rehabber coming in Monday and it's going to be pretty intense for a while with that one."

"Oh, Ricky's fantastic with horses. I think it's a good idea to see how Domingo likes him." Squeezing her eyes shut for a moment, Sandy rubbed her temples.

Sean leaned in for a closer look. Exhaustion mapped her face with fine lines, and dark circles beneath her eyes stood out like purple bruises against a pallor that had wiped away all traces of the previous summer spent outdoors. What was she having? A baby or a vampire?

"You okay?"

"Yeah," she answered slowly. "Just a little headachy. Oh, and Dad and Ryan are going up to Jackson tomorrow to see the accountant about Ricky's trust fund. Ryan's going to ask you to babysit me."

The idea of *anyone* babysitting her brought on a grin. "And you don't like the idea."

She heaved a sigh. "I've resigned myself to it. Just thinking about driving all the way to Jackson makes me nauseous. But they won't leave me home alone even though I'm perfectly capable of calling for help if I need to. Besides, according to the doctor, we've got at least three weeks. So you really don't have to do anything but work with the stock the way you normally do." A sly smile spread over her face. "You seeing Mel tonight?"

Her hormonal mood shifts were sometimes difficult to keep up with, but this time it had been fairly straightforward. *Okay, sister, consider the subject changed.* He lifted a shoulder. "Maybe."

"Umm hmm." Sandy fixed him in a knowing stare.

The back of his neck tingled, and Sean rubbed at it. "Yes."

"You get around to giving her what she really wants yet?"

Mel wanted something? Sean blinked. What had he missed?

Sandy laughed. "Never mind. I can see you haven't. If you need a birds and bees conversation..." She winked. "You should probably see your dad, since Ryan and I failed safe sex one-oh-one." She patted her belly.

"Geez!" He backed away a couple of inches. "You know I hate these conversations." Heat flooded his face, and he settled his hat lower over his eyes, pissed at himself for taking her bait.

Sandy's laughter echoed against the back of the house. "Sean, I love you, but you are about as slow a mover as your brother is a fast one. How did you two turn out so opposite?"

He shrugged and shuffled his feet.

Sandy pointed at the tree and smiled. "I'll let you get back to checking on things. You don't want to rush and end up falling." She stepped to the base of the tree and peered upward. "Dinner's on the table, Ricky."

"Yes, ma'am." Ricky's voice filtered through the lingering golden-orange leaves.

Shaking his head, Sean watched her waddle away before leaping into the air and grabbing the lowest branch. With a grunt, he swung his leg up and over, then pulled himself upright. Grabbing the next branch, his grip slipped and he almost fell but managed to snag the branch with a hooked arm. *Almost* being the important part, he acknowledged, staring out at the trees bordering their back yard from his new perspective. How the hell did sloths live all their lives upside down? His head was already thick with the blood rushing to his brain.

He grinned and headed toward the next branch. Climbing the tree again felt pretty good. A little like coming home after being gone for a long time.

* * *

Melanie slipped Sean's favorite draft in front of him with a smile. Just being near him made her heart somersault. His blond hair, a bit darker in shade than hers, was longer than usual. It curled on the ends and she wanted to get her fingers tangled in it. His jade green eyes watched her hand as she swiped a few droplets of water from the bar with a fingertip. She wished he'd watch something other than her hands, but she seldom caught him checking out any part of her these days.

"Ry's got me on baby-watch duty tomorrow morning." He swirled his beer, eyes down. Amber liquid sloshed against the edges of the mug. Mel reached for the rag beneath the bar, just in case, but he stopped the restless movement and took a drink.

"It can't be that bad. It's not like Sandy's a little kid you'll have to chase around or even entertain."

"That's what she told me." When he looked up, his engaging grin was back. "Though I'm not so sure about not having to chase her. She's been tearing through the house lately, getting the nursery ready, re-doing her and Ry's room. She reorganized the kitchen cabinets and cleaned up the pantry today. Dad keeps complaining that he can't find anything in the cupboards."

Melanie giggled. "Maybe she'll clean out the attic tomorrow."

"Aw, man, I hope not. Ry'll kill me." Sean took a drink.

"It's a light crowd tonight." Mel ran a finger along Sean's arm. "LeeAnn can close. Would you like to come upstairs for a while?"

He looked past Mel toward the other barmaid. "How's she working out?"

"She's okay." Had she answered too quickly?

One of Sean's eyebrows shot up. "Really?"

Definitely answered too fast.

Following his gaze, she lifted one shoulder and strove for objectivity. LeeAnn Shannon wore her dark auburn curls in a ponytail that sprayed from the top of her head like a bloody fountain. She was probably going for a smoky eye look with her heavy blue eye shadow and dark eyeliner, but the end result was more *Zombies in Love*.

Mel tried not to be overly critical when LeeAnn picked up a pair of beer mugs on a mini tray and stumble-swayed to the end of the bar. Maybe if she didn't wear her blue jeans so tight... A pair of young males on the hunt followed her motions, their eyes fixed on the skimpy green top that clung a bit too snugly, spilling the excess of her abundant breast tissue over the top. One nudged the other and they giggled like girls.

Those two need to be carded.

Bits of rainbow-colored feathers trimming her neckline rivaled those on the headdress of a Vegas showgirl. They fluffed and ruffed with her every movement, and a few puffed off into the air.

Oh, man, how many drinks were getting a dose of feather-to-go with them? *I hope nobody chokes.* She'd stopped asking LeeAnn to wear something with less likelihood to shed after her third day of employment, since the girl apparently wasn't listening anyway.

Mel sighed and leaned forward, whispering, "She scares me."

To Sean's credit, he didn't hoot with laughter, but it was clearly an effort as his shoulders shook and his eyes twinkled.

"You must scare easily," he managed through twitching lips. At least he didn't remind her that Sandy wouldn't have tolerated the blatant defiance.

With a smile that appeared a bit forced, LeeAnn slammed a shot down in front of one of the regulars. What had set the girl off this time? It never took much.

Mel dropped her face into her palm.

"Well, she's no Sandy." Sean lifted his beer to his lips.

Shaking her head, Mel peeked up at him through her fingers. "She's definitely no Sandy." She looked up with a sigh. "But she's a body to help with serving — when she doesn't call out. And can we please stop talking about her." She wanted to talk about things closer to home. Tracing her finger back and forth along Sean's arm raised a trail of goose bumps. *Yes!* "So how about it? You want to have some dessert up in my place?"

For a split second, she thought he might agree, but then Sean rubbed his chin. His "no" tell. Disappointment flared before he even spoke. Most times she hated that her grifter father had taught her to read people so well. It usually just made her disappointment double up on her.

"I'd better get home." The track lighting sent a fractured reflection off the mug as Sean drained the last of his beer. "I don't know what time Ryan wants to get started tomorrow but I'll have stock to take care of before they leave." He glanced up at her and smiled. It was far from the look of heated desire she craved.

"I'll walk you out." She spoke a little too brightly, hoping to mask the bruises on her heart. Rejection sucked.

It only took a minute to snag her sweater from just inside the kitchen. Sean waited near the door. Goodness, he really couldn't wait to get away, could he? As she crossed the room, she tried to emulate Sandy's sexy saunter, but from the distant look on his face, she wasn't pulling it off. Why did he always treat her like someone's vanilla-cream little sister?

"How's the horse rehabbing going?" she asked as they traversed the parking lot.

"Really good, actually." As he always did when talking horses, Sean became animated. "One of my rehabs is about to be put up for sale. Got some weight back on her. Sweet-tempered little thing now no one's beating on her. I almost want to keep her for you." He angled a glance in her direction but then sighed and gave a half-assed shrug. "But you never really get much chance to come out and ride, I guess."

Mel's bruised heart performed a cartwheel. "I could make time to come out. If you'd like me to, that is." She looked up at him as they approached his truck and decided to try one more time. "*Would* you like me to?"

A car pulled into the lot, its headlights washing over them and sending their shadows into a slow dance across his silver truck.

Sean rubbed the back of his neck. "Yeah! If you come out before next week, we can see if you and Lacey get along."

Gosh, he looked so happy. And that made her happy. When he leaned in for a kiss, she took a step forward and tucked herself tightly into his solid embrace, where she always felt safe. He sucked in a breath but didn't pull away. With that bit of success spurring her on, she snaked her arms around his waist and slanted more intimately into his embrace.

Soft lips moved over hers, tasting faintly of beer and peanuts. She outlined his mouth with her tongue. *Let me in, let me in.* The exquisite pressure when his hands squeezed her shoulders replayed as her lungs tightened in her chest. With a soft moan, he deepened their kiss, playfully stroking her tongue with his, capturing hers and sucking.

As their breathing deepened to ragged gasps, a shudder raced through him and he began shaking. His hands moved up and down her arms with feverish intent.

Score one for the home team. Finally.

Mel's nerves buzzed like a hundred honey bees hitting the mother lode of purple-flowering clover. She clutched his waist, shivering at the way his muscles jumped under her hands.

His hand scorched through the thin material of her blouse as he played along her spine like it was a flute. When had he slipped it beneath her sweater?

A physical ache goaded by emotional need welled within her.

Uttering a low, feral moan against her lips, Sean spun them around and pressed her against the door of his pickup. Her toes barely touched the ground. Mel angled her head for his kiss and wrapped her arms around his neck. A wiggle against his hips brought out a sharp hiss through his teeth.

He pulled back slowly, holding himself completely still for a minute. Then he let her slide down his body until her feet rested on the ground again.

"You're killing me here, Mel," he whispered, his voice quaking. "One of these days, we gotta do something about this — you and me."

"It's not so late yet. My room's still open."

And... she lost him. Giving herself a mental kick, she could only watch as he stepped back a foot or so. A distant half-smile played with his lips, and he kissed her on the forehead. His guard was back in place. They had just shared a very passionate embrace, and he'd definitely been turned on. Now, if he felt any sort of desire for her at all, she couldn't see it. Or feel it, the way he kept himself angled away from her. Dang it! He was so careful with her. Always keeping just one or two steps out of reach like a dangling carrot.

Sighing, she acknowledged the change between them with a nod. She couldn't remember a time since they'd been teenagers when she hadn't wanted to be Sean's girl. Yet they never seemed to get beyond a few heated kisses before he skedaddled in the opposite direction. Sometimes it was hard to tell if he really wanted to kiss her or if he was just being polite.

"Maybe I'll see you tomorrow, then?" As always, she felt a little anxious about his answer, though she usually tried to cover her anxiety with an attitude of nonchalance.

He smiled and gave her a peck on the cheek with one last warm hug. Then he rubbed the back of his neck and cast a sheepish glance her way. "Hope so."

She breathed more easily when she caught his "yes" tell. He always seemed just a little on the reserved side when he said yes to something that meant a lot to him. It was nice to imagine his slow response signaled that he considered her important.

Sean climbed into his truck but waited for her to cross the parking lot again before he drove off. She turned at the door and watched through the window. He probably didn't know she routinely stood there and watched his taillights disappear.

Mel slid the sweater from her shoulders. A white envelope fell to the floor and she groaned. Denny's letter. LeeAnn must have seen it by the register and slipped it into her pocket.

Shaking her head, she tore open the envelope as she walked into the kitchen. The letter was typed and unsigned. If not for the return address, written in her brother's familiar careful script, it might have come from anyone. But it had come from her brother, and read simply, "You should be interested in this."

A frown pinched her forehead as she peeked in the envelope and pulled out an article cut from a newspaper. For no reason other than Denny was family, her hands were shaking as she unfolded the clipping. The headline was to the point: *Prominent Oklahoma City Attorney Indicted on Adoption Fraud and Baby Selling Scheme.*

Letter and article slipped from Mel's frozen fingers.

* * *

The sitting room light was still on when Sean pulled in to the ranch yard. That meant Mr. Early-to-bed Ryan was waiting up for him. Aw, man, just what he probably needed but didn't want. Sean kicked the door of his truck closed with more force than necessary.

"Dang, bro. Shoot it and put it out of your misery already," said Ryan as he stepped from the shadows.

Juggling his keys, Sean spun about. "Aw, hell. If you're gonna jump me, can it wait 'til we're inside? It's freezing out here."

"It's October. It's supposed to be freezing." A lighter flared, harshly illuminating Ryan's face.

The acrid smell of a cigar wafted over Sean. "Didn't you eat enough smoke when you worked in L.A.?" He started walking for the house.

Ryan took a puff. "You'd think. But I guess a year or so of chatting with Dad on the porch while he lights up got me in the habit." The end glowed again. "So what's eatin' at you tonight?"

"Sandy ask you to have a go at me?"

Instead of answering, Ryan stared at the lit end of the cigar. The gesture was so like their father's, Sean rolled his eyes.

"She's worried about you." He blew out a long breath. "And so am I, a little."

The darkness hid so much. It was impossible to read his brother with only the occasional dim flare of his cigar. But maybe that meant Ryan couldn't read *him*. Sean shrugged. "Nothing to worry about."

"Horse puckey." Yeah, that was their dad's phrase, too. Maybe marriage with a kid on the way automatically turned a formerly cool guy into an old coot.

"Remind me again why I missed you for sixteen years?" Sean rubbed his jaw. Might as well get it over with. "It's Mel."

"Huh. I'd never have guessed." Ryan puffed the cigar then went for the kill shot. "Get in a fight?"

"Nope. We never fight." That didn't sound right. Even he couldn't believe such a blatant prevarication. "When we don't agree on something, one of us changes the subject."

Ryan's giant guffaw split the night. "And that *works* for you?"

"Used to," muttered Sean. What the heck, maybe talking it out would take some of his edge off. "Okay, so she keeps hinting at wanting something more."

"More than what? Like she wants to get married?"

Sean stopped walking at the bottom porch step, choosing the location for the advantage of the yellow light spilling through the living room window and over Ryan's face. "No, not exactly. As in she invited me to her place tonight, and *not* to watch a little TV."

Ryan's mouth fell open. The cigar he'd just lit tumbled to the ground in a shower of sparks. Mumbling a string of oaths, he stooped and retrieved it. As he stood, he angled a long look at Sean then shook his head. "And yet the man came home. Interesting. So, you told her no?"

"Yup."

"Why?" Ryan's gaze drifted below Sean's waist. "Everything — ah — all... *works*, right?"

"What?" Irritation flared. "Yes. Everything works. Get your mind out of the gutter, man. It's not always about sex."

Ryan's face registered total disbelief. "It's *almost always* about sex. You've been... um, *seeing* Mel steady for over two years now, right?"

Here it came. The big brother lecture about getting laid. Sean lifted a shoulder. "Yeah, 'bout that."

"And you've — *never*?"

"Nope. Never did the deed." He raised his hands surrender-style. "Satisfied?"

"No, I'm not satisfied!" Ryan jammed the cigar back in his mouth. Then he frowned and leaned toward Sean. "Ah, when you say never, do you mean *never* never or just never with Mel?"

"Geez!" Was he trying to make up for sixteen years of brotherly confidences in one night? Sean glared at his brother. "*Not...* that it's your business, but yes, I've had sex." A snarl pulled on his lips as he pushed his hand out, to within inches of Ryan's face. "You don't get to ask with whom."

A flinch then a quickly indrawn breath signaled his brother wanted to argue, but he shrugged instead and raised an eyebrow.

"It's just—" Might as well finish. "Things are different with Mel."

"You don't like her like that?"

If he stared into the darkness long enough, would it swallow him? Sean sighed. Probably not. "I love her. I want everything with her. I want what you and Sandy have."

"Then I don't get it," said his brother, as if the answer was just that simple. "Ask her to marry you."

"Can't." Sadness rolled over him like a slow, suffocating wave. "I got nothing to offer her."

There. Cards on the table. Sean didn't know what was up with Mel lately, but something was off and he felt like they were drifting in separate directions. Yet he couldn't begin to sort things out and fight for her without having his own life together. Every time he tried to bring up the possibility of a future together, she turned it around and made it about something physical. Clearly she wanted a physical relationship, and so did he, but he wanted more than that. Sean wasn't made for casual. He was done with unsatisfying, going-nowhere relationships.

And she didn't seem to want to go in the same direction.

Ryan looked stunned. "Nothing to offer? There's your share of the ranch. We're turning things around. You've got your horse rehab business. You earn a decent income. You'll be able to take care of a family."

"And we can share my bedroom here, all cozy with everyone in the main house." Sean blew out a frustrated breath and kicked at the dirt. "It's already crowded with you and Sandy, Dad, Ricky, and now your baby on the way."

"That can change, Sean." Irritation had crept into Ryan's voice. "You don't have to live in the main house to keep working the ranch. Heck, live in town at her place. Just get engaged, let her know you want to be with her. The two of you can work out the details later. And for the love of mercy, when she asks you up to her place again... go."

Sean shook his head. "Nope."

"Why?"

"Because Mel's worth more than a few vague promises and getting hot between the sheets. I thought *you* would get that." Sean spun on his heel and stomped onto the porch. A glance over his shoulder showed Ryan's mouth gaping, the cigar in the dirt again. Shaking his head at his brother's cluelessness, Sean pushed open the front door and slipped inside.

Chapter Two

"Sandy's still in bed, says she's feeling lazy today. Finally." Ryan stood half-in and half-out of his father's pickup, a frown creasing his forehead as he ticked off instructions. "Are you getting this?" he asked for the seventh — eighth? — time.

"I got it." Sean glanced at his feet as Ryan resumed his instructions. Mud caked the soles of his boots. He'd better make sure not to track that into the kitchen if he didn't want Sandy scrubbing the floor.

Rolling his shoulders didn't begin to work out the stiffness he'd awakened with, but he kept doing it just for something to do while Ryan droned on with his endless instructions.

"Are we leaving before the snow flies?" called Justin from inside the cab. His gravelly voice held more than a fair share of impatience.

Sean stole a glance at the sky and grunted. Gray, a little heavy, but the weather would probably hold for a trip to Jackson. He sniffed the air. Snow was a stretch. He could smell it in the mountains where they were heading, but more likely only rain would fall in the lower elevations. Hopefully, nothing bad enough to keep him in later so he could work in another trip to Valentine's. Mel had been on fire the night before.

And he'd spent a mostly sleepless night as a result.

Was Ryan right? Should he just let things progress to the next level? She seemed to want that. His body sure as hell wanted it. He couldn't even be in the same room with her and not feel that sense of buzzing awareness thrumming through his veins with every heartbeat.

A hand waved in front of his face, and he recoiled.

"Look, if this is going to be too much for you, we'll make it another day," snapped Ryan.

Sean stared. What had he missed? Oh, yeah, most of his brother's directives. Ryan compressed his lips and subjected Sean to a lethal glare. Sheesh. He'd seen the guy in a lot of states over the past couple of years, but nothing like the current one. He looked... frazzled.

"I've got my cell..." Frowning, Ryan patted his city slicker leather jacket, and then blew out a relieved breath as he pulled his phone from the pocket. "Okay, got it. We won't have service for a few miles up in the mountains, so call Clint Westover's office and leave a message if you can't reach me. But if it's an emergency—"

Sean allowed an edge of irritation to his words. "Geez, Ry, I don't know how I managed to take care of things before you came home. Do you want to leave a written list so I can make sure I'm doing it right?" He played in the dirt with the toe of his boot, drawing a line between them. Then he met his brother's gaze. "You're gonna be gone what, three, four hours? How much trouble can your pregnant wife get into?"

"You'd be surprised," muttered Ryan, laying a hand on Sean's arm. "She's everything to me, okay?"

Irritation evaporated. Ryan and Sandy had fought so hard to be together and it was only by a miracle that they were. Sean gave a nod. "I know. I promise I won't let anything happen to her."

Love — the incredible once-in-a-lifetime kind —
softened Ryan's eyes as their gazes held for a long moment.
"Thanks." He climbed into the truck and started it.

Sean didn't linger watching them drive off. Morning
chores had been interrupted by Ryan's lecture on the *Care
And Feeding Of Pregnant Women*. They wouldn't see to
themselves, and he'd be lucky to get everything finished
before late afternoon — especially operating one man short.

Not that he minded terribly. Sean found comfort in
working the ranch. The sameness of the daily chores
appealed to him as much as the day-to-day challenges that
made things interesting. Keeping on top of things, knowing
what was likely to happen and watching for it, being
prepared for unexpected complications — ranching required
all of that and more. Ranching was something he knew.

Women, on the other hand... he wasn't sure he got
them. At least not one particular woman.

He finished mucking the last stall in the rehab barn.
Hiking his collar against the chill of the approaching rain, he
checked on the horses in the paddock. Lacey wandered over
to the fence, looking for an apple. She was a pretty little
smoky black gal, fine-boned, with a good disposition
considering she'd been starved and abused for most of her
life. He'd planned to put her up for sale now that she was
rehabbed, but he had to be honest and admit he didn't really
want to give her up. With her ladylike manners and
sometimes coy attitude, she made him think of Mel.

Not the Mel of last night, though. Man oh man, what
was with that kiss? His heart rate bumped up again just
thinking about it. He'd been about to go off like a Fourth of
July bottle rocket when they'd stopped. Maybe he *was* as
nuts as Ryan seemed to think, but fact was, Mel meant too
much to treat her feelings carelessly. He wasn't sure if she
returned more than the physical aspect of their attraction.
And he wanted more, way more, with Melanie. She wasn't
casual sex material. She mattered.

Even if she doesn't think so.

The clatter of hooves on wood drew his attention.
Domingo wasn't especially happy today. Racing from one end

of his paddock to the other, he was kicking at the fence with each change of direction. The bottom rail by the gate was already split. If he wasn't stopped, the horse would hurt himself.

"Hey, buddy, settle down." Sean held out an apple.

For the first time since he'd come to the Cross MC, an apple didn't buy the roan's cooperation. With a toss of his head, he raced in the other direction and crashed sidelong against the fence.

Sean grabbed a lead. He'd have to put the colt in his stall, see if that calmed him. He was probably just spooked by the weather moving in. He hoped. It took every trick Sean knew to get the lead on the horse. Every time he got close, Domingo skittered away to the paddock's far side. Finally, after two apples and a lot of soft talking, Sean was able to snap the lead to Domingo's halter.

"Come on, big fella."

Domingo pranced sideways as Sean led him inside. He barely got the lead off before the horse laid his ears back and snapped his teeth.

From a safe distance, Sean looked Domingo over. No visible wounds... *He's acting temperamental, not ill.* Sean observed him for a few minutes with a critical eye. Unless he got worse, they could probably keep a close watch on him for a day or so before calling the vet to check him out. He set the latch on the stall and froze.

"Sandy!"

His instincts were screaming that something was horribly wrong as he took off for the house at a dead run.

She stood at the kitchen table, and for just a second Sean thought he must have been wrong. Then a spasm of pure agony contorted her face.

"Hey, Sean." She greeted him calmly after the wave of pain passed. "You'll never guess what just happened. My water broke all over the kitchen floor."

He glanced down at the floor, which looked surprisingly clean.

She noted the direction of his gaze and chuckled. "Relax, I mopped it up."

"Oh." Sean began edging back to the door. "Are you okay, then?"

Sandy pursed her lips and gripped the edge of the table. After a couple of long breathes, she began panting like one of the dogs rounding up the cattle. When she looked up again, she sent him a weak glare. "Do I *look* okay? The baby's coming. Now. I've called for an ambulance but I'm not going to make it. I probably have about—" Her face contorted again.

Sean allowed his eyes to drift to her belly. The simple white maternity shirt stretched taut, but the fabric didn't disguise the way her abdomen arranged itself into a shape resembling a point and then rippled as she blew out short puffs of air through pursed lips. His gut tightened and stirred, and suddenly the fried eggs and sausage he'd eaten for breakfast didn't seem like such a good idea.

"Ryan's an hour out — I got him on the two-way," Sandy panted. "But he probably won't get here before the ambulance."

"Why didn't you call *me* on the radio?" asked Sean with a frown.

"I tried. I couldn't raise you." Sandy closed her eyes and rubbed her head.

That didn't make sense. Sean pulled the radio off his belt clip and looked at it. The settings were correct. He pressed the test button. Nothing. Not even a squawk. "Dead. I'm sorry, Sandy. I grabbed this one off the charger this morning. It must be broken."

"I also tried your cell but I heard it going off upstairs."

"Sorry," Sean mumbled again. He'd been in a hurry to get at the day. And it wasn't like his cell routinely burned up with incoming calls.

"That's okay. You're here now."

Yeah, here I am... As a wave of dizziness overtook him, he darted his glance around the room. He shouldn't be intruding at such a time. If he could just get through to the hallway, give her a little privacy...

A grunt and a grimace, and Sandy's knuckles turned white where she gripped the table. "Oh man, I really want to push here."

"What?" Tremors rocked his legs, weakening his knees. The ambulance could make it. It had been known to happen. "Well, don't!"

Sandy winced and rocked back on her heels. "Sean, I need your help. Get some towels and the sterile scissors from a debridement kit. But don't you dare walk on my floor wearing those muddy boots." She made a vague gesture in the direction of his feet.

His backside met the bench in the mudroom with a jarring thud, and he slipped off his boots. He wiggled his toes against the hard, cold floor, feeling oddly naked in just his socks.

She looked a little better when he stepped into the kitchen. Right? Well, at least she wasn't panting and gasping.

"Good, you're back. I need the package of new shoelaces from my purse." She pointed to the giant leather bag on the kitchen counter.

Crap.

Sandy whimpered something that sounded like "hurry."

His stomach roiled and his breakfast made more demands for a repeat showing. He closed his eyes and drew a few deep, slow breaths.

"Sean!" Sandy's shout brought him back to the kitchen. "I'm having this baby. You. Have. To. Help. Me."

Right. A baby. Why had it never occurred to him that the result of his sister-in-law's nine-month gestation would be a little person? He didn't move, just kept staring at her. Couldn't she just will the baby to stop coming out until the ambulance arrived?

A moan, long and low, broke her panting pattern. Her face twisted and her eyes rolled back in her head as she sagged against the table, but she hung on and kept her feet beneath her.

"Whoa!" Okay, he had to help her. No getting out of it. But first things first. The kitchen chair scraped loudly across the tile floor as he dragged it from under the table and positioned it behind her. "At least sit down until I get back." He angled her in the right direction and pressed lightly on her shoulders, surprised when she slouched against the back without an argument. In the storeroom, he snagged two friggin' debridement kits, stared at the remaining plastic-coated tray on the shelf for a beat, and picked up that one as well. Then he stepped into the laundry room and grabbed some clean towels and a couple of blankets.

When he returned to the kitchen, he hesitated. "Don't you want to be in a bed or something?"

She shook her head. Sweat beaded on her forehead and streamed in little rivulets down her temples. Her dark hair was plastered to her head. "No time." She panted. *Hah-hah-hee.* "I don't think I can walk anyway."

He laid the medical kit and towels on the kitchen table. "Sandy, I don't know what to do."

Except panic. It appeared he was pretty good at panicking.

Sandy fisted a hand in his shirt. "Pretend I'm a damn cow. You've delivered baby calves, haven't you?"

Actually, he had pulled his share of calves when the mothers couldn't get the job done. But he wasn't certain now would be the time to tell her what *that* entailed. Or that sometimes the outcome for the mother cows wasn't all that great.

"I don't—" He swallowed hard over the tightness in his throat. "Don't think I can do— Sandy, you're my *sister*!" The heat of embarrassment crept into his face. He was a grown man. He should be able to be a little more worldly about the whole thing. But she was his brother's wife! It seemed like crossing a line.

She moaned again and her face became ashen. "Oh, for crying out loud, I'm asking you to help me deliver my baby, not have sex with me." With a grunt, she squeezed her eyes shut and breathed through the contraction. "If you'd have sex with Melanie, you'd know the difference by now."

Sean's choked response echoed back at him from across the room. He snapped his head up.

Mel stood just inside the kitchen, her eyes wide, twin patches of fire staining her cheeks. "I brought the final partnership papers. The door was open," she said weakly. "What's going on?"

Sandy panted through another contraction.

Another knot twisted in Sean's gut. "She's having the baby. We're waiting for the ambulance."

"Oh, no, we're not." Sandy rubbed her belly and blew out a long, slow breath. "Can *you* help me, Mel?"

Mel dropped her purse on the floor, crossed to the kitchen sink, and began washing her hands.

"Go get me an old shirt," she said. When Sean stared at her in confusion, she snapped, "Go!"

Up in his bedroom, Sean grabbed a cream-colored shirt off the first hanger he laid his hands on. It wasn't an old shirt, but he didn't care. She could tear it into strips and make bandages out of it if she wanted. All he cared about was *not* delivering Sandy's baby. He bounded down the stairs two at a time and raced toward the kitchen. When he reached the arched doorway, he skidded to a halt on the highly polished hardwood.

Sandy sagged in her seat and blew out a long breath. "Really, really wanting to push here."

With the same efficient movements she used while serving at the bar, Mel smoothed a blanket over the tabletop. She'd taken off her pink sweater and stood in just her jeans and a skimpy bra with a brightly colored pattern of... Sean squinted... *rainbow-hued frogs and pink hearts?* Curves mounded over the edge of the satin fabric like luscious muffin tops. Unable to tear his eyes away, he stood there like some kind of peeping Tom. If he lived a hundred more years, he'd never be able to look at another frog without thinking of Melanie Mitchell's underwear.

Shaking free of the spell, he padded into the kitchen, holding out the shirt like it was a shield. Erotic visuals tumbled inside his head, screwing up his thought processes. He knew he should say something but muddled as his brain was, the only thing he could think of was, "Here's a shirt." He shook his head. Yeah, what a profound statement.

Melanie slid her gaze in his direction and smiled, which had the effect of further screwing with his libidinous mindset.

"Good. Thanks." She took the shirt and slipped her arms into the sleeves.

"Oh, crap!" Sandy cried out, her hands clenched into fists. "This baby's coming *now*."

"Sean, help me get her on the table. It'll be easier to help her deliver that way."

"So... how... do you know what to do?" he asked, wondering if the floor might be a better option.

Mel's eyes were wide. She fussed with the edge of the blanket, looking uncomfortable. "I really don't. I'm kind of winging it from old TV shows."

Sean stared at Mel. Cheeks flushed, pale blue eyes glittering like sapphires. And she'd just admitted she had no idea what she was doing. They were so screwed. Ry would do him some serious bodily harm when he got home if anything happened to Sandy or the baby.

"I can— I can talk you through it," Sandy said between panting breaths. As Sean easily lifted his sister-in-law onto the table, she moaned and clutched his arm, digging her nails into his flesh. "There are a couple of pillows in the laundry room. I need them."

As soon as she released his now bloody arm, Sean escaped to the laundry room. He spotted the pillows right away and would have happily lingered in front of the dryer there, but Sandy's moan pulled him back.

"Stand up here next to me, Sean. I need you to support my back when I push," she said through the next round of panting. "Mel, have a towel ready. They're slippery suckers when they first come out."

For all his discomfort, Sean marveled at Sandy's ability to remain in control.

"This is it." With a grunt, Sandy leaned forward until her body was nothing but a tense ball. Sean braced her with his arms around her shoulders. He tried not to look at her abdomen but it was heaving in mesmerizing waves as she pushed her baby out into the world.

She stopped pushing and leaned back against the pillows, sucking in huge gasps of air. Sean flexed his fingers until the tingling stopped. The break wasn't nearly long enough. Sandy let out a shrill scream then renewed her effort to push the baby out.

"Sean." Mel's voice, low and intense, shot an arrow of dread through his heart.

In mid-push, Sandy didn't hear, thank all that was holy. He raised an eyebrow at Mel. She shook her head.

"Hold up a second, Sandy. I just need Sean to help me with something here." Mel's frantic wave spurred him forward.

Stepping in beside her, Sean took a deep breath and risked a look. Instead of a baby's head, a wad of blue-tinged tissue protruded. His heart stalled in his chest. "Oh, sweet Lord," he whispered as his blood turned to ice. How was he supposed to fix a prolapsing umbilical cord? "Sandy, don't push on the next contraction."

An amazing sense of calm settled over him as Sean assessed the situation. The cord was bulging out in front of the baby's head. With every contraction, it would be squeezed, cutting off the blood supply, and thus the baby's oxygen.

"Tell me what's wrong," demanded Sandy. "I'm not going to freak."

As if sensing their roles had shifted, Mel moved up to take Sean's place at Sandy's shoulder. "Hold my hand," she murmured. "Just don't push yet."

The first glove from the debridement kit tore as he thrust his fingers into it. The second stuck on his sweaty palm, but finally he managed to drag it into place. He reached for one of the spares and eased it onto his left hand. "Okay, San. The cord's prolapsing just a bit."

Sandy hissed a breath through her teeth. "I lied. I want to freak out."

"It's going to be okay." Speaking in a calm and gentle voice, Mel rubbed Sandy's shoulders. "Sean knows exactly what to do."

Who the heck was Mel talking about? He didn't have a clue what to do. He had no business trying to deliver a baby — at least not a human one.

Sandy began panting. "You have to — you have to get the cord back behind the — the baby."

"I know, sweetie," he murmured, trying to show confidence he didn't yet feel.

She'd told him to pretend she was a cow. She'd probably had no idea how close to that scenario they were going to come.

"I have to push again," said Sandy, her face red with the effort to remain still.

"Don't push. Breathe through it." Sean barely recognized that self-assured voice coming from his mouth.

"Look at me." Mel leaned over, blocking Sandy's view of anything happening below her chest.

Good girl, Mel!

"Just pant and don't think about anything else." Melanie didn't sound at all nervous.

"I need to elevate her hips." Sean pointed at the pillows. "Put those under her as soon as this contraction ends."

He went through the steps in his head. Elevate. Gentle pressure on the head to push it back inside a little, and then ease the cord inside. At least that's how they did it with livestock.

Where the hell was the ambulance with the dang medical personnel who wouldn't screw things up the way he could?

Mel helped Sandy get her hips on the pillows. Gently, Sean pushed against the baby's head, easing it back and taking some pressure off the cord. Oh, man, he didn't want to think of Ryan coming home to a dead baby and maybe even a dead wife.

"Honey, you need to keep your mind on your task. Worrying won't help you. Just concentrate on what is... not what might be."

That voice... so familiar. "Mom?" he whispered, darting a glance around the room. But it was just the three of them. He must have imagined it, maybe based on a long-buried memory.

A long, low moan escaped through Sandy's gritted teeth.

"Easy, honey, just a little more," whispered Mel.

Sean glanced at Mel. The flush of excitement had been replaced by a frightening pallor. "Take a breath, Mel. I need you here. You can't pass out on us."

Obediently she gulped in air, and a bit of color returned.

"Easy, now, I have this." Sean pushed a little more and the cord disappeared inside. With a grimace, he closed his eyes, picturing the cord as he followed the path it took with his fingers, pushing it to the side as he moved. A tiny round head rested against his palm. A human life was quite literally in his hand. Swallowing hard, he kept his hand in place, praying he was right about the positioning.

"Sandy, I'm guessing it's going to hurt like hellfire, but on your next contraction I need you to push with all you've got."

"Okay," she gasped. A shudder raced through her. In the final stages of labor, her legs were quaking madly.

Sean noted the ripple in her belly, knew it was coming. Even braced, he wasn't quite ready for the agony of having his fingers squeezed against his sister-in-law's pelvic bones. But he kept them in place, holding the cord away so the baby's head could progress.

Because if he didn't, the baby was going to die.

"Keep pushing, Sandy, don't stop. We're almost there." Tears filled his eyes. His hand developed a pins-and-needles sensation.

Sandy's shriek piercing the air was loud enough for both of them. Sean clenched his jaw and tried to breathe past the squeezing in his chest.

Then came a sucking-popping sound and the baby's head slipped into the world, bringing his hand out with it. *Thank God, no cord wrapped around the neck.* But the blue tinge to the face couldn't be a good sign.

"Push again, Sandy. Hard!"

"No contraction," she said between panting.

"Do it anyway. Push! Let's get this baby out." The panic had to stay tucked inside. Couldn't let it be heard in his voice.

"You're doing just fine," whispered a voice in his mind.

Sharp pain shot through his midsection, nearly doubling him over; he was tensing up, unconsciously trying to push for her. He forced out a breath through pursed lips and willed his stomach to relax some.

Sandy arched and strained and with another mighty heave, the baby slid out like a limp rag. Her flaccid body lay in his hands so still, so white. So perfect.

"It's a girl," he whispered, willing the baby to take a breath. "You have a daughter, Sandy."

"Why isn't she crying?" she asked between gasps.

Sean rubbed the baby's chest gently, hoping to stimulate her. He checked her mouth. "Come on, baby girl," he murmured. Crap. If she was a calf, all it would take was a piece of straw. How did he clean the gunk from her nose and mouth?

Mel joined him, worry clouding her eyes. Sean wrapped the baby in a towel and began to rub her briskly. Gently, he opened her mouth and swept his finger over her tongue to clear any mucus plugs. This was about as far from a foal or a calf as it could be, and he hoped he was doing it right. With a cough and a gurgle, the baby opened her mouth and pulled in a huge breath. Then she screamed with rage. Sean relaxed and began breathing again.

At the sound of a helicopter landing in the yard, Mel rushed across the room, getting to the door just as it burst open and admitted Ryan.

"Sandy!" Ryan rushed toward the table.

"You need to tie off the cord so you can cut it," Sandy said to Sean. "Use the shoelaces. Tie it in two places and cut in the middle."

Sean looked up at Ryan's pale face. His brother, the big former firefighter, was frozen halfway between the door and the kitchen table. He was strangely silent, but watching everything that was happening. Using the scissors from the debridement kit, Sean cut the umbilical cord between the shoelaces. He wrapped the baby in a clean towel and turned to his brother, holding out the noisy squirming bundle.

"You have a daughter, Ryan."

Tears filled Ryan's eyes as he took the baby and moved to Sandy's side. Sean turned away, certain he'd be crying, too, in a minute. He flexed his fingers, which seemed to be recovering the blood flow.

The back door opened, and Justin entered a couple steps ahead of a lean man with sandy brown hair. Sandy glanced over at the door.

"Oh, hi, Joe. Now everyone's here, and my day's absolutely complete. This isn't how I planned to deliver this baby. Just so you know, I'm not taking a helicopter to the hospital. We're about done here."

"Flights are grounded for fog in Jackson." Helicopter pilot Joe Griffin grinned, but he dashed a hand across his eyes before he glued them on the young couple with the new baby. "I brought up the Cross MC bird in case you needed emergency transport."

Sandy's face softened. "Thank you. But I think we're good."

Sean discreetly covered his sister-in-law with a spare blanket. Then he went to the kitchen cabinet to grab a shot. When he opened the cupboard door, he blinked at the stack of plates.

"Where's the Jack?"

"We have a little problem here." Ryan bent and kissed Sandy's forehead. "You would only consider one name, and I don't think our girl here is going to be too interested in being called Justin."

"Maybe Justine?" Mel's voice was soft. She hovered away from the crowd, near the dining room doorway, looking like she wanted to bolt as badly as Sean did. Oh, man, she looked really pale and she was shaking. She could probably use a drink herself, except he knew she'd refuse.

On his way out of the pantry, Sean's father snorted. "Don't even think about it. She's too pretty for that." He held the bottle of whiskey. "Looking for this, son?"

Sean accepted the bottle then opened another cupboard. "Where the heck are the glasses?"

Justin pointed one cabinet over.

Dang. Suddenly it was a production just to get one little shot. He poured then put the bottle back in the cabinet. Where it belonged.

"Actually, I have the perfect name," Sandy said. She looked first at Justin then up at Ryan. "I'd like to call her Bethany."

The lump in Sean's throat formed in mid-swallow. He finished downing the shot with difficulty and carefully set the glass on the kitchen counter. "After Mom."

The voice in his head that had helped bring Baby Bethany into the world. Right. Pretty sure he'd end up on the shrink ward in Jackson if he mentioned any of that.

Ryan was already nodding. Sean turned to his father and saw the tears welling. *Aw, crap.* He'd be next if he didn't take care. He started to edge toward the door.

"Sean, come here a minute."

When Sandy used that tone it was best to either listen or be prepared to run. Sean was *almost* certain she wouldn't chase him. But only almost. So he shuffled back to the table. The pink baby was already suckling one of her mother's breasts. Sean blinked back tears and averted his gaze up to Sandy's face.

"How did you know to come up to the house when you did?" she asked.

Sean smiled. That had been the easy part of the whole adventure. "Your horse told me." The room fell silent and Sean glanced around, noting five pairs of eyes fixed on him.

Great, shrink ward here I come. He shrugged. "What? Domingo was acting up."

Ryan snorted. "When isn't he acting up?"

Narrowing his eyes, Sean shot his brother a glare. "More than usual. He wouldn't calm down, even after I put him in his stall, and I suddenly knew I needed to get up here."

"You saved Bethany's life." Gratitude shone in Sandy's eyes. She looked up at Ryan and some sort of silent message passed between them. "We'd really like you to choose her middle name."

Sean gulped. "Me?"

When he noticed everyone was now eyeing him expectantly, he realized he'd have to say something. "Ah, um... well, I've always been partial to Grace."

At Mel's sharp intake of breath, the eyes shifted in her direction. But Mel was looking at Sean when she spoke. "That's my middle name."

He lifted a shoulder. "I know."

As the group crowded around to admire Bethany Grace McGee, Sean edged his way to the door again. Ramming his feet into his muddy boots, he stole one last glance at the happy family then ducked out unimpeded.

Intense longing swelled inside him as he walked to the stables. One step at a time. Maybe one day Mel would return his feelings and they could have something together... at least he hoped so.

Chapter Three

The stream of water flowing over Mel's hands had long since washed away the talc from the inside of the latex glove. Its warmth had eased the chill from her cramped fingers, but it was powerless against the block of ice in her chest.

Helping a baby into the world was a huge deal. Sharing the experience with Sean had been amazing on so many levels. It had so obviously overwhelmed him, but he hadn't let it show until Sandy and the baby were safe. Heat that had nothing to do with the steam rising from the faucet swamped her face. He'd named the baby for her.

He didn't know she didn't deserve such an honor. And she couldn't tell him. He'd hate her for sure. As it was, he'd cut out while everyone had been admiring the new baby. She couldn't blame him. As soon as she saw him leave, she'd locked herself in the powder room to wash up. But she'd been gone too long. Someone was bound to miss her — if not already then soon.

Abruptly she cut off the water. She should leave. A healthy baby was a happy occasion for families. They didn't need an intruder hanging around. But first... she'd say goodbye to Sean. She knew where he'd gone when he slipped out. Only in one place would he find calming energy. She left the tiny bathroom to find the ambulance had arrived. It was easy to slink through the kitchen and slip out the front door while the EMTs were seeing to Sandy and Bethany.

As she'd expected, Mel found Sean in the stable. With his back to the door, he was holding a conversation with Sandy's horse. She lingered in the doorway watching him, enjoying the physical appeal of his rippling biceps even as she wondered why he didn't seem to feel the cold.

"Is that why you were out of sorts earlier, big guy?" Sean scratched the horse under his ear and handed him another apple. "You seem just fine now."

Mel loved the gentle side Sean always showed his horses. He'd been wonderful with Sandy, too, though. Such a hero, saving the baby like that. Some warm fuzzy thing was still going on inside her, and seeing him pet the horse made the feeling swell to something she was still trying to figure out.

Almost like maybe she wanted to start a family of their own so she could watch him with their children. A tear rolled down her cheek. That was never going to happen. Her life was complicated enough without tossing marriage and family into the mix. She longed with all her heart for Sean to accept her and let things take a natural course without the picket fence promises she couldn't make. But Sean was an all-or-nothing man. That's why they were frustrating each other with that too-careful two-step they'd been dancing.

The horse nuzzled Sean. "I'm out of apples, big guy." But he laid his face against Domingo's nose.

She was intruding in Sean's private world, a right she didn't have. Time to make her presence known. "I love watching you with your horses."

His head popped up; she'd startled him. It was rare for anyone to surprise Sean; he always seemed hyper-aware of his surroundings.

The grin he flashed was the same one that always made her heart beat a little quicker. "Hey, you. I thought you'd have left by now."

Heat rose into her face. She probably should have, but she'd wanted to see him just once more. *Keep it light.* She laughed softly. "What? Without saying goodbye to the man of the hour? I was hoping you'd show me that horse you were telling me about."

A fascinating change came over Sean's face. He'd looked contentedly tired before she spoke. And he'd been happy to see she hadn't left. But when she mentioned wanting to see the horse, he took on the expression of a little boy showing off his Christmas loot. Almost the little boy she'd fallen in love with while sitting on a rock after his mama had passed.

Sadness threatened to ruin the moment, so she pushed it away as she followed him to the back of the barn. It wasn't at all hard to distract herself. All she had to do was keep her eyes on his rear end as they walked. In fact, the view was so appealing, Mel forgot to pay attention to anything else. She slammed into a hard wall of muscle and realized Sean had stopped walking. She threw her hands out defensively and found herself with a double handful of the butt she'd been admiring.

She let go immediately as the heat of mortification blasted into her face. The way she'd thrown herself at him the night before, he probably would think she'd engineered the move.

"Sorry," she mumbled.

Instead of the total shut-down she might have expected, he spun to face her, capturing her hand and tugging her against him with a laugh. Mel wanted to weep with gratitude. For the first time in months, she saw the heat flash in his brilliant green eyes.

A half-smile curved his lips as he walked her backwards until she hit the wall and held her there with his body. He went still, his hot gaze searing its way into her consciousness. With excruciating slowness, he leaned against her, teasing her with just the barest hint of his lips on hers. His breath fanned across her face, warm, smelling only faintly of the whiskey he'd downed back at the house.

She was unable to move, but she didn't care, for she was exactly where she'd wanted to be for as long as she could remember. His quickened breathing told her he felt the same way. Mel's eyelids became heavy and she allowed them to drift shut as she gave herself to the sensations of warmth running straight from her lips to her center. With a soft moan, he settled his mouth on hers and deepened the kiss. It was like being awakened by the prince she'd been waiting for her whole life. *At last.*

With her hunger thoroughly awakened, Mel opened her mouth and used her tongue to toy with his bottom lip. Sean's moan lent her a greater sense of daring and she nipped. His hands crept beneath her sweater but stayed at her waist.

"You have frogs on your bra," he said without breaking the kiss.

* * *

Her breathy laugh tugged at his already ragged emotions. He splayed his fingers over her ribs. Her smooth skin beneath his fingertips was surely a bit of heaven. A throaty little giggle burst from her lips as he brushed his thumbs back and forth. Finding her ticklish spots was always so much fun. They never seemed to be in the same place twice. He angled his lips to deepen the kiss and began to tickle her belly, pleased when she quivered.

"I want to see the froggies again," he murmured against her lips as he grazed her belly button with his fingertips. As he nudged her sweater farther upward, her little gasps of pleasure encouraged him. When the sweater was high enough, he stepped back to admire his handiwork, a grin tugging at his lips. There they were, grinning frogs, laughing frogs, leering frogs, even frogs sticking their tongues out, in shades of blue, red, yellow, pink, orange, purple...

Mel squirmed and grasped his arms, tugging him toward her. The frogs seemed to move with her every movement, every breath.

That bottle rocket feeling was zeroing in on him again, and he didn't care.

"I've waited forever for you to touch me," whispered Mel.

Oh, yes, he'd known that. And that knowledge nearly did his resolve in every night. Now... he had no more resolve. If this was what she wanted, he was going to give it to her. He straightened, pulling her sweater upward, while she worked at the buttons on his shirt. He hissed in a breath as she scratched her nails along his ribs, sending darts of excitement to his belly and then southward.

"Sean! You in here?"

The nice sensual buzz abruptly vanished. Ricky had some really rotten timing.

Sean bent and snatched Mel's sweater from the floor then thrust it into her hands, shielding her from view with his body as she pulled it quickly over her head. He got most of his shirt buttons done up before Ricky rounded the corner and found them.

The kid's jaw dropped and his eyes went wide. Okay, an explanation was going to take some fancy talking later.

"Ah, Justin sent me to tell you that the ambulance came and took Sandy and the baby to the hospital. Ry's following them."

Something had happened, gone wrong. As he and Mel had been indulging in a grope session, something had happened to Sandy and the baby. Heart pounding into his throat, Sean focused all his attention on the kid. "They're okay, right?"

"Yes!" Ricky locked his gaze on Sean's. "Sandy said you'd ask that and to tell you she knows everything is okay, but she wanted the baby checked out because of the complications." His forehead creased. "What happened?"

"Ahh..." The chill of dread washed away, raising goose bumps in its wake. "Remember we got that pregnant mare in for rehab, and when she delivered, the cord came out ahead of the foal?"

Ricky's face lost its color. "We almost lost that foal! Is that what happened to Sandy?"

"Yeah, but—"

"But Sean knew what to do and saved the baby." Mel moved to stand next to him. Heat radiated from her body, stirring the embers of Sean's need just a little.

"Oh, man." Ricky's gaze was full of awe and carried the weight of hero worship.

Sean sighed. *Aw, kid, don't go there.* He finished buttoning his shirt but didn't bother to tuck it in.

Ricky's sly smile was full of knowledge he shouldn't have. "Justin says it's your turn to cook and he's hungry."

His dad wasn't the only one who was hungry. Only Sean wasn't exactly hungry for food.

"I'll be in as soon as I finish introducing Mel to Lacey."

Ricky's disbelief was tangible. "Right. Okay." He slid a speculative look toward Mel. And he didn't move.

"Is there something else?" asked Sean pointedly.

"I thought we could walk back together."

Sean crossed his arms over his chest and surveyed Ricky with a narrowed gaze. "Need someone to hold your hand?"

A breathy laugh accompanied the look of disdain Ricky shot at Sean. "No."

"Good. So go take some steaks out of the deep freeze and I'll meet you up there."

Resolve settled into Ricky's eyes and he jutted his chin outward. "Sandy said no red meat for Justin."

"Sandy's not here." *Geez, was this kid ever going to get the hint?* "Go tell Dad it's his lucky day."

The smirk on the kid's face as he turned to walk away meant trouble. Lots of it.

Sean bumped his head against the wall. "I know what dinner conversation's gonna be tonight." Without looking at Mel, since to do so would stoke the fire between them, he took off for the stall at the end of the line. "Want to stay for supper?"

She actually seemed torn for a minute then finally sighed. "I wish I could. But I really hate driving these roads out here at night."

"I'll get you home," he said quietly.

When she laughed, his body tingled.

"Are you kidding? Your little brother caught us groping. Now you're going to be having the sex talk with him, and I'm so not going to be here for that."

Yeah, he didn't want to be there for it, either. Sean clucked his tongue softly and a velvet black nose poked over the edge of the stall, followed cautiously by the rest of the horse's smoky head. "There's Lacey, there's my girl."

Mel's eyes misted, filled with such love for the horse that for a split second the sharp prick of jealousy poked at Sean's heart. He'd give almost anything to be on the receiving end of one of those looks.

"What happened to you, baby?" Taking it slow and easy, Mel reached up and scratched the mare between the eyes and then allowed Lacey to snuffle and nuzzle through her hair. "Do you think she likes me?"

Was it possible to fall more deeply in love with Mel? He wouldn't have believed so, but as he watched her let the horse get acquainted, his heart tumbled even further.

"She was abused, half-starved, and acting up because of it when she was found." Sean reached over Mel and tickled Lacey under her left ear. "The owner was beating her every day because she kept getting out of her paddock. But she was just hungry. She has a few food issues yet, but she's sound."

Mel settled her gaze on Sean, and for just a second he allowed himself to pretend that loving look lingering in her eyes was meant for him. "Did you mean it? You'll keep her for me and I can come out and ride her?"

A pleasant, homey warmth washed over Sean, and his heart started a gymnastics routine against his chest. "How about Sunday? If the weather clears?" Did he sound too eager?

She moved before he knew she was going to, which was kind of a first for him. Suddenly his arms were filled with warm, squirming, sweet-smelling woman.

She trailed little nips and kisses from his throat up to his mouth. Then her lips fused to his and his sensual buzz returned with reinforcements. She drew back to look up at him but said nothing.

"Is that a yes?" He ran his hand over the pale hair that fell to her shoulders and cupped the back of her head, pulling her toward him again, stopping with his lips an inch or so from hers. "Well?"

Mel nodded. "Yes," she whispered just before he claimed her mouth again.

The moment spun into a time-stopping spiral. Sean forgot everything but the emotional and physical sensations slamming him. When he pulled back, reason slipped in.

"It won't end well if Ricky comes looking for me again." He stepped back before he wouldn't be able to.

She licked her lips and nodded, her hand shaky when she touched his cheek. "So I guess you're staying home tonight?"

Sean lost himself in her eyes and stayed there for a long time, torn between duty to his family and desire for Mel. For just a second, something flickered in her eyes. Maybe, just maybe, it was something more than physical desire he saw. "I'd give anything for Ry to talk to Ricky. But it was me he walked in on, and I'm thinking his fath— *Bull* probably never talked to him about—" He gestured between the two of them.

Her smile softened her expression even further. She touched his cheek. "You really are a good man, Sean. I'll miss you, but you do what you need to." Then she dropped her hand and walked away.

The door was about ten paces away and she was halfway there before he realized the brightness in her eyes had been the sheen of tears. He caught up to her before she made it outside, snagging her hand and tugging her back toward him. He knew better than to move in for a straight-up confrontation. That never worked with her. So he covered her lips with his once more and kissed her until she sagged against him.

"Thank you for helping today," he said when he leaned back.

The shimmer of tears remained, but there was that flicker again, too. And just as quickly, it left. He hadn't imagined it the first time. He just didn't know what it meant.

"You did everything," she whispered, tracing his jaw with one finger. "Bethany wouldn't be here if not for you."

"Mel, seriously." He couldn't resist the temptation to play with the ends of her hair. "Before you came in, I was freaking out. On the way to messing up big. You helped me get my head together. I don't think I could have done it without you."

The flicker returned, stayed a bit longer. Shoring up his courage, Sean touched her cheek. Emotion crowded his chest. "She's a beautiful baby, isn't she?"

Mel nodded, her wide eyes looking back at him.

Sean brushed a stray tendril of hair behind her ear. "Mel... have you ever thought about, maybe having—?"

Mel's eyes went wide with alarm, then her guard fell back in place. "Oh! Look how dark it's getting." She pulled free and walked outside. "I really have to go. Valentine's is going to be hopping and LeeAnn's by herself."

Sean sagged. There it was. Just the barest hint of a mention that he'd like something more permanent between them, and she'd shut him down again. He watched her leave, feeling the prick of a fresh wound on his heart. Why was she so resistant to any type of deeper relationship?

* * *

Mel kept it together while she drove away from the ranch, tossing a wave at Sean with a synthetic smile pasted on her face. When she got to the highway, she couldn't hold back the hot tears. He'd looked beyond hurt when she brushed him off. She hated it when he was hurt. Hated more that she'd been the cause of his pain. But she was in a maze of trouble without a road map, and no matter which direction she turned, someone was going to suffer.

Wind gusted, slashing rain across the windshield. The road in front of her wavered and disappeared. Mel didn't care. For just a second it didn't matter if she lived or died.

She entered the curve on the last switch before town and felt like she was on ice. Time slowed and stretched. Her body was thrown right. The road ahead became visible through her side window. Then through the windshield she had a view of the way she'd just come. Gray and brown blurred together after that and she had no idea what she was seeing. Her shoulder slammed painfully into the door as the shoulder belt grabbed her neck in a stranglehold.

God! I didn't mean it! Don't let me die!

The tires hit gravel with a nauseating crunch. Someone screamed. The little car came to a jarring stop, at a sharp tilt, its engine stalled. An inane song about a rodeo and the ride of a lifetime blared on the radio. She stabbed at the off button, missed. Tried again and missed. On her third attempt the musical twang ceased.

A hush fell over the car, broken only by the steady drum of the rain on the roof and the obscene *swish-thwack* of the windshield wipers. Something pounded in time with her too-rapid heartbeat, and after she gulped a few ragged breaths, she recognized her pulse hammering in her ears. Purple flashes began to edge her vision, so she forced her breathing to slow. Then she leaned her head against her steering wheel and broke into body-wracking sobs.

As the tears poured forth, rivaling the deluge outside, Mel tried to numb her mind; tried to forget that she loved a man who would no doubt hate her if he ever found out the truth. And the little voice in her mind whispered that maybe this near-miss would have been a fitting end after all.

The car door was wrenched open, blowing in sheets of rain. Mel screamed and frantically tried to climb over to the passenger seat, away from the intruder.

"Melanie! It's DC. Are you okay?"

Sheriff Dirk Cooley, DC to most, ducked his head inside her tiny car, bringing some of the relentless downpour with him. Rainwater rolled from his plastic-protected hat onto her shoulder.

As soon as Mel's heart settled out of her throat, she nodded. "I lost control for a minute. I just need to get the car started."

"Mel, you aren't taking this vehicle anywhere." DC nodded toward the front of the car. "You broke the axle."

With a wail, Mel buried her face in her hands and felt the sobs taking over again.

"Hey, now. Don't cry. Are you hurt?"

DC seemed discomfited. *Tough.* This was just one more thing on her crap list of life. A list that was getting too long. But it was *her* list and that meant she could cry about it if she decided to.

More water dripped as he waited without a word.

When the tears abated some, she sighed. "No, not hurt. I'm okay."

"Come on out of there. I'll give you a ride home and call Blackstone to get you towed."

In a totally useless but completely endearing act of chivalry, DC held his clipboard over Mel's head against the rain while he walked her to his cruiser.

"I'll be right back." He helped her settle in the front seat. "I need to set a couple of flares."

Mel stared at the computer setup on the dash, but it was Sean's emotionally charged face that she saw. Jacking her elbow onto the armrest, she cradled her forehead in one hand.

By the time DC returned, her tears had stopped, leaving her with a fuzzy-stuffy feeling.

DC called for the tow. Before putting the car in gear, he glanced at Mel. "You sure you're okay? You want to go up to Jackson and get checked out?"

She sniffed. "I'm good."

"Your eyes are red. Are you driving under the influence?"

Under the influence of a breaking heart, maybe. She sniffed again. "It's just from crying. It was a big day."

The sheriff smiled. "I hear Sandy had her baby, a little girl."

"Yeah." Mel smiled. "Sean delivered her."

DC laughed. "Really? That part I didn't hear. I can't wait to tell Rachel that one. She healthy?"

"Real healthy. And real pretty." Mel heard the wistful quality in her voice and closed her eyes against the emotion clouding her heart.

"Sandy and Ryan'll find life even more adventurous now," said DC.

They made the rest of the short drive to the bar in silence. But thoughts tumbled over themselves in her head. Sean wanted her. She wanted Sean. Sean wanted... more than she was free to give as long as her past hung over her. How could she bring herself and Sean to the same page — hell, the same book?

There's only one way.

The cruiser glided to a stop in front of Valentine's. Her hand on the door handle, Mel turned to the sheriff. If she was to have any chance with Sean, she would have to face her past.

"DC, do you have any idea how I can find a black sheep?"

His only reaction was one raised eyebrow. "Now, why do I get the feeling you're not talking about the four-legged kind?"

Slowly she shook her head, hoping she wasn't making a huge mistake by confiding in DC. "No, you're right. It's a man."

Chapter Four

Justin retired to the living room directly after dinner, where he'd probably sneak a cigar. And that was just fine with Sean. The only thing he could think of that would be worse than having "the talk" with Ricky would be having it with the family patriarch looking on. A black and white border collie hovered in the kitchen doorway, obviously torn between curling up in front of the fire and the possibility of more table scraps.

Sandy would probably kill him if she was there. But since she wasn't... Sean grabbed the bone from his steak and tossed it to the dog. "There ya go, Patch. Now go bug the old man."

Ricky stacked their plates and hiked over to the kitchen sink. He wasn't being particularly talkative but from the speculative gleam in his eye whenever he glanced at Sean, it was clear no bullets had been dodged.

Another of Ricky's sidelong glances caught him, and Sean sighed. "Something on your mind?"

Ricky lifted a shoulder and went back to loading the dishwasher.

Sean rolled his eyes at the kid's back and turned away. Nothing was easy with him. Nothing. He could guess what was going through the boy's head, but without knowing for certain, Sean could very well step into an even stickier situation. The kid still spooked easily over what anyone else would consider relatively uncomplicated things. And how the hell much did he know about — that?

The clatter of a plate hitting the floor startled Sean from his musing, and he spun around. The plate hadn't broken, but Ricky stood frozen in place staring at it. It had been a year and a half since he'd been rescued from the abusive home he'd lived in his whole life, but he still seemed to expect the iron fist to come down on him for simple accidents. Sean looked at the glass in his hand. Sometimes opening the door to discussion was worth a small sacrifice. He waited until Ricky turned his back then deliberately dropped the glass, watching it shatter into several pointed shards.

"Well, crap," he said, blowing it off with a shrug and a grin as he moved for the broom next to the pantry.

Ricky's blue eyes went wide as he glanced over his shoulder toward the sitting room. Then he stared at Sean for a second, opened his mouth, and closed it again.

"Relax, kid." Sean swept the pieces into a dustpan and pitched them in the trash. "It's just a glass."

"Do you have someone you want to reach out to tonight?" asked the radio DJ in a sultry voice. *"Give me a call. I'm Lilah Rae and I'm here all night."*

The soft strains of a romantic country ballad filled the air. Why the hell had they left the radio on? An itchy sensation tripped along Sean's spine.

"Ricky..." Sean cleared his throat. "Um, you know you can talk about anything with me, right?" He tossed in a soap pellet, closed the door to the dishwasher, and set it to run. "No pressure, no judgment. If something's working at you, we'll work it through together."

"Are you and Mel doing it?" Embarrassment leaked like cherry-colored paint, staining the kid's freckled face.

Well, so much for a delicate conversation and stepping lightly. Sean pinched the bridge of his nose, then dragged his hand down his face and rubbed his jaw. "No, Mel and I aren't having sex."

"But in the stable—"

Sean blew out a long breath. Delivering a baby and having a sex talk with a teen in the same day was really pushing his limits. Especially since he was the McGee brother who *wasn't* married.

"You walked in on an... intimate moment, but we weren't having sex the way I think you mean." Sean shook his head. "We haven't taken that step."

Ricky looked away. "Sorry."

"It's okay. I told you we could talk about anything." He needed to do something with his shaking hands. Pulling two sodas from the refrigerator gave him the excuse to keep his eyes averted. Sean handed one to Ricky, opened his own, and took a long swig. His mind drifted to the cold beer he would have had while watching Mel work. Maybe taking a night off from sitting at the bar and wishing she'd fall in love with him wasn't such a bad thing.

Ricky sank into one of the kitchen chairs and played with the condensation on his can. "Why aren't you having sex with Mel?"

Very carefully, Sean swallowed the mouthful of soda, managing not to choke in the process. Okay, so they were going to get plenty intense. He stifled a sigh and set down the can.

"We haven't reached that stage." He surveyed the teen, and decided to turn the tables a little. "So what about you? Are you active — sexually?" He suppressed a wince. *Great. I sound like a damn condom commercial.*

One finger drew a straight line down from the top of the can as Ricky seemed to be giving the question some thought. Geez, did that mean the answer was yes? *Say no, say no, say no.* Finally the kid lifted a shoulder in a noncommittal gesture. If Sean had to guess, he'd say that was a no. He hated guessing.

"Got someone you're maybe looking at?" he asked softly.

Too quickly, Ricky turned his face away. *Oh, joy.* No doubt that was a yes.

Maybe he should cut the boy a break. Sean offered a half-shrug. "I didn't have sex until I was almost twenty."

Ricky's head whipped up and he stared with incredulity. "No way," he whispered.

"My first time was with a girl I'd been seeing for a few months, and we stayed together for about a year before we realized we didn't have a lot of spark between us. We worked better as friends. Turns out, we're still good friends. The second girl I made love with was when I was twenty-one. That lasted about six months. Turned out she hated the small town scene and didn't actually want to live on the ranch."

"Did you love her?"

Good question. The boy was bright. Drawing in a heavy breath, Sean met Ricky's eyes and shook his head slowly. "I won't lie to you. I wish I did love her. I *liked* her a lot. I tried to talk myself into falling in love with her. And I think she wanted to love me. But if we'd really loved each other, we would have found a way to make it work." He paused to give his words time to sink in and give Ricky time to ask questions. When the teen remained silent, Sean said. "There hasn't been anyone else until Mel."

That brought on a startled blink. "You've only had two girls?"

Taking great care not to show his negative reaction to the phrasing, Sean leaned his chair back onto two legs. "I prefer to think of it in terms of I've had intimate relationships with two women. *Having* a woman, a girl... makes me think of marking notches on my bedpost. Just having sex without some sort of relationship... well, the concept's always felt shallow to me. Even if the girl says that's what she wants. So I got to know the girl without that kind of intimacy first."

The chair squeaked as Ricky fidgeted. He concentrated on moving his soda can in a little circle on the table. After a long moment, he spoke without looking up. "How do you know if it's okay?"

The boy in front of him was inches away from becoming a man. Caught now between the thoughts and feelings of childhood and the growing interest of adult thoughts and feelings, Ricky hadn't known the meaning of love for nearly sixteen years. He might as well be barreling down the interstate without a road map. Sean's heart broke all over again.

"Every time you make love with someone, whether it's a one-night thing or a long-term relationship, you give up a piece of yourself to the other person." Sean took a drink. He was so over his head. "I'm not talking about the DNA deposit you make when you have intimate contact. When you make love, it's about giving and receiving on more than just a physical level. Or it should be. You both give, you both receive. And when you do that, it's very personal. It's..." With a sigh, he spread his hands, searching for the right word. "It's kind of unexplainable — emotional. Part of what makes you who you are goes into it and stays with that other person. And part of her stays with you. You don't want to do that lightly, give away pieces of yourself. You don't want to lose the sense of who you really are. And you sure as hell don't want a woman giving you part of herself if that part of her isn't going to be special to you."

Twin lines rose from the bridge of Ricky's nose as his face screwed up in confusion. *Great, I lost him.*

The confusion dropped from Ricky's face. "How do you know if someone likes you back?"

Okay, back to easy territory. "Does she spend time with you?"

After some squirming in his seat, Ricky gave a quick nod.

"How long have you been spending time together?"

"Since summer," came the mumbled answer.

"Do you hold hands when you're together?"

A quick nod and nothing more.

"Kiss?"

"Some."

"Touch?"

Twin flames blossomed in the kid's cheeks. *Oh, crap.* Sean's heart sank to floor level. Maybe no actual *sex* sex yet, but he was on the path.

"Does the touching feel good?"

Ricky's head popped up, his eyes bulging with panic.

Sean held up a hand and smiled. "Okay, let me say that differently. I get that it feels good physically. But does it feel... *okay?* In your head. Or does it make you uncomfortable? Like you're doing something that's wrong?"

The pinched look returned, and Ricky answered slowly. "Kinda both, I guess."

"Do you feel like she's pushing you? Or... like you might be pushing her?" Sean flicked his eyes over the red and white can resting against his palm and shook his head. Man, he needed a stronger drink. The soda definitely wasn't doing the job.

Ricky shook his head. "It just kind of happened last Sunday."

Sean took a drink as he wracked his brain. *Where did the kid go last Sunday?* Memories of the white van picking him up hit with a jolt. "At the church hayride?"

"After."

"You were at Brother Bobby's house after." *Maybe make that drink a double.* Making out in the pastor's home? Not the best idea.

Ricky shrugged again. "Yeah."

"So who was there with you?" Keeping it light and casual, Sean risked a long pull on his soda, tipping the nearly empty can high.

"No one." Ricky blushed again. "I mean, it was just me and Lynn."

Sean froze, head tilted back, can still raised to his lips. Soda shot into his nose as he choked on the mouthful. He swallowed what was left, lowered the can, and set it on the counter without taking his eyes from the kid. "Higgins? Brother Bobby's baby girl? Lynn Higgins?"

It shouldn't have been possible for Ricky's face to become any redder but it did. The boy nodded, a wary look in his eyes.

Sean pushed a hand through his hair and calculated the number of steps to the bottle of Jack in the cabinet. Maybe he should just keep the whole bottle handy.

"She's really nice to me. And she doesn't care that I'm a bastard."

If Sean hadn't already been sitting down, he would have fallen to the floor. Well, crap. What had he done to piss the devil off enough to drag him into hell?

"Ricky, you're not— okay. One thing at a time." Sean rubbed his jaw and eyed the hallway that led to the living room. "About the —touching. I think because it feels kind of good and kind of not that you aren't ready to go any further." *Please, don't go any further — especially not with the preacher's youngest daughter.* Sean reached into his back pocket and pulled out his wallet. "I don't believe I'm about to do this, and I don't want you to think of this as me giving you a green light here, okay?" He pinned the kid with a hard stare. "Because I'm *not*." He pulled out a square foil packet and held it up. "You know what this is?"

The redness crept back into Ricky's face. "It's a rub— ah, a—"

Sean nodded. *Yeah, now you got the idea, kid.* "It's a condom. It's okay to call it a rubber. Heck, I don't care what you call it. Just take it, keep it in your wallet. And if you end up in a position where you need to use it — and I hope you *don't* for a while yet — but if you do, *please* use it." He slid the packet across the table, where it sat untouched. *Now what?* "Ah, do you know how to use it?" Sean squeezed his eyes shut. *Please know how to use it.* He took a deep breath and slowly opened his eyes.

Ricky stared, then finally gave one quick nod.

Relief poured through him, but he had to be certain. "Really?"

"Health class," mumbled Ricky.

Sean huffed out a breath. "I mean it, Ricky. I didn't give it to you because I'm saying go get laid. I don't want you to need it for a long time."

The condom sat untouched, but Ricky offered a quick nod.

"And it's a good idea to replace it every so often. If it's been in your wallet for a while, like more than a couple of months, toss that one and get a fresh one. If you need more, if you need a fresh one, or if you use that one, there's a box under the sink in my bathroom. You don't need to ask, just take what you need, okay? I don't count."

Again Ricky nodded.

"About that other thing, being a bas— ah, being illegitimate." Control was a struggle when he wanted to kill something. Sean gritted his teeth and breathed in, long and slow, through his nose. "Are people calling you that?"

Ricky lifted one shoulder and looked away.

"I'm reading that as a yes." Sean leaned over, trying to see the kid's face. "Who?"

"Some kids at school. It's nothing."

But it wasn't nothing. And Sean knew the speech about it just being a word was useless. "Ricky." His voice was hoarse as emotion clogged his throat. "I don't think of you like that. None of us here do. We — I..." He drew a deep breath. "I love you."

Red flooded Ricky's face again. "Aw, geez."

Sean stood up and rounded the table. "Yeah, I know. It's been a weird day. But I mean it, kid. You kinda grew on me. A little." He rubbed Ricky's hair. "Now get upstairs and play some video games."

Ricky stood, his manner more at ease. "Sean... I..." His face contorted into a mix of discomfort and confusion.

"I know, kid." Sean patted the kid on the back. "Take the condom and get out of here before we have a chick flick moment."

Still, Ricky hesitated.

Sean sighed. Nothing was ever, ever easy with this kid. "Something else on your mind?"

"I don't have a wallet."

A laugh escaped and Sean realized his heart felt a little less bashed than it had after his last encounter with Mel. "Check my top dresser drawer. Ry and Sandy gave me one for my birthday that I haven't cracked out yet. Take it." When Ricky looked like he was going to protest, Sean gave him a little push. "Hey, I said take it."

When he was alone, Sean let out a long, slow breath. Standing in front of the refrigerator, he bashed his head against the door. Twice.

"You look like someone dumped a load of manure on your garden party," Justin said from the doorway.

"I may be wrong, but I'm pretty sure I planned to be married and have babies, and *then* have the sex talk with said babies when they reached the appropriate age, preferably somewhere in their twenties." Sean banged his head again. "There's just something about being barely thirty and having the sex talk before all the rest that feels out of order."

A hearty guffaw erupted from Justin as he moved to the refrigerator and pulled on the door. "Beer? Of course, it's not like that draft stuff you'd have gotten if you'd gone to see your lady tonight." He held up a bottle.

Water actually sounded like a better balm for his dry throat, and Sean shook his head, moving to the sink instead. "Dad, did you know kids are calling Ricky a bastard? And I'm thinking they learned it from somewhere." Their parents?

In the middle of returning the second beer to the refrigerator, Justin stiffened. His hand faltered. "The boy's been calling himself that since he learned who his real father is. Old man MacKay himself started it."

Rage was hot and fierce. Sean knocked back the water and set the tumbler down with a sharp snap. "If MacKay wasn't already in prison for murdering those women and for raping Ricky's mother, I'd have to kill him just for putting that on the kid."

"And I'd have to agree with you." Justin opened the cookie jar and took out a cookie.

"Do you know he sometimes slips and calls you 'Dad'?"

A pleased smile crept over Justin's face. "I've heard it a time or two. Kinda working on something to help him out with that. Stopped in to see his mom today."

Tension coiled in Sean's middle. "How *is* Brenda?" Justin had guardianship status at the whim of Ricky's mother and it could be revoked at any time if she changed her mind, so defensiveness was a knee-jerk reaction. One he hated because it reminded him how helpless they really were. "Does she want the kid back?"

Justin shook his head. "She loves him, misses him. She'd like to see him. But no, she wants a fresh start. She thinks the boy needs one, too."

"Harsh. He's innocent in all this." Sean let out the breath he'd been holding. "He gets to stay here then, right?"

"Yup." Justin's nod bordered on giddy. "I've been thinking for the past few weeks. I know he's coming up on his eighteenth birthday next summer, but I was considering asking him if he'd let me make him my son. Legally."

Sean sat down heavily and looked up at his father. Yeah, the old man was serious. "I think... I think that's genius, and my bet is he'll like the idea."

"What about you?" Justin went for another cookie. "Do you like the idea?"

"I do." Sean rubbed the back of his neck. "I really do. He's already my brother in every way it counts. But making it official... legal. Yeah, I'd like that. I gather Ry already knows?"

"Yep. We talked to Brenda together. She's comfortable with the idea. So now it's just up to the boy." Justin rubbed his jaw. "Guess I need to find the right time to ask him what he wants."

It was rare for Sean to see his father so uncertain. That uncertainty meant he really cared.

A prickle of awareness eased into the back of Sean's head. It always happened as a subtle sensation. He didn't know where it came from or how it worked, but it was never wrong.

"You can try now." He caught Justin's eye and nodded toward the dining room. "You want to come in and join the conversation, Ricky? Seems only fair, since we're talking about you."

A few hesitant steps into the room were apparently all Ricky could manage. Hovering just at the doorway, he had that fearful expression in his eyes again, like he was certain his life was about to go to crap.

"How much did you hear, kid?" Sean leaned back in the chair and propped one leg on the table, pointedly ignoring his dad's hard stare. If this was going to be Painful Conversation Number Two, he might as well get comfortable.

"Justin and Ryan went to see my mom." The words were barely above a whisper and he was choosing them with too much care.

Sean raised an eyebrow. "That's all you heard?"

"She doesn't — want me back." Ricky's voice shook.

Without a doubt, he'd heard nearly the whole conversation, but he'd zeroed in on the one thing that hurt him the most. What he saw as his mother's rejection instead of her gift of liberation.

"Ah, Brenda's — she doesn't—" *Crap!* Sean shot a pointed stare at his father. *Feel free to chime in any time.*

Justin bit into another cookie and offered a shrug as if to say, *"You're doing fine."*

The kid continued to hold Sean in his steady stare.

Oh, hell. He pushed himself straight in the chair, dropping his foot to the floor.

"Ricky." His voice was no more than a croak. Sean cleared his throat and tried again. "It's not — it's never been a question about whether your mom wants you or not." The words formed and tumbled out before Sean even realized what he was saying. But he knew they were the right words by the way they felt on his tongue and in his heart. "She loves you and only wants what's best for you, and right now she figures we can give that to you better than she can. She knows she's pretty messed up, and she feels that she has to be able to get her own life together before she'll be any good to anyone else. That's the only reason she agreed to let you stay here."

When Sean finished speaking, Justin coughed and swiped at his eyes. For the first time in his life, Sean saw his father as vulnerable. It hadn't been contentment for Sean to lead this discussion driving the old man. Ricky's decision mattered to Justin McGee. A lot. The broken-heart-if-it-doesn't-work kind of mattered. Sean rubbed the back of his neck.

A shuffling movement as Ricky shifted his stance in the doorway broke Sean out of his introspection. "So, ah, you get that you can stay here no matter what, right?"

One quick silent nod was the only reaction. Ricky's blue eyes were so like Mac's, they sometimes hurt to look at, and that blue gaze clung to Sean now, seeking... something. Acceptance? He had that. Connection? Or maybe just love.

"What Dad wants... what we *all* would like... is for Dad to adopt you, to make you legally part of the family and give you the McGee name." Sean settled back to watch the subtle emotions play over Ricky's face.

"You'll be eighteen in just under a year." Justin finally spoke up. "So maybe it doesn't matter to you. Once you're an adult, you can legally change your name and it won't matter who your parents are. If that's what you want to do. Or if you want to stay with the name MacKay, that's up to you."

For a split second, the kid looked like he'd been given the keys to Disneyland. Then the shutters closed on his expression. He'd be hell at Friday night poker.

Ricky's mouth worked soundlessly for a minute. "I could be— You *want* me?" Aw, geez, the kid sounded skeptical, like he didn't believe anyone *could* want him.

Justin chuckled. "Oh, yeah, I want you, boy. So you know, I think of you as my son already." Justin eyed the cookie jar then shook his head and pushed it away. "But I would like to make it legal, for the rest of our lives."

"And my name would be McGee?"

Justin nodded. "If that's what you want."

"Could I — could I change my middle name?"

Sean's gut heaved and he huffed out a breath. He should have seen that one coming. Ricky's middle name was

Brody, the name of the man who'd raped his mother and fathered him.

Again Justin nodded. "Got a name in mind?"

"John."

And that made sense, too, thought Sean. The given name of the man everyone had thought of as Ricky's father for years, his mother's childhood sweetheart, Sean's cousin.

"Ricky John McGee sounds good to me," said Sean.

"Could we do it right away?" asked Ricky almost before Sean was finished speaking. So much for the worry about his answer.

The tension in Justin's features eased. "It'll take a little time for the papers to go through the court, but I've got them ready to go with our attorney. Could be you'll have that name by the end of the year." He smiled. "That is, if you're saying yes."

"Yes!" Ricky nodded. "Yes, sir."

"Good. Now, get your backside back to bed and quit eavesdropping." Justin's smile and the laughter in his voice showed him for the soft-hearted man Sean knew he really was.

Still grinning, Ricky took off out of the kitchen.

Smiling himself, Sean stood and pushed his hands over his head in an exaggerated stretch then started to follow Ricky.

"Not you, Sean." His father's voice held an air of authority that had never been possible to ignore. Apparently, he was about to be put on the spot for something.

Without a word, he dropped back into his seat. Then he waited while his father drew a glass of water from the tap, bringing it to the table and taking the chair across from Sean.

Justin swirled the glass, staring at it until the water stopped moving. Sean stifled a yawn. It was the old man's way. It was also Ryan's way, and both of them ticked him off with it. But if he said anything, his father would only take that much longer to get to the point.

"You did a good thing today, boy."

Sean felt his tension easing. Maybe it wouldn't be a deep conversation after all.

"I did what had to be done, Dad."

"Yeah, you did." Justin was watching him. "Thing is, you do that a lot. Always doing what's right, never missing your step. I figure a lot of that's because you're so dang cautious."

Sean sighed impatiently. "Dad, if this is about Mel, I swear I'll walk out. I don't want to talk about her."

"You don't have to talk. Just listen." Justin sipped his water.

Sean noted he didn't deny he was going to talk about Mel and heaved a sigh.

"You know, this house is getting mighty crowded."

Sean shrugged. "Nothing to do about it. And it's not so bad." He stood and went for the cookie jar, getting two chocolate chip cookies because he knew his dad would just take his if he didn't. When he sat again, he slid Justin's cookie across the table.

"I've been thinking since this past summer, might be there's something we *can* do about it." Justin took a bite of the cookie and smiled. "You remember that tract of land in toward town you liked when you were all of twelve?"

Sean froze in mid-bite. He nodded slowly.

"When we were at the attorney's today, I started the paperwork to have it signed over to your name. It'd be a nice place for a homestead. Got enough room for your barns and paddocks."

"Are you—?" Sean set his cookie down and stared at Justin, astonishment driving his heart like a stampede in his chest. "Are you kicking me out?"

"Naw." Justin shook his head and toyed with cookie crumbs that had fallen to the table. "I'm not kicking you out. Not even asking you to leave. I'm offering you the opportunity to start on your own life instead of always doing the right thing by others without thought to yourself."

Sean felt his jaw go slack. He knew he was staring at his father with his mouth wide open but he couldn't think of a word to say. So he abruptly clamped his jaw shut and swallowed hard over the lump in his throat.

Justin met Sean's stare with a look of understanding. "I'm saying it's your turn, son."

His turn for what? Justin's gaze was as unfathomable as it was discomfiting, and Sean shifted his eyes to the table. The cookie in front of him had seven chips visible on top. He knew that because he counted them twice while he tried to figure out how he felt about the latest development in a day full of changes and surprises. "Can I give it some thought?"

With a knowing smile, Justin lifted a shoulder and picked up Sean's uneaten cookie. "Land's yours when you want it. If you want to stay under the Cross MC or go out on your own, we'll help finance your building. One percent interest." He held up a hand against Sean's argument. "That's not negotiable."

He knew when to give up. His eyes burned, not from tears or anything. Exhaustion was more like it. Sean blinked hard a couple of times until he was certain he could speak. "Thanks, Dad."

"One more thing." Justin pulled a square brown box from his pocket and set it on the table in front of him. A jewelry box with plenty of wear around its edges.

Sean huffed out a laugh. "You're proposing to me?"

Justin chuckled. He toyed with the box. Finally he spoke, his words quiet. "About thirty years ago, your mom told me she was expecting. She was certain she was giving me another son to help carry on, and she was right. She was always right about things like that. When you were born, you had her eyes. And we all could see you had fire inside you, but it sure was a slow burn. No flash fires for you." He rotated the box so the opening was pointed in Sean's direction, but he left it closed. "You were even cautious taking your first breath. They kind of..." He drew in a long breath of his own. "...had to coax you along a little. The docs were all just a little worried, but your mom said to just give you a little time and you'd work it out. You heard her voice and gulped in your first breath. Then you let out a scream that almost brought the hospital down." He slid the box toward Sean.

Sean stared at the box but didn't touch it. Now he *was* on the verge of tears. Of all the stories Justin told, which were many, he'd never heard that one, hadn't realized he'd caused anyone concern just by being born. He rubbed the lower half of his face with a hand that trembled.

"I bought this ring for your mom that day, Sean. Because more than giving me my second son, she taught me to have faith and to be patient."

Sean opened the box.

"This belongs to you now that your mom's gone. I don't know what you'll want to do with it, but I know, given time, you'll work that out, too. Just like your mom always said about you."

The large teardrop emerald was set in white gold and surrounded by tiny diamonds. Memories flickered in his head like an old film. His mother had worn the ring on her right hand. He'd always been fascinated by its sparkle. He'd been seven when she'd died in a drowning accident — which had turned out not to be an accident after all.

He remembered her eyes, almost as green as the emerald, and her stories. She'd been even more of a storyteller than his dad. And he remembered always feeling safe when he was with her. She'd taught him and Ryan the names of flowers, watched the night sky with them, taken them on walks in the woods and told them stories of fairies and trolls. And she'd read them poetry. She'd done it, or so he understood from his dad, because she didn't want their world to be confined to just the ranch.

But it didn't really matter why she'd done it. The memories of those times gave him strength that still sustained him, especially when he ran into trouble.

Sean closed the box and shut his eyes for a moment. When he had his emotions under control, he met his father's gaze.

"Thanks, Dad."

* * *

Sean had told her he wasn't coming in that night, so Mel had no idea why she kept watching the door. But every time it opened, her head spun in that direction. Finally, it was time to close. The lights had been turned out, and she slowly climbed the stairs to her apartment above the bar.

Lots of things preyed on her mind, burdens that grew heavier with each step. She sure missed the days when she and Sandy could tell each other anything with no judgment between them, no lectures. Just silent listening and friendly advice. And maybe some delectable chocolate comfort food.

Mel thought of the letter now resting with the others in a box on top of her refrigerator. She hated her brother, loathed her father. And hoped like hell she'd done the right thing by opening a discussion with DC.

She turned the key in the lock and opened the door to her lonely apartment, jerking in surprise when a droplet of wetness splashed onto her hand. More tears? Really? She'd hated the time she'd spent away from Orson's Folly. And she knew Grandma Tilly would tell her it was unchristian, but she hated Nick DeVayne as much as it was possible to hate someone.

Mel wiped the tears with a tissue and sniffed. Damn Denny for his letters, and for dredging up the crappiest time in her life. What was in the past should stay where it belonged.

But a part of her also realized that until she addressed what lay back there, she could have no future with Sean. And Sean was the only reason she'd come home to Orson's Folly. She'd been a fool to think that the past would stay buried.

Chapter Five

Running on autopilot, Sean guided his pickup onto the highway heading for Orson's Folly. Watery sun glinting off the silver hood and shining through his windshield barely took the edge off the October chill, and it wouldn't do much to dry up the puddles lingering along the side of the road.

How the hell had his day been rustled away from him? One minute finishing up breakfast and making googly eyes at his niece, newly home from the hospital with a clean bill of health, the next bundled into his truck with a shopping list. A *list*!

He detested running errands. Handling the day-to-day operations at the ranch was a much more satisfying activity. Until the last weeks of her pregnancy, they'd counted on Sandy to run in to town. She usually spent at least four or five days a week in Orson's Folly as part-owner of Valentine's, anyway. Of course, carting an infant to make feed purchases or to the hardware store didn't make much sense, so life as he knew it would undoubtedly change. A lot. Trips to town would probably fall more on him and Ryan and sometimes on Ricky, when the kid wasn't in school or working his part-time job.

They'd have to work out a system, though, since Sean didn't plan to go grocery shopping every time they needed the pantry stocked. And considering the list tucked in his pocket with the four or five very female items Sandy had added at the last minute... he shuddered. He wasn't squeamish or anything. Hadn't he bit the bullet and helped deliver Baby Bethany? But a guy needed limits when it came to buying feminine hygiene products.

Coming off the last switch before town, Sean's eyes were drawn to the side of the road. Thick black skid marks corkscrewed across the road, then aimed straight for the shoulder where a torn-up patch showed a sudden stop in the soft dirt. Someone had spiraled out of control after that last turn. He hoped whoever it was hadn't been hurt. It didn't look like they'd gone over the embankment. It was only about a ten-foot drop, but it would have been jarring. And the river at the bottom was still running high with all the rain.

Shaking his head, he sped up again, heading for Valentine's. Should he stop? He slowed as he drove past and then frowned at the empty parking space where Mel normally kept her car.

Odd. She usually worked on Saturday mornings doing setup for one of the two busiest days of the week.

His gaze slid to the right as he crossed the intersection and a flash of red in front of Walt Blackstone's Auto Repair earned a second look. Ah ha! Mel's missing car. The front passenger wheel was caved inward. She'd broken her axle. Aw, hell, that was going to bite. When had it happened? He didn't think he'd missed her call. Maybe she'd been close to home.

It would only take a few minutes to find out how much the damage would run. Sean steered his pickup into Blackstone's parking lot and stopped next to the wrecked car. The thing sure was a mess. He dropped to the damp ground and slid on his back under the front of the car. Holy crap, the axle had been sheared right off. How long had that been waiting to happen?

Footsteps crunched alongside the car and someone crouched. "Heck of a mess," mumbled Blackstone in his gravelly smoker's voice. "I told Melanie she should just write the car off and get something else. Repairs are gonna cost more than the dang thing's worth."

The tight squeeze beneath the car made maneuvering out from under it tricky. Sean squeezed out and rolled to his feet, dusting his hands on his jeans. "How'd it happen?"

The car groaned and dipped a bit as Walt braced his hands on the fender and pushed to his feet. "Skidded herself off the road yesterday out by Five Forks switchback."

Sean struggled to drag air into lungs that didn't seem to fit in his chest. Black tire marks and the torn up patch of shoulder flashed through his memory. Frigid invisible fingers played up and down his spine.

"Mel?" he forced through stiff lips, hoping Blackstone understood what he was asking.

"DC gave her a lift."

The breath left Sean's lungs with a rush as he sagged with relief. Why hadn't she called him? He ran a shaky hand through his hair. She'd had an accident on the way home from the ranch, and a bad one. But she hadn't called to tell him about it. Not even a text. *She's slipping away by degrees,* a tiny voice whispered.

"I gotta go," he murmured, stepping around Walt.

Something was wrong, had been wrong for months. The way she'd left the day before was only a symptom of whatever was off, but he'd been too butt-hurt himself to try to work it through with her and had let her leave instead.

The drive across the street to the bar was too short to work anything through, so when he strode inside, his heart was still hammering against his chest — the way it had been since Walt had told him what had happened. The torment tearing at his senses wouldn't be alleviated until he assured himself Mel was all right.

A solitary figure perched on one of the stools in front of the bar, leaning over a newspaper, probably the *Folly Gazette*. Her face was hidden by the curtain of blond hair that reflected blue and red and green off the neon bar lights above the mirror. Mel. The world stopped whirling out of control and his heart fell back into the usual slightly erratic rhythm it seemed to adopt whenever she was near. A fresh surge of relief flushed his system of some tension.

He scuffed his boots along the polished tile floor.

With a start, she looked up and met his gaze, smiling in pleased surprise. Not even a second later, her guard fell into place.

Well, he'd about had it with that guardedness of hers. It wasn't going to get in his way, not this time. And he knew one sure way to get her to drop it. Three quick strides eliminated the distance between them.

"Hey, Sean. What brings you—?"

Her eyes widened as he took hold of her shoulders and moved in, capturing her lips in a frantic kiss born of the realization that he could have lost her, leaving all the words jumbled inside him unspoken. Her fingers fisted in his shirt. His arms slid around to her back and he pulled her tight against him, trapping her arms between them. His angst became a combination of longing and need that nudged away his customary caution.

Her lips, so warm and welcoming, her body so soft and his for the taking. He'd never felt more alive than he did as he pinned her against the bar and lost himself in the passion that always hovered between them like an ion-charged storm, ready to erupt with thunder. She went limp in his arms with a moan as he claimed the affirmation of her life that he needed for his own to continue.

* * *

The desperation in Sean's kiss clued Mel that something was wrong. Immediately, predictable scenarios stormed through her mind. Was it Sandy or the baby? His father? When the tone of the kiss rolled over to desire and he dragged her from the barstool, she swayed against him. Whatever was wrong, kissing her seemed to be fixing it. She opened her mouth to his questing tongue, enjoying the sensual invasion.

He broke the kiss slowly, retreating by inches at a time.

A contented sigh slipped past Mel's lips. "Hey, gorgeous man. Not that I'm complaining or anything, but what's going on?"

His palms were warm cupped against her face as he searched her face. His eyes lost some of his initial agitation, but they still contained an intensity she'd never noticed before.

"I saw your car and — where you went off the road." He pulled back a little and ran his hands over her shoulders, down her arms, up along her ribs, before slipping around to her back and drawing her close again, hips to hips.

Warmth spread from his touch in the small of her back. They'd never had trouble fitting perfectly against one another. She pushed the odd thought aside with a smile.

Slowly, he bent and rested his forehead against hers. "Are you okay?"

"I... had a moment. When it happened." She reached up and brushed the backs of her fingers along his jaw. He hadn't shaved and the stubble prickled deliciously against her skin. Ever so slightly, he pushed into her touch. "Yeah... I'm okay," she whispered, holding onto his gaze. But she hadn't been okay, not really. Not until he'd walked through the door.

And now he was there. Caring. Strong. And because she felt herself not only leaning against him, but leaning toward letting him take care of her through her latest crisis and maybe the rest of her life, Mel recoiled. She had to get her life in order before she could entertain any idea of happily ever after — if such a thing even existed for her. She straightened and turned back to the newspaper, folding it without righting it.

Before she could cram it under the bar, Sean stilled her movements. "What's this?" He tapped a finger on one of the red circles she'd drawn.

"It's nothing. I'm looking for another car. It's going to be cheaper than fixing my old one." She reached for the paper but he held it out of her reach, reading it.

"In the barely-running, never-safe, piece-of-shit section of the classifieds?" Sean shook out the paper. "This one's as old as I am and has over three hundred thousand miles."

"But its transmission's been replaced."

"Replaced with what, a couple of squirrels instead of just one?"

"And it's only five hundred dollars."

He grunted. "It's not worth five hundred cents." He went back to reading. "Okay, this one's a little newer. Runs but needs engine work. *Some* front end damage. The guy probably hit a tree and screwed up the engine."

"It's only six hundred." The heat of embarrassment was beginning to creep in, pulverizing the sliver of confidence she'd found upon convincing herself she could afford another car if she just searched hard enough.

Shaking his head, Sean turned the paper over and read the next ad she'd marked. "No, Mel. Just — no. Why are you looking at such crappy cars? Are you on a tight budget?"

"Technically, yes." She tried to snatch the paper again but he only held it higher. "I'm partner in this place now."

"You get a partner's salary, don't you?" He frowned. "Sandy would have made sure of that."

"It's not as much as I was making hourly."

Confusion clouded Sean's stare. "How can that be? I know Sandy. She plays fair. She wouldn't make you partner and cut your cash flow."

Mel sighed. "She didn't exactly. She wouldn't take anything from me for the partnership. Just made me partner, signed half the bar over to me for nothing. When payday comes, I sign half of my check back into the business as payment for my half of the bar." And oh, she really hated making that admission with all the questions it was going to raise.

The twin lines across his forehead deepened as Sean stared at her, his mouth open. After a few beats, he shook his head as though to clear the cobwebs. "Are those the terms Sandy wanted?"

Mel quickly shook her head. "She doesn't know about it. I've been doing the books."

Sean tossed the newspaper onto the bar and grabbed Mel on the shoulders. He gave her a little shake. "Are you screwing with the books?"

"No!" When he only raised an eyebrow. "Okay, it's all there, documented as my monthly payment for the partnership. I'm not screwing with the books, and I'm not taking money that isn't mine."

"No, you're only giving Sandy money she doesn't need, didn't ask for, and she's going to be mad as *hell* when she goes over those books and finds it."

Panic rose in Mel's throat. She grabbed his hand on her shoulder and squeezed. "Sean, please. Don't go to Sandy."

His eyes narrowed, and his voice chilled. "Tell me why I shouldn't."

"I can't accept this partnership for free, Sean. I can't." Her voice stank with desperation and bordered on hysteria. He'd probably think she was losing it, but she couldn't help it.

"It's not free, Mel." His tone softened, but his frown remained. "Ryan told me she set it up like a profit-sharing deal."

What had begun as a small thump in her temples blossomed into full-throttle pounding. Mel stepped back, pressing the heels of her hands against the pulsing. "It's still too easy. I can't get things handed to me like that. I can't explain, but I need to earn my way."

* * *

Sean rocked back on his heels. He actually understood her reasoning. It was exactly how he felt about his share of the ranch, and was the reason he'd chosen to pay Ryan back for his stake in the horse rehab part of the business. He eased her hands away from her head and tugged her close again, cradling her against his chest.

"Okay," he murmured, kissing the top of her head and smoothing her hair. "Okay, I won't go to her. But you have to."

She pulled away sharply. "Sean—"

"Mel!"

Their gazes tangled, locked. Mel looked away first.

"You have to go to Sandy." Patience was becoming a struggle. On the outside, he was pretty sure he was successful. Inside, he was all knotted up. Something was going on with Mel. She had changed. Again. They no longer had their little game of mutual chase going on, which had once felt like they at least shared a common goal, that being a relationship.

Because he still needed the contact, Sean laced his fingers through hers and settled her against him with gentle pressure to her back. Her heart beat so hard and fast in her chest he could feel it against his own. He held her silently, nestling his face in her soft hair until the pounding settled into a slower, lighter rhythm. "Go to her, Mel," he said softly. "Explain your reasoning, and work out a plan with her. She's going to be miffed if she finds out on her own that you've already put several thousand dollars into this place without telling her."

Mel's breathing slowed, steadied. Her trembling diminished to an occasional tremor. Finally she nodded and leaned back in his arms, lifting her eyes. His body reacted instantly to her charged blue gaze and her change in position, fitting them more intimately together, but for once, if she noticed, she didn't push the envelope.

"I'll talk to her next week. Let her enjoy being a mom for a few days, okay, Sean?"

Her request made all kinds of sense. Some of his apprehension eased, and he nodded. "Okay. But you aren't getting one of those heaps. Let me help you — stop shaking your head."

"I'm not shaking my head."

"You were shaking it in your mind." He kissed her, quick and hard. "Give me your budget and let me help you find a car. Do you care what you drive?"

"I originally wanted it to have four wheels but I'm no longer that picky."

He just stared at her. She stared back. Her tropical-ocean blue eyes were so wide, he could almost fall into them. Slowly she shook her head and sighed. "No, I don't care what I drive as long as it runs. But I was trying to keep to five hundred or less. I can go up to seven-fifty if I don't eat next week."

Sean dialed back his acerbic response in favor of gentle teasing. "Do me a favor and eat, sweetheart. You're already too thin." He kissed the tip of her nose. "Okay, I have... grocery shopping to do. But I'll come back after and look through the classifieds."

Her melodic laughter filled the room. Some of the shadows fell from her face. "Did you draw the short straw? You hate shopping."

Now... how to best move in for the kill. Sean smiled. "Ryan only brought Sandy and Bethany home from the hospital this morning. Dad could do it but he buys stuff he wants that's not good for him. Ricky has work later today."

She was nodding. "So... you drew the short straw."

He shrugged and schooled his features into what he hoped was an appealingly helpless smile. "I don't suppose you'd have time to help me out, would you?"

After directing a glance around the bar, Mel shrugged. "LeeAnn's in the stockroom. I'll get her out here. If we hurry, I can help you before the Saturday rush."

"Thanks." Sean slid the list from his pocket. "We can go more quickly if we divide this up." He tore it in half and handed her the bottom section. The one Sandy had written.

Mel looked it over in silence. Suddenly her eyes flashed up to him. She tossed back her head and laughed. "I am so tempted to demand we trade halves just to watch you pick this stuff up. In fact, I've already decided. I don't care if it does take longer. We're doing the shopping *together*." With a wicked smile, she reached in the drawer beneath the bar and pulled out a roll of clear tape.

His topsy-turvy heart suddenly righted itself when he saw his Mel again for the first time in months.

* * *

Positive energy that had been missing for a long time surged through Mel. Just being in no-demand mode with Sean again made her want to dance and sing her way across the parking lot to his truck. She settled for walking at a sedate pace and smiling up at Sean as he held the door for her.

They talked about trivial things on the way to the grocery store, how the weather was turning colder, how the red lights should be a little shorter through town, how traffic was light. Had he seen the post office was getting a makeover but they were closed on Saturdays now? How AJ'S General Store still had the best ice cream... and it was too bad the weather was getting cooler, though, making ice cream not so appealing.

Trivial things.

The kind of small talk acquaintances forced into the conversation to make the silence go away because it was unbearable.

So much for her burst of energy. Maybe she should have danced to his truck.

Finally they made it to Little Bob's Market. The place was crowded.

"Guess we found where all the traffic went," murmured Mel as she hopped to the ground. She studied the stretch of blacktop between them and the store. They couldn't have parked any farther out and still be in the same county.

As she walked around to the rear of his pickup, Mel cast a sidelong glance at Sean. His step was light as he caught her glance and shot her a grin.

So the mundane conversation hadn't really killed anything. The boy-man was still there. Maybe she could persuade him to play.

Grinning back at him, she chose a shopping cart that had been left at the edge of the lot. After a quick glance for trolling cars, she put one foot on the back bar and pushed off with her other, like she was on a scooter. The cart started rolling, slowly at first. She gave another kick then hopped on the back and aimed down the long hill toward the store. The breeze kissed her face and tickled through her hair, and laughter bubbled up. Leaning outward, she steered the cart around Mamie Schmidt, pulling her two-wheeled personal shopping basket.

Mel heard a whoop from behind her. On the back of his own cart, Sean drew even. He was about to pass her!

"Oh, no, you don't!" Mel touched her toe to the ground and gave herself an extra push, laughing triumphantly as she pulled ahead again. "Take that! You'll never catch me now."

She glanced over her shoulder. The expression of horror on Sean's face was comical. But then he jumped off and pulled his shopping basket to a stop. Still smiling, she turned back to face forward.

Her cart slammed to an abrupt halt when it ran into the six-foot wall of muscle blocking her path. Her gut wrapped around the cart's handlebar, and the breath whooshed from her lungs. One scuffed brown boot had been planted on the cart's rounded front bar. Slowly Mel skimmed her gaze up, over the dark brown pants, the hands firmly gripping the other end of the basket, and the tan shirt with the shiny gold star over the left pec.

Finally her eyes met the scowling countenance and she smiled weakly. "Hey, DC." Her voice came out too airy, and she turned her lips in to keep them from curving into a smile. The blacktop was about six inches away, and she eased first one foot down, then the other, managing to stand up straight just as Sean sedately pushed his cart up next to hers. Right. As if he hadn't just been riding it like he was a NASCAR driver.

"Melanie Mitchell, what are you doing?" DC crossed his arms over his chest.

Beside her, Sean snickered, and Mel elbowed him in the ribs.

"You know, I expect this kind of crap from little kids." DC straightened the cart and wheeled it onto the sidewalk.

"Not from a responsible business owner." His glance latched on to Sean. "Or a conscientious rancher."

Sean, the rat, fixed an earnest look on his face. "I was trying to catch up with Mel. She had obviously lost control of her basket."

DC glanced from one to the other. "Lost control, huh?" He shook his head. "You're both lucky I don't write you tickets for reckless operation of a shopping cart in a crowded parking lot."

"Does that mean we can come back when it's not crowded?" asked Sean, grinning.

Mel aimed for his ribs with her elbow again, missed, and grabbed her shopping cart to keep from tumbling over.

Not even a hint of amusement graced the sheriff's face. With his brows drawn together, he split another glare between the two of them. "Go on, do your marketing. And how about you stick to the speed limit in there?"

"Yes, sir." Subdued, Mel edged the cart past DC, sinking her teeth into her lip to hold back the laugh that was trying to burst from her throat.

As soon as Sean followed her through the door, she caught the light of laughter in his pale jade eyes and lost her resolve. The giggle bubbled up like a spring-fed stream, pushing out into a full-blown chortle, and she clung to him helplessly while she struggled to recover. He didn't help matters any when he joined in the laughter. For a moment, they stood just inside the doors, hanging onto one another. Then he lowered his mouth to hers and gave her a soft kiss before he stepped back.

"Excuse me." The cold voice of Earlene Higgins came from behind Sean.

Mel peeked around him to see Brother Bobby's wife glaring at them, condemnation in her eyes.

"Sorry, Mrs. Higgins." Mel drew in a deep breath and pulled Sean out of the woman's path. "We just thought of something funny, and we were laughing because it was — funny." She grabbed Sean's arm and tugged him away from the door. "We're just going to get shopping now. Nice seeing you."

They rounded the corner of the first aisle and broke into fits of hilarity all over again.

Breathless, Mel finally averted her gaze, refusing to look higher than Sean's shoulders. "Okay." She held out her hand. "Give me the list."

Silently, Sean handed her the taped-up piece of paper. She scanned the items then began pushing the cart toward the back of the store.

"I'm sorry, but you're traveling a hair over the speed limit." Sean's arms closed on the cart handle from behind. "I think you definitely need to go back to driving school." He nuzzled the back of her neck.

Mel slapped at Sean like a mosquito. "Stop it. We're never going to get your shopping done." She led him down the first aisle. "Okay, Sandy didn't put any specific brand name on her maxipads. Do you know what she uses?"

"What?" Sean froze. His face was as red as the exit sign behind him. "No," he choked out.

"Okay, why don't you call home and ask—" She broke off when he simply stared at her. "Never mind, I'll... just wing it." She pointed to the end of the aisle. "Breast pads will probably be with the baby things. Get her the economy size so you hopefully won't have to get them for her again."

His mouth worked soundlessly. Finally, he fixed her with a narrow-eyed death glare and stalked to the end of the aisle.

Chapter Six

"I'll see you tonight." In the tiny vestibule by Valentine's front door, Sean pressed Mel against the wall, enjoying one last kiss before he hit the road. Brushing his lips back and forth ever so lightly hitched her breathing every time. Her lips were warm and he didn't want to leave, even for an hour. For the first time in months, her eyes weren't filled with shadows and secrets. Their time together that afternoon had been about the moment; no past, no future. She'd been his Mel again.

The outer door opened to admit a young couple Sean had never seen before. Quickly, he stepped aside to let them pass.

"Tonight, then..." Mel lifted one hand and wiggled her fingers in a wave. A faint smile lingered on her lips.

He turned and walked away before he lost his resolve to leave.

On the drive back to the ranch, Sean's smile lingered as well. He hadn't had so much outright fun with Mel since they'd been kids together. He pulled up to the homestead and sat for a minute, sorting through the emotions slamming him, knowing if he didn't, they'd be hanging out there for the whole family to see and analyze.

A tap on the side of his truck jerked Sean from his contented musing. He pushed open the door and hopped to the ground.

Ryan frowned "Why are you sitting out here?"

"Working through some stuff." Flicking a warning glance at his brother, Sean ambled to the rear of the truck and opened the cap. Bags and boxes of groceries lined the truck bed.

Ryan whistled. "We order all that?"

"Nope."

"Planning a party?"

"Nope. I also don't plan on doing the marketing for a good long spell." He handed several packed bags to Ryan, choosing his next words with care, lest he show too much distress. "Mel sheered the axle on her car."

Concern etched into Ryan's face. "She all right?"

"Seems to be." Sean picked up a box. "Thing is, the car's not worth the cost of the repair. She's trying to work out how to get another one on a fixed budget. She's looking through the classified ads—" He shook his head and started for the house. "Most of what's in her budget aren't worth the price of a tow to the scrap yard."

"Hey, I saved my 'Vette from the junkyard."

Sean stopped walking and caught his brother's eye. "And spent what? Two years making it drivable? During which time you had another ride, I'm guessing."

With a smile and an unapologetic shrug, Ryan silently conceded the point, and they started walking again.

"Thing is, she's limited herself to five hundred bucks, and there's no way she'll let me help her."

Ryan whistled. "She won't get squat for that." He rubbed his face. "You know, Ford was selling his Jeep. It's pretty old with high mileage, but he always makes a fair deal. I think he wanted in the range of twelve hundred for it. But he'd probably let her pay some now and the rest later."

Sean was way ahead of his brother, already punching buttons on his cell. "That's the Jeep he used for his work with search and rescue." He put the phone up to his ear and continued toward the house with his burden of groceries. "Damn fine vehicle."

"Hello?" answered a feminine voice.

"Liv? It's Sean."

"Hey, Sean. Run anyone over with your shopping cart yet?" asked Olivia Ford.

"I see the grapevine is as healthy as ever." Sean chuckled. The package of chocolate chip cookies crackled as he withdrew it from the bag and set it on the kitchen counter. "I was wondering if your brother still has his Jeep up for sale."

"Oh, yeah, it's still sitting out there. Let me get him."

Cold air rushed from the fridge as Ryan opened the door and placed a gallon of milk on the shelf. Sean carried the box of canned goods into the pantry, his movements awkward as he held the phone to his ear.

After a few moments, Colton Ford's voice came over the phone. "So you're looking for a Jeep?"

Sean explained what had happened to Mel's car, and mentioned her cash flow issues, skipping the details. "We're looking for something cheap but safe."

"It's twenty years gone. Got high mileage, but I had it in for regular maintenance. Engine and tranny are solid, and there's no rust on the body. What's she looking to pay?"

Ah, here was the sticky part. "I understand you're asking twelve hundred."

"I was but I'll cut Mel a deal."

Sean shook his head. "A deal's not the problem. I'll meet your price, Colt, but Mel needs to believe you're dealing her down to five hundred. The rest'll come from me but..."

Ryan's eyebrows shot up.

"You don't want her to know," said Colt.

Sean turned his back on his brother. "I know I could work at her and wear her down, Colt, but I'd rather not. If you'll agree to sell it to her for five, I'll run by tonight with a separate check for seven hundred."

"Make your check for an even five," said Ford. "Come on by right now if you want. Check it out, see if it's what you're looking for."

Sean disconnected the call and turned around to find Ryan staring at him thoughtfully.

"You sure you know what you're doing?" he asked finally.

Sean lifted one shoulder. "It's win-win. She gets a reliable vehicle, Colt sells his Jeep."

"And you don't see anything wrong with going behind her back to add in the funds to accomplish this win-win?"

Sean's mind drifted to thoughts of Mel secretly paying Sandy for the partnership. *Goose, meet Gander.* He shook his head. "Not really."

* * *

The man next to Sean at the bar plowed into him for the third time, mumbled yet another apology over his shoulder, then turned away again. Sean shook his head. No sense getting mad. It wasn't the guy's fault. It was the damn bar. It was hopping-crazy, even more than usual for a Saturday. Sean usually didn't care. It was, after all, Mel and Sandy's livelihood. But the current excess of humanity was crowding his personal space in a big way. Surely all kinds of fire codes were being broken.

At the rate things were going, the place would still be insane at last call. Sean stared at the amber liquid in his mug. When would he get Mel to himself again? They were going riding the next day. Would he have to wait that long? Dang.

"Hey, Sean. I guess this isn't much fun for you, is it?" She leaned over the bar and caught him by surprise with a quick kiss to the lips.

He grinned, immediately wishing she'd do it again, pleased when she seemed to read his mind. She prolonged the second kiss, her soft mouth molding against his, warm and welcoming. When she drew back, she brushed her upper lip with the tip of her tongue.

"That makes it worthwhile." Sean slipped his cell phone from his pocket and pulled up the picture he'd snapped earlier. "Tell me what you think of this."

Her whole face wrinkled into a frown as she peered at the screen. "I... don't know. Tell me what I'm looking at."

"If you want it, this is your new ride. Colt Ford's selling it. Got high miles, but he's kept it in good shape. We can have Walt look at it if you want, but Colt had it in the shop for a thorough inspection before he put it up for sale."

She sighed longingly. "I wish, but it's probably more than I can afford."

"Five hundred."

Mel blinked. "Really? It seems like it should be more."

Shrugging, Sean took a long pull of his beer before he answered. "He's been trying to sell it for a little while now. He reduced the price." Funny, he hadn't anticipated feeling that tiny twinge of guilt when he misled her.

But when Mel looked at the picture again then back up at him, she was wearing a smile that made him forget the rest of the world existed, so anything remotely guilt-like got a heave-ho to the back of his mind.

"When can I get it?" Her eyes danced with childlike excitement.

"You don't even want to look at it before you decide?"

Wide eyes surveyed him with complete trust. "Not if you think it's worth it."

"We can swing by and take a look at it tomorrow if you still want to come out and go riding. I'll pick you up about ten. Colt said he's more than happy to deliver it to you on Monday, give you time to get it licensed and insured."

"You've thought of everything." She leaned over and kissed him again. "Oh, Sean, I do love you!"

If he never drew another breath, it was worth it to hear those words. Mel's eyes went wide. Her hand fluttered to her mouth.

"Um, I mean..."

With his gaze never leaving her face, Sean took hold of her hand and laced his fingers through hers. Then he brought her hand to his mouth and pressed a tender kiss. He smiled but didn't say anything. Obviously, she'd only gotten carried away on the waves of her excitement. He ignored the little ache of yearning. Mostly.

"Hey, did you eat?" Mel's composure returned, proving him right. "Kitchen's still open."

So he did what he always did. He went with the flow. "Finally. I'm starving."

Mel bounced away, returning several minutes later with a burger and fries.

"I'm afraid you'll have to eat it alone. My break's about o—" She squinted toward the front door and her face turned pale as ash.

Sean whirled to follow her gaze but no one was there. "What is it?"

"Oh, ah... nothing." She spoke softly, her attention locked on the door, her forehead wrinkled into a frown. "Just someone I thought— excuse me." She moved quickly, slipping around the end of the bar and heading for the door. It took Sean a few extra moments to make his own way through the crowd.

* * *

Why couldn't crowds part like the Red Sea the way they always did in movies? Mel led with her elbow, muttering apologies as she pushed through the mass of humanity jammed into the bar. The night's receipts should look good.

But she didn't give a hoot. Another few steps, another squished toe. And goodness, did no one know how to use deodorant? No sooner had the uncharitable thought settled in than the overpowering scent of what had to have been a whole bottle of Choice 420 aftershave smacked her in the face, invading her nose and eyes, and good grief, she could even taste it. She averted her face from the noxious perfume cloud and gave a little cough. *The ad says make 420 your choice. Doesn't say anything about using a whole bottle at a time.*

Finally she got her hands on the heavy door and pushed outside into the parking lot, gulping in the chilly air.

She couldn't be certain it had been him. It had been almost eleven years since she'd last seen her brother. He'd been all of seventeen then. It wasn't so much that she had recognized the kid as she had noticed signs of their father in his stance.

He'd never left the family business, she reminded herself. If that *had* been him, he was up to no good. If he had come to see her, would he explain his cryptic letter? Or had word gotten to him that she was now partnered in the bar? Either way, best she remember Denny and her father both served themselves first, and there was never anything left for someone unfortunate enough to come second.

Scanning the parking lot revealed nothing but a sea of empty cars. Mel stomped her foot like a stupid kid. *Okay, breathe.* More than likely it hadn't been Denny. But he *had* sent that letter, which meant she was on his radar. A thousand imaginary insects marched along her spine, leaving an unsettled feeling with their passing. She shuddered and turned to go back inside, startled to find herself up against Sean.

"Oh, you scared me."

"*I* scared *you*? Why'd you take off running like that?" He brushed the hair out of her eyes and cupped her face in his warm hands. "What did you see?"

The moment had arrived. She could lie or she could set the groundwork for what she knew she would have to tell him soon. Concern knitted itself into his brow as he studied her.

No pressure there. Closing her eyes, Mel decided to stop running. "My half-brother," she whispered, searching Sean's face for his reaction.

He jerked backward, clearly surprised. "I didn't know you had a half-brother."

"He's my father's son." She let him put an arm around her shoulder. "My *biological* father."

Green eyes flashed in the yellow sodium vapor lamps as Sean blinked a few times. "Todd Mitchell wasn't...?"

Mel shook her head. "I promise to explain the whole thing to you, but if I don't get back to helping LeeAnn, she'll either quit or Valentine's will go bankrupt. Come on back inside." When he remained where he was, looking out over the parking lot, she tugged his arm. "Please."

Just inside the door, she waited for him to catch up. She'd just dropped a huge bomb. What was he thinking? The interior lighting was too dim to read his face.

In that peculiar way he had, Sean seemed to know she needed reassurance. "Hey." He used one finger to push her chin up, and looked into her eyes. "Whatever it is, it's going to be all right."

It never felt more right to hook one hand around the back of Sean's neck and pull him to her. She kissed him very softly, realizing in that moment more than she ever had that she would be devastated if she lost him. "I hope so. But it turns out Nick DeVayne — my real father... is a class A jerk. And my brother is just like him."

* * *

He'd been right about the place hopping until last call. That was still a couple of hours away and Sean watched as the crowd thinned then grew again. Apparently she didn't catch sight of her brother or brother's look-alike again. But was that a blessing or a curse? A few of Mel's shadows had come back, so what did it matter if she'd seen the real thing or a doppelgänger? But on the off chance it was the real thing and he returned, Sean had hung around past his normal time.

That spooked look on her face hadn't allowed any other choice.

"We don't close for two hours." Mel slid a glass of water his way. "But you don't need to stay and babysit me. You look really tired, Seanie. Will you be okay to drive home?"

He *was* tired, too tired to object to her childhood name for him. He squeezed his eyes closed for a moment and pinched the bridge of his nose. "Yeah, I'll be okay."

"Or." She touched his arm and caught his gaze. "You can sleep at my place."

Disappointment washed over him, stealing his earlier pleasure, and leaving a bitter taste. Sean shook his head. Were they going back to the same old dance after all? With his desire for more emotional intimacy and her offering a physical relationship?

But she squeezed his arm. "Just to sleep, okay? I worry about you driving home when you're this tired."

He laid his free hand over hers and squeezed back. "You don't need to worry about me."

She smiled, rolled her hand over, and threaded her fingers through his. "I won't worry if you stay. I'll even take the couch."

Sean understood she could have pushed his buttons; she knew him well enough. She could have played the helpless woman in distress, afraid because she might have seen her brother. But she hadn't. She wouldn't.

"I'll have to leave early to take care of stuff at the ranch."

"Then go up now." Mel slid a key ring from her pocket and singled out a key. "There's an alarm clock on the nightstand. And I promise not to take advantage of you when I come up. Although," she added, giving him a wink as he took the key, "I can't promise not to take a peek."

* * *

Sean had only been in the efficiency apartment above Valentine's once, when he'd helped Ryan move Sandy's things out to the ranch. As Mel's home, it looked vastly different. Sandy'd had a lot of things. Mel had very little and most looked to be the wrong side of secondhand. An ugly purple sofa divided one end of the room from the rest of the apartment, apparently designated as the living room. One ancient end table held a brass lamp. Another end table, in a different style, was serving as a TV stand for a tiny television set. A wooden box, about the size of his mother's old jewelry box, sat next to the TV, piquing his curiosity.

It didn't seem likely she'd keep her jewelry in the living room. His fingers twitched. He could lift the lid, just take a quick peek. She'd never know.

Shaking his head, he stepped into the kitchen area instead.

Looking around her place, Sean got the feeling she was used to living lightly, like she never stayed long in one place. But he'd known her all his life. She'd lived in Orson's Folly from the time she was born until she'd had to go live with relatives after her mother died.

His lips curved into a smile as he remembered Melanie as a young girl. He'd been enchanted by her. She'd reminded him of the fairy princess his mom had always told him he would marry. When she'd had to leave, he'd missed her desperately, and at first he'd been determined to find her. But at fourteen, looking for her wasn't feasible, and life had moved on. Then, one day just after his twenty-second birthday, she'd shown up in Orson's Folly again.

He'd been involved with Savannah about that time, a petite, blond city girl looking to fulfill her fantasy of marrying a rich goodtime cowboy.

Well, he'd had the goodtime part of that equation anyway. A snicker slipped out as he opened a cupboard and grabbed one of her two tumblers.

He'd always known Savannah wouldn't hang around. And from the moment Mel had re-entered his life, he'd been painfully aware that Savannah was no more than a replacement for the only woman he would ever love. He hadn't mourned when the goodtime gal went back to the city. He had been hurt deeply, though, to discover that Mel wasn't the same person who'd left. She'd changed, hardened. But as time passed, she had regained her delicate fairy princess softness.

They'd had a shot again.

Until the past few months. Did the darkness that seemed to grip her have something to do with the brother he hadn't known about? He turned on the tap and let the water flow until it chilled a bit then held the glass in the stream.

Dread poked insistent fingers at Sean when he thought about her years away from Orson's Folly. Where had she been? What had happened to her? She'd promised to talk to him about it. He wondered if she really would.

Numbing chill stole over his fingers and he looked at the glass in his hand. Water bubbled into it, flowing over the rim and saturating his fingers. Cursing under his breath, he shut off the faucet and lifted the glass to his lips for a sip.

When he was satisfied, he tossed the rest of the water down the sink and set the glass on the counter next to the sink.

A state-of-the-art coffee maker with a timer on her kitchen counter seemed to be her only luxury. He located her coffee canister next to an ancient, questionable-appearing microwave. Setting the coffee maker for four o'clock in the morning seemed logical. The smell of the coffee would motivate him to get up and leave — he hoped. If it didn't, he'd take a lot of crap for not being there. As it was, the simple text he'd sent to Ryan telling him he'd be home the next day had probably raised an eyebrow. He flipped the switch down, killing the light over the sink. As he edged past her bistro-style table, his foot caught the lone chair that wasn't quite tucked under it. Not exactly set up for private dinner guests with only one chair. Then again, the whole apartment was a little close.

And yet... He sighed as he took in the room again. It was blessedly private.

The queen-sized bed had been left behind when Sandy moved out to the ranch. It was neatly made up, with a pale blue chenille bedspread and about a dozen throw pillows in a mishmash of colors and patterns that should have jarred the eye but somehow seemed to be crying out in welcome.

In the bathroom, Sean found the first evidence of Mel's whimsical personality. A huge bathtub with whirlpool jets ruled a corner of the room, and she'd placed candles and jars of bath beads on the triangular shelf in the corner. Brass wall sconces and copper filigree butterflies adorned the walls. The window on the far wall of the bathroom was covered by curtains in a butterfly pattern. Sean glanced at the rug in front of the tub and blinked. *Oh, boy! Frogs on lily pads.*

Back in the main area, Sean pushed the button on the bedside lamp. A faint rosy glow spilled from beneath the raggedy lace lampshade. The alarm clock was exactly where she'd told him it would be. A newspaper clipping tucked underneath the clock caught Sean's eye — obviously something she'd saved. After setting the alarm, he made sure the piece of paper stayed safely where she'd left it.

The bed dipped a bit under his weight as he sat on the edge and slipped off his boots. After a moment's hesitation, he unbuttoned his shirt and shrugged out of it. He loosened his jeans but left them on. He'd probably be more comfortable if he removed them, but that didn't feel right. Or maybe it felt a little too right.

* * *

Mel slipped into her apartment, closed the door behind her, and set the lock with a little snick. A tiny thrill raced in a direct circuit from the goose bumps on her arms to her stomach, where the electrical current roused hundreds of fluttering butterflies.

I have a boy in my room. She suppressed a giggle that probably would have awakened that boy. Well, technically a man, but having a man in her room didn't sound as appealing. Nor as innocent.

She'd all but promised she *would* peek, so peek she did, standing at the foot of the bed.

He lay on his back, one arm flung to the side, the other over his head. The covers had slipped down to his waist. In the pinkish glow of the lamp, his tanned skin took on a coppery sheen. His lean body and well-defined muscles had come from years of physical labor.

No, technically not a boy... and not even hers. But the serenity on his face, so open, so innocent. Would they ever get their chance? Her heart wrenched just a little at the thought. Because at the moment, it sure as heck didn't feel like it.

Mel padded to the bathroom, where she washed away the smells of the bar, and then donned a pair of flannel PJ pants and a soft navy blue T-shirt. She pulled a blanket from the linen closet and returned to the main living area. She couldn't resist stopping at the foot of the bed again. He hadn't moved. His breathing was deep and even. At least he was getting good, solid rest.

She eased her way up along the bed and reached for the lamp to turn it off.

"Your couch is ugly and lumpy," he said quietly.

Mel jumped, sucking in a huge gasp of air. "I thought you were asleep."

He didn't move, didn't open his eyes. "Was. But you were watching me and it woke me up."

Now he wasn't making sense. Was he talking in his sleep?

"You've got a big bed." He opened his eyes and rolled onto one side, propping his head on one hand. "There's no reason you should sleep on that lumpy couch."

Mel stared at him, uncertain what to do. Why was he offering to share the bed?

Green eyes glinted in the dim light and he chuckled. "Just sleeping here, Mel. Your bed's big enough we probably won't even bump into each other." He pulled a pillow from beneath his head and dropped it on the other side of the bed.

She hesitated, but was unable to stop looking at him.

"Scared?"

Mel nodded. "Yes." Scared of her desire, scared of her feelings. Scared of the emotional intimacy the act of sleeping with someone promised.

"Of what? What are you afraid of, Mel?" His voice was soft. He was talking to her the way he spoke to the horses he helped heal from physical and emotional wounds.

The persuasive tone whispered over her like a comfortable old blanket, and she trembled at the soft caress of the words.

"Are you afraid of me?"

Mel nodded. "Of you... not so much. But everything..." Everything he represented that she wanted but wasn't sure she'd ever get. Everything she didn't deserve.

"I won't hurt you, Mel," he said softly, holding her gaze.

A smile tugged at her lips. "You won't mean to," she corrected in a whisper.

His answering smile mirrored her uncertainty. "Lie down on your bed, Mel. We'll sleep, just like you offered. I promise."

Her movements seemed sluggish, as though she were operating in slow motion as she crossed to the other side of the bed and sat. With a deep breath, she eased onto the pillow, sticking to the extreme edge of the mattress. She didn't draw down the covers, instead pulling the blanket she'd carried from the linen closet around her. She could feel his eyes on her the whole time. Then she rocked her head to the side and looked at him. And found herself trapped in a gaze that made her forget to breathe.

"Good night," he said in his gentle voice. Then he reached over and killed the light.

Mel rolled onto her right side and closed her eyes. Big mistake. She was facing him. Her first breath was filled with him, earthy, faintly musky... intoxicating. Only a couple of feet and she'd be touching him. Her palms tingled, her fingers twitched. His skin would be warm from sleep. She could... *Please do,* whispered her body, and she fought the urge to squirm. Another deep breath, more torment.

A soft sigh came from the other side of the bed.

Oh, geez, was he still awake? Could he hear her sniffing him up? Maybe if she turned over. She flopped onto her back and then to her other side. Better. A little lonelier but it cut the temptation.

Had Sean set the alarm clock? She hadn't checked. Maybe she should just make sure. No. If he woke up and caught her, it would look like she was checking up on him. She forced her eyes closed.

A sigh slipped past her lips. She hated lying on her left side. It always felt awkward and uncomfortable. The pillow was flatter than she liked. Folding it over just made it too fat and a little hard. The splash of moonlight coming through the window was brighter than the bedside lamp had been. And she noticed because she wasn't keeping her eyes closed. She squeezed them shut.

The hard pillow pinched her ear. She had to get off her left side. The bed never creaked as she eased onto her back. A smile spread over her face. Success!

"Are you going to bounce around for what's left of the night?" he asked in a mild tone.

"I... didn't know you were awake," she mumbled.

"Hmmm, 'sokay." He adjusted his pillow and let out a long sigh then went back to deep, even breathing.

Why couldn't he be snippy? She could deal with snippy. But lying in a bed so close to him... If she got up, he'd either think he was imposing by taking her bed or he'd know how much he was affecting her.

This was a mistake. I should have taken the couch. But she couldn't seem to will herself to climb from the bed. Instead, she concentrated on her breathing. Nice and slow, in then out, in then out. Like waves lapping against a shore. Sean's breathing matched hers, their breaths becoming one. Heated yearning raged through her like a tropical flash flood. A shudder rocketed through her.

Definitely a mistake. She flipped back to the left.

Sean heaved a deep sigh. "I can feel your tension from here." The bed dipped and creaked softly as he shifted and moved to the center of the mattress. Then his hand brushed over her arm, and he hooked her around the middle, easing her toward him until they were spooning. Warm breath fanned the back of her neck. "Go to sleep, Mel," he whispered.

Being held by him was infinitely worse... and infinitely better. She willed herself not to move. Any moment she'd wake up and find she'd been alone the whole time.

His hand began a slow, lazy caress, traveling the length of her arm from shoulder to wrist then back. Fine tremors began where he touched, flowed outward on little electrical currents.

"Relax," he murmured. "Nothing's going to happen."

And *that* was the problem. She didn't want *nothing* to happen. Her whole body was winding up for the pitch. The one he'd just told her wasn't going to happen. She forced those tightly wound muscles to relax. "Did you know when I was not quite thirteen I stopped thinking of you as my best friend?"

He froze but only for a moment. Then his hand began its spellbinding caress again, moving higher, toying with her hair where it touched her shoulders.

Mel's skin tingled. She made herself keep talking when all she wanted to do was turn in his arms. "I decided when the time was right I was going to take you as my lover instead."

The hitch in his breathing might have been a hiccup, but his hand stopped moving again. Oh, yes, she had his attention.

"Of course, I hardly had any idea what that meant. I only knew it was special and personal. And I knew it would be good with you because I really, really liked you. I always felt safe with you. But you didn't seem to notice me like that."

"I've never stopped thinking of you as my best friend." His murmur rumbled in his chest, the echo vibrating against her back.

So that was it. Friends. Hope deflated and a tiny crack etched across her heart. "I under—"

His fingers flexed against her arm, the grip an exquisite, bruising pain. It only lasted a moment before he released a shuddering breath and relaxed his hold. "But I noticed you, Mel," he choked out. "There's never been a time I haven't noticed you. And for the record, when you were almost thirteen, I not only noticed you, I wanted you. And I *did* know what it meant, just as I knew it'd have to wait." He shifted his hand higher and traced the outline of her ear as he spoke. "We've always had a connection. But when I was thirteen, fourteen... man, it was intense. All those budding hormones." He chuckled. "And sometimes it was downright painful." He drew a deep breath and blew it out, and the warm puff tickled the hairs on the back of her neck. "Kinda like now," he whispered.

Had she heard him right? Mel's heart rate ramped up. Maybe... just maybe—

"And then," he choked out, "you had to go away. One day... you were just... gone."

Chapter Seven

Mel seemed to freeze in his arms, and Sean sighed. They'd been constant companions since early on. The same gentle comfort she'd offered when his mother died had also been there to ease the pain and emptiness he'd experienced when Ryan left home. But only one year after Ryan's departure, Mel herself had been yanked from Sean's life. Though his father had tried to fill in the gaps, Sean had been inconsolable. It hadn't been a great time. In fact, it had been a mighty confusing time. And very lonely.

Mel had never spoken before about where she'd gone, who she'd lived with. And they hadn't immediately taken up their companionship again when she returned. She hadn't been the Mel he'd grown up with. She'd come home a girl with a lot of mileage and a bite to her personality. But even that bite hadn't killed Sean's love for her. He'd simply waited her out. Was still waiting her out...

He stilled the restless brush of his fingers on the soft skin just below her ear, but he couldn't bring himself to break the contact. "Where did you go? Where did they take you, Mel?"

She brought her hand up and laid it over his. Her palm was hot. She flexed and contracted her fingers reflexively. Her breathing was shallow and quick and he knew without feeling it that her heart rate had bumped up.

"My whole life, I never knew Todd wasn't my real father. Mama never told me, not even after he died."

Sean remembered the accident that had claimed Todd Mitchell's life. It had happened a few months after Ryan left. Mitchell's pickup had skidded off the road on the way to Jackson and slammed into a cliff face. The truck had been mangled beyond recognition, its driver dead on impact. Twelve-year-old Mel had been crushed at the loss of her father. With the need to provide for herself and her daughter, Mel's mother had gone to work as a waitress at Carol's Diner in town. Sylvia had worked long hours, and in a freakish coincidence, almost a year to the day after her husband's death, she had been driving home late one night when a logging truck broadsided her tiny car. She hadn't had a chance.

"Everyone thought I would live with Grandma Tilly. I wanted to. I loved her so much," whispered Mel. "But she was Todd's mom, and not really my grandma at all."

Her light sniffs and barely perceptible shudders told Sean she was crying. Torn between wanting to know what had happened and the need to soothe away her pain, he brushed a tender kiss over the top of her head.

And waited.

"One day, this man showed up. He said his name was Nick DeVayne. He and my mom had been — together before she married Todd. He said I was his daughter. I didn't want to believe him. It was like — I'd lost my parents and now this man was trying to take away who I was." Mel stopped talking and inhaled deeply, then blew out the breath. "Grandma Tilly sent him packing, but Nick came back the next day with proof. He had my original birth certificate naming him as my father, and notification from the state of my adoption by Todd in lieu of back child support. Oh, he had a story about why he hadn't paid, and the story always changed."

"But if you were adopted, weren't his parental rights terminated?"

"He had an emergency order of custody signed by a judge in Oklahoma City."

Mel rolled out of Sean's arms and turned to face him. Silver light from the full moon slanted through the window and bathed her face. The dim glow and the pale blond hair splashed across the dark pillowcase made her appear ghostly. He couldn't see the shadows in her eyes, but he knew they were present.

"Are you sure you want to hear all this?"

Sean propped his head again. Needing the contact, he reached out and smoothed her hair. "Only if you want to tell me."

"After Nick took me away, I met my half-brother, his son, Denny. I don't know what happened to Denny's mother or how Nick ended up with custody. Denny was a year younger than me, and exactly like his— *our* father. It was all about making a fast buck with both of them. We never stayed in one place very long. Nick ran cons. And then we'd have to leave before he got caught. He changed our names so many times, I lost track of who I was supposed to be. He used me and Denny in his cons." She buried her face in the pillow, her sudden movement severing the connection between them. When she turned back to Sean, she tucked her hand under her cheek. "I helped him screw so many people over. I got good at it. I got really, really good at seducing older men to be interested in me with my virginal innocence, and then Nick would move in for the kill, all blustery, 'what are you doing with my fifteen-year-old daughter?' And they would pay him so much money to make sure he didn't go straight to the police." A harsh chuckle tore from her lips. "I stayed fifteen for almost three years."

Oh, sweet Lord, he hadn't expected *that*.

Emotions he couldn't define, didn't understand, were slamming Sean like a jackhammer, accompanied by body-engulfing cold and the taste of bile in his throat. Her pain became his, and he couldn't breathe. How had she stood it? "Did they — the men — did they — *hurt* you? Touch you?

Ra—" The words felt like they were being ripped from his throat. He wanted to pull her back into his embrace but he sensed the distancing had been intentional.

After a moment, Mel surprised him by sliding an arm across his chest and up to cup his neck. "I love you for a lot of reasons, Sean. Just now, I love you so very much for caring about that." Her fingers flexed briefly. "No. No one hurt me, no one touched me. Not — like that."

He eased out the breath he'd been holding. Maybe they hadn't physically hurt her. But no one could suffer that without mental and emotional scars left over from that sort of abuse. And the hot and cold chase between them suddenly made sense.

"The day I turned eighteen, I left. I was almost broke. Nick never let Denny or me have any money. But once, when I was fifteen, we stayed in a town so he could run a long-term con. I got a job at a local fast food joint. He never knew, and I was able to hide the money I made. I knew I had to get away. It wasn't enough, wasn't nearly enough. And then I found out Grandma Tilly had died just a few months before I left. I was alone."

Sean's lungs squeezed against his heart. She hadn't needed to be alone. If she had called him, he would have found her. But she hadn't called him. And she had left DeVayne when she was eighteen, yet she hadn't returned to Orson's Folly until she was twenty-one. The date she'd come back was inscribed into his memory. "Where did you go? Why didn't you come back here?" *Why didn't you call me?*

"As soon as I found out Grandma Tilly was gone, I *couldn't* come back here. I felt — dirty. I didn't want you to see me."

"No, Mel," he whispered. Every word stabbed like another knife in his soul.

"I went to Las Vegas. Found work as a cocktail waitress." She shivered. "The customers all wanted so much more than drinks."

Sean's heart seemed to hover between beats. He wasn't sure it would start again. He couldn't talk. The question he most wanted to ask stuck in his throat.

She sighed heavily. "And because I didn't let them cop their feels and wouldn't go home with anyone after hours, I kept my job, but my tips weren't very good."

The band around Sean's lungs loosened. But he wasn't certain the damage to his heart would ever heal. Had he really thought he wanted to know the sources of her shadows?

With a tiny sigh, Mel continued speaking softly. "Then I got a huge break. I found out Grandma Tilly had left me her estate. She was very smart, though, and put it in trust for me until I was twenty-one. It wasn't much but it was mine. Nick either hadn't known about it or knew he couldn't touch it."

"Who held the trust?"

Mel pulled in a long breath. "Your dad," she whispered. "He tracked me down in Las Vegas and told me about it. Told me Grandma Tilly would have wanted me to come home. And I decided I needed to... I *wanted* to come home."

"I remember Dad's trip right before you came back," murmured Sean. He'd thought Justin had gone looking for Ryan. When his father had refused to answer any of Sean's questions about the trip, he'd assumed it hadn't gone well. Sean smiled into the darkness. *You made sure she came home, didn't you, Dad?*

Mel shrugged. "Sandy had just bought Valentine's when I pulled into town, and I answered her ad for a bartender."

Sean lay still. Mel's hand on his neck heated skin that had chilled. She'd lived a horrendous life for eight years. No wonder she had shadows. He dragged a hand over his mouth, ending at his jaw, and rubbed his chin. Her reaction when she thought she'd seen her half-brother now made perfect sense.

"You're wrong about one thing." Sean tried without much success to temper the rawness in his voice. "I don't care who donated the DNA, your real father was and always will be Todd Mitchell."

Mel hugged him then, tightly, as if she never wanted to let go. And he sure as hell knew he didn't want her to. No more than he intended to let *her* go.

He trailed his fingertips along her arm where it lay across his chest. After a brief hesitation, he slid his hand to her waist. He'd meant it as a simple caress, a gesture of comfort. But her skin was so soft, so heated. For a moment she stiffened in surprise. Then she seemed to melt into him. Love and desire surged, knotted together, and tore through his system until nothing else occupied Sean's mind except his awareness of Mel at the most visceral level.

"You always did kiss like I'm the only woman in the world," she whispered against his lips. Then with a soft moan, she threw back her head, opening up all new possibilities for exploration of her slender neck.

Her skin quivered beneath his lips as he roamed, pausing to enjoy the madly beating pulse at the base of her throat. A unique blend of lingering bar smells and something lightly floral wafted about him, leading him to the edge of her soft T-shirt. It was in the way. He allowed one hand to drift toward the bottom hem of the garment while he used his teeth to push the neck out of his way. He'd known. He had known waiting for Mel would be a reward in itself.

"Sean..." Melanie sighed. "I don't want to *sleep*."

"I know," he murmured against her shoulder. He didn't want to sleep, either. Abandoning the task of removing her shirt in mid-lift, he reached toward his wallet on the nightstand.

His erotic fantasy slammed against stark, eye-opening reality.

He'd never replaced the condom he'd given to Ricky.

Gulping for air, Sean flopped back against the pillows, snagging her hands to still her caresses. "Stop. Please stop." He was so close to the edge; very soon he wouldn't care about responsibility. He trembled with the effort to push back his desire.

The moon had moved on, away from the window, leaving them in almost complete darkness. But he sensed her looking at him, knew her face would be decorated with confusion.

The words wouldn't form, hung up on his frustration. He sucked in a quick breath and blew it out, repeated the process twice more. "I can't do this. We can't do this. Not now." He pulled her closer, although it was sheer torture.

A little cry of distress wrung itself from her throat, and she began to tremble. "You always put the brakes on. I thought — I thought it would be different this time."

"Mel." He spoke through gritted teeth. "I don't have any protection. I don't have a condom."

Her body began to shake more violently.

"Aw, Mellie... please. I just want—"

A soft snuffle-snort brought him up short.

Laughter.

Not tears.

She was laughing. At him? Or their situation? He drew back and stared but still couldn't make out her face. But he didn't have to.

"I've waited most of my life for this moment and it's all falling apart over a stupid piece of latex?" More laughter bubbled forth.

"Something like that," he ground out.

She moved from his arms with a groan, sat on the edge of the bed, and turned on the light.

"Where are you going? Do you have something here?" If she said yes, he'd wonder why later.

She chuckled. "Hardly. There's been no need."

Relief and frustration twined hands and skipped through his system.

"I'm going for my best friend in times like this. Snickers."

He laughed out loud. Chocolate. She wanted chocolate.

She looked in his direction. Her voice was tinged with leftover amusement. "And later today, you and I are going to invest in the biggest box of condoms they sell."

Yeah, probably not the time to tell her he already had one of those. But he *would* make it a point to shove a condom or several into his wallet when he got home. Coherent thought deserted him as she leaned over and pressed her mouth against his in a sizzling kiss. Sensation slammed upon sensation. Heat, then chills. Emotion welled, and love pushed itself into the mix. The alarm clock next to the bed began to scream. With almost simultaneous precision, the smell of brewing coffee filled the room.

Mel retreated, slapping a hand across the top of the clock. She stood up and stretched. With a husky little laugh, she walked to her kitchenette.

He watched her go with a lot of regret. For the first time he could remember, Sean cursed the chores that were calling him from a warm bed.

* * *

At the rustle of movement from behind him, Sean paused with his hand on the saddle and glanced over his shoulder in time to catch Mel scrubbing at her eyes as if to wipe the sleep away.

"You should have stayed and gotten some sleep. I would have gone back for you." Sean double-checked Lacey's cinch then gave her a pat on the neck.

"Don't worry. You don't have to tie me in the saddle or anything. I won't fall off." Mel stifled another yawn as she stepped closer to the horse and accepted a boost up. "I want to be here. I like helping." She sent him a slow smile. "Besides, I kinda-sorta like hanging out with you."

Warmth spread on a direct current from her smile to his heart. "Kinda-sorta, huh?"

She'd told him that once when they were kids; by his estimation with the information he had now, just about the same time she'd decided they should be lovers. Satisfaction spread warmth through his system and his lips twitched into a grin. With a soft chuckle, he swung his leg over the back of a large-boned chestnut filly. Ginger was a little more skittish than he would have liked, but she desperately needed the exercise. Hopefully she'd calm down on the trail. He'd only had her in the stable for a little over a month.

"Feel up to a ride all the way out to the Fords'? We can look at his Jeep." He shot her a sidelong gaze. "And if you wimp out on the ride over, maybe Liv'll truck you back here."

"Not likely. I'm not a wimp." Mel smiled sweetly. "But in the event my ass ends up sore after this ride, you have my permission to kiss it." Clicking her tongue, she urged Lacey forward.

Sean stared after her, temporarily struck dumb. That had become a recurrent malady of late. He nudged Ginger into a brisk walk to catch up with Mel and Lacey.

It was warm for October, and the sun was strong. They weren't on the trail long before Mel pulled up to take off her denim jacket. The simple pale blue polo shirt she wore beneath hugged her body, and enticing curves pushed against the fabric as she moved. Sean's nerves tied themselves in knots.

A surprise gust of wind stirred the brush beside the trail, and Ginger spooked sideways, bumping Lacey. The older horse, by far the more passive of the two, balked and hung back, allowing Ginger to take the lead. Sean turned to check on Mel, smiling in approval when he saw she was patting Lacey's neck and talking to her in a reassuring tone.

Another breeze hissed through the grass and this time Ginger laid back her ears and snorted. She half-reared, kicking out at the swaying grass and nearly unseating Sean. It took him a few minutes to get the filly under control, and then a few more seconds while he mentally kicked himself. He knew better than to succumb to distractions on the trail.

"Why is she so nervous?" asked Mel, pulling alongside him.

"She hasn't had a lot of training and what she's had's been half-poor." Sean firmly pulled Ginger back onto the trail. "Someone probably took it in their head to beat her down because they thought she was too frisky."

He stroked the nervous filly's neck and clucked his tongue.

"Then they're stupid," said Mel flatly. "Every good horse trainer knows kindness and patience win the game." She and Lacey dropped back again as the trail narrowed.

And just what was he to make of that? Because it sounded like she was talking about more than horses.

* * *

Sean was still mulling over her statement a half hour later when they arrived at the Ford place. Colt was in the yard with his head under the hood of a red Jeep. As they drew near he stood, dropped an old blue rag on the fender, and approached them.

"Mel. McGee." He nodded at each of them in turn. "Nice day for a ride."

Mel stared at the Jeep, a reserved expression on her face. Sean slid off Ginger and tethered her to the fence. He turned to help Mel off her mount, but Colt was already there, large dark hands spanning Mel's slender waist, catching her as she slid from Lacey's back, and setting her safely on the ground.

Slowly he unlocked his jaw and unfurled his fists as he let out a long, slow breath. *Get a grip, man.*

Mel walked around the Jeep once, her face completely unreadable.

"It's obviously in great shape. So why are you selling it for so little?"

Sean stiffened, but Colt merely shrugged. "It's taking up space here. And I knocked a couple hundred off because you're a friend." He shrugged. "You can pay more if you insist, but I'd cut any friend a deal."

Dang, he was a smooth liar. No wonder he often won at Friday night poker. Sean still couldn't get a read on Mel, but he didn't think she was suspicious. Opening the door, she waved it back and forth as though assessing its sturdiness. Then she sat on the driver's seat, and finally cracked a smile.

"Feels pretty good sitting here."

Colt handed over the key. "Go ahead and start her up, take a drive if you want."

Mel started the engine, listened for a minute, then eased the Jeep into first gear and inched forward. She pulled the brake and turned off the engine.

Colt raised an eyebrow. "Not going to drive it?"

"I wouldn't have the faintest idea what to look for on a test drive, so I'm just going to trust you."

Colt's lips twitched into one of his rare smiles, and he glanced in Sean's direction. "You're right. She's definitely not one you want car shopping on her own."

"What's that supposed to mean?" Mel handed the key back to Colt.

"Sean told me about some of the ads you were considering."

"Oh, he did, did he?" She angled a speculative look at Sean. Then she sent Colt such a sweet smile it was a wonder he didn't spin into a diabetic coma. "I'd very much like to buy the Jeep. Sean said you might be able to help me get it to my place?"

Colt nodded. "Sure. Tomorrow about noon okay with you?"

"Perfect."

"Sean!"

He spun about at the shout from the barn and grinned when he recognized the willowy figure and straight, waist-length brown hair of Olivia Ford as she walked in their direction.

"I'm sorry I missed you yesterday." She bounced into his arms and kissed him on the cheek, then stepped back. "Glad you came back." She turned around. "Hi, Mel."

Mel's reserve had come up again and Sean wondered why. She and Olivia had been pretty tight when they were kids. Liv showed no sign of recognizing the guardedness, and Sean wondered if he was just being sensitive.

"I put Sean's check on your desk," Liv said to Colt. "You left it on the kitchen table last night."

Sean closed his eyes, hoping Mel hadn't heard.

"What check?"

Crap!

"Sean left a deposit on the Jeep for me to hold it until you could get here," said Colt.

Mel looked between the three of them, probably guessing that something was going on. "Oh, thanks, Sean. How much do I owe you?"

Sean rubbed his jaw. Keep it casual, he reminded himself. "Just twenty-five dollars."

"Fifty," Colt said at the same time.

A narrowed gaze landed on Sean. "Which one of you can't do the math?"

Sean shot a look at Colt. "He's right. It was fifty. He only asked for twenty-five, but I already had the check written." Because he wanted to shuffle his feet in the dirt like a seven-year-old caught with an extra cookie, Sean forced himself to remain absolutely still.

Colt and Liv seemed to be holding their breaths as well. Finally, Mel shrugged and her face lit up with one of her killer smiles. "Okay, then."

* * *

Sean didn't move a muscle. Not. One. Forget deer in the headlights. The man standing in front of her was a rat with his pointed snout and beady eyes caught in the corn bin. He was trying so hard to maintain a poker face, he'd be lucky if his face *didn't* freeze into the macabre mask of horror he'd affected. Her bullshit sense rose to full alert. But after no more than a long stare, she smiled and looked away. She'd figure it out soon enough. She always did.

She made arrangements for Colt to deliver the Jeep to the bar the next day and they'd go from there. Then Mr. Ants-in-his-pants Sean decided they needed to hustle on out of there.

Back on the trail again, she watched him. Poor Ginger spooked at just about everything. Sean wasn't having a very good ride. He'd been right about Lacey, though. She was a real sweetheart. Mel had fallen in love with her.

"You feel up to a detour?" asked Sean when they were nearly back to the Cross MC. "Just a short one. I want to show you something."

She followed him around a stand of yellow-leafed cottonwood trees and onto a small rise overlooking a gently rolling field. The afternoon sun turned the tall grass golden. The field was rimmed by pine trees, outlined by wood and wire fences, and along one fence a rough two-rutted trail wound in from the main road. Distant mountains formed a backdrop for the cottonwood trees with their dwindling yellow-gold leaves.

"What is this place?"

His smile seemed a little less sure. "Do you like it?"

"I do," she breathed, awestruck. "It's so peaceful and pretty."

Sean dismounted, looping Ginger's reins around an old log, before turning to catch Mel as she slid off Lacey. His hands lingered on her hips. Unable to resist, she leaned toward him. He pulled her close, raising his hands to cup her face. He looked deep into her eyes, then slowly bent and brushed his lips across hers. It was one of his emotionally devastating, feather-light kisses that caused her heart to race and always left her wanting so much more. When he pulled back, she sighed.

"I've loved this place since I was a kid. Dad's been saving it for me." Sean pulled Mel around to stand in front of him, easing her back against him and crossing his arms in front of her at her waist. He turned them both. "I want to build a house here someday. Over there by that one big cottonwood." He turned them again. "And out that way, I'm going to put up a horse barn so I can keep the rehab stable going from here." He turned them again. "And over there, a play yard with a swing set."

Mel's heart exploded into a staccato cadence. He was showing her a future he wanted to share with her.

"Oh, Sean." Just for a moment, she wanted to believe. She wanted to believe they could have the piece of heaven together that he was showing her. Her breath stalled in her lungs as the icy truth poured over her. As soon as Sean found out her secret, he probably wouldn't want anything to do with her.

"We should probably get back." She slipped from his arms and headed for the horses.

She almost made it. But he grabbed her hand and she came to a dead stop. Slowly, he pulled her back toward him, turning her around and looking into her eyes. "Please don't do this. Don't shut us down again, Melanie."

She forced a light laugh but even to her ears it sounded weak. "I'm not shutting anyone down." Suddenly Mel didn't know what she was doing or why. She was afraid and apparently hid it so well that the man she loved didn't even see it. She opened her mouth to tell him. When the words wouldn't form, she closed it again.

He held her gaze for a long time. Then he shook his head. "You already have." He let her go, turning away, but not before she saw the hurt and confusion in his gaze.

"Wait!" Mel caught up with Sean next to Ginger, just before he swung into the saddle. She laid a hand on his shoulder. His muscles tensed beneath her touch.

"I don't know who you are any more, Mel." His hand fisted around the saddle blanket. "One minute I see the girl I've always loved. The next you're all closed off." Slowly he relaxed his fingers. "I brought you here, showed you this place because I thought—" He shook his head. "It doesn't matter." He took hold of the saddle and prepared to mount the horse.

Mel put her hand over his, stopping him. "It does matter. It matters a lot. I don't want us to fight like this."

"Is there an *us*, Mel?" He turned, fixing her in his pale green stare. "Because lately it doesn't feel like it. I thought after this morning you might—" A spasm of pain rolled across his features. Abruptly, he dug in his pocket and pulled out a small brown box. "I brought you here to show you what we could have, a dream we could build together. But if there's no us, there's no dream. Here. This is never going to belong to anyone else." He thrust the box into her hand. "I wanted to give this to you, right here, where I wanted to build a life with you. I thought we had something this morning. I thought we finally reconnected." He shrugged.

"Guess I was wrong. All you wanted was a physical hookup, after all. A little friendly benefit fu—"

The sharp crack of her slap filled the meadow. Screaming a harsh protest at the disturbance, a blue jay rose from a low shrub and winged into the pine trees. Mel raised a hand to her mouth, horrified at her behavior. "Sean..." She reached for him but he evaded her touch with a step backward, holding up his hands as though to ward her off.

"If you ever feel you want more, if you ever decide you want to marry me, put my ring on and come find me." He turned away without bothering to mask the flash of disgust on his face.

Mel closed her eyes. She didn't stop him, just watched as he climbed into the saddle, wheeled Ginger around, and took off toward home at a fast gallop.

The box he'd shoved into her hand was old and small. Something he'd been hanging on to? She traced a finger around the edge but didn't open it. He was wrong. It wasn't hers. It never could be. She shoved it into her pocket, then she mounted Lacey and steered in the direction of the ranch.

Chapter Eight

Sean wasn't at the stable when Mel arrived. Ricky was grooming Ginger, who finally looked worn out and less skittish. Mel felt Ricky's gaze on her as she removed the saddle from Lacey's back. He continued to brush Ginger, keeping his thoughts to himself, though clearly he was *having* thoughts.

"Do you want me to take care of Lacey for you, Mel?"

Surreptitiously dabbing at her teary eyes, she shook her head. "I can take care of my horse, Ricky, thanks." She picked up the grooming mitt and began to use it on Lacey.

The horse's neck was warm. Mel pressed her cheek there, breathing in the horsey scent. Lacey nuzzled her as if to commiserate.

"You're such a sweet girl. I don't know how anyone could have hurt you, but I promise I never will." Tears spilled from her eyes and rolled over her cheeks, moistening patches of the horse's hair.

The hand on her shoulder was warm and firm. Startled, Mel looked up with Sean's name on her lips. But it was Justin's kind eyes looking at her, the lines crinkling at the corners deepened with concern. Hastily, Mel scrubbed the tears from her cheeks. Ginger was back in her stall and Ricky was gone. How long had she stood there hugging her horse and crying?

"I guess it's silly to cry over a horse when she's not being mistreated anymore."

Justin continued to look at her in silence. Deep inside, Mel squirmed just a little under his scrutiny.

"Even sillier to cry over a man with a foul temper and mean with it," he finally said.

So he'd seen Sean. Mel couldn't let the blame for her mood fall on the man she loved. "It's not like that."

Justin took the curry mitt from her hand and set it in the grooming bucket. "Let's go for a walk and you can tell me how it is."

"Lacey needs—"

"The boy'll take care of her."

She forced a smile, well aware of how shaky it felt on her lips. "Ricky went and got you?"

Justin's answering smile was wide and sure. "We met halfway. My second son came up to the house all butt-hurt and acting like a jackass. It doesn't happen often, but when it does, no point in talking to him. I figured there'd been words between you two." He settled an arm around Mel's shoulders and steered her into the yard.

They stood without touching at the back fence, near the trailhead. Justin said nothing, just looked out over the pasture. That squirmy feeling in the pit of Mel's stomach returned.

"He's not being a jackass, not without reason, anyway . I hurt him. Very deeply, I think."

Justin set a foot on the bottom rail of the fence, keeping his eyes forward. "Do it on purpose?"

"No," she said on a long sigh. "He's not — we're not in the same place. I don't think we're even reading the same map. And I know he doesn't understand why."

He turned his head and Melanie found herself trapped in his stare. "Got a problem with telling him why?"

"I started telling him. But it's complicated, and telling him got — complicated." Mel laid her head against the top rail of the fence.

Justin's arm slid around her again. For the first time since Todd Mitchell had died, Melanie felt safe in the arms of fatherly love.

"It's going to be as complicated as the two of you make it," he said. "Did he react badly to what you told him?"

Mel looked up again and met Justin's eyes. "No, he was sweet, and he got — and we—" Heat rushed into her face.

Justin's eyes twinkled. "So you got ahead of yourselves."

Smiling in relief, Mel turned and gave Justin a hard hug. "Exactly. Well, almost. And he saw that as us making a connection. So today, he took me to this really pretty place where he thinks he wants to build a home with me." She stepped back and pulled the box from her pocket. "And he gave me this."

Justin regarded the box, his brow furrowed. "He just gave that to you? He didn't ask a question to go with it?"

"I think he was going to. But we were fighting by then. He told me I was shutting us down. And I was. I didn't mean to. I don't want to. He just shoved this in my hand and told me it would never be anyone else's. I didn't open it. I don't even know what it is."

Justin took the box from her hand and lifted the top. With a sigh, he closed it again. "It's the ring I gave his mother the day he was born."

"Oh," whispered Mel. Justin held out the box and she shook her head. "No, that's not mine. He should have never given it to me."

Justin picked up her hand and pressed the box into it. "But he did give it to you. If you don't want it, you need to give it back to him yourself."

Mel looked at Sean's father. He was right. He shouldn't be the messenger. She nodded and closed her fingers around the box.

"Before you do that, though, you need to tell my son the rest of your story. Because I don't think you're on different maps, just different highways." He laid his hand on her shoulder and waited for her to look up at him. "Sometimes highways meet and become the same route. Sometimes, you have to find a connecting road. How you do it's up to you." He laid his arm over her shoulders again and gave her another quick hug.

"Do you know that Todd Mitchell wasn't my real father?"

Justin gave her another one of his considering looks. This time she braced against the squirming sensation.

He shook his head, looking a little sad. "Todd Mitchell was a good friend of mine. I'll wager he'd have something to say about you thinking he wasn't your *real* father."

Mel squeezed her eyes shut, took a breath, and then opened them again. "Sean said almost the same thing. But my real father was a man named Nick DeVayne."

Justin ran a hand over his jaw. "Nick DeVayne. Now that's a name I never thought I'd hear again."

"You knew him?"

"He raised some hell through here years ago."

"He isn't a nice man," whispered Mel.

Justin chuckled without humor. "No, girl, that he is not." He turned her to face him. "But that doesn't mean there's anything wrong with *you*. I meant what I said. You are Todd Mitchell's daughter. No biological connection's gonna take that from you."

"I was with Nick for almost five years."

This time, Justin's laugh was genuine. "Have you met our Ricky? He was with his blood kin for a lot longer than five years. What do you think of him?"

Mel smiled. "Ricky's wonderful."

"And so are you, Melanie Grace Mitchell."

He said it so simply. If only it really was that simple. "I told Sean about a lot of it. But not everything. I did some horrible things — *one* — really horrible thing."

"Is this about the cons DeVayne ran that he got you mixed up in?" asked Justin. "Or is it about that baby you had when you were — what, fifteen?"

Mel's legs were suddenly the consistency of wet spaghetti, long and skinny, and very limp. She would have slumped to the ground if not for Justin's steadying hand.

"How do you know about that?"

Justin heaved a deep sigh. "Your *real* father, Todd Mitchell, and I were best friends growing up. His mother was a second ma to me. After she had to send you off with DeVayne, I visited with her a couple times a week."

Melanie covered her face with her hands. "She knew? Oh, I must have been such a disappointment to her."

"No, girl. Never that. She loved you. She knew about your circumstances because DeVayne told her when he tried to sell you back to her."

Mel sat on the ground and put her head on her knees. "I'm going to be sick."

Justin laid a hand on top of her head, rubbing lightly with his fingertips. "I'm sorry, girl. If she had come to me, I would have helped her. By the time I found out, DeVayne had disappeared with you."

Mel looked up. "Does — does Sean know?"

"No. But I think he should." Justin tilted his head. "Is that what you're afraid to tell him? Is that what's keeping you apart?"

Shaking all over, Mel nodded. "Mostly."

"Tell him," Justin said again. He extended a hand. After a brief hesitation, she took it and he pulled her to her feet.

"Denny's been sending me letters. I only opened the last one. I think — I think whoever adopted my baby, it wasn't legal." She met Justin's gaze and saw only kindness and understanding. "I think my fath— Nick sold my baby," she whispered. The first tear fell, then the second.

"Damn asshole."

Mel stared. Justin McGee rarely cursed.

"Sorry, girl." Shaking his head, Justin hauled Mel into his arms and cradled her against his chest. "Hush now," he whispered. "We'll sort that out, too. It'll all be okay."

* * *

Up at the house, Sean watched them from the front porch. He leaned over the railing and craned his neck to keep them in sight. What were his father and Mel talking about? Why did Justin keep hugging her?

Then they were heading toward the house. Together. Crap damn it! He knew he'd have to face her sooner or later. He'd hoped for later. When he wasn't raw inside. Looked like it was going to be sooner. Fine. But it sure as hell wasn't going to be on the porch where it would be obvious he'd been watching them. He hustled his tail inside, closing the door behind him a little harder than he'd intended.

Oh, well.

He turned away from the door and ran straight into his sister-in-law, for once without the baby glued to her shoulder.

Her gaze swept downward then up to meet his. "You look like the devil rained out your baseball game. What happened?"

Sean tensed. He didn't need a family psych session. Not today. Not ever. So he put on his best surly face and answered her. "*Nuh—thing.* Got that? Nothing happened. Not a damned thing. Nothing's wrong."

Sandy rolled her eyes. "Whatever you say, but your *nuh—thing* is my best friend and the closest thing I'll ever have to a sister."

Okay, message received. Hurt Mel and my life is over. Too late on both counts, Sister.

Sean looked behind him, just wanting to escape. His nothing was also about to come in the front door, and Sean had no intention of being caught arguing with Sandy about her when she did.

"She's fine. I'm fine. We're all just fuh-reakin' fine."

Sandy's eyes narrowed. "You're being a jackass."

"Yeah, now that seems to be the consensus. You, Dad. Whoever."

Sandy shook her head and turned away. One hand on the balustrade as she started up the steps, she looked over her shoulder. "This isn't who you are, Sean. And it's not who you have to become. If you ever care to talk about *nothing*, or the fact that you're not *just fuh-reakin' fine,* I'll be here."

Stunned, a little less blustery, Sean watched her make dignified progress up the stairs. He managed to duck through the dining room into the kitchen just as the front door was pushed open.

Ryan stood at the range over a pot of chili. He took one look at Sean and silently stepped to the back door, pulled it open, and left it that way. Then he returned to his cooking.

Sean stared. "What'd you do that for?"

Ryan lifted a shoulder. "Just being a good big brother and helping you run away."

Casting his "good big brother" a scathing look, Sean stalked to the door and gave it a shove. It closed with a solid bang. "Jackass."

Ryan's laugh dripped with contempt. "No, sorry. Only room for one jackass at a time here, and you've got that covered for the day. Maybe the month." With a final stir, he put the spoon down, lowered the heat under the cooking pot, and set the lid in place.

"You know, boy, you can be all kinds of stupid when you get one of these moods on, but I've never known you to be a coward." Justin stood in the door to the dining room. His mouth was pulled into a grim line. His blue eyes had gone hard and taken on a gray cast. He raked Sean up and down with an openly derisive expression. "You think I didn't see you gawking at us off the front porch?"

Sean glared. He should have known his eagle-eyed father had spotted him. "Hey, Dad. Don't hold back or anything."

"Oh, I'm holding back plenty right now. You think you're the only one hurting here? You ran a hay mower over that girl's feelings without a thought to what you were doing." Justin walked to the range and lifted the lid on the chili pot, sniffing appreciatively. He turned back to Sean, only slightly more in control. "Son, you have no idea what she's been through or why she's holding back. And yeah, she's holding back. She wants to explain everything to you, but she's hurting and afraid of what you'll think."

Sean clenched his fists. "So she doesn't trust me. Doesn't trust what I feel for her." And didn't that just make his day? He peered into the dining room. Where the hell was she?

"Well, listen to the high and mighty Sean McGee. Son, have you ever told her how you actually feel? Does she have any reason to trust you? Because near as I can tell, you didn't give her a proposal, you gave her an ultimatum."

Standing near the sink, Ryan snickered. He stood up straight and went silent when their father threw him a quelling glance.

Justin sat at the table and eased his legs out in front of him with a sigh, apparently relaxing.

Sean knew better. His dad was setting him up for the kill. He backed up a step and bumped into his strangely silent brother.

"Melanie loves the hell out of you, son. Why? I don't know. Because just now, I don't see much lovable about you." Justin rubbed his jaw. "If you lose her, it'll be because you threw her away. So now you have two choices. You can go to her, ask her to tell you everything and listen to the whole story, and then tell her what you feel for her. You can accept that what she's offering is all she *can* offer right now. Or you can break things off with her and miss her for the rest of your damn fool life. Those are your choices. Period."

Sean looked at his feet. He felt like he was eight again, caught lighting one of his father's cigars. Justin had given him two choices then, too. Tell the truth and take his punishment or lie and disappoint his father. And still receive his punishment. He'd opted for not disappointing his father then and his punishment had been tolerable, just some extra chores. Sean worked at unclenching his jaw. Drawing a shaky deep breath, he met Justin's eyes, and reeled backward at the anger he read there.

"Where is she?" he finally muttered.

"She's visiting Sandy and the baby." Justin sat up straight, pointing a finger at Sean. "Go take a walk and think about things before you go looking for her. And son, I'd like to suggest the words 'I'm sorry' would make a good start to what you have to say to her."

Justin turned to Ryan, effectively dismissing Sean. "Does Joseph still have the detective connections he used to find your Angel?"

"More than likely." Ryan pulled a sack of corn meal from the pantry and set it on the kitchen counter. "Why?"

"Got someone I need to find." He glanced pointedly at Sean, obviously expecting him to leave.

Sean stepped onto the back porch and pulled the door closed behind him.

* * *

He walked. He tried to think, to sort things out. Everything was all mashed together between his heart and his head and not much was making sense. Sean found himself at the main road, so he then turned around and walked back. The fence along the drive was new, replaced just the year before after a fire had burned it and threatened the main homestead. Ryan had almost lost Sandy in that fire.

Sean's love wasn't being threatened by fire. It was being threatened by his own stubbornness, his sudden and uncharacteristic impatience. From the time Ryan had settled down with Sandy, Sean had longed for the same thing with the woman he'd loved from the first time he saw her when they were children. He hadn't told Mel how he felt and what he wanted, though. He'd just assumed she wanted the same thing.

His dad had said Mel loved him. He could only hope the old man was right. And he hoped it wasn't too late to accept her on her terms.

Early evening sun slanted in from the west. It would be dark soon. As he approached the main house, a feeling, a particular awareness, made him look up. She was standing at the top of the drive, watching him.

He wanted to beg her to forgive him. He wanted to kiss her and hold her. He wanted to give her everything she needed. He wanted to accept whatever she could give in return. Mostly he just wanted to run into her arms. Instead, he walked the last hundred feet at a normal pace. But he never took his eyes from hers.

Mel's expression was completely bland, her body language unrevealing. Except for her fiery blue eyes. It might have been the heat of anger or hurt. Or passion. Or something else entirely. But she wasn't freezing him out.

Only when he got close did her gaze falter, but only briefly. Then she seemed to regroup, lifting her chin and looking him in the eye. The late afternoon breeze ruffled hair the color of summer sunshine, reminding Sean of when they'd met as children.

She'd given him innocent comfort then, and over the years, they had provided comfort for each other through some really heavy stuff. Somehow, during the time she'd been away, he'd lost touch with that special connection they'd had.

He wanted it back.

When she opened her mouth to speak, he stilled her with two fingers on her lips.

"Mel, I'm sorry. I was a jerk. I lo—" He stilled his panic, slowed his breathing, and tried again. "I love you." He dropped his hand. "I don't want to lose you."

Pain flashed in her eyes, followed by fear, and yes, the shadows were there. How had he not realized that the shadows were caused by deep pain, the kind of pain that shattered hearts and kept them from ever becoming whole again?

Mel reached out, hesitated for a second, and then cupped Sean's neck. Her thumb traced a back-and-forth motion along his jaw as she held his gaze. "We were always friends first, weren't we?"

Captivated by her touch, by the look in her eyes, Sean could only nod.

"Somewhere, sometime, while I was away, I lost that part of us. And when I came back, we didn't reconnect that way. *I* didn't reconnect that way." Her eyelids fluttered closed. Then she bit her lip and opened her eyes again. "And that wasn't your fault. I think it's harder to be friends than it is to be lovers. When I first came back, I couldn't find the person I used to be. I didn't like who I was, and didn't want you to see who I'd become. I wanted you to always think of me as — as your sunshine girl." A tear spilled over.

Sean raised his hand and captured the tear. For a moment, it glistened on his fingertip. "You are," he whispered.

"I want to be." Her voice trembled as a shudder tore through her. "But there's more to the story I started telling you. I need to finish."

Sean couldn't stop looking at her. "Okay."

"Nick kept us in Oklahoma City for a year when I was fifteen. I got a job at a dive diner without telling him, and I hid all my money. And there was... a boy there. Glenn Moss. We started seeing each other and—" She grimaced, then drew a fortifying breath and continued. "I got pregnant."

Somehow, Sean had known it was coming. He'd steeled his emotions against the pain and jealousy. Then he oddly found he hadn't really needed to. It was good she'd found someone.

Mel shivered. She stared off into the distance. "We weren't ready to be parents. Oh, I would have. I'd have sucked it up and raised the baby if I'd had any kind of life to offer. But being dragged all over the country behind Nick, being used in his scams and schemes. What kind of life was that for a baby?" Her voice broke and so did the dam holding the emotions inside of Sean.

He pulled her against him and held on tight. His tears mixed with hers. They stood that way until the breeze picked up and chilled them both. Mel pulled back and just looked at him.

"Did you love him? The baby's father?" he finally croaked out.

Mel closed her eyes. When she opened them, they were just a little brighter with hurt that had been too long suppressed. Slowly, she shook her head. "No. And he didn't love me, either. He wasn't unkind. He was just a teenage boy who wanted to get laid and had no clue what love was. I... liked him. But it's always been you, Sean. Was always meant to be you from the time we saw that wild stallion together."

He didn't want to know. He had to know. "What happened to your baby?"

She stood up straighter. "I hid my pregnancy for as long as I could. I almost made it." Her voice broke and she took a deep breath before she continued. "Nick had that stupid scam with me being hit on by older men going on, and one of them got too close, got his hands on me."

Sean's vision hazed red for a second.

"He asked how innocent I could be if I was already pregnant." She gulped in air, full-out shaking.

Sean rubbed his hands over her bare arms to warm them. "Do you want to go inside?"

The only indication she gave that she'd heard him was to shake her head. "I was going to have the baby in the hospital and then just leave it. I knew that was technically abandoning the baby but I knew it would be safe in a hospital. Nice and anonymous. When Nick found out I was pregnant, that wasn't going to happen. He kept me hidden. I had the baby, a little girl, on Christmas Eve, in the dirty apartment Nick was keeping us in. His girlfriend at the time helped me deliver her."

Cold assaulted Sean from the inside out and he shivered violently. A baby born outside of a hospital might as well not exist.

"They left me behind to clean up the mess I'd made," said Mel flatly. "And they stole my baby girl. I don't even know what she looked like. I only know she was a girl because Nick had wanted her to be a boy. Said he'd promised someone it would be a boy. And he had no problem expressing his — disappointment." Mel broke contact with Sean.

Sean was raw. His voice was raspy, choked with emotion he couldn't get in check. "He hit you?"

"It was mostly verbal."

Mostly, not only. Sean clamped his jaw hard rather than spew the vulgarities crossing his mind about the man. He wanted to hunt him down. Only Sean's response wouldn't be mostly verbal.

But there was more to the story, he realized, forcing his attention back on Mel. She continued speaking, her voice flat. She sounded numb. "I'm pretty sure Nick and his girlfriend sold my baby. And, God help me, I let them, because all I could think — pray — was that wherever she ended up, it *had* to be better than being with me. It wasn't until much later that I realized he could have sold her to monsters who would hurt her."

Sean stared, frozen, unable to move. Horror gripped him; for the baby, for the girl Melanie had been, needing to make such a choice. "Mel." He could barely get her name out. "All this time, you've been holding onto this. Did you think I wouldn't understand?"

"How could I expect *you* to understand when *I* didn't?"

Sean closed the gap between them again. He caught her hand and laced his fingers through hers. Shaking, he brought her hand to his face, pressing it against his cheek while he held her with a look.

"I love you, Melanie Grace Mitchell. I always have and always will. Nothing is ever going to change that. Do you understand me?"

Very slowly, she curled her fingers to clasp his tightly. "I love you, too," she whispered. "Always have, always will."

Turning his face, Sean pressed a hard kiss to the back of Mel's hand.

Chapter Nine

Somewhere out in the world, Mel had a nearly fourteen-year-old daughter. A child she had never been allowed to hold or even see. Sean held onto that intellectual fact as a means to keep the cauldron of swirling emotions inside him from boiling over. Truth be told, he had no idea how he felt about Mel's revelation. If he stopped now to analyze his feelings, no doubt he'd only over-think the whole thing as he normally did with unsettling news. He did know his feelings for Melanie Mitchell hadn't changed. Nothing would ever destroy his love for her.

He was that sure.

He had no idea how Mel had survived during the years she'd been gone. But at least now he understood why she'd been a stranger when she'd returned home. He couldn't make those years go away, but he would damn well make sure she never had to live through anything like that ever again.

His hand lingered on her knee after he saw her into the passenger seat of his pickup. He wasn't sure if he meant his touch to be comforting to Mel or if he was seeking reassurance from her. Maybe both.

She brushed her fingers over his knuckles, met his gaze and smiled. The band of uncertainty squeezing his heart up into his throat lessened its grip. She understood him. She always had.

* * *

Sean started the pickup and turned on the headlights. The high beams cut a path ahead of them as they drove toward the main road in silence. Mel could tell he was still disconcerted. She didn't know how to change that. It was just something he would have to work through. For now, she held tight to his words of love and prayed the rest would come.

Just after he turned onto the main road, a trail led off to the right, its entrance nearly obscured by overgrown brush.

"Sean, stop! Please."

He maneuvered the truck to the side of the road and they rolled to a gentle stop. "Did you forget something?"

Mel shook her head. Then she nodded. "Yes. Yes, I did." She breathed in deeply, aware that she was about to risk everything. She pointed to the twin ruts. "Can we go there?"

Sean raised an eyebrow, obviously mystified, but he put the pickup in reverse and aimed them onto the tracks. He drove with caution, avoiding the deepest of the ruts, stopping when the track dwindled to nothing. He cut the engine but left the lights on. Then he shifted in his seat and waited.

Mel slipped the ring box from her purse. Sean's expression turned wary.

Drawing in a deep breath, Mel set the box on the seat between them. "I didn't open this. I know what it is because your father told me." She took a deep breath. "I'm not going to put your ring on, Sean."

He inhaled sharply and his body tensed. She laid her hand on his arm and squeezed, knowing he probably thought the worst, but she needed to do it her way for both of them.

"Come with me." Mel opened the door and jumped out. Picking her way through the tall grass to the front of the truck, she stopped in the glow of the headlights and looked back. She could only pray he'd follow.

He did, but more slowly. *Cautious all the way, huh, Seanie?* His steps faltered a few feet away.

"I know it's dark now." The mad pulse in her throat gave her voice a breathless quaver she couldn't quell. "But I'm hoping you'll help me see something." She fitted her back against him until she could feel the heat of his body there. He still didn't move, so she pulled his arms around her waist and held them in place. "When you come home, you pull in the driveway. You stop right here. What do you see over there?"

He drew a deep breath. When he spoke, his voice was as shaky and uncertain as hers. "The front of a house."

"What does the house look like?"

"I... don't really know." He tensed. "Mel... what is this?" He tried to turn her in his arms but she leaned back instead.

"Do you want some help?" she asked, looking upward over her shoulder.

Sean hesitated then gave a barely perceptible nod.

"Brick and stone? Or logs?" she asked.

"Logs and fieldstone?"

"A good compromise." Mel smiled. Just maybe... "One story or two?"

"Two." His answer came easier this time. Some of his tension eased.

"With a long front porch?" Some of her own tension lessened.

"Yeah, all the way across, maybe around to the side."

"Look." Mel gestured vaguely in the general direction of the imaginary house. "Someone's waiting for you at the front door. What does she look like?"

His breath caught but he recovered quickly. "She's the most beautiful girl in the world. She has hair the color of sunshine and eyes that reflect the sky." His arms tightened, and he pressed a kiss just below her left ear.

Mel shifted inside his embrace until she faced him. "I like this dream you're showing me, Sean. I like it a whole lot." Standing on her toes, she kissed his neck, his jaw, the side of his mouth. "Please tell me there's still time for me to share this dream with you."

He swallowed. "Melanie," he whispered, making her name sound like a song on his lips. "There's all kinds of time."

"I'm not going to put your ring on, Sean."

He closed his eyes, pulling in a long, steady breath before he opened them again and nodded.

She kissed the corner of his mouth once more. "But if you put it on me, I'll never take it off."

Framing her face with his fingertips, Sean leaned forward, hesitated, searching her eyes. Mel let down her barriers, accepted the vulnerability that came from trusting him as she met his gaze.

With a groan, Sean captured her lips in a fiercely possessive kiss. He backed her up against the front of the truck, repositioning her head and angling his own for a deeper kiss. Her arms stole around his waist, and she hugged him close as the hunger that had been gnawing at her for years took over.

The feral growl that started low in his throat sparked a flash of longing that radiated straight from her core and rushed through her body like a starburst.

His lips were hot and soft, demanding and giving. But she wanted much more than those lips she knew so well. She wanted the whole package: one often ornery, frequently funny, sometimes infuriating, always loving cowboy named Sean McGee.

When Sean retreated, he grabbed Mel's hand and led her to the passenger side of his pickup. Moonlight flashed on silver as he yanked open the door. Setting his hands at her waist, he easily lifted her up onto the seat. Then he reached beyond her for the box she had left there.

"This belonged to my mother." He opened the box and slid the ring out, holding it so she could see the heated fire of green emerald, the cool ice of white diamonds. His gentle laugh was a little breathless. "There's a story that goes with it that I'm sure Dad will tell you when he sees you wearing it." He paused. "Melanie, will you let me put this on you? Will you wear it and agree to marry me? It can be tomorrow, next week, next year, ten years from now. Whenever you're ready. You're worth waiting for. I've never loved anyone the way I love you."

Had she thought she would be ready for him? Her heart thumped painfully and squeezed into her throat, and her chin quivered as tears filled her eyes. Her breath hitched; she couldn't pull in enough air to speak. So she held out her shaking left hand, and despite her tremors, he slipped the ring onto her finger.

"We've waited so long already," she whispered, hooking her arms around his neck. "What do you think about January?"

"Happy New Year?" He leaned in and took her lips again, pushing her backward onto the seat and crawling in after her.

His body provided warmth against the cool October night, but Mel generated heat to match from deep within. Sean nuzzled her neck, spinning sensations that rocketed into her center, stirring the yearning of years and the emotions of decades. She snaked her arms around his back and arched into him. His hand dipped under her shirt and moved to the snap on her jeans. His fingers were warm where they grazed her belly button.

In an instant, his slow burn flashed over into a recklessly ignited fuse that mirrored her own. And she reveled in the knowledge that she had sent him there.

No, they hadn't had the connection Sean had craved that morning, but it was present now as two hearts welcomed each other home.

* * *

Sean cradled Mel next to him. Her breathing was more a series of deep sighs. Every so often, contentment rose from her throat in a soft purr. He didn't know how long they lay on the seat of his truck, but he wasn't in a hurry to break that long-awaited connection.

She shifted, brushing the velvety soft skin of her breast against his chest, raising goose bumps that trailed to his belly. Chuckling softly, he bent and nuzzled her there, seeking her nipple and drawing it into his mouth.

Gentle sighs became low moans as she stirred against him and threw a leg over his knee. "Again?" she murmured, tracing light circles along his rib with her fingernails.

Hell, yeah, again. And again. And again.

And after that, again.

He rolled slightly, wincing as his bare butt hit the cold vinyl seat. Again could wait just a bit. Until they got to her place. He'd take it slow, show her how much he loved her in the best way... They had plenty of time, all night if they wanted, or at least as long as the—

No!

He raised himself, abruptly pulled away from her, knowing it was already far too late to be doing so. He should have done that first. *Before* anything happened. *Stupid! Stupid!*

He clambered over the seat and scrambled out of the pickup, stooping to retrieve pieces of abandoned clothing. His hands shook for very different reasons now. After righting a stubbornly twisted leg, he hauled his jeans up over his hips. His shirt lay draped over the side-view mirror. He snatched it and shrugged it over his shoulders.

Mel sat staring at him. The dome light cast a golden glow over her pale skin. She didn't even make an attempt to cover herself, so he averted his eyes as he grabbed her jeans and shirt from the floor of the truck and tossed it onto the seat. Without bothering to locate his boots, he left her, pushing the door closed to protect her from the mountain chill.

The grass was damp and cold beneath his bare feet as he stalked to the rear of the truck. He stood in the dark, resting his forehead on the cap. The mountain wind washing over him was tropical in comparison to the chill in his gut. What had he just done to her?

Mel's approach was nearly silent, but he felt her moving up behind him. Her arms began to sneak around his waist, but he jumped forward and slammed into the truck. Away from her touch.

"Don't, Mel. Don't touch me just now."

She snatched her hands back. "What is it? What's wrong? Did I do something?"

The fear in her voice was obvious and it killed him. He had to touch her after all. He whirled, tugging her against him, his hands sliding up her back. "No, Mel. No, you did nothing wrong. I'm sorry. I'm so sorry. I went at you like a runaway train and—"

"But I liked that! I want to do it again." She wiggled against him and giggled. "Only… maybe not in the truck next time. As exciting as that was, we're not kids anymore, are we?" She leaned back, pressing her hips harder against his. "And I have my own place…"

Her words and movements made him think of everything he'd always wanted to do with her. But he had to maintain sanity now. "Listen to me, Sweetness. We didn't — I didn't use anything. Protection — I didn't use a condom."

She went completely still.

"Mel." He angled his head for a better look, but it was too dark to see. She was so quiet. "*Melanie?*"

Damn, he was losing his mind. What kind of stupid, insensitive, selfish ass was he? She'd accepted his marriage proposal. That hadn't given him license to take her to bed — and not even *in* a bed. What was he thinking? She was right. They weren't hormonal kids any longer.

She drew a shaky breath. "Is that all?"

"Isn't it enough?" he muttered.

"It's okay," she murmured. Then she added, speaking louder with more assurance, "Sean, it's okay. I'm healthy, you're healthy. We're going to get married. And it's not the right time of the month for me to get pregnant."

* * *

Alone in her little apartment, Mel looked at the calendar. She counted again, though she had no need. Even as she had reassured Sean out by the back of his pickup, she'd already guessed the truth.

It was *exactly* the right time of the month to get pregnant.

"Okay," she said to her reflection in the bathroom mirror. "Chances are nothing happened. Lots of people trying to get pregnant have sex at the right time and it doesn't work."

Fate wouldn't be so cruel as to allow history to repeat itself. Right? Her own face mocked her from inside the mirror.

* * *

Sean stopped his truck in front of the house, still berating himself for not taking care with Mel. It was late, but a dim light shone through the living room window.

"Oh, *hell,* no."

He pushed the pickup door closed with just a whisper of sound, then eased his way into the shadows and around the side of the house to the cottonwood tree. Peering up its length, he shook his head. Some things never changed.

With a sigh, he jumped up and grabbed the lowest branch.

* * *

Just as she was pulling the covers on her bed back for the night, Mel's cell phone chimed. Sean's number blinked insistently and she smiled at the warmth rushing through her with the memories from earlier in the evening.

"Hey, lover," she murmured, flopping back against her stack of pillows. "I miss you. I wish you could have stayed."

His chuckle tickled her ear and inched along her awareness, and she knew everything would be okay. No matter what.

"I wish I could have stayed, too. But I've got a problem-child horse arriving tomorrow, and I have to be here." He waited a beat. "Colt's delivering your new ride tomorrow, right?"

"Yep. Not that I mind spending the time with you, but it'll be nice having my independence back."

He chuckled again, sending more happy little zings of sensation to her heart. "I was just hoping you'd find your way out here after you have wheels under you."

When she twisted her hand and wiggled her fingers in the soft glow of her bedside lamp, fire flashed off emerald and diamonds. She smiled. "Chances are pretty good I'll find myself heading in your direction tomorrow."

"Good," he breathed into the phone. "Did I tell you I love you?"

"You may have mentioned it once or twice." Mel deliberately prolonged her hesitation then gave him what they both needed. "I love you, too, Sean."

* * *

"Anyone heading into town today?" Justin entered through the dining room arch and crossed the kitchen. After a quick glance at the oatmeal warming on the range, he went directly for the fresh pot of coffee. "I need some nails for the windows around here. Got critters sneaking in at all hours."

Sean tunneled his vision on his own bowl of oatmeal. The stuff was disgusting. Dang, Sandy needed to get off the health kick.

"That right? Critters?" Following on Justin's heels, Ryan stirred the pot of oatmeal, made a face, and left the spoon standing straight up in the sticky mess. Casting a cautious look behind him, he pulled out a frying pan and moved to the fridge, from which he withdrew a carton of eggs and a package of Canadian bacon. "Are you sure they won't just chew their way in like rats if you nail the windows shut?"

Well, keeping a low profile wasn't going to cut it. Sean sighed. "Someone have something to say to me?"

Rubbing his eyes, Ricky entered the kitchen. He froze at the range and stared into the pot of congealing oatmeal then eased backward. "Ah, I'll just—" He sniffed and wrinkled his nose. "—get something on the way to school." He shook his head sympathetically at Ryan. "Sandy's changing Bethany's diaper. She said she'd be right down."

Heaving a sigh, Ryan put his intended breakfast back into the refrigerator. He turned back to Sean. "You really okay?"

Sean held onto Ryan's gaze for a long time, watching the emotions play in his brother's eyes, a hint of humor, mild interest, and a whole lot of concern. Big brother stuff, he reminded himself. The kinds of things Ryan still seemed to feel he needed to make up because he hadn't been there. An itchy sensation began at the base of Sean's neck and spread upward. Being the younger brother in that equation wasn't always comfortable. Finally he nodded, averting his gaze to the right. "I'm good. Mel's coming out later. So in case you get the urge to grill her, she's good, too." A smile that wouldn't be denied spread over his lips. She'd been very good.

"So she doesn't have a huge vampire bite on her neck like that one?" Ryan gestured vaguely at Sean's collar.

Hand sliding to his neck, Sean angled himself away from Ryan. Oh, she undoubtedly had bites, plenty of them, and not all on her neck, either. His body tingled into primitive awareness as memories of the night before rushed to the front of his thoughts as he carried his bowl to the sink and rinsed it thoroughly. Warm water coursed over his hands, and he thought of Mel's heated responses to him, but he tucked that particular memory back where it belonged. When he turned from the sink, Ricky was staring at him, a thoughtful expression on his face.

Sean's composure slipped a little and he considered that condom. The one Sean hadn't been able to make use of the night before. The one now in *Ricky's* wallet. He'd made good and sure to replace it with several that morning. He could only hope it wasn't too little, too late.

"You ate the oatmeal." The kid spoke slowly. His eyes were wide with awe. "You *hate* oatmeal."

"Hey, sometimes I get hungry, kid."

Shooting him a look that suggested he knew exactly what Sean had been hungry for, Ricky shook his head.

Not at all comfortable, Sean grabbed his denim jacket from the hook next to the door. "I'm expecting Devil's Advocate in about an hour. I'll be in the stable."

"Devil's Advocate?" Justin added more sugar to his coffee. "Is that a horse or a lawyer?"

Sean threw his father a sarcastic smile. "Thoroughbred. Got hurt in a stable fire. He won't be racing again but they're hoping he'll work out as a stud."

"Aw, geez." Justin set his coffee cup on the table and eyed the oatmeal on the stove again. "Racing's just the waste of a good horse."

"Yeah, well, this job's gonna pay the bills for a long time."

"Ha! Know what else pays the bills?" asked Justin. "Getting the cattle to market."

"Got the trucks coming out beginning of next week," said Ryan.

Oh, thrills. His least favorite activity in the world, shipping cattle to be slaughtered. Sean's smile felt a little tight, but he sighed and nodded. "I'll clear my calendar."

"There's Daddy." Sandy entered the kitchen, one shoulder occupied by a bright-eyed Bethany struggling to focus on her surroundings. "Need me to freshen up the oatmeal?"

"No!" Justin, Ryan, and Ricky answered at the same time.

Hiding a snicker, Sean ducked outside, pulling the door closed behind him.

* * *

The unopened letters in her hand bore postmarks from different cities, all of them west of the Mississippi River, most in the Southwest, though a couple were from Kansas and the last had come from Iowa. Denny. He probably hadn't written to her out of any sense of family ties. So what was he after? She'd read his last note. Now she needed to find out what he'd sent to her over the last several months.

A flutelike warble filtered through the screen door as a meadowlark greeted the morning. It was a happy sound, in obscene contrast to the task before her. Mel sat at her tiny kitchen table, enjoying the cool autumn breeze that occasionally fluttered the papers on the table. Her hands shook as she tore open the oldest letter and slid out the single folded sheet of white paper.

Chapter Ten

Mel needed a lawyer. She needed to talk to DC, and probably needed the investigator Justin had suggested. She had no clue where to start.

And she had to have another uncomfortable conversation with Sean. He'd been understanding about her pregnancy as a teenager, hadn't thought less of her. Would he understand that she needed to find out what had happened to her daughter?

She looked at the letters on the table in front of her. She'd been right. They were snakes. She was pretty sure the things Denny had written would be considered evidence in the investigation of the attorney in Oklahoma — if he'd actually been involved in selling her baby, that is. The one thing that worried her was that she had made no attempt to find her child before now, hadn't reported the birth or that she'd been forced to give her away. And according to her brother, that made it look like she'd had a part in the selling of her baby.

Not a single day had passed since her baby's birth that Mel hadn't thought and worried about her, prayed for her.

But with Bethany's abrupt and memorable entry into the world had come a sense of urgency to find her own baby. Well, not so much a baby any longer... Mel didn't want to disrupt whatever life her child had. She had always tried to convince herself her daughter would have a much happier life without her in it. That didn't need to change.

But a glimpse, the knowledge her little one was safe. Surely that wasn't too much—

Her cell phone chirped and she answered it without looking.

"It's been eight hours, thirty-seven minutes, and... fourteen seconds since I kissed you goodnight. Miss me yet?"

A grin slid across her face. "Justin, I thought I told you not to call me at this number."

"Ha, ha." Sean's voice oozed with sarcasm. "Not that I begrudge my dad some action — as long as I don't have to hear about it — but not with my girl. So, do you want to try that again or do you have something to tell me?"

Suddenly she didn't want any more teasing. "I do miss you. A lot."

"What's wrong?" The laughter had gone from his voice as well.

"I'm really just missing you." She blinked back the tears. "Turns out—" Her voice cracked. "Turns out I'm pretty attached to you."

Concern crept into his tone. "Are you sure that's it? I can get Ry to wait for the horse I've got coming in this morning."

"You just take care of your horse so you can give me my alone time tonight."

"Okay." He didn't sound convinced.

"I love you, Seanie," she whispered and disconnected the call. Would life ever be uncomplicated for them?

The sharp rap at her screen door interrupted her irritation, and Mel blinked in surprise at the man on the other side.

"DC. Hi." She held the door open so he could enter.

The sheriff looked uncomfortable. "Sorry for the early hour, but I've got something you're going to want to hear, and I'm guessing you'd rather hear this in private."

She pointed to the sofa and followed him over.

"There is no easy way to say this." DC opened a small black notebook and read from the top sheet. "A speeding ticket was issued by state police to a Mr. Dennis DeVayne on US-189 out of Jackson last Saturday afternoon."

"Oh." Mel's heart dropped to the pit of her stomach, where it continued to beat rapidly. "So he is in the area."

"He was around last Saturday, at least." DC closed his notebook and tapped it with his fingers. "He also ran a red light in Jackson, got caught on a camera." He met her stare. "Back in July."

Could it get worse? She squeezed her eyes closed for a second and prayed her life would pop back into her control. Except if she was honest, it never really had been in her control. Uneasiness tightened her throat. "He wants something. He's been hanging around."

DC rubbed his jaw. "Well, you know him and I don't. I can't really say anything other than he appears to be a lousy driver."

"I've been getting letters from him since May but they've been from different cities, out of state."

A frown creased DC's forehead. "So... he's on the move a lot, and yet he keeps coming back here, or he mails them to an accomplice to mail to you. Nick DeVayne, maybe? I haven't found anything in the system on him at all. Maybe he's being careful." He gave her a pointed look. "Or something might have happened to him. Do you want me to look at the letters? If there's anything remotely threatening, we can at least get it into the system and start looking at Dennis."

Decision time. Mel drew a long breath. "I... think I should bring them to you later. I think — maybe I need a lawyer."

As she finished speaking, he was already shaking his head. "I'm sorry. I didn't hear what you just said. Were you looking for me to recommend an attorney for an unrelated matter, Mel?"

Mel flashed a grin. "If you weren't married already, I'd so go after you."

With a quick laugh, DC stood. "I'm guessing your boyfriend would have something to say about that."

"Actually, we've had a development." She held out her left hand.

A wide grin split his face. "Well, I'll be damned. The boy finally got around to asking. Congratulations, Mel. You set a date?" He held up a hand like a stop sign. "And I'm only asking because Rachel will have my head if I come home with this news and no date."

It felt good to laugh. "We're thinking January."

"It's been a long time coming." He stepped back and examined her face, nodding with approval. "You look happy."

She was happy. But she was also scared. Mel bit her lip. "Can I ask a hypothetical question?"

"Sure." He bent to retrieve his hat from the coffee table.

Mel took a deep breath then let the words out in a rush. "If a fifteen-year-old girl has a baby and lets her parents put her up for adoption... and it turns out the baby was sold illegally by the parents, how much trouble can the girl get in?"

DC straightened, leaving his hat on the table. He regarded Mel in silence, a speculative glimmer in his eyes. Finally he answered. "I'm not a lawyer. But hypothetically, I think it would depend on how much the baby's mother benefitted from the sale, whether she was a willing participant. If she spoke up at some point to protect the child. Selling babies is human trafficking."

Mel closed her eyes against a wave of nausea. "Okay. Thanks."

"What's this about?" asked DC gently. "Are you in some kind of trouble, Mel?"

"I'd be real appreciative of that lawyer's name now."

The sheriff gave her a long, hard stare. His battle between duty and friendship was easy to read. Mel met his gaze with a level look, letting him see her fear without openly admitting to anything.

DC nodded. "Steve Wilson. He has an office on Angle Road. He used to be a damn fine criminal attorney in Laramie, but he does more family law now. He handled Lisa's adoption for me and Rachel. Tell him I referred you if you need to see him right away."

Relief weakened her muscles and Mel grabbed the back of her sofa to keep from sagging to the floor. "Thank you."

DC crossed the room to leave but he turned at the door. "You're not alone, Mel. You need help, don't be afraid to ask."

She smiled against her sadness. "I know."

As DC pulled open the door, he exclaimed in surprise. "Hey, there, Ford."

A little thrill of excitement set up residence in her stomach. The Jeep might be a used vehicle, but it was nicer than anything she'd ever been able to call her own. "He's delivering my new ride." She grabbed a jacket, and they all moved outside.

"I didn't think you'd ever sell this old thing, Ford. Used to think it was surgically attached to you." DC moved around the Jeep, smiling appreciatively, running his hand over a fender. "You put a lot of miles on this baby with search and rescue. You still gonna be working with them?"

The sigh that escaped Colt's lips sounded almost wistful, but it was hard to tell since his eyes were behind sunglasses. "Yeah. This one's still got some life in her, but SAR takes a bit more equipment these days, so I'm upgrading."

Nodding his agreement, DC popped the hood. "If I'd had the twelve hundred, I would have taken this off your hands for sure." He sighed. "But then Rachel would have killed me for not getting something more practical."

"What's more practical than a vehicle that can go anywhere in rain or snow?" Colt asked with an easy grin.

DC barked a good-natured laugh. "Tell that to a mom with a four-year-old. Practical has four-wheel drive, four real doors, and a roof that stays in place." He closed the hood, turned to Mel, and winked. "Try not to shear the axle on this one, girl."

Resisting the urge to stick out her tongue, Mel shot the sheriff a narrow-eyed glare. Then she smiled.

As DC drove off, she studied Colt, speculating on the deal he'd cut her. Darn it, she'd known something was going on between Colt and Sean the day before. She should have pinned Sean on it then and there. "What did DC mean about twelve hundred dollars?" she asked bluntly.

"That was the original asking price last spring." Colt's answer was smooth and easy, just as it had been the day before. "I dropped it over the summer."

She'd never been able to read Colton Ford's face as easily as she could read the faces of most other people, even without the dark glasses he had in place now. Mel darn well intended to never play poker with the man.

She'd have to call him out.

"You didn't drop the price that far." She leaned against the Jeep, crossing her legs and folding her arms, sending the message that she didn't intend to move until she received a satisfactory answer.

He stepped back, apparently sizing her up from behind those irritating glasses.

Tack two. Mel tried for an engaging smile. "Come on, Colt. What's the real price on this thing? Can I really afford it?"

"You have the five hundred?"

Drawing a deep breath, Mel blew it out impatiently. "Yes, I have the five hundred."

Colt lifted a shoulder. "Then you can afford it."

But Mel's mind clicked into overdrive. Olivia had mentioned a check from Sean the day before, and the two men had each stated a different amount when she'd asked about it. She dug her heels in.

"Colt, what did he do?"

The inscrutable man shifted his stance, and she thought he was going to cave. Instead, in a soft voice, he asked her a direct question. "Would you do anything for him if he had a need?"

She replied without hesitation. "Of course."

"And you know he feels the same way about you?"

This time she was more cautious. "Yes."

"Then what does it matter?"

She'd never felt more like stamping her foot and demanding to be treated like a grownup. "He can't just swoop in here and take care of me, Colt. I can't accept that."

Colt spread his hands. "Why not?"

Typical man, like everything was so simple. "It's personal and Sean knows all about it."

Ford slid his sunglasses off and trapped her in his dark-eyed gaze. "He loves you, you know."

"I do know that." Nodding, Mel allowed herself to thaw a bit. "And I love him."

"Apparently, you gave him a budget, and the only things in your price range aren't reliable or safe." He cocked his head to the side. "Sound about right?"

She sighed. "Yes."

"He wants you to drive something he's sure of. Would you want less for him?"

Mel huffed out a breath. "No."

"He offer to help you?"

"Yes." She rolled her eyes with impatience.

"Why did you refuse his help?" When she shook her head in denial, Colt held up a hand, a knowing smile on his face. "If you hadn't turned down his offer, we wouldn't be having this conversation."

Avoiding his too-perceptive stare, she stared across the parking lot as a logging truck rumbled by. "I need to do things for myself."

"Taking care of yourself is good, builds self-reliance." Now Colt leaned himself against the Jeep. "Pride's not a bad thing. Unless it gets in the way of your happiness."

With a jolt, Mel realized he wasn't speaking of just her situation. He had some kind of experience that was coloring his assessment of the whole thing.

Colt looked Mel in the eye. "A few years ago, I was in a position where I needed help. Someone offered and I said no. I made sure she wouldn't — couldn't help. I got it all worked out my way, the harder way. And I lost a good — friend because of it." Colt touched Mel on the arm. "Sean's loved you probably since the day he met you, when his mom died."

The same day your father died...

A flicker of emotion played across Colt's face, but she suspected he'd said all he would on that topic. She nodded silently.

"Sean takes care of people, Melanie. He always has," said Colt. "It's not just what he does. It's who he is. And I'd guess it's one of the reasons you love him."

All her arguments caught in her throat. She dropped her gaze and stared at Colt's boots. In the light of his reasoning, she was suddenly embarrassed by her reaction. "You'd be right about that."

"He's not doing this to hurt you or to take away your independence. He tried to spare your pride by making a private deal with me." The glasses slipped back into place. "He wants to help you take care of yourself. Don't blow this all up in his face unless you want to throw away what you two have together."

Mel sagged against the Jeep, deep in thought. She hated it, but she also realized Colt was right. If she had talked things over with Sean and worked out a plan to repay him in the first place, there would have been no subterfuge. He hadn't done it to embarrass her. He wanted to protect her. As messed up as that was, it also felt good to know he cared.

With a heavy sigh, she reached into her purse for the bank envelope. "I can't argue with that. Let's do this." She held the money just out of reach. "But first, tell me how much he's carrying me."

Colt stared for another long space of time. Finally, he blew out a long breath and gave a nod. "He matched you."

"That damn stupid jackass!" More curses slipped out with amazing ease. After she sucked in a couple of deep breaths, Mel smiled and handed Colt his money.

He accepted the cash, folded it without counting, and stowed it in his wallet with deft motions. He looked up and returned her smile. "Can you swing a ride to the feed store? Olivia's meeting me there."

* * *

Devil's Advocate arrived hours late, in a state-of-the-art horse trailer, complete with air-cushioned ride, climate controlled boxes, and a motorcycle parked in one of the open boxes.

And, according to the accompanying paperwork, the horse came with a personal attendant, who was expected to stay on-premises. *Oh, joy. A bodyguard.*

The attendant was a sharp-eyed weasel. The thought was so random, Sean blinked in surprise the second it popped into his mind. He shook his head but the thought was still there. It wasn't so much the man's appearance, though for some reason he seemed vaguely familiar. It was more in the way he carried himself. Sean was probably a year or two older than the other man, but the weasel had an edginess about him that suggested a lot of hard mileage. His gaze wandered as he walked, and he stopped frequently, as though checking his surroundings for danger.

Definitely a weasel.

Sean got the idea that the attendant's eyes saw everything and knew the exact whereabouts of everyone in his vicinity. While his smile seemed amiable, his nearly black eyes were openly assessing, as though looking for weaknesses to exploit. Beyond that, the man was a dandy of sorts, all flash and show, but without much substance. His nut-brown hair was cut in one of those careful styles designed to look like it hadn't been styled at all. His clothing was more suited for a New York cowboy than one in Wyoming.

"Dallas Northrop." The man held out his hand.

Sean reached out and clasped it without bothering to first wipe the stable grime from his own. A small measure of satisfaction rippled through him when Northrop surreptitiously rubbed his palm on his designer jeans after their hands unlocked.

"We don't really have accommodations for guests, Mr. Northrop."

The designer dandy shook his head and smiled. "Not necessary. The trailer has adequate quarters in the front. I'd be appreciative if you can give me a place to hook up for electricity and allow me the use of shower facilities."

Sean gave the man a long appraising look. He didn't carry himself like someone who followed the U.S. Thoroughbred racing circuit, eastern or western. Nor did Sean think he came from the international scene. He definitely wasn't rodeo or ranch. Oddly, he seemed to struggle to fit into his own skin.

Shifting his attention to the rear of the trailer, where the driver cautiously opened the doors and pulled out the ramp, Sean could already feel a sense of trouble. He was aware that Devil's Advocate had extensive injuries. Pain from burns wasn't easily forgotten, not to mention the terror the animal had undoubtedly felt when he'd been trapped in the flames.

As Sean had read and re-read the history of the incident, the one thing that always stood out was how the reports really gave no information beyond a vague mention of injuries and a horse who had what amounted to post-traumatic stress disorder.

Devil's Advocate was already snorting and agitatedly shuffling his feet. Not necessarily a bad sign. Some horses didn't travel well and became anxious to get their feet on solid ground.

"Sorry. I guess the tranquilizer wore off," said Northrop.

"So you tranqued him?" No surprise there. Sean suppressed his anger. He'd reserve judgment. Some horses needed sedation to travel and this one had been through a major trauma.

Northrop huffed out a sarcastic laugh. "Freakin' thing's not amenable to being handled unless he's shot up with feel-good drugs."

Okay, maybe a little judgment after all.

Sean pointed to the main stable. "He's got the first stall on the right through there. You can unload him and get him settled."

When Northrop simply stood and stared, Sean raised an eyebrow. "Problem?"

Northrop shrugged. "I'm just here to oversee his rehab. I'm not his handler."

And you sure as hell don't give a crap about the horse either, from the look of things.

Sean shook his head and subjected the man to another long stare. What did this dude's job description actually entail? And how much was he being paid to loaf on the job?

"Thing is, Mr. Northrop, the horse doesn't know me at all. He's just had a long trip from California, and he's coming off a tranq. He's gonna be looking for a familiar face."

Northrop shrugged. "Truth is, McGee, I'm not all that familiar to him. I never saw him before last week."

Inside the trailer, the clatter of hooves began to escalate. If they didn't get the horse out soon, Devil's Advocate would have to be sedated again. Sean figured he'd be having an interesting phone conversation with the owners later, and odds were his fee was about to go up substantially.

Either way, he wasn't going to continue the dance of words with the useless attendant. Ignoring the ramp, Sean swung himself up into the trailer. In the dim light the horse could barely be seen, but his ears were flattened and he was shaking his head from side to side.

"Hey, buddy, take it easy." Moving slowly, Sean got close enough to see the horse was cross tethered, inhibiting some of his restless movements.

When Sean reached up, the horse snorted and pulled his head back. "Calm down, big fella. You're safe. No one's gonna hurt you now."

He kept up a running monologue of reassuring murmurs as he unclipped the tethers from the sides of the box. Devil's Advocate was tall, at the upper limits of height for a Thoroughbred, probably seventeen hands or just under.

His chest was deep and his long neck led to a finely chiseled head.

Once Devil's Advocate was off the tethers, Sean was able to coax him forward one shuffling step at a time. At least he wasn't behaving aggressively, so Sean divided his attention between the horse and the path they were taking to the outside. The sunlight at the door to the trailer grew closer as they edged along. As they drew closer to the door, Devil's Advocate snorted and tossed his head, but he kept up the slow forward momentum.

With a hollow thud of metal-shod hooves on the rubber-matted ramp, they were out of the dimly lit trailer. The glare of midafternoon sun momentarily blinded Sean, and he faltered at the top of the ramp so his eyes could adjust. When he started walking again, leading the horse into the light, Devil's Advocate tugged hard on the lead, but the light seemed to dazzle him, too, and he calmed enough to keep moving forward. His ears were pricked forward now, his eyes showing white.

"Careful, big boy. Easy." Sean stepped back, but kept a firm hold on the lead. From his vantage point, the horse's seal brown coat was unblemished, if in need of a good grooming. He followed Sean with a suspicious gaze, his left eye rolling just a bit.

Mindful of those long, powerful legs, Sean maneuvered Devil's Advocate toward the stable. His "attendant" seemed to have vanished.

A movement toward the house drew his eye and Sean felt a prickle of uneasiness edging into his awareness. What the devil was Northrop doing, lurking near the back door? And who was he talking to? A flash of sunlight on red hair provided the answer. Looked like the attendant would require some reining in. Northrop had no reason to be talking to anyone in the family but him. Certainly the weasel had no business with Ricky.

Taking advantage of Sean's distraction, Devil's Advocate snorted, then squealed, rearing and lashing out with a solitary kick of his forefoot.

"Easy," murmured Sean.

He pulled the horse's head sideways and down, firmly bringing Devil's Advocate back under control. Keeping the big horse's head tilted downward and to the side, Sean convinced him to stay on all four legs. The horse would only pick up on any angst, so he forced an outward calm though his heart raced. That had been close.

"Okay, bud. That was my warning. I get it." Focusing his complete attention on the horse, Sean got him into the stable and turned him in to the waiting stall. He let out a slow breath as he unclipped the lead.

As soon as Devil's Advocate was off the lead, he moved to one of the rear corners of the big box stall. Sunlight slanted through the window, falling across the center of the space, but he avoided it. The big Thoroughbred protected his right side, keeping it against the rear of the enclosure and sticking to the shadow.

Sean slid the door closed, not so much to protect himself from the horse but to provide a greater sense of security for the scared animal. He stood quietly for a while, just watching. Gradually, the horse began to calm. He snuffled his way around the box and checked out his surroundings. Good. He was interested in living. As first steps went, that was a big one.

"I can't keep calling you Devil's Advocate, dude. It's just too long." Sean leaned against the door, refusing to consider the obvious choice of shortening the name to Devil.

"Why don't you call him Dev?" Mel's soft voice floated on the air.

Nerve endings tingled with delicious anticipation, but Sean didn't move, just kept watching the horse. "Dev, huh? How about that, big guy? Seems easy enough."

She lingered in the doorway until Sean signaled her to come closer, and then she inched forward, stopping an arm's length away from him.

"He's beautiful," she whispered. "But so sad."

"Yeah, the kind of pain he's had'll do that." Sean turned, his gaze falling on Mel, and he felt an instant rush of heat. She still took his breath away. Every time he saw her, it was like looking at her for the first time all over again.

She'd left her pale blond hair free the way he liked it best, and his fingers twitched with the desire to bury themselves in all that sunshine. A thin, plum-colored sweater flowed over her trim figure and hugged her in the places he wanted to hug.

Melanie's smile swept the shadows from her face. Her eyes lingered on him for a few heart-stopping moments before she turned to look at Dev. When he saw her expression change to one of concern and sadness, Sean followed her gaze.

The horse had finally presented his other side.

"Aw, man." With his stomach in his throat, Sean forced himself to keep looking without showing any reaction. "He should have been put down."

Dev's entire right side was the exact opposite of his flawless left. Much of his hide, from his shoulder to his flank, had been burned off, replaced now by whitened scar tissue. A smaller scar covered most of his right hindquarter. His neck also bore evidence of scarring.

By Sean's estimate, roughly a third of the colt's total skin had suffered deep burns. He swallowed hard against the lump in his throat.

"Why didn't they?" whispered Mel.

Sean gritted his teeth as he absorbed the animal's pain and terror. "Greed. He was a winner, and winners breed winners. Though why they didn't just put him down and take the insurance payout, I don't know. He must have been insured against the loss of future race earnings and future stud fees." He rubbed his jaw, trying to put it together. "For some reason, they're laying out a huge amount of money on the chance I can help him so they can send him to stud." He shrugged. "The longer they can keep him alive, the more they can get in stud fees. But they need him to be happy and amenable to mating, which means no pain and no anxiety. They can't take a chance he'll hurt the mares."

"Artificial insemination?"

Sean shook his head. "Not allowed."

Mel made soft clucking noises that Dev responded to with small twitches of his ears. "Why don't they just sedate him for mating?"

Sean chuckled, casting her a sidelong glance. "The kind of tranqs he probably needs, it'd be like asking me to perform after giving me Valium and a bottle of whiskey."

Mel giggled. "Yeah, well, don't take this wrong, but I don't think I want to see what that's like. I kind of like the Energizer Bunny version of you from last night." She captured his gaze and held it while she caressed her upper lip with her tongue.

Every thought in Sean's head vaporized as all the blood left his brain for a trip south of the belt. He widened his stance slightly and folded his arms over his chest. "Okay. New rule. No talking dirty in the stable."

"That wasn't dirty." Mel's smile turned vaguely catlike. "Dirty would be if I said come by my place tonight and I'll—"

Sean clapped a hand over her mouth and kept it that way while he walked her backwards out the door.

"*You* are a distraction." Once outside, he pressed her against the side of the stable and held her in place with his body.

She gazed up at him, challenge in her eyes.

Challenge accepted. Game on.

He shifted, settling his hips against her more intimately, sending the message of just what her "dirty talk" was doing to him.

Her pale blue eyes widened then lit with passion as she squirmed closer. Sean removed his hand from her mouth and replaced it with his lips.

* * *

Embers flamed instantly, his initial burst of passion animated by her nuclear response. The kiss was deep, hot, and wet. As they both lost themselves in it, the embrace became just a little rough. And she liked that a lot. When he pulled back, Sean's eyes were twin points of emerald fire. Mel moaned and wound her arms around his neck, pulling him back for more.

He tried to break the kiss, and she sank her teeth lightly into his bottom lip. *Oh, no, you don't, mister.*

He moaned from deep in his throat. His mouth lingered but he eased his body away from hers. Finally he retreated and she allowed him to do so. "I'll be at your place for a private dinner tonight. Be waiting for me?"

Mel followed him off the wall, but carefully kept her distance. Was it possible for someone to erupt into flames from the heat of a kiss? She slipped her key ring from the pocket of her jeans and removed a key. "Here."

"What's this?"

"The spare key to my apartment. Let yourself in and I'll have... dinner... waiting for you."

He inhaled sharply and deeply. "Is six o'clock too early?" The fire in his eyes dwindled but the smolder remained. Oh, yes, he would be thinking about her for the rest of the afternoon.

Chapter Eleven

Sean was late. For years he'd been careful to check and double-check stalls and occupants, set locks and alarms. He'd never resented taking care of the horses he owned or those he was rehabbing. But that part of his job had made him later than he cared to be, and getting to Mel's place had become his single goal. Finally he arrived, breathless and excited, and feeling like a hormone-ridden teenager with his libido doing somersaults through his system. He glanced at his watch; forty-five minutes late.

The dinner Mel had promised might be burnt by now, and as Sean slid his key into the lock, he wondered if he'd at least get dessert. He pushed the door open and his mouth watered instantly. But it was a toss-up whether it was because of the smell of food infusing the air, or the sight of Mel lounging on the foot of her bed wearing a form-fitting corset in black trimmed with pink satin over a pair of barely-there black panties. Every muscle in his body tightened, and he forced his gaze to move on quickly lest the evening be over before he joined her on the bed. Black lace stockings led down to — *have mercy* — five-inch stiletto heels in the same shade of pink as the corset.

His mouth fell open and he dropped his hastily packed duffel bag on the floor with a *thunk*. "Honey, I'm home."

* * *

"I went up to Jackson and did a little shopping today." Smiling, Mel slid one foot along the edge of the bed in what she hoped was a suggestive manner. "I found a sale."

Sean stood rooted by the door. When he spoke, his voice was hoarse. "I feel like I should want to come over there and peel you out of that, but you look so good... I just want to stay here awhile and enjoy looking at you."

His words sent little arrows of anticipation to all the right places. She wiggled a little, trying to ease the building ache for his touch.

Her movements seemed to break the spell he was under. Sean crossed the room in two paces, dropping to the bed and sprawling on top of her. Laughing out loud, he rolled them over in one easy movement. "I've been thinking about you since you left the ranch earlier. You're making me crazy for you."

Mel giggled and rubbed her cheek against Sean's. "I thought shopping would calm me down but all I could look at was lingerie and that only made it worse. The more things I bought, the more I thought about you, and... wearing them for you."

"Lingerie?" He almost choked. "H-how much did you buy?"

She winced. "A few days' worth."

Sean inhaled sharply. "You shouldn't say things like that." He rolled them again so he ended up on top, supporting himself on his forearms.

She touched her tongue to her lips; his breathing grew ragged. He pulled her lower lip into his mouth and suckled gently, released her, then settled his lips against hers for a heated, toe-curling kiss. When their gazes locked, the tenderness in his eyes made her sigh.

"Sean." Mel brushed the back of her hand along his cheek. "Thank you."

His half-smile was warm. "For?"

"For loving me so well."

"Oh, darlin', you make that easy to do." His lips lingered, planting butterfly kisses between each word he spoke. "Melanie Grace Mitchell soon-to-be McGee, I love you so very much. You're the only person who makes my world right."

Shuddering at the intensity of his declaration, Mel traced her fingertip along the edge of Sean's ear. "I get all caught up with you and I don't even care." She slid her hand around behind his head and urged him down again, meeting his lips for a kiss she felt in her soul.

With slow, tender strokes, he explored. Soft kisses against her eyelids made her tingle. He trailed butterfly kisses over her temple, down along her jaw, that raised answering flutters in her middle. His breathing became ragged as he lingered at the base of her throat, tickling her with his tongue. Yearning filled her. And just as she believed she couldn't love or want him more, he roamed lower, placing kisses along the top of her corset, dipping his tongue beneath the edge.

A moan slipped from her throat as he found the laces along the front of her corset and tugged at them with his teeth. As the lingerie gapped, he gave a little nip along the swell of one breast. Exquisite pain was quickly soothed by his tongue, sending hot darts to Mel's pleasure center.

"You're overdressed," she whispered, tugging at the buttons on his shirt. She freed one, then two. Gasping, he reared back and helped her dispense with the garment. Her hands were already moving to his belt. "This, too." She tugged. A mischievous thought brought out a giggle. "Though maybe later we can play a little game..."

A feral growl exploded from his chest and his busy hands took on fervid intensity. Cool air washed over her hot skin as the remainder of the corset fell away. And then Sean fell upon Mel as though she were newly discovered treasure. Licking and nipping, kissing and soothing.

Reveling in each sensation, for the second time in as many days, Mel welcomed Sean home.

* * * *

The splash of cool air as Sean drew back and sat on the edge of the bed raised goose bumps in Mel's sensitive places. Oh, how nice it would be if he'd come back and warm her chilly skin. She stretched and sighed, hoping to entice. But he only drew the blanket up around her breasts.

"Where are you going?" she mumbled, watching him through veiled eyes.

He stood, casual in his nakedness.

Which was fine with her, since he presented quite an enjoyable view.

"I love you, Mel."

"I love you, too." She patted the empty space next to her. "I'm getting cold."

"So's dinner," he murmured. "And I skipped lunch."

Laughter burbled out as she sat, allowing the blanket to fall to her waist. "Need some fuel for round two?"

"Mel... It feels like — like we're doing it all backward." Sean swallowed hard. "I love making love with you. I feel like I'll never get enough of you."

Warmth blossomed in her center and fanned outward. "It's the same for me."

"The thing is..." He snatched his jeans from the floor. "...the next time we make love, I want you to be my wife."

Mel's breath caught. She should feel the sting of rejection, but something staved it off. This was Sean, her lovable, loving, very careful Sean. And his caring nature was one of the things she loved most about him. She could have blown him off, maybe even convinced him he was being silly.

Something even more precious than love was taking root.

She respected him too much to work the angles just to get her way. And from his words, it was apparent he respected her, valued her.

A huge grin spread across her face as the emotions inside her mushroomed. "So, which one of us is getting the ugly, lumpy couch?"

* * *

They ate dinner on the sofa, in front of Mel's tiny, ancient TV set. She amused Sean by tuning in to a child's Halloween marathon with nearly as much enthusiasm as she approached kissing him. But that was his Mel. Everything with her was about life and living it all out. Having changed into a pair of oversized plaid flannel PJ pants and a long black T-shirt, Mel now more closely resembled the childhood pal Sean remembered and he found himself smiling so often throughout the evening his mouth started to hurt.

"How did you know one of my favorite dinners was roast chicken?" He swirled a piece of biscuit through some gravy and put it in his mouth. The subtle flavors teased his palate as he chewed.

Mel sat beside him on the sofa, cross-legged and facing in his direction. She lifted a shoulder and smiled shyly. "I just imagined it would be anything but beef. Like chicken farmers probably get their fill of poultry."

He chuckled. "Right. And pig farmers probably get more bacon than they care to think about."

The clatter of her fork being dropped onto her plate accompanied a shocked gasp. "Oh, no... A person could never have too much bacon."

An easy laugh slipped out. "Good point." He finished his last bite of dinner and stood, snagged her plate and tucked it on top of his, and then walked to the kitchenette. "No dishwasher?"

"Ri-i-ight." She giggled and gestured around the room. "Like there's room for one. Dishes get done the old-fashioned way here."

"Well, okay, then." He shrugged and turned on the tap. As the water spluttered and splashed into the white plastic dish pan, he checked under the sink and scored some dish soap.

Mel stood next to her bistro table, just staring. "What are you doing?"

Before he answered, he squirted a measure of soap into the pan, watched it bubble and foam, then said without looking up, "Doing our dishes the old-fashioned way."

Arms around his waist and warmth reached out to him from behind as Mel laid her head between his shoulder blades. "You realize I can never let you go now, right? I mean, you do dishes, probably even take out the trash."

He spun in her arms and cupped her face, searching her eyes and finding all he'd ever need in them. He dipped his head and gave her a quick, hard kiss then took a step back and winked. "Apparently my plan's working."

"Oh, you think so, eh?" She crossed her arms over her chest. "You still haven't told me if you take out the trash."

With a grin, Sean scooped a handful of foam and deposited it on her nose.

"Oh!" she said with a squeal, scraping up her own handful. White foam landed on the cabinet door behind him. But she was quick and another handful landed on top of his head.

So he gave her a white foam goatee. And then a pair of foamy earmuffs.

Laughing so hard tears formed in her eyes, Mel held up her hands in surrender.

"Ha! I wi—"

A grin of pure evil spread across her lips and she leaned in, nuzzling her face against his, spreading sudsy wetness across both his cheeks. Then she tossed back her head and cut loose with maniacal laughter.

A fierce wash of sensual hunger swept over him like a tidal wave, and his knees buckled. He caught her around the waist with one arm and ran his free hand through the soft strands of her hair. Their bodies pressed together, he dipped her back in his arms and kissed her with a burst of intense heat, moaning into her mouth when she surrendered, and she became pliant against him. She wiggled until she freed her arms, which had been caught between them. Sighing, she twined them up and around his neck, where she simply held on and returned his deep kiss.

Desire edged past reason, and with the sureness of a striking rattler, he placed both hands at her waist and lifted her onto her tiny kitchen counter.

At her sharp intake of breath, he drew back and met her gaze. Twin flames of blue burned in her eyes. She rimmed her lips with her tongue and then rolled her lips inward, kicking Sean's heart into overdrive.

The shirt went first. He didn't even bother with subtle caresses and a gentle lifting of the hem. Just grasped it and yanked it over her head, tossing it somewhere behind him.

In the glare of the overhead light, he studied her. Pale skin, slender body. And nothing under the shirt. Goose bumps trailed from her neck down to her pebbled pink nipples. Groaning, Sean buried his face in the valley between her breasts as she placed her hands at the sides of his head and massaged the shells of his ears, shooting hot bullets of need on a path south.

The bed seemed miles away. But somehow he'd get them there. He drew back only to find himself trapped by her hold on his ears.

"No," she moaned. "Don't stop..."

"Shhh, it's okay." he murmured, covering her hands and making an attempt to pry them loose. "I'm not stopping. Just... not here."

"Yes, here." She used her hold to bring him closer to her. Breathing in ragged gasps, she worked the buttons on his shirt while trailing teasing little nips and kisses along his jaw and neck.

Cool air whispered across his shoulders when she pushed his shirt back. Then she was pressed against him, skin to skin, and her feverish fingers were attacking his belt.

If it was going to be on the kitchen counter, so be it. He grabbed her flannel PJ pants and tugged.

* * *

Mel was still breathing heavily as she padded across the kitchenette to her door, then bent and picked up her T-shirt. Self-consciousness had made a surprise appearance, and it didn't set too well. The burning in her face warned that her emotions were still plain as day on her face — something else that was new and unexpected.

Three times she'd made love with Sean McGee, and that last time— The temperature in her face rose by several notches. They'd done things she'd never in her markedly unsheltered life imagined. Who knew Sean McGee could be so freakin' — inventive?

An arm snaked around her waist and Sean leaned his chin on her shoulder.

"Too much?" he asked in a soft voice.

She gave a quick shake of her head. When she spoke, it was a fight to keep her voice steady. "Nothing will ever be too much with you."

His hold tightened for a heartbeat. His hot breath tickled her ear. "We should get to those dishes."

"Let 'em soak." She pointed to her one kitchen chair. "Sit. I have apple pie for dessert."

"You made apple pie?"

The giggle slipped out as they found their natural rhythm. "Charlie made apple pie. I just absconded with it from the kitchen downstairs."

He chuckled as he sat. "You need another chair."

"But there's only one of me." She sliced the pie and scooped it onto a plate. With a smile, she set it in front of him. "Why would I need another chair?"

"Maybe for times like this... when two of us are eating?"

Brandishing a fork, Mel headed for the tiny table. "You're so sweet. Is this like asking me for dresser space? Because *that* I can actually do something about."

He shot her a stunned look, and she chuckled as she perched herself sidesaddle in his lap. The side of the fork sliced easily through the juicy pie as she cut off a piece and popped it into her mouth. Tart sweetness exploded over her tongue.

"Hey! That's mine." He reached for the fork but she held it out of his grasp.

Blinking with feigned innocence, she gazed up at him. "Was it?"

The next bite of pie went into Sean's mouth. He closed his eyes. "Mmmm." His tongue flicked at a crumb that clung to his upper lip.

"This is almost better than..." His smile was slow, the look in his eyes sizzling.

Unbelievable. Shivers of awareness rocketed through her all over again, and Mel squirmed. Two could play like that, though. She leaned forward and used her own tongue to swipe a bit of filling he missed at the edge of his lower lip.

Sean leaned into her touch, capturing her tongue between his lips. Mel lost track of where she was, and the plate she held dipped. Sean snagged it just before the remainder of the pie slipped to the floor, and set the dish on the table.

When she pulled back, his eyes were heavy-lidded and glazed. Mel swallowed hard and pushed back the desire he could incite with just one of those looks.

She hated to ruin their evening. She really did. But she'd promised herself they would talk just a little.

"Sean..." She pulled in a bracing breath, then another. "I need to find my daughter."

At the same time, Sean spoke. "I think we should look for your daughter." His brows drew together. "Wait. What?"

Mel shook her head, not certain she'd heard him correctly. "You first."

Sean spoke slowly, his eyes holding her gaze. "I want to help you find your daughter. Hear me out." He lifted a hand to shush her. "It might be she's happy and everything's good. Then it'll be up to you to contact her or not. But if she's not okay, you need to know so you can make things right for her."

Pie completely forgotten, Mel squealed with happiness and threw her arms around Sean's neck. "You just keep getting better and better."

Before they got carried away again, Mel rose and walked to her closet. She took out a long sweatshirt and pulled it over her head. Then she stepped out of her PJs and into a pair of jeans.

At first, Sean stared at her in confusion, but he quickly glanced away. "What are you doing?"

Mel shrugged. "I've got a couple of things to show you and I'm going to talk about my family. I'm not doing that when I'm in my pajamas."

Sean's lips twitched at her explanation. Then he frowned. "Mel, if you mean Nick DeVayne and his son, they weren't your family."

It took her six steps and about as many seconds to cross the room to where he sat waiting. Cupping his cheek, she gazed deep into his eyes, needing him to understand everything. "The thing is... we were together as a family unit for almost five years before I could leave. As sucky as it was, as we were... we *were* a family, Sean. We did — things as a family. Denny and I worked the grift. It was expected of us like other kids are expected to do household chores."

She could tell the idea was distasteful to him. His frown deepened, his mouth set into a grim line. His most hurtful reaction of all, though, was when he averted his gaze.

A wistful sigh escaped her lips. *Oh, Sean.* His reaction was exactly why she'd never wanted him to know about that part of her life. In silence, Mel moved her hand to toy with his ear, and then she hooked the back of his neck. Bending to him, she brushed his lips with hers. When she lifted her head again, his dark thoughts weren't as apparent in his eyes.

"Let's go sit on my lumpy sofa." She grabbed Denny's letters from the top of the fridge. Sean followed her in silence.

* * *

It was for the best, Sean reminded himself. He'd already broken his resolution not to make love to her again until they were married. If they'd kept up the game with the pie, who knew where things would have led again?

Strike that. He knew exactly where they would have led.

Projecting an air of mystery, Mel set some letters on the coffee table then pulled the small wooden box from next to her TV over to the sofa. So he was about to find out what she kept there after all. She sat with it on her lap, absently tracing an invisible pattern on the top. Finally, after several deep breaths, she raised the lid.

"There wasn't much worth bringing with me when I left Nick." She lifted out a stack of what looked like check stubs, paper-clipped together, and set them aside. She pulled out a white and black plastic name tag bearing an unfamiliar logo with a steaming cup of something and the name Monique DelRay. She set that on top of the check stubs.

He couldn't see the next object she picked up. She kept it in her palm for a second, then extended her hand and opened her fingers. "Remember this?"

With a jolt, he recognized the red pebble in the shape of a heart. He'd found it outside the funeral home and given it to her to hold onto at Todd Mitchell's funeral, hoping it would give her comfort in some small way. He'd have done anything back then to make her smile.

Still would.

He traced the rounded edge. "I don't believe you kept this."

"It was one of the few things I had of you. This was another." She slid out a photograph, bent and worn around the edges. In faded color, it showed the two of them playing on the tire swing that still hung from the tree in the McGee backyard. She sat on top of the swing, clinging to the rope for dear life, and he stood on the swing, one leg on either side of her, his head thrown back in an obvious war cry. They'd been incredibly happy all those lifetimes ago.

He struggled for breath, remembering exactly when his father had taken the picture. Sean had teased Mel without mercy until she climbed on the swing and let him push her higher than she was comfortable going. Then he'd jumped on behind her and together they had whooped and laughed until the swing had slowed down.

Reaching into his pocket, he slid out his wallet and flipped through the plastic picture section until he came to the photo he sought. Then he turned it and showed her the same picture. "Life was a lot simpler then, wasn't it?"

Mel's chin quivered.

"Don't, please." He stroked her jaw with a forefinger. "If you cry right now, I'll lose it."

She bit her lip and held her breath. After a moment, she seemed to get herself back together. "I don't have any pictures of my mom and dad. Nick found them one day and burned them in front of me. He didn't find the one of you and me because I always kept it in my pocket."

Would there ever be an end to the heartbreak? Sean finally understood why it was taking her so long to talk about the time she'd been away. Each word probably picked at an emotional scab. "Dad has pictures of your parents. They're older ones. My mom took them before she died. I used to go through all the pictures she took so I could feel close to her. I'll get them for you."

Her eyes glistened again and he shook a finger in warning, unable to speak over the lump of emotion caught in his throat.

She lifted out another picture and caressed it with her finger before letting him see it. "This is Glenn. This is my baby's father."

Shock drove icy ripples through his body as he stared at the picture. The face that looked out at him could have been mistaken for his own at about age sixteen. The kid had worn his hair longer but his features and coloring were so similar they might have been Sean's.

He cut his gaze up to Mel.

She leveled her gaze back at him, her smile a little regretful. "Yeah, he was kind of your replacement. But he was nice, too. He deserved so much more than to be a fill-in boyfriend."

"What happened to him?"

Mel shrugged. "No idea. He knew about the baby, but he was so freaked out and scared, he agreed to let me handle things. Nick never knew who the baby's father was." She sighed heavily. "I never told him, no matter how many times he asked. He would only have gone to Glenn's parents for money."

"So, he just disappeared?" Sean set his teeth, struggling to hold his tongue. *He* wouldn't have disappeared. Not for anything.

Mel nodded, the sadness in her eyes shredding his heart. "It was what I wanted him to do, Sean. He didn't abandon me. I don't think he would have. But Nick would have hurt him in more ways than you can maybe imagine."

So she'd protected the kid. But no one had been there to protect her when she'd needed it most.

She reached into the box again and removed something wrapped in green and gold Christmas paper. "This is the only other thing I kept."

Did he dare hope...? He'd used that same paper... He held his breath until she revealed the tiny brass horse. The air escaped on a long sigh. It *had* meant something to her. He'd worked around the ranch for two months, doing extra jobs for his father, so he could pay for the Christmas gift he'd given her when he'd been twelve. About two inches tall, the proud horse stood, alert and watchful. It had reminded Sean of the mustang stallion they had seen together the day they'd met.

"Mel..." He opened his hands, palms up, at a loss for words.

She shook her head and smiled for the first time. "I didn't show you these things so you would feel sorry for me. I want you to know that even though Nick tried to take away who I was, he didn't succeed. He couldn't. And a big part of that was because I held on to *you*." She touched Sean on the hand. "I need you to understand that even though I helped Nick run his cons, I tried very hard to hold on to who I was. I lost pieces of me, a lot of me, actually, but not all of me." She swallowed hard. "Not the part that's always belonged to you."

"You survived, Mel."

Leaving the things from the box scattered across the coffee table, she picked up the letters.

"Denny's been writing to me. Just since last May, and only two or three lines in each letter."

Pain shot through Sean's jaw as he clenched it so hard a muscle jumped. May was about the time Mel had started to act a little more desperate about their relationship. Was that a coincidence? No, probably not. He shoved his feelings on the subject to the back of his mind. "What does he want?"

"He hasn't revealed that yet," she said dryly. "In all but his last letter, he mentions cons we pulled together. Some of them he's exaggerated the things I did, some he got right. He wants me to know he can rat me out at any time. Wants me on edge, not feeling safe. He's made his presence known. And he's just like Nick, so he wants something. The thing is... he's in the area. His last letter was postmarked from Des Moines, Iowa, but DC told me he's had tickets from different places in Wyoming. The last one was Saturday afternoon."

Sean let out a breath. "So you really may have seen him."

"Probably. In his last letter, he sent me a newspaper clipping." She slid it across the coffee table.

Recognizing it as the clipping that had been tucked under her alarm clock, Sean picked it up.

"*Prominent Oklahoma City Attorney Indicted on Adoption Fraud and Baby Selling Scheme.*" He continued to read the short article, noting the date was within the last couple of weeks. Allegedly, the adoption lawyer had been accused of selling one baby, so all of his arranged private adoptions since the start of his practice fifteen years earlier were being investigated. "It doesn't really say much. Do you think this is the attorney DeVayne worked with when he stole your daughter?" He skimmed the article again until he found the name. "Elias Hood?"

"The time and location fit. But the name means nothing." Mel rubbed her temples. Her face had grown pinched, her eyes drawn and tired. "I don't know if Denny would have known where my baby was taken, though I suppose he could have just found out. It's not like him to give me this information without getting me to give him something first, so I'm confused."

"May I read the other letters?"

Without uttering a word, she handed them over. He could tell she was reluctant for him to see this aspect of her life, so he took hold of her hand while he read, hoping to reassure her.

The letters didn't say much. A few mentions of the virginal con she'd already told him about, a couple with specific descriptions of the men. The descriptions were so specific they stood out, and Sean wondered if they had been blackmailed more heavily or if there was another reason these two had been mentioned. One letter near the end mentioned a time they'd worked together to score some free fast food.

"Why are they all typed?"

Mel picked up the top letter and ran her fingers over it. "This is a paper trail. Denny took a huge gamble, mailing me anything at all, but for some reason he needed to reach out, to build up to whatever it is he's after. Sends me letters, not quite threatening me. To anyone who doesn't know him, it's just remembering good times."

"But why are they typed?" he asked again.

"So they can't be tied directly to him. He types the letter, deletes it from the computer, destroys the computer — no more connection." She shifted to meet Sean's gaze. "He handwrote the envelopes, maybe because he couldn't print them from the computer for some reason, but more likely hoping I'd recognize his handwriting. Since the first letter isn't threatening or incriminating in any way, there would be no reason for me to not open the next."

"Except you didn't," said Sean softly. He traced the tops of Mel's fingers where she clutched her brother's letter.

"Nor did I toss them in the trash." She set the letter back onto the pile with a sigh that shuddered through her body. "He took a calculated risk that I'd have no reason or desire to go to the police with his unopened letters, and I'll bet an expert couldn't pull even one of his fingerprints off the letters themselves because he would have worn gloves. He would have been careful never to send anything he touched directly. No way to prove he's the one who sent them."

Mel drew her knees up in front of her and laid her forehead against them. Whatever wounds were being opened, they ran deeper than maybe even Mel knew.

"Do you remember the two men he describes here?"

Mel lifted her head and shook it slowly. "I tried to forget everything. It could be he only described them because that's all he remembers." She plucked at the piping on the edge of the sofa.

Tried to forget, she'd said. Which meant she remembered way too much. He laced their fingers together again, a small gesture of comfort, and far too late to offer it, but it was all he had.

"DC recommended an attorney for me. Steve Wilson. And your dad was going to see about hiring an investigator for me."

Sean smiled, finally understanding Justin's query about their helicopter pilot's investigative connections. "I overheard Dad and Ryan talking the other day. Dad was going to talk to Joe. He's got friends in the business."

Mel sighed. "I can't explain this, but I have a hunch whatever Denny wants, it has absolutely nothing to do with my baby. This is a smokescreen."

"Then we'll figure that out, too. But for now, we're going to concentrate on locating your child." Sean flipped the last letter over and saw a calendar beneath. "What's this?"

"Oh, that's nothing." Mel reached for it, but he held it away from her.

He'd seen the same system of dots and letters seven months earlier on the calendar his sister-in-law had used to prove to the whole family that no way was she pregnant. Only this one had a small red X marking the day before, and a question mark in two weeks.

Sean's gaze flew to Mel's face, and he was assaulted by a sudden influx of emotion he was at a loss to define. She sat frozen, her eyes wide, fingertips resting against her lips, and she looked like she was terrified to take her next breath.

Although her body language gave him the answer, he had to know, had to hear it from her lips. So he spoke slowly, careful to keep his voice even. "Last night? You told me it wasn't the right time of the month to get pregnant."

Closing her eyes, Mel pursed her lips and blew out long and slow. Canned laughter erupted from the TV as she met his gaze. "I needed to check before I was sure. But yes, I suspected I was wrong even when I told you that."

Her honesty took him by complete surprise and inflated his emotional response into anger. "Why? Why didn't you tell me the truth?" He grabbed her arm a little more roughly than he'd intended. "Were you ever going to tell me?" She flinched but didn't pull away, and he instantly loosened his hold. "I'm sorry." He rubbed her arm. "It's just... you aren't alone in any of this."

"I know I'm not alone." She sighed and took his hand. "If it turned into something to be concerned about, yes, of course I would tell you."

"Then why not just tell me the truth last night? That it's possible I got you pregnant." He laid the calendar back on the coffee table, pissed to discover that his hands were shaking.

Mel threw a leg over him and moved onto his lap. She cradled his face in her soft hands and met his eyes again. Her fingers tickled his ears. "There was nothing we could do about it. You had just made amazing love to me, in a way I hoped you would do again. I didn't want to ruin that moment. We'll have time to think about it later if we have to."

He had to say something, but she was playing with his ears. His suddenly very erogenous ears. He closed his eyes, giving himself over to her touch. But only for a moment before reality intruded in the form of a blond teenaged boy. A missing baby girl. The possibility of yet another new life having been created.

"No." He covered her hands with his own, stilling them. "Wait a minute. Mel, I came at you like a freight train last night. I didn't even *think* about using protection. We need to talk about that. About the possibility of—"

Mel slipped her hands free and laid them on his bare shoulders. "It wasn't like it was assault, Sean. Not even close. It was pure passion and... I loved it. I wanted what happened at least as much as you. And unless you stopped somewhere on the way home last night, I got in at least one good bite." She caressed his neck with her thumb. Her voice lowered, took on a husky quality. "And you came back for more. Tonight. Even after you said you want to wait... you came back again after *that*. Do you have any idea how... *incredible* it feels to be wanted so much that all reason goes away? To know that someone you love feels that strongly, that passionately about you?"

Her eyes were wide, amazed. *And amazing.* Sean struggled for control, but when she licked her lips, he almost lost the battle.

She continued in a soft whisper. "And how wonderful it feels to be loved so much by you that you want to take care with me?" She melted against him. "Please hold me for a while."

Protective instincts sparked to life. He smoothed a hand along the back of her head. "For the rest of your life, Sweetness."

* * *

Sprawling next to Sean on the sofa, Mel lifted her head, feeling even more well-loved from the emotional closeness they were sharing than when she and Sean had actually made love. She chuckled.

Sean's eyes flew open. "What?"

"You have a new bite." She kissed him where his neck met his shoulder. "Right there."

His hand flew up to the dark mark. "I'm never going to hear the end of this." He raised serious eyes to hers. "And you know if I got you pregnant last night, we're going to end up sitting through a lecture."

She laughed. "First of all, if I did get pregnant, *we* made it happen, not you. Second, it would probably be a whole intervention we'd have to sit through. But third... it wouldn't be the end of the world... would it?"

Sean's jaw dropped. He looked confused and maybe just as conflicted as she felt.

"I'm not saying we should try to have a baby," she added quickly, feeling just a little breathless when she considered the possibility that it was already out of their hands. "I'm just wondering if— if you'll—"

"Oh, Sweetness." His hands moved to her shoulders. "My preference is to have some time for just you and me. But if we made a baby? Darlin', how could I not love our child?"

Tears flooded her eyes. "Right answer."

Chapter Twelve

Work with Devil's Advocate was slow-going but steady. The horse still took his time warming to Sean before each training session. He sometimes snapped his teeth a bit when taking an apple, but Sean counted it a plus that Dev no longer tried to kick his head in when being turned out in the paddock.

Dealing with Dallas Northrop, on the other hand, was beginning to piss Sean off more than was probably healthy for the horse's attendant. As far as Sean could tell, Northrop didn't do anything but use up good breathing air. He never worked with the horse. In fact, he steered clear of all the horses. He frequently disappeared, which actually Sean didn't mind. Except, unfortunately, the man never stayed gone. Dev wouldn't tolerate Northrop in his presence. The few times he was around, Sean had ended up cutting the training sessions short.

When Northrop approached just after Dev had sidled his way into the paddock, Sean couldn't resist maneuvering them so the other man's back was toward the fence just to see what would happen. Dev's ears had already gone flat against his head the second Northrop appeared.

"Did you get my note?"

"You've left several notes, Northrop." Sean kept his eyes fixed on the horse and his tone deliberately cool. "I assume I got them all, but maybe you'd like to let me know which note you're concerned about."

Northrop made an impatient sound. "Do you have an idea when this horse'll be ready to go?"

Using his forefinger, Sean tipped his hat back and regarded the man, keeping a carefully blank expression. Whenever he spoke with Northrop, Sean intentionally adopted a slow, lazy drawl, and he tended to exaggerate that even further when Northrop tried to strong-arm him in any way. "Now that depends on where y'all want him to go."

In the door to the stable, Ricky coughed back a laugh and turned his attention to rearranging the harnesses on the wall.

"He's been here four days." Northrop leaned against the fence. "All you've done is put him outside, talk to him, then put him back inside."

"Rehab training isn't an exact science. The horse hasn't been comfortable since he got here. He's not eating well, and he's still too skittish to do more than exercise him in the paddock. He needs a few days just to get used to new surroundings." *And to people who give a shit, you jackass.* Sean fixed a smile on his face that was as phony as the man he smiled at.

Dev edged toward the fence, his eyes tracking Northrop's movements. The man in question remained oblivious.

"Well, do you have any idea when he'll be calm enough to go to stud?"

The horse was within biting range but still behaving.

"Like I said, it's not an exact science." Sean shrugged. "You're gonna want him at his best. Mating's stressful."

Watching Dev for signs of an imminent strike, Sean considered moving the horse's intended victim to safer ground.

Then Northrop spoke again, making a critical error in his word choice. "Yeah, I guess you'd know about that, given how much time you're spending with that pretty little bartender in town."

Irritation blossomed into rage, and Sean narrowed his eyes, taking a step forward. As he expected, Northrop stepped back. When he spoke, Sean used a soft tone that anyone else would have recognized as an angry warning. "I'm here on-site to work with the horse. I'm not your personal servant, and my business is none of yours. Long as I do my job."

Northrop held his hands up in apparent surrender that Sean saw right through to its rotten core. "Hey, yeah. No problem. I just noticed that sweet thing and how you spend a lot of time with her. Didn't know you had your brand on her."

Fists loosely clenched, Sean stepped forward once more, and Northrop tried to step back again, his retreat halted by the fence. He stiffened but didn't flinch.

Dev moved quickly, teeth snapping on air just as Sean, jumping with nearly equal speed, pushed the irritating man to the side and down. Sean remained on his feet, though his hat went flying.

Northrop was visibly shaken as he picked himself up off the ground, brushing the dust from his fancy city jeans.

"That horse don't much like you, Northrop." Sean bent over and retrieved his hat, slapping it against his leg a few times to dislodge the dust. He resettled it on his head before casting a narrow-eyed glare at the horse's objectionable attendant. "I can't think why that might be."

His face red, his eyes still wide with shock over the sudden attack, Dallas Northrop moved carefully past the fence. "Just get me an estimate on when you plan to be finished with the horse," he ground out before he stalked off toward his trailer.

From inside the stable, Ricky sniggered.

Sean turned his back on Dev's angry attendant to look at the horse. Dev eyed him back. Blowing softly, he waggled his ears back and forth, shaking off some unseen fly.

Almost nonchalantly, Dev turned his head in the direction of the open pasture beyond the paddock. He twitched his ear again and blinked.

"Yeah, I know," Sean said to the horse. "Not my finest moment. Nice work, though."

"Did he just wink at you?" Mel's voice came from behind him.

"*You* are a distraction." Sean tossed a grin over his shoulder. "Are you going to behave, or do I have to ban you from the stables?"

"Oh, you're not nice. I came to see my big guy."

Sean spun around, a suggestive comment at the ready, only to find Mel had moved to the fence.

"And he's happy to see me, aren't you, Dev?" Mel leaned on the fence, clucking her tongue gently.

About to pull her back to a safer distance, Sean dropped his arm. Dev was responding to Mel. His ears pricked forward, showing interest. With a quiet whuffle of greeting, he took a cautious step in her direction.

The interaction between Mel and the troubled horse enthralled. Sean forced himself to still his protective instinct as the huge horse took another two steps closer to Mel. Something powerful was happening, and Sean stood back to watch, though he remained vigilant. When the horse came close to the fence, Mel extended her hand. Sean held his breath but Dev only snuffled expectantly at her palm then nuzzled her hand.

"Next time I'll bring an apple." She slowly ran her hand along the top of Dev's nose and upward to gently rub the space between his eyes. Sean's jaw slackened as the big horse pushed into her touch.

Mel had a natural connection with Dev. If Sean could figure it out, maybe he could use it to help the poor horse. Because as much as he didn't want Northrop to realize it, Sean had sure as hell been wracking his brain just trying to find a way to reach Devil's Advocate. Maybe the ability to connect wasn't so much in any expertise he'd managed to acquire. Maybe the secret was in finding common ground.

Love welled as Sean watched the two wounded souls begin to forge a bond.

Oh, man, Mel was beautiful. She wore jeans and a simple gray sweatshirt; nothing at all special. In fact, she looked pretty buttoned-up, and with her slim figure, almost boyish. But he found it incredibly sexy, more for what it didn't show than what it did. The wind gently teased at her hair, occasionally blowing stray tendrils into her face, but she ignored them.

As she worked her magic on Dev, Sean found his eyes drifting to her flat abdomen, wondering if they'd created a new life. He tried to picture her belly growing more round as the months passed, the way Sandy's had. Mel was right; it wouldn't be the end of the world. In fact, it was part of a dream he'd had for a long, long time. Home, Mel as his wife, children. He just hadn't planned for it to happen out of order. So far he had a piece of land with no house, and marriage tentatively planned for a couple of months.

Dev suddenly snorted and danced away from the fence. Mel looked confused but not shaken. Movement in the distance caught Sean's eye, and he looked up to see Northrop skulking near his trailer.

The horse was getting too agitated, so Sean stepped forward to urge Mel back some. "Better let him work his mad off."

She sighed. "I thought I was getting somewhere."

"You were." Sean looped an arm over her shoulders, enjoying her closeness. "It wasn't you. He saw Northrop. For some reason he hates the man." He snickered. "Not that I blame him."

Creases formed across Mel's brow as she stared at the trailer.

Grinning, Sean playfully flipped the ends of her hair. "Hey, why the frown?"

"I don't know." Smiling, she shook her head as though to clear it, and her face became sunny again.

The growl of Northrop's motorcycle signaled his departure. Already agitated, Dev tossed and shook his head, pawing the ground. A single, shrill scream echoed through the yard. But when Mel moved back to the fence and clucked her tongue again, tension deserted the horse and he extended his neck as far as he could in her direction.

"There, see? It's okay, baby. The nasty man's gone now. You can come back over here, sweetie."

Sean stood behind Mel, his arms loosely around her waist. Dev approached them slowly, more suspicious of Mel with Sean nearby but clearly much less agitated.

"Did you talk to the lawyer?"

She nodded. "He made copies of the letters and told me to turn the originals over to DC. Apparently, because I was a minor, he doesn't expect too much in the way of consequences on me. Especially since I'm cooperating now and if any prosecution comes of it, I can promise to testify. It helps that I walked away when Nick no longer had any legal control over me, and there were no assaults or injuries on my record." She wrinkled her nose. "Or murders."

At her last word, Sean rocked back on his heels and stared. She was serious. He'd never given any thought to the possibility that DeVayne might have been involved in some cons that turned violent. Apparently, her attorney was considering all angles.

"DC's going to forward copies of Denny's letters to Oklahoma City in case they turn out to be relevant to any investigations." She inhaled deeply, leaning into Sean's embrace for a moment. "And I just dropped off copies up at the house in case Joe's investigator can help."

No longer showing any trace of agitation, Dev wandered to the other side of the pen.

Mel watched for a few moments longer then faced Sean, pushing her arms beneath his jacket and around his waist in a tight hug. "I have such a bad feeling about all of this. Something's up. And I can't help but think Denny's involving me somehow, but that it has nothing to do with the baby." She leaned back to meet Sean's gaze. "That's the way Nick always ran the grift. It was smoke and mirrors. It's misdirection, like a magician uses. I can't get away from the thought that Denny wants me to concentrate on my daughter so he can get away with something else."

"Maybe he's keeping your mind off of some*one* else? Like where Nick DeVayne might be and what he's doing right now?"

She stared at him with solemn eyes. "That's entirely possible."

If something didn't break soon, Sean would explode. He hated seeing the worry clouding Mel's face. And he felt just a little bit of resentment — no, a lot of resentment — because what should have been a very happy time for them was being rained on.

* * *

Mel absorbed the tension radiating off Sean. Too much of it was related to her. A smile spread over her face that was at once hopeful and a little scared. "I'm a lot of trouble, huh?"

He touched her mouth with his fingertips and shook his head. "No."

But she stared into his green eyes, thinking he probably had no clue just how easy he was for her to read. Most times, anyway. Not so much lately. "I'm not really sure I believe you, but okay. For now." She slid her hands over his chest. "Promise if it ever gets too much, we'll talk before you kick me to the curb?"

Irritation flickered in Sean's eyes, but Mel slid her hands upward and teased his ears with soft caresses.

Desire replaced the annoyance in his gaze, thawing the chills that had settled in her stomach. She'd only just discovered his whole ear thing, but it worked as a diversion every time.

He snaked his hands up to grab hers and still their tormenting. "I said you had to be good. No distractions."

"I'll stop distracting if you'll tell me what's on your mind." She wiggled in his arms one more time but then stepped back and waited.

Sean lifted one shoulder. "Okay. It's a gut thing with me, too. Only it's not about you. Sorry." He stopped and kissed her nose then gestured toward Dev with his head. "It's about this horse. It's unreal that they sent along an attendant to stay on the premises, let alone an attendant who doesn't actually do anything with the horse. He spends most of his time watching me. When he's not off the ranch. That's just one thing that's bothering me about this whole deal."

Mel laughed. "Maybe they should have sent along a girl instead. You never seem to mind me looking at you."

Sean made a sour face at her and flipped the ends of her hair with his fingers. "I like *you* watching me."

"You said Dev hates the man, too. Why would they send him with someone he doesn't like?"

Sean shook his head. "I don't know. But if he's not here to look after the horse, then why *is* he here?"

"How does Dev act around you?"

Sean returned his attention to the horse, who was working his way back in their direction. "He tolerates me. At least he doesn't hate my guts like he does Northrop. And he likes Ricky nearly as much as he likes you. Then there's this thing I noticed the other day." Sean rubbed his jaw. "His conformation's off. Chest isn't as deep as a runner's chest ought to be, and he's severely bench-kneed."

"That last one you'll have to explain." Mel peered around Sean to look at Dev. His knees looked fine to her.

"The bones in his front legs aren't lined up properly." Sean steered her back toward the fence. Dev was standing still, eyeing them with interest. "See his front legs? You should be able to imagine a line from his shoulder to his hoof and the leg would look symmetrical. I saw it almost immediately. When you look for that line on him..."

He gestured with his hand. Following the gesture, Mel drew an imaginary line and frowned as it seemed to zigzag. "I see it! His knee looks strange, kind of square. His hoof is more to the outside of the plane. What does that mean?"

"The bones above and below the knee aren't lined up properly. It gives the knee the look of a shelf or bench, and it makes him unstable, especially for anything strenuous, like running a race." Sean shook his head. "I don't see how he's got such a good win record. Or how he hasn't fractured his carpal bone by now."

"Maybe he was injured in the fire?"

Sean shook his head. "Nope, this is congenital. I've contacted the Racing Commission for his medical records. Something's wrong here. I know it. No sane owner would have raced him, let alone bred him or expected any mare's owner to send her courting." Curling his lip with distaste, he glanced over at the horse's trailer. "Then again, I'm not entirely convinced this horse has sane owners."

In spite of the fact that she suspected he was serious, a giggle slipped out. "Why not just take a pass on the job? Is the money that good?"

Sean leveled a look on her, one that spoke volumes without saying a word, and when he did speak, the words were wistful. "The money is that good, but — you know, it's hard to just give up on him. He's got a look in his eye."

Mel met his gaze. "It's going to be hard for you this time. Giving him back. This one's going to hurt."

Sean pulled in a deep breath, held it. Then he nodded once, quickly. "He's got all kinds of heart. He's not in much pain now, but he went through some rough shit."

"I suppose buying him is out of the question."

He chuckled. "Given what they're paying me for rehab training, that's a good bet."

The sound of rotors overhead had them both looking up as the Cross MC helicopter breezed directly over them and settled on the small helipad.

"What was Joe doing out today?"

"Probably checking for strays. Ryan's got market trucks coming next week."

"Ouch. Your least favorite thing to do." Mel laughed softly. "Need some help? It's been awhile, but I remember most of it."

"Well, Sandy's out of play this year, so maybe..." His eyes drifted to Mel's abdomen.

Another laugh bubbled up. "Hey, eyes up here."

Color rushed into his face and she actually felt sorry for him. "Sorry. I was just thinking about..."

"I know what you were thinking. But even if I am, it's not likely riding a horse to run a few cows onto the trucks would bounce it out of me." She shook her head. Her cell phone chirped and she dug it out of her pocket.

"Joe's here," said Sandy. "He says he might be able to help, but he wants to ask you some questions. Can you come up to the house?"

"On my way." Mel pocketed her phone and smiled at Sean. "It's LeeAnn's night off, so I'm closing."

His lips formed a lopsided smile. "Are you telling me not to come out?"

"Never! I'm telling you it'll be late, so I'll understand if you stay home."

Sean groaned and suddenly Mel was wrapped in his arms. His kiss was hot and hard. His hand in the small of her back held her tightly against him. When he broke the contact, the heat was back in his eyes. "You know, Sweetness, more and more, home's starting to be wherever you are."

"Back atcha," she whispered. Then he released her and she started toward the house.

"Hey, Mel!" Sean called across the yard.

She turned.

His grin was bright and carefree. "You're right. It wouldn't be the end of the world."

She smiled back at him, wondering how he would feel if he knew she was — just a little — beginning to hope she *was* pregnant.

* * *

Mel sat between Justin and Ryan at the kitchen table, listening to the slender man with the sandy brown hair and tawny gold eyes as he paced the length of the kitchen.

Joe spoke with animated style and a lot of hand gestures. "We don't know if a birth certificate was issued, and even if one was, I doubt you were listed as the birth mother. But we can look at all adoptions around that time frame, concentrating on the attorney in the clipping."

Sandy shot Joe a warning glance when he almost bumped into her at the sink slicing carrots, and he stopped pacing.

The energy he exuded made Mel's head spin.

His glass of iced tea sloshed dangerously close to the brim when he picked it up and took a long drink. With a sigh, he set the glass back down and lounged against the counter next to Sandy. Then he started speaking again. "It's more than likely hers will have been a private adoption and, assuming it even went through the courts, closed. DeVayne wouldn't have wanted you to be able to find the child, or her you."

"How many infants could have been adopted in the immediate area during that time frame?" Ryan shifted in his seat, stretching out his long legs.

"You're assuming she was adopted in Oklahoma." Joe snagged a carrot slice, easily avoiding Sandy's slap at his fingers. "There's no real guarantee that she wasn't adopted across state lines." He spread his hands. "I'm really sorry."

Mel wanted to cry. "You're saying she could be anywhere, and there really is no way to find her."

Turning from her task, Sandy laid a warm hand on Mel's shoulder. "We'll find her."

"I'm saying it might take a long time, and there aren't any guarantees." Joe picked up his tea. "We can try to find DeVayne so we can question him. Obviously, if your brother sends more letters, I'll want to see them. It sounds like a kind of kids' game, like he's teasing you about knowing something you don't. You know, nanny-nanny boo-boo."

Mel rubbed her forehead, trying to ease the headache. "That's precisely what he's doing. And he's expecting me to get so desperate to find out what he knows that I'll give him what he wants in return."

"What does he want?" asked Sandy.

Mel shook her head, feeling miserable and hopeless. "It could be as simple as he wants money from me to as complex as he wants me to work with him again." She laid her head down on the table.

"Mel, do you get the feeling Denny's working on his own?" asked Joe. "From everything you've told me, Nick DeVayne was always the one who ran the show in the past. Would he be so far in the background that he didn't contact you?"

Mel sat up and met Joe's gaze. "That's what bothers me the most. Nick was always more intimidating to me than Denny, and both of them knew that. They used to get me to do what they wanted with the bad dad, good brother routine."

Joe's features went grim. "And Nick was the bad guy?"

"Yes." A shudder shot through her as she recalled some of those bad dad moments when he'd used his fists, and she drew a calming breath to ward it off. *That's over. You're safe.*

Joe steepled his fingers. "So Denny contacting you like this... does it feel like he's trying to take on an intimidating role? What was traditionally Nick's role?"

Fingers of chilling realization clawed at Mel's spine. "That's it exactly. Nick would say or do something, get me upset, then Denny would move in, play the understanding brother, and somehow convince me that I should do things I didn't want to do. For the longest time, I trusted him. I thought it was the same for him, that he didn't want to be there either." She grimaced at the little twist in her gut when she considered her brother's betrayal.

They'd been in Santa Fe, New Mexico, only two states away from Wyoming and the closest she'd been to her home for two years. She'd told Denny of her plan to slip out and call Sean for help. She'd managed to skim some of the take from the homeless kids scam she and Denny had run on various street corners. She had enough to get them both bus tickets to Cheyenne, and she knew Sean would find a way to get her. Only Denny had been missing when it was time to leave, and when she'd decided to leave without him, he'd been waiting with Nick at the bus station. Nick had told her if she had been resourceful enough to figure all that out, she could run bigger cons, and her don't-touch-the-virgin con had been born.

Mel shook her head and blinked back tears. "I was wrong. Denny was exactly where he wanted to be."

Justin rubbed his jaw. "Nick DeVayne was always a rooster. He wouldn't run things from behind the scenes. If there's a scam going on and he's involved, I'd expect him to be front and center."

"The fact that he's not is quite a script change, isn't it?" Ryan spoke quietly, turning in his seat to look directly at Joe.

"I'm afraid it is. And that makes Denny a wild card. Unpredictable." Joe drained his glass of tea. He caught Mel's gaze. "My contact will probably want to get in touch with you and really pick your brain. His name's Ben Jamison."

Relief that her current debriefing appeared to be coming to the end brought on a sigh. "Sure. I appreciate everything, Joe."

"I know. That's why I do what I do." With a cocky grin, Joe settled a Dodgers baseball cap on his head and tugged the bill lower over his eyes before he pulled open the back door and stepped out.

Justin cleared his throat. "I came across these the other day." He slid a large gold envelope tied with red string across the table. "Just some pictures. Happens some of them are old. You're even in a couple, got a handful of your parents in here. They were with Tilly's things. I plumb forgot I had them until Sean mentioned you didn't have any pictures of your family."

Fighting to keep the hot tears in her eyes from spilling over, Mel traced the edges of the envelope. "Thank you," she whispered, not trusting herself to say much more.

The baby monitor came to life with Bethany's lusty cry and Sandy sighed. "Sorry, guys. I was going to peel the potatoes for dinner but the boss is calling." She handed Ryan the vegetable peeler.

"Wait!" Mel stood. "Please let me see to her."

Sandy looked startled. "Okay." She opened the refrigerator and retrieved a pink bottle, which she handed to Mel. "Put this in the bottle warmer and set it for two minutes. Call me on the intercom if you need anything."

* * *

After Mel left, Devil's Advocate wandered over to the fence, apparently looking to be friends. Sean managed to get a lead on him and walked him across the stable yard and back without incident. When Sean unclipped the rein and settled him back in the paddock, the horse shied from the offer of a nose rub.

"Can't say as I blame you, big guy."

"Sean!"

He glanced up and smiled. Sandy strode across the yard with determined steps.

"What's up?" he asked when she got closer.

"I need to talk to you about Mel."

Annoyance drove a scowl onto his forehead. "Look, I know I was a jackass on Sunday. Everyone made a point of letting me know. But even Mel's forgiven me."

Sandy shook her head. "This is something else."

"Okay." Sean looped Dev's lead over the gate and gave Sandy his full attention. "I'm listening."

It took a few moments and a couple of deep breaths before Sandy was ready to explain her mission. "I think she's pretty fragile right now. All this crap with her brother and then worrying about her little girl."

"No argument there." Sean started walking toward the stable, where other horses awaited his attention.

Sandy fell in step next to him. "It occurred to me when I listened to her tell her story that in a very real way, she was violated. She may not have been actually raped, but the violation is very similar."

Horror settled like a dark cloud. Sean stopped walking and stared at his sister-in-law. "I..." He took a deep breath and tried again. "I hadn't thought to look at it that way."

"I'm not a professional counselor or anything." Sandy touched him on the arm. "But she gets a look in her eyes when she talks about it, especially about the times she was forced to scam the older men."

Sean sighed. So he hadn't been the only one to notice. He'd hoped he was imagining it. "I've seen that look, and it's scary as hell." He rubbed the back of his neck. "What can I do to help her?"

"She's going to hate this..." Her lips flattened into a thin line as she seemed to struggle. "I think she should see a counselor. Someone trained in domestic violence and PTSD."

Cold fingers reached into Sean's heart and squeezed. "You want me to convince her, don't you?"

"Ah, no." Smiling, Sandy shook her head. "I think she'll get pissed at you if you bring it up."

The sharp crack of flesh against wood echoed across the yard as Sean slapped his palm against the stable door.

Dev tossed his head and broke into a trot around the perimeter of his paddock.

"I don't know what to do, Sandy. I don't know how to help her."

"*I'm* going to suggest counseling to her." Sandy touched him on the arm. "She'll get mad at me. But if I open the door, you can maybe reinforce the suggestion if you get the opportunity, and she won't be as mad at you if you aren't the one to bring it up."

That could work. Sean nodded. He wanted badly for Mel's world to right itself, but he knew it wouldn't happen on its own, and he was completely powerless. "She doesn't have much hope of finding her daughter, does she?"

"Joe's good, Sean. He took seven years to find me for Ryan because they had the name wrong. But he's starting with no name, and in some ways, that might be easier." She gave his arm a couple of pats. "Just be there for her. In fact..." She angled a glance at the house. "She's in the nursery with Bethany right now. And I sure would love the chance to visit with Domingo. You should go to her. She's feeling a little raw after talking about her baby."

Sean didn't have to hear that suggestion twice.

Chapter Thirteen

Just as Sandy had said, Sean found Mel in the nursery. He hung in the doorway, the tears he'd been struggling against for the past week filling his eyes. Apparently oblivious to his presence, Mel sat in the old wooden rocking chair that had once belonged to his mother, the baby cradled securely in her arms. Her blond hair spilled like a curtain of sunshine around her face as she bent close to Bethany, singing a lullaby about pretty horses in sweet, lilting tones.

Two people sat in that chair: a fifteen-year-old girl with the daughter she'd never had the chance to hold, and the mother she might yet become, holding their child. She was a natural mom. Maybe he'd known that from the moment she'd put her arm around him after his mother died.

Slowly, he scrubbed at his eyes, absolutely unwilling to be caught in such a vulnerable emotional state by anyone in his family. He watched until Mel finished the song and kissed the baby on the forehead.

"That makes a mighty pretty picture, Sweetness," he whispered.

Mel didn't look up right away, but she smiled. She brushed her cheek against the sleeping baby's, then stood and laid Bethany in her bassinet. The smile widened when Mel turned, but her eyes were bright with unshed tears. She'd always seemed so strong, even during the rotten times. And it was there still, but so was the fragility Sandy had talked about. Moving with care, the way he would with one of his frightened horses, Sean closed the distance between them.

He traced a fingertip along the line of her jaw, stopped at her chin, and raised her face, falling into her gaze. "Hard day?"

"Yeah, a little." Baby lotion teased his nostrils when she laid a palm against his cheek. "I have all this stuff going on in my head. About my little girl, and about..." She looked around him toward the door and shrugged. "...the other thing. And sometimes I think what if I am... and then I wonder, what if I'm not, you know?"

Yeah, he knew. Ever since he'd discovered the possibility, he'd been tormenting himself with the same conflicting thoughts. And not for the first time, he considered that if they did have a child, it might in many ways be just a replacement for the baby she'd never even been allowed to meet. He hated that thought. Selfishly, he wanted any child they created to be special to them both because of their love for one another.

"I might have to let her go, Sean." Her voice was quiet. Her chin quivered as a single tear welled and spilled over. "I might never find her, might have to just accept that I'll never know."

"Is that what Joe said?"

"Not in so many words."

"So they'll keep looking?"

She nodded. "Yeah, but—"

"Then we hold onto hope." He folded his arms around her and held her close. "Don't give up on her yet, okay?"

Don't give up on you.

Don't give up on us.

She nodded again. "I want to believe we'll find her, Sean. I'd give almost anything just to know she's okay." She sighed then seemed to melt into him, bunching his shirt in tightly clutching fingers like he was her personal lifeline to hope.

Sean had been a problem solver his whole life. Give him a troubled horse, and he knew exactly how to approach it to get it to trust again. Give him a complex logistics problem or financial question, and he had the skills to fix what was wrong. Whenever his brother needed him to watch his back, Sean was there without question.

He didn't have the first idea how to make Mel's life right again.

And that was killing him by inches and feet.

* * *

Mel arrived at Valentine's fifteen minutes late to relieve LeeAnn. The disgruntled employee wasn't shy about her feelings in the matter.

"I thought I might end up working your shift again." She aimed an ugly scowl at Mel as she tugged off her green apron. "I washed the last of the dishes and stacked them *all*. I thought that kid was supposed to come in today to help with setup."

"Ricky's not here yet?" Mel frowned. It wasn't like him to be even a minute late. "Thanks for covering until I got here. I really appreciate it."

"Whatever." LeeAnn flung the words over her shoulder on her way out the front door.

I see you didn't let the door hit you in the...

Mel sighed. LeeAnn's attitude sucked eggs, and if she kept it up, she wouldn't last much longer. Even if she was good with the drinks and knew her stuff, Mel had no idea what Sandy had been thinking to take the girl on. But then, Sandy had taken a chance on Mel some years back. And she'd had at least as big a chip on her shoulder.

Still, it was time to talk with Sandy about hiring some more help. They were busy enough that they might be able to afford two more part-time employees. Then, if LeeAnn quit, they could move someone up to full time.

For all the complaining she had done, at least LeeAnn had accomplished the setup so everything was ready for the evening's customers, who would begin to arrive within the hour. Thursday wasn't their lightest evening, but it was seldom hard to handle the folks who came in. Mel actually enjoyed being the only bartender on her nights, and with Ricky serving the food, they made a good team. He was a hard worker, liked the customers, and always got excellent tips.

Working out the problems of the bar and making plans for the future steadied Mel. Thinking of things other than her screwed up family helped give her distance from the troubles and a calming perspective on her life. When she was here behind the bar, she was Sandy's partner, half owner of Valentine's, one of the most successful businesses in Orson's Folly. She didn't feel like a victim when she dealt with business matters.

The front door opened, and Mel looked up with a welcoming smile, ready to serve the first customer of the evening.

Her smile and professional attitude vanished as icy crystals formed in her veins. She kept her voice careful, emotionless. "Denny."

"Hiya, Melanie."

The brother she'd walked away from had been a tough boy with scruffy dark hair and eyes, still somewhat awkward at seventeen, but already developing the suaveness needed for life as a professional grifter.

The hard man who sauntered across the space between the door and the bar had his hair cut in a flashy style. His clothing was Western style but all designer-made. A day of riding would strain those fancy single-stitched seams. And those genuine alligator skin cowboy boots wouldn't hold their shine after a day on the range, either. Expensive sunglasses dangled from the collar of his pricey shirt. He'd either hit it big or he had a benefactor who was willing to cater to his tastes.

"What are you doing here?" She struggled to maintain an even tone. She wanted to jump over the bar, grab him, and make him tell her what he knew about her daughter. Instead, she crumpled a towel and wiped the polished oak down while she waited for his answer.

"Aren't you going to offer me a drink?"

"You planning to pay for it?" she countered.

Denny flinched and clutched his chest. "Ouch. Harsh."

She raised an eyebrow, not for a moment fooled by his playful attitude. The organ beating in the chest he clutched was as cold and dead as last year's Easter ham and as rotten as an old egg.

With a smirk, Denny slipped a pricey-appearing leather wallet out of his pocket and removed a twenty, then slid it across the bar. "Whiskey sour. And, ah, keep the change." He took a seat on the nearest stool.

Not on your life, you little prick. Mel smiled as she held the bill up to the light and checked the security strip. Spotting it, she nonetheless grabbed the iodine detector pen and drew a line across the twenty. No stain made an appearance, not that she'd expected one would, but double checking sent a clear message: *I don't trust you.*

Smiling, she placed a glass on a bar napkin, then poured his drink and passed it and the correct change across the bar in front of him.

Denny took a drink without touching the bills. "Did you get my letters?"

"You mean your cryptic little trips down your version of Memory Lane?" Mel tossed the cloth beneath the bar, suppressing a flinch when it knocked over a row of shot glasses. "Yeah, I got them. What do you want, Denny?"

"Whoo-hoo. Straight to the point, aren't you?" He looped his arms lazily over the back of the barstool and sat back, never taking his slitted dark eyes off her.

"I may be, but apparently you aren't. Either get to it or get out."

"You've gone cold, sis. Used to be a time you wanted to take care of me."

"You don't much look like you need taking care of these days." She'd never bully him into making his pitch outside of his own timing, so she did the one thing that had always worked when they were teenagers. She walked away.

Her steps carried her to the other end of the bar and almost to the kitchen before he caved.

"Okay. I sent you information I thought you might be able to use to find your baby."

Mel looked at him over her shoulder and affected a tone of indifference. "What makes you think I'm looking?"

"Because you cried yourself to sleep every night from the time they took her away until you left us."

Her composure slipped, and she turned so he wouldn't see that he had surprised her. Too late.

"You didn't think I'd noticed, did you?" His voice softened, became almost seductive. "When I found the stuff about the baby in Nick's things, I passed it on to you, thinking it might help you find her."

Mel stopped walking. She turned but didn't move back up the bar. "In his things? Where's Nick? Why are you going through his belongings?"

A troubled look that was probably as genuine as any of his promises settled over Denny's face. "He's gone. Last April."

Gone... as in Nick DeVayne was dead? Denny hadn't said as much but still... Unsure how that made her feel, Mel changed tacks. "Why don't you get out of the business, then?"

Keeping his eyes locked on her, Denny pushed to his feet and walked closer. His smile didn't reach his eyes; it never had. "I'm working my last job right now."

Mel stood still, waiting. Getting the marks to come to the con instead of the other way around kept them on the hook and allayed any growing suspicion. The best grifter not only avoided showing desperation, but actually put on an air of disinterest in the outcome.

As she studied her brother, Mel almost believed he was interested in getting out. Almost. So much so the thought crossed her mind that maybe he believed that himself. But it was always just one more job with a grifter, and then after that, just one more. The lure of the game was nearly as powerful as the payout.

"And what *is* this last job you're working?"

Down came the shutter. "It's just a little shell game."

"Here, Denny? Where I happen to live?" She rolled her eyes and started walking again, tossing the challenge over her shoulder. "No one in Orson's Folly has the kind of money *you'd* need to retire."

He showed his teeth, but it would be a mistake to call his expression a smile. "The money's not here, Mel. Just the con."

She schooled her features into nonchalance before turning around. "And you need my help with something?" It was so easy to inject that little warble into her voice, the one that said maybe she'd make a deal... for the right price.

The triumphant flash in his eyes was brief. He was getting good at concealing his thoughts. But she was still better at reading him than he was at hiding. That was why Nick had often put her on as the lead in their scams. She could read people and spot those who would be vulnerable to the grift. Those who would eat from her hand and believe every lie she told.

"I don't do that stuff anymore." The thought of getting involved in a con again was nauseating, but Mel sighed, pasted a look of longing on her face. "I've been out a long time. I wouldn't be good enough to help you."

Denny's smile turned cunning. "That's the beauty of this job. You don't have to do anything but stay out of the way when you run into me. Pretend you don't recognize me."

"Oh? And where am I likely to see you?"

"Look, you don't have to stay away from anywhere, and you can't change your routine. You'll see me around town, and whenever you do, unless someone introduces us, you just pretend you don't know me."

Mel smiled. "And if I don't blow your operation, what do I get? A cut?"

"Is that what you want? Money? I was going to let you go through the rest of Nick's things to see if you could find out where he took your baby." His smile was easy.

And completely false.

"I don't know," she hedged. "You didn't really give me much to go on with your notes. Give me something else, something that'll be obviously helpful. Then I'll think about keeping my mouth shut."

Denny slumped in his seat the way he always did when he'd been beaten. But he'd have lost that trait as he got deeper in the game, so he was figuring to play her by doing what she'd expect.

He'd figured wrong.

Still, Mel suspected she'd overplayed her hand and backed off a step. "I see. You don't have anything else." Shaking her head, she disconnected from the conversation, continued walking, and slipped through the silver doors into the kitchen. Once the doors swung closed, Mel sagged against the stainless steel counter, holding on to the edge to keep from crumpling to the floor.

"Melanie, are you ill?" asked a sharp voice from the prep area.

She shook her head. "No, Charlie, I'll be okay in a minute." She knew she wouldn't put off the cook for very long, so she took a deep breath and blew it out. Awkwardly, she pushed to her feet and squared her shoulders.

Charlotte Morrow Haines was slim, somewhere around Justin McGee's age, though she looked much younger with her salt-and-pepper hair stylishly cut in short, feathery layers. Widowed and at loose ends, having sent her three daughters off into the world, she'd been working in the kitchen at Valentine's since Sandy had first bought the place and expanded the menu. Charlie had a natural tendency to mother, which explained why she was comfortable in the kitchen. But more to the point, she'd taken on both Sandy and Mel as her own and tended to be over-protective.

And she was on the way toward Mel with a glass of water and a concerned expression, her white cook's apron looking a bit incongruous over her faded jeans and simple yellow blouse. "You're tired. You work yourself too hard. And that useless sexpot Sandy hired said something about you being late, didn't she?"

Mel glanced up and frowned. She accepted the glass of water and sipped. "Thanks. I'm just tired. Did LeeAnn say something to you about me being late?"

Her lips set in an angry line, Charlie made an impatient gesture. "That girl was fretting about you being here on time or not being here at all starting a half hour before her shift ended."

Charlie's disdain for LeeAnn was nothing new. They hadn't gotten along from the time the young woman had walked in looking for work. Mel sighed. It might be a moot point if the waitress ended up quitting.

"I should have called to let her know I was running behind." Mel looked around the sparkling kitchen. "Has Ricky called in?" It would have surprised her if he had. The boy attended school full time, worked part time for Valentine's and put in long hours alongside Sean and Ryan at the ranch, but he had never once called in sick since he'd been hired at age fifteen.

Charlie's face registered alarm. "No. He hasn't called you?"

Mel pulled her cell phone from her pocket and dialed Ricky's number, frowning when it didn't even ring once. "Straight to voicemail." She looked at her watch. "Give him another fifteen, then I'll call out to the ranch. I've got to get back out front. If he comes in the back way, have him pop his head out to let me know he got here, okay?"

"Absolutely," agreed Charlie.

Mel drew a breath for strength then exited the kitchen. It was anticlimactic to find that Denny had left. Leo Pickens and Ed Lantree were just taking seats at the end of the bar. Thursday was the day the two local proprietors typically took supper together at Valentine's. They'd need a moment with the menu before ordering the same things they had in the whole time she'd known them.

She sent them a smile and a wave and then began bussing the place where Denny had sat, but paused at the sight of black ink on the white napkin. *In case you forgot, Nick's girlfriend when you had your baby was Vicki Forrester. More where that came from. –D!*

Instead of his usual freakishly neat script, he'd written each letter block style, possibly striving to alter his handwriting for some reason. She shook her head. That signature was classic Denny.

"Sloppy, really sloppy, brother dear."

He'd made certain not to mention that "more" came with a price, though, and he'd said nothing about needing her help to run a con. She folded the napkin carefully and tucked it into her back pocket. At this point, it was something to give to Joe rather than DC.

She forced another smile onto her stiff lips and approached her two customers. "Gentlemen, what can I get you this evening?"

Always the kidder, Leo Pickens, owner of the feed and tack store, looked around at the empty bar. "Gentlemen? Oh, you mean us?"

The normalcy of work settled her nerves. She sincerely hoped Denny opted to stay away, at least for the evening. Stepping into the kitchen, Mel caught Charlie's eye as she turned in the dinner orders.

Charlie shook her head. "Still no sign of him. I'm worried, Mel. It's not at all like the boy."

Nodding grimly, Mel dialed Ricky's cell again and when it went to voicemail, she stepped out to the parking lot, hoping to see him pull in. But he wasn't out there, either. She chewed her lip as she dialed Sean's number.

She could hear the smile in his voice when he answered. "Hey, Sweetness, I was just getting ready to leave."

"Sean." She chewed on her upper lip. Oh, how she hated giving him worrisome news. "Ricky never showed for work... and he hasn't called."

His answer was immediately serious, his tone sharp. "When did you expect him?"

"He's scheduled for four o'clock but he's almost always here by three-thirty. His phone goes right to voicemail." Mel blew out a steadying breath. "I know that doesn't seem too late, but—"

"But it's not Ricky's style. I know, Mel." She heard him draw his own deep breath. "I'll check with Ryan and Dad to see if they know anything. Call me if he shows?"

"Of course."

As Mel slipped her phone into her pocket, a troubled feeling settled in her stomach. She pressed the tips of her fingers to her temples and rubbed in a circular motion, hoping to stave off the killer headache that threatened.

Sixty minutes later, still no Ricky, and nothing from Sean. It took less than an hour to get from the ranch to town, so Mel knew something was wrong. Cold on the inside, trembling on the outside, she kept mixing up orders. Thankfully, the bar had fewer customers than normal, even for a Thursday. When her cell phone chirped, she whipped it from her pocket, almost dropping it in her haste.

"Sean?"

The service was spotty, and she only heard some of the words between clicks on the line and bursts of static, but she got the gist. "Got him... sending... home... explain when... get there."

By the time Sean pulled open the front door and walked in, some ten minutes later, Mel had calmed down. His grin seemed a little strained, but he'd said Ricky was going home, not to the hospital or the police. She wanted to run over to him, but something in his demeanor kept her rooted behind the bar.

She delivered a beer to Henky Tenbaum then met Sean at the other end of the bar. Her lips twitched when she noticed the black smudge extending from one cheek up over his nose. "You been overhauling an engine? You're covered in grease."

"Ricky had engine trouble." Sean wiped at his cheek and managed to smear the mark. "He was stranded in the one dead cell zone between home and town, and he'd grabbed the broken two-way."

"Is he okay?"

"Yeah. He'd have had a long walk if you hadn't been worried about him, though." Sean scratched his jaw. "I think that old truck's a goner. Ricky and I got it to Blackstone's and I sent him home in mine." He winked at Mel. "I thought I might use my spare key to your place and crash here so I can check with Blackstone tomorrow when he opens. What do you say, Sweetness?"

A slow smile tugged at Mel's lips. "Oh, and I bet you're picturing yourself using that key about now, running up there, maybe soaking in my tub, then kicking back, aren't you?"

Sean answered back with a sheepish grin. "Kinda, yeah."

"Yeah." She nodded twice, morphed it into a headshake. "Uh-uh. I don't think so. See, you just sent my only waiter home, leaving us very short-handed this evening."

"Yeah, Ricky was really shaken. Sorry about that, but I don't see what I... can..." He caught sight of Mel's secret smile. "Oh, no. *Hell*, no. I'm no waiter."

Mel sighed and set a sorrowful look on her face. "Oh. Okay. I know you worked hard all day. You go ahead and take yourself off and have a rest. I'll sneak in so I don't wake you later." She allowed her shoulders to fall in a defeated slump and started toward the other end of the bar.

"Okay," he called out.

She spun and flashed him a huge grin. "Really?" Then she allowed her laugh to bubble out. Sean added infinite levels of delight to her life. When she was with him, her heart did funny acrobatics in her chest. And teasing him was just one of those perks that made life so interesting. "Relax. I'm messing with you. I've got this covered. You go on up."

"Oh, no. You were right. I can't leave you without help." His voice was smooth and he sent her a sweet smile. A little too sweet.

She was about to regret teasing him in the first place. Excitement stirred miniature butterflies in her stomach.

"Give me ten minutes to clean up and you've got yourself a waiter for the evening." His smile widened into a grin.

Chapter Fourteen

"You did good tonight." Mel flipped the lock on the front door and killed the light on the OPEN sign. The jukebox played one of her favorites, a lively pop song, but it would wind down on its own.

Sean chuckled. "Better than you thought I could. Admit it."

She turned to take him in, looking him up and down, unsurprised by the need to temper the hunger he stirred within her. He should be exhausted. He'd been up before the sun, worked all day and then all night with her, refusing to go up to her apartment early even when they'd had only a couple of customers left. Yet he looked like he could go another couple of hours. Where did he get his energy?

"You were better than I thought you'd be. But Ricky's shift ended about six hours ago." Mel walked slowly toward Sean, holding his gaze. Her heart raced with the intensity she saw. When she stood in front of him, she reached up to touch his cheek. "You should be asleep on your feet."

Sean glided his hand upward along her arm and eased her toward him. But his exploration didn't stop there. Over her shoulder and down to play along her spine, he used his hands in ways that made her stomach butterflies take flight and perform a ballet as he molded her against him. "Do you know what I need?"

Pressed so tightly against him, she could think of one thing... She wiggled suggestively, and he sucked in a sharp breath through his teeth. *Score: one to one.* Should she move in for the kill? "Yes, I think I do know what you need." She lifted her gaze to meet his. "Is my new waiter looking for a little bar sex?"

Flames rose from the embers in his eyes. He moved against her with a little more urgency as he pushed one hand into her hair and gently tugged her head back. With her face completely exposed to his intense scrutiny, she ran her tongue across her upper lip. His breath hissed again, and he dipped his head to touch her lips with his.

He tasted so good, his lips warm and comforting. Her feelings had long since passed merely being in love with him. He was her constant, her steadying influence. He was the one person who had been and would be there for her, the one she would come back to no matter where life took her.

He turned them so she was pressed against the bar then lifted her up onto it in one swift move. He kept his gaze on her face as he allowed his hands to roam along her denim-covered legs, stopping just above her knees. The pause held her on the brink, made her ache for him in both body and heart.

His smile was gentle. His eyes held a glint of awe. "You'd do this, wouldn't you? If I asked, you'd make love with me right on this bar."

She lifted a shoulder, keeping her eyes locked on his. "At the moment, I'd do anything you asked of me," she said very softly, trusting him with all of her.

The jukebox lapsed into silence. Sean went silent, too. He looked at her for several long moments, almost as if he were seeing her for the first time and was trying to memorize her face. Finally he laid his head against her chest, and his arms stole around her waist. He drew a deep, shuddering breath. Standing back, he slid her off the bar and set her gently on the floor.

With his fingertips, he grazed her cheeks, watching her with a half-smile. "Melanie," he murmured.

She tilted her head and smiled back, feeling suddenly shy. "Sean?" His mood was strange tonight, but in a good way.

"I want to get married."

Mel blinked. A smile tugged at her lips. "We *are* getting married." The butterflies in her stomach picked up again.

Sean shook his head. "I don't want to wait until January." He dipped his head and slid his lips along hers, teasing them both before he claimed her mouth with devastating persuasion.

Mel's heart did a flip-flop. He'd said he'd wait until she was ready. Why did he want to push things up? She skimmed her hands over his chest, bringing them to rest on his shoulders, leaning back to catch his eyes. His heart was right there. It blew her away to see so much love on one person's face. And it was all for her.

"I don't understand. Why?"

The glow in his eyes faded just a little and his smile faltered. Mel stretched her hand and used her thumbs to caress his lips. Her own smile still in place, she pushed the corners of his lips upward. "Is it because — I mean, are you worried I might be pregnant?"

His lips lifted into the smile she wanted. "No." But he pulled back a ways and glanced downward then up to look her in the eye. "Not worried at all."

"Then why do—?"

He swallowed her question with another kiss, tender and sweet, and packing more punch than the hottest caress. This time when he drew back, Mel's thoughts tumbled over one another in an incoherent mishmash.

"I love you, Mel. It's that simple. I love you and I want to be with you. I want to lie down next to you at night and wake up next to you in the morning. And I want to do it as your husband."

A stray coherent thought formed one word. "Okay."

Sean's lips twitched. The soft glow from the track lights over the bar made his hair look nearly white. "Is that okay, I can love you? Or okay... something else?"

The butterflies quickened, became a storm. She was going to do it! Breathless, she nodded. "Okay. I'll marry you tonight if you want to run away with me."

His tender smile widened into a huge grin and he gathered her against him so tightly, he lifted her feet off the floor. He twirled them both, and then set her down again. "Hold that thought, Sweetness, and let's get up to your place."

She hurried through her closing routine and double-checked the front door. Then she grabbed his hand and pulled him through the kitchen to the rear exit. Her hands shook as she set the lock and pulled the door closed. Then they were on the stairs to her apartment.

She cast a glance back at him as she led the way. She had one foot on the top step, when Sean's hands settled on her rear end, giving her a light push.

"Oh!" Mel leapt forward onto the deck with a laugh bubbling from her throat.

When she whirled around, she bumped into him. His lips captured hers in an ardent kiss that stole her breath and set her mind to spinning again. He walked her back against the closed door, pressing her there with his body, while his hands began to wander. When icy fingers snuck beneath her blouse and teased the bare skin at her waist, Mel's shrill squeal echoed across the parking lot.

"Oh! That's cold!" And it tickled. And it was making her shiver but not with the chill.

She squirmed against him, trying to avoid those freezing fingers, but only managed to push his hands higher, to the bottom of her ribs, then higher still as he grazed the lower curves of her breasts.

A burst of heat exploded in her belly and radiated outward, counteracting the chill. Breathless, she fumbled her keys and lost; they landed on the deck with a clatter. "You're in trouble now, mister," she gasped and gave him a gentle shove, then bent to retrieve the key ring.

When he caught her around the waist from above, she shrieked again, falling limply into his hold amid gales of hysterical laughter.

"Gotcha!" Sean hoisted Mel over his shoulder, laughing when she struggled.

"Put me down, troglodyte!" She smacked ineffectively at his ass.

He turned around, dangling her in front of the door. "You can keep slapping at me or you can unlock the door with that key you're holding and let us in." Her own rear end was well within his reach, perched as she was on his shoulder, and he gave it a gentle pat.

She fumbled with the lock, her excitement and the cold making her fingers uncooperative.

Finally, key and doorknob turned, and she pushed the door open. Sean carried her through, kicking the door closed behind them, then waited while she turned the lock. He aimed straight for the bed.

"Put me down." Mel wiggled. "You are so getting put in time-out."

Sean's biceps bunched as he lifted her off his shoulder and dropped her onto the bed, smoothly following her down and supporting himself over her. He dipped his head and took her lips, sliding his tongue against hers.

She moaned, filling herself with his taste and texture.

He surfaced briefly, rubbing his lips lightly across her cheek to whisper in her ear. "So you're gonna put me in time-out, huh?" Then he took her earlobe into his mouth, using lips and tongue until she fisted her hands in his hair and arched against him, unable to do more than hang on for the ride he was taking them on.

She gasped as he moved to her shoulder and sank his teeth in lightly then quickly sucked away the sting. "Maybe not."

Busy fingers wound themselves into her hair, tugging gently until her neck arched, exposing her tender skin to his kisses.

"*Maybe* not?" He teased with his lips then drew back and hovered a millimeter away.

Mel fidgeted, trying to move into his touch, but he wasn't budging. "Are you sure about that time-out?" he murmured, running his thumb along the sensitive place just beneath her ear.

"Okay." She moaned and pressed against his hand.

"Okay what, Sweetness?"

"Okay, no time-out."

He trailed kisses along her neck, stopping at the base of her throat. His voice was no more than a seductive whisper. "Do you trust me with you, Mel? Trust me to do anything I want?"

She would explode from the inside out if he didn't do something with her soon.

He shifted and met her eyes. "Well?"

At the naked hunger in his gaze, her pulse slammed against her throat. She wasn't afraid of him, never would be. But she'd only met the wild side of him a few days earlier. It was sometimes like kissing a stranger. Except it wasn't a stranger. It was Sean. Her Sean. But it was always different, always exciting. And she wanted him in that moment more than she wanted her next breath.

No longer capable of speech, Mel nodded.

Sean stood, tugging Mel to sit on the edge of the bed. Crouching in front of her, he held her eyes with his. "I am so in love with you, I can't think straight. After tonight, I can't stay here with you. Not until we're married."

Mel blinked. He'd surprised her again, and yet... what he said felt right. With a tiny cry, she threw her arms around his neck. "Please tell me you meant it that you want to move our wedding date up."

* * *

In the wee hours, Mel rose and pulled on a sweatshirt and flannel PJ pants to counter the October chill. "I'm going to have to break down and call Foster's to top off my oil tank so I can turn on the heat." She crossed to the kitchen and poured a glass of apple juice, lifting the carton toward Sean where he lounged shirtless against a mound of pillows, his hands laced behind his head, not looking in the least chilly.

He shook his head. "We could just generate more of our own heat."

"Ha-ha. Probably not a good idea until after we get to City Hall next week," she said, returning the juice to the fridge. "I'm as human as the next person and I kind of like your idea of waiting." She'd never felt so cherished... or so safe.

"Ummm, that was my idea wasn't it?" He shook his head and wagged his eyebrows suggestively. "Best laid plans..."

The tang of juice as she took a sip puckered her lips, so she turned the action into a kiss and blew it to him. "You need sleep."

"Can't. Not sleepy." After a little maneuvering beneath the mussed-up covers, he grabbed his T-shirt from the floor and slipped it over his head. Inside out.

Mel chuckled but kept the information to herself. "Where's all this energy coming from all of a sudden?"

He stood, and the dark boxer briefs covering him revealed what he'd been doing under the blanket. With sure movements, he rearranged a couple of pillows and straightened the bedding, then sat again. "It's not sudden. I was energized all night watching you work the bar."

"Huh! What's new about that? Every time you come in I'm working the bar." She set her empty glass on the counter and started across the room.

"Yeah, but you were giving me orders tonight. That was hot." He went back to rooting under the covers and came out with her black and pink bra. A leer crept over his face as he held the bits of silk and lace up to his chest. "Would have been even better if I'd known what you had on under your blouse." He tossed it in her direction.

Mel snagged her bra from midair and threw it onto the dresser. "You are entirely too obsessed with my undergarments."

Flopping back into the pillows, he rolled onto his side and buried his face. He muttered something that might have been, "You have no idea." But before she could ask what he'd said, his breathing became deep and even.

Not tired, huh? She lowered herself to the bed and pulled the blanket over his shoulders.

* * *

Sean woke in the dark, wondering where he was. As he came to full awareness, the soft sigh from the warm body next to him brought him to full alertness. Mel's apartment. He ached for her but the ache was beyond physical, an exquisite pain he'd never known with any other woman. Life hadn't been easy for them. Much worse for her, he reminded himself.

He knew her worries weren't gone, and hadn't even been forgotten. But just for a while, they'd put the worries out of the way and enjoyed one another's company, joking and teasing, settling into the same give-and-take routine they'd had as kids. He'd had to sit on his hands, though, when she'd decided to get more comfortable and reached beneath her T-shirt to unhook and remove her bra without taking off her shirt, in that mysterious way women possessed.

Then he'd lost his control altogether when she'd spun it around on one finger and swayed her hips suggestively.

That was why taking a step back and sleeping in separate quarters had to be. They weren't kids any longer. But he couldn't wait to have the legal right to call her his wife. He already thought of her that way.

For Sean, it was simple. He loved Mel with what he knew was the world's most perfect love. The innocent love of their childhood had changed, become stronger. But it was still as permanent as it had ever been. She was his center. Her smile alone turned him inside out, but her love kept his feet steady on uneven ground. He'd do anything for Melanie Grace Mitchell. Anything.

But he was terrified that he wouldn't be able to do the one thing she needed most: help her right a mistake she'd had no choice but to make when she'd been just a child. The prospect of seeing those shadows in her eyes day after never-ending day was killing him.

His eyelids felt heavy again, and he drifted off to sleep to the sound of Mel's light snores. He should tease her about that. The sound was such a comfort, though, he knew she could snore like a chainsaw and he'd want to hear it every night.

* * *

The smell of coffee hit Mel on the way out of the shower, bringing on a smile. She hadn't set the coffee maker, so Sean was awake. She opened the door and bumped into him just on the other side, holding a mug of coffee aimed in her direction.

"Black and insanely sweet." He kissed the tip of her nose.

Mel wrapped both hands around the mug, enjoying the warmth against her palms. She took a sip, then another, closing her eyes as the syrupy liquid began to work its magic.

Chuckling, Sean touched the mug. "You know this here loop thing is a handle, right?"

Mel simply settled her hands more tightly around the outside of the mug and stared at him over the rim as she took another drink.

Sean smiled and pulled on his jacket. "I'm running over to Blackstone's now. I'll give Ry a call to come get me. Maybe I'll see you later? Tonight for sure."

"I can give you a ride out to the ranch, if you want." Mel took a longer drink. "I need to see Joe if he's out there, anyway."

Sean's gaze was suddenly sharply alert. "Has something happened?"

Mel chewed her lip, took another drink.

"Mel?"

"Denny came by the bar yesterday."

"When did you plan to tell me?" he asked sharply.

Irritation flashed, then was gone. She kept her voice even. "I'm telling you now."

Sean stared at her, shaking his head. "You don't think — *maybe* — you should've told me a little sooner?"

Stunned at his reaction, Mel had no idea how to respond. So she didn't. She set her mug down on the counter and walked slowly to her closet. She didn't even pay attention to what she chose. Grabbing the first shirt she came across, she let her terry cloth robe drop to the floor.

Behind her, Sean coughed. "Still here, Mel. Why didn't you tell me last night?"

Mel shrugged into a pink shirt but left it unbuttoned while she slid a pair of skinny jeans from a hanger. Maintaining her silence, she tugged those over her feet and shinnied them up her legs. She was fastening her shirt as she turned around.

Sean stared, but she noted with dismay the shutters had been drawn on his expression.

"When do you think I should have told you, Sean?" she asked carefully." When I was training you how to wait tables? Or maybe when you were kissing me against the bar? I know! When you were asking me to push the wedding date up! Or, how about while we were romping between the sheets?" She tucked her shirt and pulled the edges of her faded jeans together. With a small sense of defiance, she pulled on a canvas loop-buckle belt and cinched it tightly. She sat on the bed and drew on first one sock, then the other, and then she stepped into her boots because they were handiest.

To complete her outfit, she grabbed an oversized hoodie, jerked it over her head, then grabbed her purse and keys on her march to the door. She tugged the door open and stood waiting for him.

Sean preceded her across the threshold and stomped down the stairs without waiting for her. "You could have called when he showed up. Or how about right after he left?" he tossed over his shoulder.

"Sure, that would have been convenient, since I already had you on the phone because I was worried about *Ricky*." Her shrill shouts echoed off the building. Clamping her mouth shut, she whirled about and locked her door, then followed him. In a more subdued tone, she continued. "It slipped my mind because Ricky is more important to me."

Sean halted at the foot of the steps to greet Charlie, who was just getting out of her car. *Oh, just great. Let's make this a public argument.* Mel kept silent, hoping the cook hadn't heard anything. No way would her protective mama bear keep out of it.

"Charlie, what are you doing here?"

The cook clucked sympathetically and shook her head, then explained carefully as though Mel had gone soft in the head. "It's Friday, honey. Food order's coming in so I'm here for my split shift."

"It is, isn't it?" Mel frowned. How had she lost track of the days so easily? "The week went by fast."

Charlie smiled. "Since I'm here, why don't I get some breakfast going? Maybe some hotcakes and ham?"

"Thanks, but I don't eat breakfast." Mel's stomach rumbled. She felt more than saw Sean's glance at her abdomen and peeved with it, shifted her stance to angle away from that look. They didn't even know if she was pregnant, and he was already considering every little influence. She was more than a freaking baby factory. If she didn't want to eat, she damn well would not be forced into it.

Even if Charlie's hotcakes did sound appealing.

Sean didn't take his eyes off Mel as he spoke. "Miss Charlie, whatever you can whip up in that kitchen would be most appreciated. I'm just going to run over to Walt's to see about Ricky's truck."

He fired a look at Mel that said they'd talk when he got back and without offering another word, he stalked across the parking lot toward Blackstone's Auto Repair.

Fine. She had a few things she felt like talking about. Grumpily, she moved to unlock the rear door to the bar, frowning when she found it was already hanging open.

"Charlie, have you been inside?"

"Inside." Once again, the cook shot Mel a curious look as though she was losing it and shook her head. "I just got here as you two were coming out."

Mel pushed the door open with one finger and peered over the threshold. In the dim light, nothing appeared out of order. Moving with caution, she reached around the edge of the door to turn on the light. Charlie stepped in behind her and pulled a baseball bat from just inside the door. Mel blinked in surprise.

Charlie shrugged. "My equalizer. In case things ever get too rowdy."

Mel didn't have to ask if the cook knew how to use it to defend herself. She was holding the bat like a martial arts expert.

Inching forward, Mel entered the bar and flicked on the main light. But nothing seemed out of the ordinary there, either, and she eased out a breath. That left the office, just down the hallway toward the rest rooms. Mel could already see from where she stood that the office door was wide open. And she distinctly remembered closing and locking that door. She pulled out her cell phone, ready to dial the sheriff's office as she moved toward the hallway.

The hand on her shoulder startled her, and she would have screamed, but another hand clamped over her mouth. Mel struggled until she recognized Sean, and then went still. He tugged her backward, propelling her through the kitchen and then outside to where Charlie was pacing fretfully.

Sean's face was dark red with anger. "Are you out of your freaking mind?" He kicked the gravel. "You don't go investigating a break-in by yourself!"

That was it! She was done with his caveman tactics. Stiffening her spine, she positioned herself toe-to-toe with him. But as she opened her mouth, he yanked her against him and took her mouth in a not-quite-savage kiss.

Wires crossed in her brain as his kiss sparked her own emotional response, and she forgot what she'd been going to say.

Sean broke the kiss abruptly, taking her by the shoulders and looking into her eyes. His own eyes seemed almost crazed. "Geez, Mel. You scare me sometimes. We don't know if anyone is still in there or what they might have done — or left in there."

Gasping for breath, she stared at him. "*Where* did you come from?"

"I asked Walt to look at Ricky's truck then came back here for breakfast and almost got clocked in the head by Charlie's baseball bat."

Mel activated her cell phone. "Fine, I'll call the sheriff. Satisfied?"

Sean took her phone from her, hit END, and handed it back to her. "I called. The point is, you should have called when you saw the open door."

Mel shoved her phone back into her pocket and rubbed her tired eyes with the heels of her hands. As her heart rate slowed to a more normal pace, the world tilted then spun wildly. Her legs gave out, and she plopped down onto the curb, clutching her head at the temples.

"Mel!" He was beside her in an instant, crouching, supporting her with an arm around her shoulder. "What is it?"

Charlie handed him an open bottle of water, and he held it to Mel's lips.

She took a sip then pushed it away. "I'm okay. I'm just so tired and so—" *Scared.* "This was just one more thing I—" *Oh, crap.* She felt like she was all of six years old again, and sporting a skinned knee. Tears filled her eyes and she sniffed back her runny nose. Reaching into her bag, she pulled out Denny's note and shoved it into Sean's hands. "Here. Denny left this stupid note on a napkin when he was here yesterday. I need to get it to Joe. Just — *please* — go away for a while."

"Mel." His voice was soft and caring, all traces of anger gone. "I'm not leaving you alone."

"I won't be alone. I'll be here with Charlie. Just go *away*. And take the Jeep. You own half of it anyway." She looked into his eyes, challenging him to deny the truth, letting him see the hurt she'd felt since he'd snapped at her earlier over keeping Denny's latest visit to herself.

Sean seemed to sag. "You weren't supposed to know about that. Who told you?"

Mel cupped his cheek and sighed lightly. Her smile softened her words. "Oh, Sean. Haven't you ever heard the saying that you can't con a con? I knew something was up. Then DC was here when Colt delivered the car, and he mentioned the original price was twelve hundred. No one drops their price that far. All I had to do was think about what five hundred was going to get me from the classified ads to know I was getting a deal. I put the pressure on Colt and he admitted you matched my funds."

"You didn't say anything." Sean looked away. "I thought you'd be pissed."

Her laugh held no humor. "Oh, I was livid. But Colt talked me down, and he made sense. You're just trying to keep me safe, and I'd do the same for you."

He leaned forward and touched his forehead to hers. "I'm sorry."

"Don't do it again." She pulled back and met his eyes, giving him a smile. "Please?"

The sheriff's patrol car pulled in to the parking lot and came to a stop nearby. Sean stood, offered Mel a hand, and when she took it, easily pulled her to her feet.

Deputy Penny Sherwood climbed out of the cruiser. "Mel. Sean. Hi, Miss Charlie. Got a call about a break-in?"

"The door was open when we got here this morning." Mel brushed the last of her tears away. "I locked up myself last night. I've been inside to check things out. The office door is open, too, and that's always locked at night."

Sherwood unsnapped her gun holster and stepped through the back door. She returned in less than ten minutes. "It's clear. Mel, I need you to go through and let me know if anything's out of place. I didn't see any obvious damage."

Mel handed Sean the key to the Jeep. "I mean it. Go away for a while. There's nothing you can do. I'm filing a sheriff's report. I'm not leaving today. I have to get the locks changed, and I don't want to leave Charlie alone. You'll find a way to get the Jeep back to me."

"I'll see you tonight," said Sean.

Did that mean he'd stay again, despite his intention not to? Mel sighed. "You will if you get here and don't close your eyes."

Willing herself not to look back, she followed Penny into the bar. When the Jeep growled to life, she squashed the little stab in her heart that he was leaving. After all, she'd been the one to send him away, hadn't she?

* * *

An uneasy feeling crept over Sean as he watched her walk away without saying goodbye or giving him a kiss. He sighed, knowing he'd screwed up with her again. Would he ever get his shit together and stop stepping on his own feet with the woman?

He looked at the napkin Mel had pushed into his hand. The note from her half-brother. *In case you forgot, Nick's girlfriend when you had your baby was Vicki Forrester. More where that came from. –D!*

Not the usual content for a cocktail napkin note.

What did Denny DeVayne want? It was apparent from his message that he was holding information about Mel's baby hostage, so he obviously wanted something. Sean frowned. Something about the writing was weird, even allowing for the fact that it was written on a cocktail napkin. Almost perfect, straight not slanting, evenly spaced, boxy block letters, each one perfectly crafted; it seemed to mock him for his helplessness. The writing hid behind anonymity. The letters Denny had mailed to her had been typed and he hadn't signed his name, but the note written on the napkin was signed with a dash next to the letter *D*, followed by an exclamation point. Something about that nagged at him. Where the hell had he seen that signature mark before? It must have been on one of the letters. The man must have signed one, after all. He laid the napkin on the seat next to him and started the Jeep.

Chapter Fifteen

Mel closed her eyes and tilted the old leather chair back, resting her feet on the antique oak desk. She enjoyed talking shop with Sandy again, even if it was just over the phone.

"I may be on maternity leave, but I can make a few phone calls," said her partner. "I'll have a security company out by the beginning of next week. I can't help with roundup anyway, so Bethany and I can come in and spend some time there."

"In the meantime, I'll run out and make a night deposit of some of the evening's take earlier in the evenings instead of waiting until the next day, just in case Denny gets any ideas about helping himself," said Mel. "It'll be a change in script that he might not expect."

"You make sure Sean goes with you," Sandy advised.

"Yes, ma'am." The proceeds from the latter half of the evening would go home with her until the next morning. Sandy would worry herself sick if she knew, so Mel kept that part of the plan quiet.

"So, Sean didn't come home again last night."

"He didn't?" Mel feigned shock. "Where on earth could he have gone?"

Sandy chuckled. "You sound happy."

Mel stared across the room, but instead of seeing the ancient office furniture, Sean's face floated in front of her.

"Mel?" Sandy's sharp voice brought her back to the office and the phone call.

Of its own accord, her mouth began speaking without first engaging her brain. "He wants us to move our wedding up and get married right away."

"Wha-at?" Sandy drew the word out. "Why? You two've waited so long already. He can't wait another few months?"

She might as well finish what she'd started. "I said yes."

"You said — why? Mel! You're pregnant!"

Mel's heart jumped. "No!" she said quickly. With a sigh, she sat up straight. "That is, we don't know. It's too soon. But he swears that's not why he asked."

No sound came from the other end of the connection and Mel looked at the receiver before tapping it on the desk. She put it back to her ear. "Sandy? You there?"

"It was Sunday night, wasn't it?" asked Sandy. "You and Sean made love the first time after your big argument."

Mel leaned over and knocked her head on the desk blotter twice before she answered with a sigh. "In the cab of his truck. We didn't — it happened very quickly and we didn't use — protection."

"*That*... actually explains a lot," said Sandy. "He snuck in late and acted really strange Monday morning." She chuckled. "Ry's gonna give him so much crap."

Alarm had Mel's heart racing all over again. "You can't tell Ryan!"

Sandy laughed again. "I won't have to. He'll just know. It's the brother thing. So... what are your chances of being pregnant?"

"A little too good." Mel picked up a red pen and began doodling on the tablet in front of her. "I'm pathetic, aren't I? Pregnant as a teenager, possibly pregnant right now out of wedlock."

"You really don't think I'm going to judge you on any of that, do you?"

Mel inhaled deeply and blew out again. "No. No, I know you're not."

"So, a baby isn't the reason he asked you to move the date forward?"

Mel drew another line on the paper. "That's what he said."

"Then you should believe him. These boys never lie."

"That's just it." Mel moved the pen and another line appeared. "He already did. Lie, I mean." She told Sandy about the funds for the Jeep.

"Ouch."

"Exactly. But I got over it, and even moving the wedding up doesn't bother me. I like the idea. But Denny was here yesterday afternoon and I didn't tell Sean about it until this morning. He freaked out on me, and now..." She sighed.

"Do you love him?" asked Sandy.

"You know I do."

"Don't read too much into his eagerness, then," advised her partner.

"I'm trying not to. Sandy... I want to marry him. And I think — under any other circumstances I'd be really happy if I found out I was pregnant."

Sandy chuckled. "Really. In the cab of a pickup." The chuckle became a laugh. "You kids!"

"You know that's not how I would've wanted it to happen. We should have time together. A baby should be planned and wanted and... wanted." A tear dropped onto the blotter in front of her.

"Mel!" Sandy's sharp exclamation drew her away from her pity party. "You wouldn't want the baby?"

"No, no— I mean— That came out wrong. Yes, if there's a baby, of course it will be a wanted child. Just not a planned one." She sighed. "And maybe not a convenient one."

"Sweetie..." Sandy spoke in gentle tones. "It would be a baby with the man you love and plan to marry, not the end of the world. Will you love him or her?"

"Babies are new life… a gift from God. That's what Grandma Tilly used to say." Mel sniffed and rubbed her eyes. "Even though she was talking about the stupid old barn cats and their kittens at the time."

"You didn't answer my question." Sandy's voice grew softer. "Will you love your child any less if he was conceived during your reckless moment?"

Mel pressed a hand to her flat stomach. She closed her eyes and pictured herself as she'd been years earlier, a teenager, belly swollen, no resources, nowhere to turn for help. She'd loved that baby before she was born. Loved her enough to make plans to get her away from a detestable lifestyle.

"Yes," she whispered. *But am I trying to replace one child with another?* She couldn't put voice to the thought. Somehow, that would make the possibility all too real.

"There you go. Big sister says stop worrying." Sandy's soft chuckle was balm to Mel's frayed nerves. "I hear Bethany stirring. But Mel… it'll work out. All of it."

"I suppose it will."

She hung up the phone and tapped her chin with the back of the pen. At least Sandy had agreed with her about hiring two more part-timers. Mel twirled the pen between her fingers like a baton. Then she dropped her gaze to the page in front of her. The stick figure she'd drawn had a huge pregnant belly and a tiny stick baby inside. A short burst of half-hysterical laughter escaped.

Sandy was right. There was absolutely no point in wondering or worrying about something that had either already happened or hadn't. With a sigh, she tore off the top sheet of paper and set it aside before beginning to draft the ad for additional help.

Mel's eyes drifted to the wall safe across from her. It hadn't been opened, or if it had, he'd left everything untouched and closed it again. At any rate, the evening's proceeds had been left intact. The desk drawer, however, had been forced open and left that way. Mel was certain this was Denny messing with her. He could have easily opened the outdated safe with their entire take from the previous evening, but had apparently chosen to leave it alone. He also could have opened the desk drawer without breaking the lock, but the lock had been jimmied and was now useless.

"What are you doing, Denny?" She tapped the pen against the top of the desk, replaying the conversation she'd had with him the day before. Some kind of shell game, running somewhere close by, but the money was apparently separate from the scam itself.

What kind of scam was he involved in?

"The money's not here..." he'd said. *"Just the con."*

That suggested a third party. Shell game, three-card Monty, now you see it, now you don't. Some kind of fraud? What about his traffic tickets? Was he just a careless driver? Auto insurance fraud? That was typically more of a big city scam. Orson's Folly was ranching, a handful of small businesses. And Valentine's. Was he after the bar, thinking he'd have an easy time of it because of her partnership stake?

She massaged her temples.

Deputy Sherwood had been kind and filled out the report. She had also been honest and told Mel up front that without evidence, they could do little more than question Denny *if* they happened to find him. The state police had been by, checking for fingerprints and other miniscule bits of forensic evidence, but Mel knew they wouldn't find Denny's. He'd have been careful. They did find prints on the safe, and since it was highly likely these would turn out to be Mel's, she had to suffer through the indignity of having her own prints collected for comparison, even though they were already on record with the state as part of her partnership in the liquor license.

She'd spent fifteen minutes washing her hands and cursing her half-brother, though the ink had washed down the drain in the first thirty seconds.

When her cell phone chirped, she set her pen down and checked the caller ID, but didn't recognize the number. Her heart took up a crazy, erratic beat as she answered. "Hello?"

"Is this Melanie Mitchell?" asked a deep male voice.

"Yes, who is this, please?"

"My name is Ben Jamison. I'm a friend of Joe Griffin."

Her eyes closed in relief and she eased out a breath. "You're the investigator."

He chuckled. "That's one thing I do. I needed to touch base with you, ask a couple of questions. Is this a good time?"

She shifted to a more comfortable position. The creak of her desk chair cut through the silence, startling her, and she forced herself to sit still. "Does this call mean you'll take the case, Mr. Jamison?"

"Call me Ben." He spoke easily and his deep voice was soothing. "And yes, I'm going to try to help you. Let's start with telling me your story in your own words."

With halting words and phrases, Mel told Ben Jamison the same story she'd told Sean and then Joe and the others. It never got any easier to say.

"My brother came in to the bar yesterday and let me know he was in the area running what he's calling a shell game. He wants me to keep quiet and pretend I don't know him if I should run into him." Mel finished speaking quickly then drew a shaky breath.

"Did he give you incentive? Offer cash? A cut, maybe?"

The room was suddenly too hot. Warmth invaded her face. Sweat tickled the back of her neck. It was October. She'd dressed for October. Fanning her face didn't help at bit. Sandy should have a ceiling fan installed. It was too close in the tiny office.

"Ms. Mitchell?"

Right, the phone call. What was wrong with her? "Ah, yes, I'm here. He um... He said if I help him, he'll give me more information about my daughter and implied if I don't cooperate, I'll never find her."

"What makes you believe he's holding out on you?"

"I don't know." She weighed the question carefully. "He's harder to read than he used to be, harder to work. He said our fath— that Nick DeVayne is dead. If that's true, then Denny'll be out of his depth. He'll have developed a style of his own, but the specifics will depend on who he's working with. He's still a follower."

"You think he's working with someone?"

The memory of his expensive clothing, his cavalier manner with money played in her mind, and she shook her head. "He's not working alone."

"Interesting."

"After he left, I found a note with the name of our father's girlfriend at the time I had the baby. I'd forgotten her name but the name he left sounds familiar. Vicki Forrester. She won't be in my father's life now. He has — *had* them on a revolving door system."

"I'm going to need a copy of that note."

"I gave it to Sean McGee to give to Joe." Crap, she should have turned it over to DC. What had she been thinking?

"Good." The sound of shuffling papers came over the phone. "Were there any cities or states DeVayne stayed in longer while you were with him, or maybe kept going back to?"

"We were in Oklahoma City for a year. That's where I had the baby. There were a couple of places in Texas we went back to more than once."

Her cell beeped, indicating a call was waiting. She pulled the phone away from her ear to check the caller ID. Sean. She'd call him back.

"Would you say you stayed in the Texas and Oklahoma area?"

"Sometimes Arizona or New Mexico. A couple of times when I was first with him, we went to Nevada, but he stayed away from Las Vegas." Which was the main reason she'd chosen to go there when she'd left him. "Denny told me once that they'd had trouble there." Her headache was definitely taking hold now. "And we went to New Orleans for Mardi Gras once, but things didn't go well for him. We ended up leaving in the middle of the night." His face had been a swollen mess of cuts and bruises. "I think he got beat up."

"Did he ever have steady employment?"

The guffaw exploded past her lips before she could restrain it. "Never. It was always the grift and usually things we could all run together at first. Later, he would go off on his own for bigger things and leave us either waiting or working a minor con."

The phone on her desk rang, but she knew it was also ringing in the kitchen and Charlie would pick up. After three rings, the line lit up and the ringing stopped.

"After you had the baby, what made you think he sold her?"

Mel tapped her foot against the bottom of the desk. "He never said anything other than adoption, but one time his girlfriend said something about after the baby we would be on easy street."

"Okay, just a couple more questions for now, I promise. I know this is hard. Did it seem to get better financially after he took your baby?"

"A little but not much, and Vicki wasn't too happy afterwards. I remember thinking they were working a con and she obviously expected to tap into the mother lode." Mel stood and walked to the wall safe, studying the dial, wondering if her brother had touched it, invaded it, the way he was invading the rest of her life. "Right after I had the baby, she and Nick argued all the time, and just a few days later, she was gone."

Ben was quiet for a moment but Mel could hear the sound of computer keys being struck at lightning-quick speed.

The typing stopped. Ben returned to the conversation. "Did any of you ever use aliases?"

Mel moaned out loud. "Oh, I can't believe I didn't think about that. Yes, we all went by several names. I was Monique DelRay a lot of the time. Denny was Davey DelRay. And Nick was Ned DelRay. One time he was Donald Nichols. I don't remember all the names he used but he stayed with his initials or his initials in reverse." She sighed heavily. "That's going to make it harder, isn't it?"

With a sinking heart, she heard Ben blow out a breath. "I won't lie to you. It's definitely not going to make it easier. But knowing his pattern of choosing names will help."

* * *

Sean's violent curse as he stabbed the END icon with his finger then stuffed his cell phone into his pocket earned him a vindictive stare from Dev. The horse stood in the center of the paddock, apparently awaiting their daily cat-and-mouse game of trying to build trust. Sean jammed one foot on the bottom fence rail and stared back.

What the hell had Charlie meant when she'd said Mel was *busy*? She'd never been too busy to take his calls before. Not even when they'd barely been dating. It was just one of those little things he'd taken for granted.

"She's in her office and requested not to be disturbed," Charlie had informed him after he'd broken down and called the bar's landline.

What are you doing, Mel?

He tried to stem his irritation but had only marginal success. She'd been hurt by his accusations of keeping her brother's visit a secret. He got that. And he *had* been wrong. That was why he needed to talk to her, to apologize. She'd asked him to leave — told him to go away.

I was a jerk. Again.

But he didn't think that would prevent her from taking his call. His mind drifted to the break-in. More than likely she was dealing with the aftermath of that. He'd seen the look on her face. She was convinced Denny had been the intruder. And, knowing the way her mind worked, she would take that on as her responsibility. Sean's hands curled into fists. If he could get his hand on that brother of hers, he'd—

"You got a late start working Devil's Advocate this morning. For the price you're charging to fix this damn horse, I'd think you'd be able to pay a little more attention to a regular schedule."

Crap in a sack! How had Northrop managed to sneak up on him? Pleasing visions of dragging the irritating jerk across the prairie behind his horse rolled through Sean's mind, and his mouth pulled up on one side. He drew in a deep, steadying breath, wiped his face into a carefully blank slate, and turned in the direction of the voice.

"Just so we're clear, Northrop. Again." Sean allowed some of his irritation loose when he spoke. "The services this horse's *owners* are paying for don't come with my punch card to your personal time clock."

"I haven't seen you do any training since he's been here." Derision dripped from his words. Northrop was either stupid or spoiling for a fight himself.

Sean tipped the brim of his hat upward and tilted his head back, regarding the dandy boy through hooded eyes. When he spoke, he allowed his voice to creep along in a slow drawl. "Well, Mr. Northrop, you'd probably have an easier time seeing me work Devil's Advocate if you stuck around to watch." *Not that I want you here, you pompous ass.*

"Look, just tell me your best guess when you think you'll be finished with him." He brushed at something on his jacket sleeve, looking in Sean's general direction but somewhere over his left shoulder rather than meeting his eyes. "I'll need a written progress report."

Oh, you are definitely displaying a tendency toward a death wish.

Rage had curled Sean's hands into fists; he forced them to relax and offered a lazy shrug instead of a punch to the jaw. "Case as bad as Devil's Advocate? Minimum of two months, probably much longer." He smiled. "But don't worry. My fee covers as long as it takes. Why? Got someplace else to be?" He couldn't resist poking the weasel.

Northrop muttered a string of curses and glared at Sean for a hot minute. Sean returned his glare beat for beat without flinching. Finally, Northrop kicked at the dirt with his fancy city boots, turned, and stalked away, muttering under his breath.

A glance into the paddock revealed Dev had moved to the far side. Great. Back to square one.

Sean's cell vibrated, and thinking it might be Mel, he almost tore the pocket of his jeans getting to it.

"Sean, this is Walt Blackstone."

Letting out a long breath, Sean felt his heartbeat steady. "Yeah, Walt. Did you look at Ricky's truck?"

"I have, and I've called DC about it, too, son. The engine overheated and seized because the radiator was bone dry."

Sean struggled to catch up. Like Justin, Walt often talked in circles and started his thoughts in the middle instead of the beginning. "Why does a dry radiator warrant a call to the sheriff? And Ricky swears the temperature gauge never registered above cold before the engine started blowing steam."

"Wire to the gauge was cut," said Blackstone. "Recently. But the engine blowing may have saved that young man's life."

Icy fingers walked down Sean's back and settled in the base of his spine. "Why is that?"

Walt coughed. "Because someone put a tiny screw in his brake line. Boy was about out of brake fluid and on the way to failing brakes."

Sean hung up, not sure whether the ice running through his veins was due to fear or rage. Maybe both. Deep in thought, he dimly registered the sound of Northrop's motorcycle driving off. *Yeah, that's right. Tuck your tail and run off, weasel.*

The crunch of gravel under Sean's boots made him think of breaking bones. *No brakes. A deliberate act.* Blackstone's words reverberated through Sean's brain. *Ricky could have been killed.*

Whatever was going down, Ryan needed to know. But for the life of him, Sean couldn't recall where his brother had said he was heading. Sandy! She'd know where to find him.

Sean caught up with her as she tidied the kitchen. Bethany, securely fastened in her infant seat on the table, was putting up a fuss. Justin sat making goofy faces and speaking baby talk.

"Where's Ry?" Unable to resist, Sean stroked one of Bethany's feet and was rewarded by a kick. His heart kicked at him in response.

"West pasture with Joe. Oh, and there's a letter for you in the office. Came overnight mail." Sandy placed a cup in the dishwasher and closed the door, setting the switch to start. The soft swish of running water filled the room.

Bethany stopped fussing and jammed a tiny fist into her mouth, making wet smacking sounds around it.

Sandy sighed and gestured to the baby. "The sounds of running water and machinery calm her every time. Works with the washer, too."

Sean stared at his niece. For one so tiny, she had a dynamic personality. "Uh, is that normal?"

Sandy shrugged. "You've got me. But if it ever stops working, I'm going to go insane."

"A drive in the truck used to settle Ryan when he was little," said Justin. He stood and stretched, giving his granddaughter's cheek a rub with a forefinger. "Used to take him out in the truck to drop hay when he got colicky."

"That may be next on the list." Sandy opened the freezer and pulled out some chicken. "She seems to have a hard time settling sometimes."

Sean froze with his finger in mid-tickle. His heart did a strange little flip. What if Ricky's truck wasn't the only one that had been sabotaged? He marshalled his emotions and maintained outward composure as he edged toward the back door.

"Sandy, promise me you won't go anywhere before I get a chance to look at your truck."

Always astute to the smallest detail of behavior, Sandy focused a questioning gaze on him. "Why?"

It was never a matter of not telling Sandy what he knew. Lives depended on complete honesty. He'd just hoped for some backup when he let her in on the news. "Someone messed with Ricky's truck. That's why it broke down. If it hadn't overheated, his brakes would have failed."

Sandy's face turned pure white with tinges of green. "Who would do that?"

"I don't know. It might have happened anywhere. Just — don't go driving." Without waiting for a response, he stepped into the hallway, heading for the study. The west pasture had no cell service, but his brother would have taken a hand-held radio.

"Damn it!" He exploded as he entered the business hub of the ranch. The malicious acts and violence had ended when the whole MacKay thing had blown up. Had Bull

MacKay resurfaced from under his rock in rehab and returned to cause trouble?

"We're on the way in," Ryan said after Sean raised him. "Something wrong?"

"Are you on horseback?"

"Yeah, why?"

"I'll explain when you get back, but don't let Joe take off in the chopper. Someone's messing with equipment on the ranch again."

"Shit," Ryan muttered. "Okay, sit tight. We're about thirty minutes out."

A cough sounded from the doorway. Sean turned to see his father leaning on the jamb, watching him. "You're going to want to look at your horse man real hard, son."

Sean dragged a hand down his face, pausing at his mouth. "Yeah." He rubbed his chin. "That's exactly who I'm looking at first. Have you seen him doing anything that seems off?"

Justin laughed. "I've hardly seen him at all, unless it's when he's going in the opposite direction. The man sneaks around like a dang barn cat after a mouse."

"Dad..." The lump in Sean's throat made speaking difficult. "If it's him... I'm sorry. I knew something was off and—"

"Don't." Justin's lips thinned as he sliced the air with one hand. "What's done is done. Just get to the bottom of it and make it right."

But as Sean strode out to the stables to meet his brother, fear that he was missing a crucial piece of the puzzle settled in his gut. He tried calling Mel's private line one last time but gave up when she didn't answer, and instead lifted the hood on Sandy's SUV.

Ryan and Joe arrived soon after he started. They must have double-timed it. Never much of a mechanic, Gus tended their horses.

The thorough inspection of every vehicle and piece of mechanical equipment on the ranch, including the helicopter, was a tedious process.

"Clean," Sean said, crawling out from under his own pickup. He stood, meeting his brother's eyes, noting they mirrored his own concern. "That's everything. So it looks like Ricky's was the only thing that got hit."

"I don't get it. If you're thinking about Northrop, why would he care about Ricky's ride?" Ryan leaned against the driver's side door of Sean's truck, stretching out his long legs.

"Walt said the brake tampering was designed to be a slow leak, so there's no telling when it was done." Sean rubbed his jaw. "He only drives it to work at the bar and to run an occasional errand."

Joe doffed his Dodgers cap and toyed with the hard brim. "Maybe his was just the easiest to get to."

"It's usually parked farthest from the house." Sean turned to stare thoughtfully at the trailer where Northrop had been staying.

"What if it didn't happen here?" Joe's eyes slid to Mel's Jeep, the only vehicle they hadn't checked, since it wasn't a ranch vehicle. "What if it was tampered with at Valentine's?"

"Son of a bitch!" Sean took off at a sprint. He was already under the Jeep, looking at the brake line, when a creak signaled the hood lifting, and splotches of waning autumn sunlight filtered to the ground around him.

He saw it almost immediately, the brake fluid leaking around the connection at the front of the vehicle. And right behind that, a small hole in the metal brake line.

Muttering several ripe curses, Sean slid from beneath the Jeep. One look at the faces of his companions, and he knew something else was wrong. "What?"

"Start it," said Ryan.

Slipping the key from his pocket, Sean did as he was instructed.

Joe pointed. "There it is. See how the lower hose is spraying fluid? It's been loosened, but it only leaks when the Jeep's running."

Ryan twisted the radiator cap and peered inside. "And already the radiator looks about half drained."

"Geez! If she'd been driving it..." Sean squeezed his eyes closed, visions of Mel driving along and then losing control of the Jeep flickering like an old movie reel through his brain. A vivid picture of that stretch of road where she had lost control and driven off the road filtered through, sending shards of ice to his heart.

With frenzied hands, he pulled out his cell and called the bar, actually grateful that the cook answered.

"She's still in the office," Charlie said. "I can check if you want."

"Charlie, listen to me. Call Blackstone. Get him to come over and tow your car back to his place and give it a thorough check."

"What's this about?" asked Charlie, mild alarm tingeing her voice.

"Someone tampered with Ricky's pickup," Sean told her. "That's why he broke down. And we just found the same tampering on Mel's new Jeep, so we're thinking it probably happened at the bar. We want to get your car checked out."

"I'll drive it over right now."

"No. Call Blackstone to come and get it. Don't drive it until you know it's safe."

He ended the call and met Ryan's questioning look. "I gotta go."

"I can tighten the hose and replace the brake line on this." Joe tapped the fender. "Save towing it to town."

Sean glanced over his shoulder but didn't stop his race to the truck. "Thanks, man."

Ryan caught up with Sean just as he reached his pickup. "You're thinking of Mel's original accident, aren't you?"

"Yeah." Sean shot his brother a level stare. "I am." He yanked open the pickup's door.

Ryan laid a heavy hand on Sean's shoulder. "Watch your back. We only know the brake line and radiator are good on your truck. We don't know if something else might have been tampered with." Ryan's fingers flexed. "I don't want to lose you."

Sean swallowed over the lump of emotion. He glanced into his brother's green eyes, saw his own looking back at him. He nodded once and pulled the door shut.

As Sean started the truck, Ryan held up a hand to stop him. His eyes held a speculative gleam. Sean rolled the window down and waited for Ryan's chuckles to subside enough to be able to speak.

"Hey, you know when we were kids how we used to crack jokes about the people driving around with pieces of coat caught in their doors?"

Sean frowned, unsure where Ryan was going with his question, but irritated by the delay. "Yeah, I remember. What the hell, Ryan?"

Ryan lifted a shoulder. "Yeah, we've all been kind of wondering that, too. But I'm gonna take a wild guess here that Mel wouldn't want you driving around town with her panties blowing in the wind."

Heat rolled into Sean's face. "What?" He opened the door and looked down, spotting a bit of pink satin and lace fluttering in the light breeze. Growling, he snatched it up and shoved it onto the seat next to him then slammed the door. He glared at Ryan, who hooted.

"Geez, Ry, grow up."

Ryan chortled and wiped tears from his eyes with the back of his hands. "*Me* grow up? I'm not the one apparently *doing it* in my truck. Now I know why you climbed in the window Sunday night." He took a deep breath and suppressed his laughter, but it remained just below the surface. "At least tell me you had safe sex."

The heat in Sean's face crept up a notch and he shifted uncomfortably. Unfortunately for him, his keen-eyed brother picked up on his discomfort immediately and choked. "What the hell are you doing, Sean? Did you miss the lecture?"

Ryan's hand was clamped firmly on the door of the truck. Unless Sean wanted to drag his brother along with him quite literally, he had no immediate escape. "Once. It happened that way *once*." Sean looked straight ahead, refusing to meet Ryan's gaze. "I gave Ricky the condom from my wallet and forgot to replace it," he mumbled. Sean huffed out a breath. What the heck? Ryan might as well know the whole story. "Turns out it was a good time of the month if you're trying to get pregnant."

Ryan sobered. His laughter died completely. "Whoa! Mel's *pregnant?*"

"No! That is, we don't know. Yet." Sean finally peeked at his brother, who was frowning in concentration. "Geez, man! You're doing the *math?*"

Ryan's wince became a sheepish look. "Sorry. And I'm sorry I teased you. I can see why you've been distracted."

Sean shifted again and looked away.

"Is there something else?" Ryan's voice was sharp.

"Not really."

Ryan leaned toward Sean and studied his face, and understanding dawned. "You're not worried. You want this?"

"That's the thing, isn't it?" Sean tapped his fingers on the steering wheel. Then he shrugged. "I don't *not* want it."

Ryan was clearly surprised. He scrubbed a hand down his face while he continued to study his brother. Then he dropped his other hand from the truck and stepped back. His eyes and his voice softened. "You need anything, you let me know, okay?"

And that *was* the thing, Sean thought as he pulled onto the main road. At some point in the past day or so, he'd gone from not caring to actively thinking in terms of what a baby would mean to their life together.

He set the hands-free on his phone and dialed Walt Blackstone. "Hey Walt, you still got Mel's old wrecked car?"

"Sure, I towed it out back until the scrap yard takes it next week."

"I need you to check something for me. I need to know if Mel's car was tampered with the way Ricky's truck was."

Walt's voice sharpened. "You got something going on, boy?"

"I don't know, Walt." Sean pressed down on the accelerator. "I don't know. But if DC's still there, tell him I'm on my way in and I need to talk to him, okay?"

Chapter Sixteen

Standing in the doorway of the office at Valentine's, Sean lost track of how long he'd been watching Mel sleep at her desk. Hunched over a notepad, she cradled her head in the crook of one arm. The pen loosely clutched in her fingers had tilted sideways and its tip had left a few red lines on one cheek.

He smiled. Had she been making one of the lists she loved so much? She sighed, and Sean held his breath. Maybe she was about to wake up. But she only resettled her arms and burrowed her face more deeply. The pen slipped from her fingers with a tiny clatter.

Sean entered the room for a closer look and noted a couple of balled-up pieces of paper on the edge of the desk, with another on the floor next to the trash can. He bent to pick up the one on the floor when he spotted another page, this one still on the notepad, with the outline of a stick figure. A very pregnant stick figure. A grin pulled at Sean's lips and he chuckled quietly, emotions swelling in his heart.

But then thoughts of Walt Blackstone's news intruded and Sean sighed. He didn't want to think about vandalized vehicles. He wanted to think of cozy nights and the prospects of a family. The reality of the danger Mel was in, though, meant he'd have to tell her in order to keep her safe.

He'd talked to Walt about the extent of the damage, while the state police had loaded Ricky's truck and Mel's wrecked car onto flatbed trucks. They'd been ready to go out to the ranch to pick up the Jeep as evidence, but he'd informed them the damage was already in the process of being repaired. That admission had earned him a steely-eyed stare, so he'd calmly dug out his cell and called Joe. The sabotaged parts would be saved and Mel would still have her vehicle. The state cop had shaken his head and muttered about compromised evidence.

Mel stirred again but still didn't wake up. Sean suppressed the urge to smooth back her curtain of sunshine-colored hair and kiss her awake. On top of the worry her brother was causing, Mel had been keeping up with her late night responsibilities in the bar. A twinge of guilt niggled at Sean. She'd also been getting up early with him when he left in the mornings, often going out to the ranch with him. Usually so full of energy, she must be exhausted to fall asleep at her desk.

He sighed and jammed his hands in his pockets. For now, he'd let her sleep. Content in the knowledge that he was sticking close and she was safe, Sean eased from the office, pulling the door closed. She'd be pissed off that he hadn't disturbed her, but Friday was one of the busiest nights of the week and to go into it already worn out couldn't end well.

As Sean passed through the main barroom, Ray Dan Beckley and his band, Cowboy Blue, were setting up equipment for the show later. Sean nodded a greeting to the musician. The band was good. They could probably make a go of it traveling or even cutting a recording. They were definite crowd pleasers, but they seemed satisfied to work their various day jobs and spend Friday and Saturday nights on the stage at Valentine's.

Charlie and Ricky were in the kitchen, prepping for the dinner rush.

Sean plucked a sliver of green pepper off a vegetable platter and bit one end. "Hey kid, whose ride did you borrow?"

Glancing up from chopping what appeared to be a hundred onions, Ricky made a sour face. "Sandy's."

Sean winced. Her mini SUV definitely screamed family rather than hot teenaged cowboy. "Why'd you draw that one?"

"Da— ah, Dad's idea. It's got an alarm system and GPS service."

Actually, the idea was genius. After Sandy had been caught in the middle of an old feud, she'd found herself pushed over a cliff in Justin's truck. The GPS tracking would have been helpful back then, and it had been a selling point when she and Ryan had bought the SUV in preparation for their baby. Sean had no further worries about Ricky getting home safely.

"Dad's usually on top of good ideas. So it might cramp your style, but you probably won't find yourself broken down on the way home."

"Oh, man, it's got a *baby seat* in the back." Ricky scraped the chopped onions into a plastic bin and moved on to cutting up lettuce for salads. His hands were sure and steady as he drew the knife through each head of lettuce twice then dropped the quarters into a bin before grabbing another head.

Sean's lips twitched. As far as he was concerned, that was just added insurance Ricky wouldn't be following in his own footsteps and *"doing it"* in the car. "You'll live. I think that's Dad's point."

Sean turned to Charlie. "Blackstone look at your car?"

Her hands faltered over the strips of chicken she was filleting. "He did. Everything checks out."

The tight band squeezing Sean's lungs eased some. He was glad Charlie apparently wasn't being targeted, but that left him wondering and worrying about the reason behind the tampering. Was it just a matter of opportunity, or had the vehicles been hit for a specific reason?

Charlie set her knife down, wiped her hands on her long white apron, and walked slowly around the counter. Her voice was quiet but firm. "Does this have something to do with Nick DeVayne or the fact that his son was in here yesterday?"

Sean jumped in surprise. He rubbed the back of his neck. "Mel told you about that?"

Charlie shot him a long considering stare, the kind that said she quite possibly knew more than he did about the situation and was trying to figure out how much to tell him. Finally she sighed. "No, she didn't say a thing. It only took one glimpse at the man for me to know he's Nick DeVayne's son. Not only looks like him but has the same arrogant, cocksure attitude."

Charlie steered Sean toward the door, her eyes sliding in Ricky's direction.

Catching the look, Sean nodded agreement.

"Justin hasn't said anything about this to you, has he?" she asked in a hushed tone.

Shock sent Sean rocking back on his heels. "My *dad*? What's he got to do with Nick DeVayne?"

A wry smile twisted Charlie's lips. "Very little, actually. He was already married to your mom, had Ryan, and you were on the way when Nick breezed through. But we'd all been friends since we were kids. Justin used to date Sylvia in high school."

"Wait, what?" Sean's jaw went slack. His dad and Mel's mom? He shuddered. Something felt significantly wrong about that arrangement. He didn't even want to think about their dating activities.

Charlie lifted one shoulder and let it fall. "And I dated Todd Mitchell before I met Henry. Orson's Folly's not that big a town."

Sean rubbed his eyes and dragged both hands down his face. Oh, hell, things were taking a seriously weird twist. Thoughts of his dad going on dates with Mel's mother, maybe even sneaking in the window when he came home after curfew — mind blowing.

"None of us were really involved with Nick. When he and Sylvia took up with each other, they spent all their time alone."

"Until he got her pregnant then left?" guessed Sean.

Charlie let out a wry chuckle. "Oh, he did so much more than get Sylvia pregnant." She sat on one of the bar stools.

Sean sat next to her but said nothing. Charlie was holding court, and she commanded his full attention.

"He got Sylvia involved in some hustling up in Jackson. She was in deep. Then she got pregnant and had a baby girl. That was Mel. Nick tried to sell Mel out from under Sylvia, had a buyer all lined up, but turns out she was an undercover police officer. Sylvia left Nick when Melanie was just a few days old, after he got arrested for trying to sell the baby on the black market. They thought she was involved. And because Nick had her so deeply wrapped up in the scams he was pulling up there, Sylvia almost went to jail. Justin and Beth went to your Grandpa Rushton for help, and they got her a good lawyer. She came home and stayed with her parents. Took up with Todd Mitchell — truth is, Todd had loved Sylvia since high school himself. I know *that* for a *fact*." A gentle smile lit her eyes. "Sylvia settled down real well with him. I think they were happy. He adopted her daughter and the rest of the story you know."

Any second his brain would explode. "Holy hell on fire. This is getting so f— ah, messed up." If DeVayne had been successful in selling his own daughter, Mel wouldn't be there, wouldn't be *Mel*! He ran a hand through his hair, shook his head, trying to clear it. "How much of this does Mel know?"

"I think she probably knows very little," answered Charlie with a tired sigh.

"What do you think her brother wants with her?"

Charlie shook her head. "I wouldn't be able to hazard a guess. But, Sean..." She sent him a look filled with warning. "It can't be anything good."

Sean slammed his open palm on the bar. "What is it with DeVayne and selling children?"

"Sylvia loved that girl. She might have stayed with DeVayne if he hadn't tried to sell the baby."

At the startled cry from behind him, Sean whipped around. Mel stood in the hallway leading to the office. Her face mirrored horror. There was absolutely no hope that she hadn't heard what he and Charlie had been talking about.

He leapt from the stool and crossed the distance between them, pulling her into his arms. She buried her face against his chest and rubbed it back and forth, obviously still waking up. The shudders tearing through her mirrored the ones assaulting his system.

"It's okay," he whispered. He smoothed a hand over her hair as he talked. "It's okay. He wasn't a good man. You already knew that. You're safe and he'll have to go through a lot of people to even get near you."

The lie made Sean physically ill. Someone had already gotten near her. Someone had tampered with her car, and she could have been killed. He had to tell her. But when?

Now. They had too many misunderstandings between them as it was. Over Mel's head, Charlie signaled that she was going to get back to work.

He leaned away from Mel but just a little. "Sweetness... can we go to your office and talk?"

In wide-eyed silence, she nodded.

He got the message loud and clear. *When will it all end?*

* * *

From the seat at her desk where Sean had put her, Mel stared in disbelief. "But I thought I just skidded in the rain."

Sean paced the room. "You lost control of the car but the skid wasn't caused by the braking. You had no brake fluid by then."

"They tried to kill me." Mel couldn't keep the tremor from her voice. Her composure was about gone. Struggling to stay in control, she studied Sean. He looked haggard, beyond tired. Her heart gave a jerk. He hadn't signed on for her crazy family problems. He was a rancher and a horse trainer. His life was supposed to be about cattle and horses, getting married and having a family. Building a legacy. It wasn't supposed to be about sabotaged cars and babies being sold. What had she dragged him into?

Abruptly Sean stopped pacing and swept a gaze over her, warming the ice flow in her veins. "Whatever you just thought about, don't think it again." He shook his head. "I love you."

How the heck had he picked up on her musing? Mel bit her lip to stop her chin from quivering. "But—"

"Now see, there's that look again. What are you thinking?"

Mel sniffed down the choking feeling in the back of her throat. Could she feel more miserable or pathetic? "I was only thinking that you didn't sign on for the kind of crap I'm bringing to your life."

He was at her chair in seconds. She barely even saw him cross the room. He knelt on the floor and laid his head in her lap. His arms slid around her and beneath her shirt to lock at the small of her back. One restless thumb stroked back and forth, sending vibrations along Mel's spine.

After a few breaths, he looked up at her. His face was a mix of love and torment. "Mel, you are my whole life. I've loved you from the time we were kids. I thought I'd lost you once. If I lose you again — now... it'll kill me." His hands flexed. "When you look like that, say things like that, it feels like you think you should disappear."

Shock waves rolled over her in alternate bursts of hot and cold. Her stomach performed flip-flops. He knew her better than she knew herself. She *had* been working herself up to taking her troubles out of his picture and leaving him behind. Panic entered his eyes, evidence that her thoughts were as clear to him as they had been to her.

"Sean, no," she whispered. "I do sometimes think I have more problems than you need in your life; that you deserve so much better than me. But... I can't let you go." She laughed softly. "I keep waiting for you to figure out that I'm so not worth all this trouble."

Relief washed over his features; a corresponding echo settled in Mel's heart.

"Mel." Sean's voice was soft. His eyes were filled with emotion. "There is no one better than you. No one. You're worth whatever it takes for me to be with you."

His hands traveled along her spine, and Sean moved up in the same motion, stopping to lay his face against her shoulder. Mel cradled him close, enjoying his warm puffs of breath on her neck. His spicy woodsy scent surrounded her in a comforting embrace as she breathed in deeply.

They'd see it all through, because neither one of them had a choice. A bond more powerful than time, distance, or the machinations of others had formed from the time they'd sat on a big boulder together as kids.

At a soft knock on the door, Sean stood and gestured for Mel to sit still as he crossed the room to answer.

Mel straightened her blouse with slow, precise motions, not particularly concerned about her rumpled state. However, she stood as soon as she glimpsed Charlie. The cook wouldn't interrupt unless it was for something critical.

"LeeAnn called in sick." Charlie's lips were tight, her mouth set in a straight line.

Yep, it was something critical. Mel sighed. "Okay, thanks for letting me know."

"I can stay late," said Charlie. "But I've never been good behind the bar." She gestured along her body. "Not sexy enough, I guess."

"Thanks, Charlie." Chuckling, Mel sent her an encouraging smile. "I don't want to interrupt your evening. I'll work something out."

The cook clamped her hands on her hips and narrowed her eyes. "Melanie Mitchell, if I didn't want to do it, I wouldn't offer. And you know it."

A warm sensation rushed Mel as her mama bear shook a finger at her. Even with Charlie's help, though, they'd have a hard time. "Okay, Charlie. As long as you're sure." They'd figure out something.

"Okay, then." Charlie backed out of the office.

Frowning, Mel looked over at the yellow notepad she'd been using to draft a help wanted ad. If only she and Sandy had decided to hire new help a week earlier. She blinked back tears that were as much from exhaustion as they were from frustration, but no amount of resolve seemed to still her quivering chin.

It took two to work the bar except on the slowest evenings. Without one person tending bar and another waiting tables, the customers couldn't be served on busy nights. Apparently she was about to let her partner down the same way she'd let down so many other people in her life. Sagging back in her seat, she blew a wisp of hair out of her face. So that was what a deflating balloon felt like.

"Hey, what's that look?" His voice one step shy of harsh, Sean stood by the door with his arms folded across his chest.

Mel had never seen him like that when he wasn't ticked off at her, and she blinked in surprise. "Please, Sean. I don't want to fight with you over this."

His attitude didn't change. "What do you think I'm angry about, Mel?"

"I don't know, maybe because I can't open short-handed tonight... I'm letting Sandy down."

"If you think I'm mad because an employee called out on short notice, you'd be right." He shrugged and stepped back into the room. "But if you think I'm mad at *you* because of it... well, then you'd be wrong. You and Sandy always spread yourselves thin here, but I figured it was something you had to do — for economic reasons."

"It was at first. Now... not so much. It's poor planning on my part."

"I'm not starting an argument. And I'm not mad at you because you have an unreliable employee. But, Sweetness, you look like you're about to throw in the towel over being short-handed. What's up with *that*?" Sean's gaze raked her top to bottom then came back up and settled on her eyes. "You used to look at stuff like this as a challenge." His voice softened. "I've never seen you back down from a challenge."

"I'm just — I'm tired, Sean. I can't think. I can't figure out how to make it work."

"I'll stay late," Ricky said from the doorway. "I know I can't serve alcohol but if I stay late, I can help with closing."

"No, Ricky." Mel cut him off with a slash of her hand. "We'll figure something out that doesn't include you driving home at two in the morning."

"He can come back to my house with me." Charlie returned to the office on Ricky's tail.

Mel looked from Sean to Ricky to Charlie and smiled at their obvious conspiracy to help her. Apparently Valentine's was holding an impromptu strategy meeting.

"I live right here in town," said Charlie. "If I have someone with me, it won't be so hard to go home in the dark."

Mel shook her head, but Sean nodded and she glared at him.

He shrugged. "I don't see a problem with that. As long as Ricky calls Dad. That leaves waiting tables and running the bar. Mel, if you can take the tables, I'll work the bar."

She began to voice a protest, but Sean cut her off again.

"The drinks are usually fairly straightforward here. I can pull a draft and pour a shot."

Mel stared. It was a simple plan, and it could work. "I'll have to do some quick training for the register and show you where everything is."

Sean indicated the door. "No time like now."

"Mel." It was Ricky, shifting from foot to foot. "Lynn's sister needs a job. She wanted me to ask you last week."

"Bertie Higgins?" Mel shuddered at the thought of the preacher's daughter working the bar. "I don't know. She'd be what, twenty-two or twenty-three now?" Mel chewed her lip. Then she shook her head. "No, I don't think so. Her father's liable to kill her and maybe me, too, if I hire her."

"Why not?" Sean spread his hands and divided his glance between Mel and Ricky. "She's a big girl, right? An adult? She needs a job and you need an employee."

Mel opened her mouth, her argument all ready, and then realized Sean made sense. "You know, she's a huge flirt."

"So she'll take home some good tips." Sean winked. *Winked.*

Mel felt a smile coming on, but she forced a frown instead as she struggled to imagine the preacher's daughter working at Valentine's, even on a temporary basis.

"We can kind of keep an eye on things, make sure they don't get crazy. Let her know you expect her to work, not go home with any customer for any reason." Sean shrugged again. "I know she seems flighty, but she's really got a lot going on in her head."

Mel huffed a breath and grimaced. "Okay, Ricky, give her a call. We'll see how it goes tonight, maybe tomorrow night, even if LeeAnn comes back."

* * *

It felt good to be working the floor again. Mel enjoyed being behind the bar, but that had always been Sandy's place. The regulars all had favorite seats, some at the bar itself, some at tables out on the floor. Working behind the bar, Mel had missed some of her favorite customers.

Roberta Higgins actually managed to surprise Mel. She was strikingly beautiful, at only twenty-two, with waist-length honey brown hair and an hourglass figure that she knew how to use to good effect on the male customers. She flirted just enough to get some great tips, but she was on top of the orders, delivered them quickly, and never mixed any of them up. In fact, she was better at the job before one night was out than LeeAnn had been after two months of employment.

Mel loaded her tray with a round of beer for a table of four just as Bertie arrived with a new order. She was flushed and grinning, obviously happy about something. But she was also looking a bit tired around the edges.

"Go ahead and take a break, Bertie," said Mel. "We don't have a break room but there's a place in the kitchen where you can eat. Order anything you want."

"Sure, just let me fill this one order." Bertie loaded the tray with a beer mug and a couple of mixed drinks. "Got a new arrival. Cute guy at the table by the door."

Mel smiled and allowed her eyes to follow Bertie's gesture across the room. Her breath caught in her throat. "I'll get that one. You go on your break before things pick up again, okay?"

Mel delivered her round of drinks and stopped back at the newcomer's table. "Hello, Denny. What do you want?"

Her brother looked up with a smile that didn't reach his dark eyes. "Mel. Friendly as ever."

She raised an eyebrow. "Just taking your order, Denny."

He looked around. "You're busy tonight."

"Which is why I'm taking your order and then walking away. I don't have time for chit-chat."

"Right. I'll take a house draft. But tell me one thing." The dim lighting made the glitter in his dark eyes a reflection of pure evil. "Have you had a chance to think about my proposal?"

"The one where I pretend not to know you so you can screw someone over?" Mel leaned over the table, forcing herself to look into Denny's daunting eyes. "Not going to happen."

He shrugged. "Suit yourself. I should tell you, I know where your baby went, and she's okay... for now. But she's just hitting that age where she'll be finding herself on the wrong side of her adopted *Daddy's* interest. You know all about what it means to have men look at you that way, don't you, Mellie? Only this guy... he does a lot more than look."

Bile rose in Mel's throat and she swallowed it back. Denny was messing with her. His use of that name and his tone of voice were no accident. Nick had spoken in the same falsely affectionate tone and called her by that innocent-sounding nickname every time he'd "caught" those older men attempting to cop a feel.

Mel couldn't fully suppress a shudder when she recalled the way those older men had raked their lewd glances over her tender body. They'd intended to do so much more than look, too.

What name had her little girl been given? Did she even have one? Would someone swoop in at the last minute to save her over and over? Did she have anyone at all?

Mel backed up a little. No! Denny *was* messing with her. He had to be. Somehow she managed to still her shaking. With supreme effort that she could only pray Denny didn't recognize, she injected a distinct chill into her next words, though she wanted to throw herself at her brother and beat the truth out of him. "What are you doing here, Denny?"

"Just making a deal." He stretched, leaned back in his seat like a jungle cat about to pounce. "I'm almost done here. No one'll get hurt if you don't say anything about who I am. Keep that to yourself so I can finish this job, and I'll give you all the information I have on your little girl."

Her mind screamed. *He's lying! He's lying! He's lying!* Her heart was going to explode. For her daughter's sake, she forced a calm demeanor, lifting a shoulder and affecting unconcern. "Tell me what you're running and I'll consider it."

"Like I said, just a shell game. Of sorts."

Her stomach threatened her again. She raised an eyebrow. "That's it? There's no money in the Monty."

He smiled without showing his teeth. "That depends on what you're using for a pea."

"What exactly *are* you using, Denny?" *Besides my daughter...*

He only shook his head. His face remained a mask. "The less you know, the better. Just trust me, keep your mouth shut, and no one'll get hurt."

"And if I don't? If I walk over to the phone and call the sheriff on your sorry butt?"

"So far no one's been hurt." Denny's smirk bared the tips of his teeth, deadly white fangs of the wild animal she knew him to be. "That's subject to change the second you bring anyone else into this. A damaged car is a minor inconvenience compared to what I can do to you and your new — family."

A chill rode in on the back of Denny's laugh and settled itself in Mel's gut. Her lungs struggled for oxygen and she trembled with fear. He noticed. She saw it in his eyes. But his next words confirmed it. "If you don't believe me, open your mouth. That sure is one pretty little girl your partner just gave birth to. Sure would be a shame for her to be hurt, or... stolen away."

Fury rose, replacing her fear, and the rage exploded, fueled by the memories of all the hurt she'd suffered with Nick and Denny. Her impotence to help herself and her inability to keep her daughter safe simmered in her core. If her brother could be believed, the child had been sold into a bad situation. Loathing for Nick DeVayne sent a haze of red through her mind. Mel forced a smile. Hatred would only threaten her ability to finish the con.

Denny had every reason to lie and no reason to tell her the truth about her baby's circumstances. But could she take that chance? And could she take a chance that he wouldn't somehow get his hands on Bethany? That had been a pretty specific threat.

With Denny's nonchalant mention of damaged cars, all sense of liberation from her old life was dashed on the rocks of his not-so-veiled threat toward the people she loved. Even as Mel glared at her brother, she knew the truth. Denny's words were no idle warning. Either she played his game or people would be hurt. Perhaps starting with her unknown daughter, but certainly not ending there.

Had she really thought he was inept and awkward at this game? She'd managed to trap herself. So what did that make her?

Mel flashed to the vision of her mangled car, of the way it had skidded off the road. She thought of Ricky's truck, how that could have been him losing his brakes and skidding, like her dad had, into a cliff. Her stomach turned. What if Todd Mitchell's accident hadn't been an accident after all? Or her mother's?

He knew he had her. A grin of triumph showed off his perfect white teeth before she'd made a conscious decision. "I've changed my mind. Don't think I'll have a drink after all." He stood and laid a fifty dollar bill on the table. "For your time."

Mel stood frozen as he walked out, staring at the bill he'd left. If Denny was throwing money around, he either had lots of cash or thought he was about to score a bundle. Given how invested he was in her silence, her bet was on the latter.

"What was Northrop saying to you?" asked Sean when she stopped by the bar to fill another order.

Mel shook her head, numbed by the encounter with Denny. She scanned the room, trying to figure out who Sean was talking about. He spoke again, but she barely heard him, didn't really register what he'd said. Fear filled her to overflowing. She had to tell him about Denny. Now. Mel drew a deep breath.

Sean set a mug of draft on her tray. "I'd love to pound the crap out of him before he leaves."

Mel blinked in surprise. Had he known what she was going to say? "He's not worth it."

Sean shrugged. "I don't know. It might screw up my contract, but giving him something to go home with other than Dev might be satisfying enough."

Mel set her tray on the bar and stared. "You lost me. Who are we talking about?"

Sean shook his head and chuckled. "Earth to Mel?" He pushed her tray away from the edge. "Dallas Northrop. The man you were having the conversation with."

No! No, no, hell-damn-it, no! Everything fell into place like lock tumblers. His latest job involved Sean and his family. And he was already close to them. Her heart settled somewhere in her throat as she tried to articulate. Breathing came in hot, tortured gasps.

"Sean, I—" She blinked, shook her head. Something was wrong.

The band's rhythmic beat began to fade into a dull thump in the distance. Sounds of clinking glasses and animated conversation echoed as her surroundings became an amalgam of disharmonic chaos. Sean studied her, concern etched into his features. His mouth moved but she couldn't hear his voice. Colors spun. Rainbow swirls shot out from the overhead lights, trailed in front of her eyes, then receded into nothing, consumed by the widening black holes in her vision. She pitched forward, became vaguely aware of Sean's hands on her arms.

Chapter Seventeen

"What the hell?"

With Mel's collapse into his arms, Sean's heart stalled. He lifted her and strode down the hallway to the office, where he laid her on the old leather settee. She was already stirring and he blew out a breath of relief as fear eased the squeeze on his heart.

"Sean?" Ricky stood in the doorway.

Without turning around, Sean took charge. "Have Bertie stand behind the bar. Mel never got to close out the register and there's a lot of cash in the till."

Mel rubbed her forehead and tried to sit up, but Sean pushed her back down.

"Easy, there. Don't try to sit up too fast."

"What happened?" Her voice sounded thick. Her eyes seemed to be focusing, though. She tried to sit up again and this time he helped her.

"You passed out." He kept a steadying hand on Mel's shoulder.

"That's ridiculous. I don't faint."

A harsh laugh slipped out. "Yeah, apparently you do. Do you remember anything?"

She shook her head and swung her feet to the floor. "Not really. Everything got kind of fuzzy. Then I saw you but you looked so far away." She grimaced and gestured around the room. "And here I am."

"I'm calling Doc Trent."

"That's not necessary. I'm just tired."

"Your other option is the hospital in Jackson. I'll drive you there myself."

"Oh, geez, no!" She touched him on the arm, speaking slowly and with force. "I'm just really tired. I'll be fine in the morning."

Sean was unconvinced. "You're pale and shaky." He touched her forehead, flinching at the feel of cool damp skin. "And clammy."

"I haven't eaten. That's all." She shot him one of her brilliant smiles. "Just get me something from the kitchen and I'll take my break now to eat."

He laughed without feeling it. "Oh, no. You're finished for the night."

Mel's sigh sounded like one of long-suffering.

Oh, yeah, he'd irritated her.

"Please don't tell me what to do."

He took in Mel's pallor with a growing sense of unease. She was exhausted and her eyes held a hint of trouble. Something was clearly bothering her. "What did Northrop say to you?"

Mel wrinkled her nose. "Who?"

"The guy you were talking to before you passed out."

"Oh, him." She shook her head and made a dismissive gesture with her hand. "Nothing, really. He asked if this was all the night life around here."

Sean snorted. That didn't surprise him in the least.

Charlie pushed open the door and came in with a plate. "Sorry, honey, we don't have much light food here. Got a club sandwich, easy on the tomatoes, just the way you like it."

"Thanks, Charlie. I'll be out as soon as I eat this."

Sean caught Charlie's look of concern and nodded. "I'll be right back," he said to Mel.

In the hallway, the noise from the bar was overpowering, so Sean slipped into the kitchen. Pulling out his cell phone, he punched in Sandy's number.

* * *

The sandwich helped fill the emptiness in Mel's stomach. It did nothing to ease the hitch in her soul brought on by the lie she'd just told Sean. Somehow she had to find a way to make things right — to protect Sean and his family and also find out what Denny knew about her little girl. But first she had to tell Sean the truth about Denny. What was she thinking, lying to him? Her brother wasn't going to play fair. Whatever scam he was pulling, it involved Sean, and that wasn't acceptable.

The band rolled into playing the last call song, and Mel frowned, checking her watch. They were still two hours away from closing. She stood quickly and moved toward the door, yanking it open to find a wall of muscle on the other side.

"Sean? What the hell's going on?" she demanded, speaking more sharply than he deserved.

"You're closing two hours early tonight." He was solidly in her way and apparently not intending to step aside. His hands clamped on her arms when she tried to slip by. Firm. Determined. Unmoving.

She wasn't going anywhere.

"Fine." She was too tired to fight a decision that had already been made anyway, so she stopped struggling and sagged against him. "Just tell me why."

"Sandy's orders." Sean walked her backwards into the office. "I told her what happened with LeeAnn — the girl's fired, by the way — and she likes the idea of hiring Bertie if she still wants the job. But the crowd is already thinning down, and it's not going to kill anyone to close two hours early."

She opened her mouth to speak and a yawn popped out. "You're right. I don't like it but I am tired." *Beyond tired.*

"Then you're going to like this next part even less." He kissed her, hard and quick. "We're going back to the ranch tonight."

"But I don't—"

He kissed her again, this time softer, lingering until she was certain she'd melt into a little puddle at his feet. "I don't want to leave you alone, but I have to get up early."

That would also put her out there, where her brother was apparently about to start something. Whatever it was, she could only hope to put a stop to it. So she shrugged and nodded her head. This was her opportunity to tell him about Denny. Mel drew a steadying breath. "Sean, I have—"

The door opened and Ricky walked in with the register drawer. "Band's packing it in. Mel, do you want this in the safe tonight?"

No, she didn't. Realizing her opportunity had slid on past for the moment, she motioned to the desk. "I'll bring it with us. I just need to get the bank bag. Thanks, Ricky."

Sean left with Ricky, and Mel decided she could wait until they were in the car. She slipped out of the office to find that Bertie, Ricky, and Sean had almost finished the nightly cleanup. Charlie had secured the kitchen. Their coordinated efforts rivaled those of an emergency team performing a disaster drill.

Mel slipped outside and stole up the stairs to her apartment to grab a change of clothing. A few minutes later, she exited, bag in hand, and made certain to lock the door behind her, though she was well aware that no lock would keep Denny out. Clouds hid the stars and she was certain she smelled an early snowstorm on the air.

Sean lounged at the base of the steps. He pushed off when she reached him and draped an arm over her shoulders, steering her toward his truck. "Ricky and Charlie are making sure Bertie gets home."

Mel felt like royalty as Sean settled her in the passenger seat. She chewed on the need to talk as he drove through Orson's Folly, past all the shops closed up tight, beneath the town's single flashing yellow traffic light. They finally hit the highway and Mel turned in her seat. He flicked a glance in her direction before returning his eyes to the road. Her heart swelled so full of love, her resolve to talk to him nearly crumbled like an old stone wall. She didn't want to break the mood, but...

"Sean—"

His cell beeped once. Sliding it from his shirt pocket, he pulled to the side of the road and answered. After speaking a couple of sentences Sean said goodbye and hung up. "Ricky got Charlie home okay but decided not to spend the night, so he's right behind us."

Mel sighed. "That's good. They've gotten close since Ricky started at Valentine's. I think she misses her kids and needs people to mother. It was nice of him to see her home."

"Ricky's a good kid."

"You love him."

In the light of the dashboard, Mel saw Sean's lips curve into a gentle smile. "Yeah, I do. But he doesn't like people saying that to him just yet."

"He'll get there. No one can resist your family."

A comfortable silence fell. *Now would be a good time to say something.* But she didn't. It was going to change everything and just for a few moments more, she wanted things to seem normal.

"How are you feeling now?" Sean asked after a few miles.

"Less tired and not hungry." She smiled over at him. "Thinking I wish we'd stayed at my place so we could... you know... cuddle and talk."

His chuckle made her toes curl in anticipation. "We can still... you know... cuddle and talk. Just in my room instead of yours."

Mel felt the heat flood her face. "Um, I... don't think so. Not in your dad's house."

"Really... because...?"

Mel's face flamed. Right, like Sean's family didn't already have ideas about them anyway.

"I can bunk in with Ricky tonight if that makes you feel better," suggested Sean.

She should have been relieved, but instead she felt instantly lonely. "You know, it really doesn't. I don't want to sleep alone ever again."

Of their own accord, the words had spilled out more forcefully than she'd intended. Sean glanced over at her.

"Hey, are you okay?"

Mel needed to talk. Now. But the words didn't come. She knew she couldn't trust Denny. More than likely, he would leave town without telling her anything at all about her daughter.

If he even knew anything.

But if she crossed him, she could be risking her child's life. When had she come to care so much?

And then she had to consider Denny's threat about the continued safety of Sean and his family, especially his insinuation that something could happen to Bethany. *What should I do?* Her breathing clutched as emotions seared an agonizing trail from her heart outward.

She caught Sean's movement as he turned to look at her and realized he was waiting for her answer. "I'm okay. How about you?"

He redirected his attention to the road ahead before he spoke. "You scared me tonight, Mel." He was direct, and even though he tried to cover it by speaking lightly, his voice carried an underlying tone of anxiety.

Unshed tears stung her eyes as her heart broke. She could cheerfully send Denny to play in hell with the devil for coming back into her life and putting such an impossible dilemma in front of her.

They turned onto the ranch driveway. This was it. Now or never. If Sean got mad and ended up bunking in with Ricky, then at least he would know the truth. He wouldn't be defenseless, and in the morning maybe they could figure things out.

"Sean, I need to tell you something..."

* * *

As they drew close to the house, the back of Sean's neck prickled. Whenever that popped up, the sudden feeling of uneasiness never failed to leave him disconcerted, mainly because that particular sensation was always associated with trouble of some kind.

The glow at the end of the drive wasn't normal. He squinted, struggling to make sense of it. It was far too bright to be coming from Northrop's luxury accommodations.

Mel touched him on the arm. "Sean, the man in the bar tonight. Dallas Northrop, he's—"

"Stables are on fire!" The words exploded out of Sean's mouth as he recognized the source of the light. He punched the gas on the pickup.

Mel's cry of distress echoed through the cab as he pulled his cell phone from his pocket and dialed for emergency assistance. He had to go through the motions even though he knew in his heart it was already far too late. As they flew past the main house, he laid on the truck's horn to alert the people inside.

"We have to get the horses!" Mel pushed her door open before they came to a full stop.

A pair of headlights barreled along the drive behind them. Had to be Ricky.

* * *

She'd left it too late. Mel's heart rose into her throat, pounding so hard she was certain it would blow up. Denny had made his move, and so much for his promise that no one would get hurt. Sean was about to race headlong into a blazing inferno.

Light from the main house spilled from the front doorway as four figures poured from inside. Ryan and Joe raced across the yard toward the blaze, followed by Sandy. Justin took up the rear, his faithful canine pal Patch nipping at his heels.

Denny's words about Sandy and Ryan's baby echoed through Mel's brain. "Go back!" she screamed at Sandy. "Go back in the house! Don't leave the baby alone."

"I'm the only one who can get Domingo out." Sandy was almost to Mel. Her steps faltered for just a moment, and then she began to run again.

Mel jumped into her path. "You have to go back! You can't leave Bethany. My brother is here, and he might be after her!"

Sandy skidded to a halt. "No!" Horror blossomed across her face. She glanced back at the house then cast a tortured gaze at the stable, where horses were screaming in fear. Everyone knew how much she loved Domingo, and Mel knew to abandon him would be agony for her friend, but Sandy clearly had no choice. She had to protect her child.

As Sandy whirled around and started back to the homestead, Mel shouted after her. "Take Justin with you. He shouldn't be out here — his heart!"

Sandy tugged on Justin's sleeve. Whatever she said convinced him. Once she was certain Sandy and Justin would make it back to the house and Bethany would be safe, Mel sprinted after Joe and Ryan as they ran toward the stable where Sean had disappeared.

Glowing gold smoke swelled from the doorway, breathing and billowing, like a genie just released from the bottle. The roar of the fire didn't quite drown out the piercing shrieks of the terrified horses. How many were in there? Where were they? Where had Sean gone?

The wooden structure hissed and crackled as it burned. Ominous groans issued from stressed timbers. Dark shapes began to boil in the center of the brilliance, and shadows took on the form of grotesque faces floating in the plumes. Mel's steps faltered at the doorway. The smoke stung her eyes and she lost track of where she was. Someone's hands yanked on her, hard, pulling her back away from the opening just as the doorway roared to fiery life and flames exploded over her head.

"Sean!" Her scream was lost in the howl of the fire. She tried to run in again, only to find it was Joe's hands on her, firmly tugging her back. She pointed to the stable. "Sean's in there — the horses—"

Ryan sprinted the last few steps toward the blazing building. For several heartbeats he hung in the doorway, a dark silhouette against the white-hot glow. Then he stepped over the threshold and was swallowed by the raging beast.

"They know what they're doing!" shouted Joe. "Sean knows horses and this definitely isn't Ryan's first fire."

Please, God... Please... Tugging out of Joe's grip, Mel pressed a hand to her mouth. She couldn't even finish the prayer... the words just kept repeating themselves in her head.

Flames licked out of the windows and curled over the roof. On a cloud of yellow haze, a shadowy figure emerged from the building.

Sean!

He led two horses. Mel ran forward and grabbed one of the leads.

"Lacey. Come on, baby."

Thrusting the other horse's lead into her hand as well, Sean disappeared back inside the inferno. Ginger squealed and struggled, pulling Mel up almost off her feet.

"Mel, this way!" Ricky called from the other end of the cow barn.

Spurred into action, Mel pulled the pair away from the burning building. Ricky tugged open the metal gate to the stock pen and helped her coax the horses through the chute and around the side of the barn into another pen.

She raced back, hoping to spot Sean, but instead found Joe and Gus pulling burning chunks of wood and hay away from the doorway with a pitchfork. More shadowy figures came through the door. This time Ryan led two horses. Mel recognized the older geldings, Buck and Galaxy. Grabbing the leads, she pulled the nervous animals across the alley to the other enclosure and turned the geldings into the same pen as Lacey and Ginger.

Ryan had disappeared again by the time she got back. Screaming and crashing sounds emanated from the interior of the stable, and Mel's pulse increased to heart attack level. The black smoke choked her. All around them, cinders and ash rained down. Flames framed the edges of the roof now.

The outline of the building was barely discernable in the clutches of the writhing, roaring monster consuming it.

The whole stable was going to cave in any minute.

Ryan stumbled out, coughing, looking disoriented.

Mel stared at the glowing orifice, watched the coiling tendrils of gold snaking into the night, and willed Sean to appear.

Joe yelled something to Ryan, but the fire's angry bellow drowned out his voice. Ryan shook his head and moved toward the door, jumping back as flames at the top of the doorway twisted out and up into the darkness.

Giant white flakes of snow began to drift downward. Blowing ash mixed with the fluffy flakes, forming swirls of snow and ash. It was impossible to tell which was which.

The fire was a wild, pulsing serpent now, its white heat singeing its way along Mel's skin. Sean was somewhere in the heart of that beast.

A huge shadow filled the doorway and Sean rode out on Domingo's back. The horse no sooner cleared the doorway than he reared and pawed his front legs. Sean's jacket was around the frightened horse's head, covering his eyes. As Sean rode him across the alley between buildings to the other enclosure, Ricky ran behind him.

The unmistakable sound of a horse screaming in pain and terror came from inside the conflagration.

"Dev!"

Mel dashed through the stable doors into her worst nightmare. Above her, hundreds of golden-orange vipers hissed and crept across the ceiling. Smoke stuck in her throat, tasting of burnt wood and hay. Mel fought for each breath. Incessant howling completely surrounded her. Dizzy with disorientation, she performed a slow pirouette, seeking some sort of landmark. What direction had she been traveling in?

The alarmed horse shrieked again, then again, and she pinpointed the direction. Mel felt her way along the heated wall toward the sound. Rhythmic thuds were sandwiched between screams as Dev kicked at the walls of his stall.

By the time she stood outside his box, Mel could barely make out more than a shadow. The frenzied horse reared and threw himself at the back stable wall. Mel shrugged out of her jacket and grabbed the lead from the hook on the stall door. When she touched the latch, searing pain assaulted her right hand and she screamed. The giant horse on the other side of the door answered her in kind.

Her heart thudded uncontrollably fast, but she tried to keep her voice soothing. "Come on, baby boy. Let me just snap a lead on you, and I'll get you out of here." She clucked her tongue and kept talking to Dev, unaware of exactly what she was saying, just making sounds that seemed to calm him.

She managed to get the lead on him but it took three tries. He tugged backward hard, shying away from each new lick of fire, obviously disconcerted by the hellish surroundings. Mel threw her jacket over the big horse's head and loosely tied the arms beneath his chin. One agitated foot kicked out, grazing her on the shin.

Sudden tears filled her eyes at the sharp stab of pain radiating upward. She limped toward the stall door, tugging the horse's lead.

"Come on, Dev. Come on, big guy."

He balked at the stall door, rearing blindly and shaking his head in an attempt to dislodge her jacket. She couldn't persuade him to move forward and she didn't have the strength to force the issue.

"Please, baby, you have to come out with me." Coughing, crying in pain and frustration, she had to keep trying. She wouldn't give up and let Dev die in such a horrible way. "Come on, big boy. It's okay. I'm here with you."

The burning in her right hand grew, began creeping up her arm. She kept glancing at it, expecting to find it engulfed in flames. Working with only her left hand wasn't doing it — she wasn't strong enough. But she couldn't make her right hand work to get it around the lead.

A large, soot-covered hand closed over hers. She'd know that touch anywhere: Sean, adding his strength and persuasion to hers. Together they managed to get the horse through the stall door and into the wide hallway. Flames reached for them from the walls, edged along the floor, chasing them out into the cold night.

It took both of them to get the agitated horse across the alley. Sean walked them farther down to a different enclosure before tying the lead firmly to the metal fence rail.

"He's the last one," Sean yelled over the roar of the fire.

The volunteer fire department had arrived. The building was a complete loss, so the battle turned to the task of protecting the other outbuildings.

Mel looked beyond the aging pumper truck and saw Denny skulking at the entrance to Dev's trailer. A snarl began low in her throat, and she ran at him, launching herself from about five feet, tackling him to the ground. Because she caught him by surprise, he ended up on his back. Mel punched him once with her left fist, then with her right, ignoring the molten waves of pain that shot into her arm, then slammed him again with her left. His nose gave under her last burst.

Then someone pulled her off him by the waist.

Sean shook her until she stopped fighting his grip. He shoved his face into hers. "What. Are. You. Doing?"

"This is my *brother*." Mel looked beyond Sean to where Joe was helping Denny to his feet. "He's Denny DeVayne, and he promised no one was going to get hurt." She pulled free of Sean's grip and approached the brother she loathed. "What are you doing here, Denny?"

"You weren't supposed to be here. You never close the bar this early. Why'd you change the plan? You were supposed to stay away tonight and keep your boyfriend occupied like you've been doing." He moved toward Mel, but Joe restrained him with a grip on one of his arms. "Why did you have to save that freakin' horse? You knew he was supposed to die. You knew the plan, sis. We can't collect on his insurance unless he's dead."

She stared at Denny, struggling for understanding. What was he saying? Another growl issued from low in her throat, and Mel tried to go after him again. Black rage took over, and she had no doubt that she would kill him. But Sean held her fast by the waist, her feet barely touching the ground. Denny aimed himself at Mel, but Joe yanked him backward, forcing some distance between them.

The red and blue lights of the sheriff's cruiser lit up the yard just as the first arc of water left the pumper truck to hit the raging flames.

* * *

Handcuffed and Mirandized, Denny sat in the back of DC's cruiser. His last taunt to Mel before the door closed on him was a slice into her heart.

"You didn't keep to the bargain, sis. Too bad. You'll never find your kid now."

"You working with him, Melanie?" DC's face showed a mix of professionalism and friendship. Mel tried not to hold it against him that he had to ask. After all, she had been more or less working with Denny by covering up his presence at the ranch.

"I knew he was in town, but I didn't know until tonight that he was pretending to be Dev's attendant." She shivered, more from nerves than the cold, although steadily falling snow stuck to her eyelashes.

"I'll take him in tonight." DC gave her a hard stare. "Why didn't you trust me, Melanie?"

Mel dropped her eyes and gave a half-shrug.

"I've gotta tell ya, girl," continued DC, "I have no choice but to question you tomorrow."

"Please." Mel laid an urgent hand on DC's arm. "I need to talk to him."

"You can see him tomorrow."

"Please," she repeated, desperate for answers. "He says he knows where my baby is."

The sheriff cursed under his breath. "Two minutes. And Mel, I'm standing right here, so anything I hear will go in my report."

She nodded, then yanked open the car door.

"Where is she?"

Denny turned to look out the other window.

"Bastard!" Mel screamed. She would have gone for him again but DC held her back. "Where is she? Where's my little girl?"

Her brother turned cold eyes on her. "You stupid, gullible bitch. You really believed I ever knew? Or cared?" His insane laughter blasted into the night, and DC gently pulled Mel away from the car. With a flick of his wrist, he slammed the door.

"I'll see you tomorrow, Mel. We'll try to sort through the bull. I know I don't have to tell you not to leave town." He tipped his hat and got into the cruiser.

Mel fell to her knees as the car drove off. Tears rolled freely. She'd been such a fool to trust Denny even a little bit. At the cough from behind her, she looked over her shoulder. Sean watched her, his eyes frozen chips of jade. She rose slowly and walked to where he stood.

"I'm sorry. I should ha—"

"Don't," he snapped. "Don't talk to me with more excuses and rationalizations tonight, Mel. I've had about enough of your lies and schemes."

He pivoted on one heel, presenting her with his back as he moved off toward the horses. Ricky and Ryan were already leading them into the extra stalls in the cow barn.

Mel stared after him as he became a shadow moving amid the smoke from the still-glowing stable. Bursts of flame shot from the blackened ruins, but were quickly drowned by water from the pumper. The rumble of a large engine drew her attention to the driveway as another pumper truck rolled up. The side was emblazoned with a gold crest and the words *Oslow Volunteer Fire Department*. Two pickups followed the truck in, neighbors most likely. The cavalry arriving in force.

She gazed across the yard. Sean had blended into the background. If he was one of the figures scurrying about leading horses or stomping pop-up flames, she couldn't tell which.

Ice settled in her gut. She hugged her arms around her waist and shivered. Sean hated her. And he had every right to do so. Because of her, he'd nearly lost everything. And she'd lost him.

A leather jacket was laid over her shoulders, and she snuggled into its warmth, but it did nothing against the chill inside. When she looked up, she found herself under the regard of Joe's soft golden eyes.

"He was scared he'd lost you tonight."

She shook her head. Her own voice sounded small to her ears. "No. That's not it. I let him down. He thinks I did this — caused it. He thinks I was helping my brother." Mel didn't bother stemming the tears.

Joe steered her toward the house. "Let's get you inside and cleaned up."

Chapter Eighteen

"The bank bag's in Sean's truck," mumbled Mel as she sank into a chair at the kitchen table. "I forgot about it when we saw the fire."

"I'll take care of it." Sandy laid a light blanket over Mel's shoulders. "Your arms are like ice."

"She's in shock." Justin set a cup of steaming black coffee in front of her. "This'll help warm you."

The dark liquid sloshed against the edge of the cup. Mel's unsettled stomach echoed the sentiment. Bile rose in her throat and she pushed the cup away a little too violently. Some of the contents sloshed over the edge. "I'm sorry." Mel tried to rise so she could clean up her mess, but Justin settled a hand on her shoulder and gently shoved her back into the chair.

Sean's father crossed to the sink and grabbed a sponge, quickly dabbing the spilled coffee.

"I-I'm sorry. I c-can't drink that." Mel rubbed her forehead with her left hand. "Can I just have some water, please?"

Sandy set a tumbler of water on the table. Mel reached for it, winced when she made contact with the glass, and quickly switched hands. She laid her right hand in her lap, keeping it out of sight.

"You're hurt. Let me see." Sandy's voice was sharp and firm.

Reluctantly, Mel eased her hand out from beneath the table.

Sandy turned the palm up and cried out. "When were you going to get this taken care of?"

For the first time, Mel looked at the hand causing her so much pain. The skin of her palm was white and ragged; it wept clear fluid with areas of blood showing in patches beneath the torn skin. The outer edge of her thumb was angry and red with a line of pale blisters extending toward her wrist.

"It's nothing," she murmured, trying to reclaim her hand.

Sandy held on firmly. "Mel, these are deep second degree burns, maybe even some third."

"You're an EMT. Can't you just bandage it for me or something?"

Sandy turned the hand over, shaking her head. "You have to have these looked at in a hospital. How did this happen?"

"The latch on Dev's stall. I had to open it and it was hot."

"Does it hurt?"

"Just a little. It's no big deal."

"Burns like these are dangerous." Sandy moved to the storage area and brought out the medical kit. "If you get an infection, you can actually lose your hand."

Mel shrugged. What did it matter, anyway?

"I'm going to clean this and then it's the hospital for you." Sandy looked over her shoulder at Joe. "Go get Sean. Tell him he needs to take Mel to the emergency room."

"No!" Mel nearly shouted the word, then felt foolish as everyone turned to look at her. "He's busy seeing to the horses. I'll take myself." After all, she'd taken care of herself for years with no help — proof she needed no one.

Sandy laid out the items she would need: sterile saline, medicated gauze, a basin. "Mel, he's going to want to know."

With a sad little laugh, Mel shook her head. "Trust me. He won't."

Joe eased his way out of the kitchen, and Mel shook her head. They'd find out. And when they did, maybe they'd blame her, too.

Sandy spread her fingers apart, putting stress on the burnt tissue, and Mel moaned. Too bad her hand couldn't be as numb as her emotions. Sandy tipped the irrigation bottle. Cool sterile saline flowed over the burns, first stinging then soothing. Mel buried her face in the crook of her other arm while Sandy worked on her injuries.

* * *

Standing alone in the night, Sean could only watch as the stable burned itself out, taking everything he'd worked for with it. He turned at the sound of his name and watched Joe's approach.

"Sandy sent me out here. Mel needs to go to the hospital."

Sean's already tilting world threatened to shatter completely. Mel had looked just fine when she'd walked up to the house with Joe. Multiple disastrous scenarios rolled through his brain in the space of one heartbeat, at the forefront the possibility of her pregnancy.

"What..." He cleared his throat. "What's wrong?"

"Second and maybe third degree burns to her right hand." Joe's voice was calm but his face reflected urgency.

Mel's betrayal, so recently revealed, stung deeply. Sean didn't want to hear her rationalizations for why she'd chosen to work with Dennis DeVayne, AKA Dallas Northrop. The fact was, she'd kept it from him that her brother was the man staying at the Cross MC. The man who'd set fire to a stable filled with horses, apparently in an attempt to kill the heavily insured horse he'd brought with him to the ranch.

As he looked over at the blackened, smoldering remains of the building, wisps of flames still occasionally sputtered, only to be put out by a blast of water from the volunteer fire department's pumper truck.

Everything he'd been trying to build, for himself, for them... just gone. And Mel might as well have lit the match that had taken it all away.

"I guess it's a good thing she's left-handed, then." Bitterness welled inside, spilling over into Sean's voice. "I'm busy here. She'll have to find someone else to take her."

"She doesn't want to go at all." Joe jutted his chin out. "Sandy's hoping you'll convince her."

A wild need to run to the main house and see her, take care of her, rose but he squashed it. Shrugging, he turned back to the ruined stable. "That would be her choice, then, wouldn't it?"

"No, I'm not sure it is," Joe said, disapproval heavily lacing his voice.

Sean refused to look at him. After a few heartbeats, he glanced over his shoulder. Joe was halfway back to the house.

Good.

"Sean?" Ricky's uncertain voice came from the darkness. How long had he been standing there? He stepped into the blue-white yard lights, head angled in query. "What's wrong with Mel?"

With an impatient wave of his hand, Sean blew off the concern. "Nothing, just a couple of burns."

"Joe said she has to go to the hospital."

"So?" Sean lifted a shoulder. "She'll find someone to take her."

Ricky's eyes went wide. "What's up with you?"

"I can't take her." He shrugged again. "I have work to do here." Putting a decisive end to the conversation, Sean moved toward the smoking ruins, seeking Ryan. His brother was in that mess somewhere performing mop-up with the VFD.

"What happened, Sean?" Ricky's voice challenged across the distance between them. "You got in her pants and now she doesn't matter as much?"

Red clouding his vision, Sean froze. Whirling around, he stalked back to the teenager. "You don't know what you're talking about."

"I know you say one thing and do another." Ricky's hands were balled into very effectual fists. "So what's the deal? Isn't she as good in bed as you thought she'd be? Not a good enough lay for you?"

Sean's hands clenched, but he kept his mouth clamped shut.

"One screw and you're through?"

It was one taunt too many. Snarling, he swung on the kid.

But Ricky was young and quick, and he ducked to the side. He bobbed in the other direction on Sean's second swing. Then he stepped back a pace.

"I've been dodging fists my whole life." His blue eyes glittered. "Never figured I'd have to dodge them *here*." Casting a look of revulsion in Sean's direction, Ricky whirled and stalked toward the house.

He couldn't have scored a more direct hit if he'd actually thrown a punch.

Bile pushed into Sean's throat as the rest of his world began to crumble away in chunks. "Where are you going? We have work to do," He managed to shout at Ricky quickly retreating back.

"I'm going where *you* should be going, *big brother!*" Ricky called over his shoulder without stopping. "To the hospital with *your* girl."

* * *

The nerve block was wearing off, and with it went the pleasant numbness. Mel inhaled sharply as the nurse finished wrapping her hand.

"I'll be right back with your discharge instructions."

"You need something for the pain, girl?" Justin stood next to her, a fierce protector.

"I'm good." There was only one thing that would take her pain away, and Mel was pretty sure Sean wasn't going to show up. "What time is it?"

"Eight a.m.," said Joe, currently slumped in a chair near the door with his eyes closed, but apparently not sleeping.

Ricky, Joe, and Justin had taken turns sitting with her through the night while a plastic surgeon had examined her and then cleaned and treated her wound. Ricky had often been sent on coffee runs for Joe and Justin, though Mel suspected that was more to spare him from seeing the ugly wound or hearing her moans than because they actually wanted more hospital swill.

"I'm keeping you from the ranch."

Justin snorted. "It's not going anywhere."

The nurse returned with discharge papers just as Joe's cell phone beeped. Mel watched his face as he answered it, looking for a sign that maybe it was Sean calling to check on her.

"Are you sure?" he asked, his voice sounding dubious. Then he left the room.

Paperwork and prescriptions in hand, Mel was beyond ready to leave. But when Joe returned to the little room, the look on his face told her something else had happened.

"I need to talk with you a minute before we get going."

"Ricky and I can go get your prescriptions filled." Justin picked up the paperwork and they left the room.

"Mel, that was Ben Jamison on the phone." Joe urged her to sit on the edge of the bed again. "He found your father."

"Nick? Denny said he died last April."

Joe slowly shook his head, his kind tawny eyes holding hers.

"He lied? Of course he did. He doesn't know what truth is." With her stomach tying itself into knots, Mel knew she wasn't going to like the rest of the story. "Where is he?"

Joe ran a hand through his thick brown hair and swallowed before looking back at her. "Right here in Jackson. In a state-run nursing home. Right in this complex, in fact."

"Nursing home!" Mel was suddenly glad she was sitting.

"He's in the advanced stages of liver cancer and probably doesn't have long to live."

Why would Denny have told her Nick was dead?

To keep her away from him so she would think Denny was the only way to find her daughter. And she had walked right into the trap. Mel wished she could say she was sorry, but she found herself with no sympathy. "Is he— can he have visitors? I need to ask him..."

"Mel, I'm sorry." Joe looked away, drew a deep breath then met her eyes again. "The cancer has caused dementia. He doesn't even know who he is. He probably won't remember anything about your daughter."

"Oh." Mel bit her lip, trying to push back the disappointment.

"She has to try!" Ricky stood in the doorway. His face showed intense emotion. He glanced at Justin's stony expression and tempered his tone. "I'm sorry. I didn't mean to eavesdrop. I don't know the whole story, Mel. But if you have a little girl somewhere, you have to try to find her."

Justin laid a hand on Ricky's shoulder. "I agree with the boy. She'll never know if she doesn't try."

As one, all three men looked at Mel. She nodded. "I want to see him."

* * *

Sean kicked a piece of burned wood. A twisted piece of metal that had once been a horseshoe was still nailed to it. He picked it up and ran a finger over the blackened metal. Warmth still radiated off it, as though it were alive but dying. They'd been kids when Ryan had nailed it up above the doorway. It was supposed to have been for luck. *Yeah, right.* Sean's lips twisted into a grimace as he pitched the damn thing onto the scrap pile. The dull thud it made was

the echo of his dying dreams. It had brought luck, all right...
bad luck.

Weak sunlight flashed off his watch as he checked the
time. Almost nine. His body screamed for rest, but he kept on
moving. Watering and feeding the stock. Checking the
horses. The vet would be out later to make sure, but
miraculously, they all seemed to be in one piece with no
major injuries. Even Dev, though the fire had sent his
disposition issues over an edge he might not return from.

Ryan helped with cleanup, but Ricky and Joe were
still in Jackson with Mel. For the third time in fifteen
minutes, Sean checked the call log on his cell. Nothing. No
one had called to tell him how Mel was.

Mel hadn't called to let him know she was okay.

What if she wasn't okay?

"Hey, here's a novel idea. Why don't *you* call *her*?"
Ryan stood on the other side of the ruins, staring at Sean
with a knowing look.

"Maybe because I don't care."

"That's not true," said his brother. "Why don't you let
her explain?"

Sean shook his head. He kicked at another board.
"There's nothing to explain. She lied about her brother. She
knew he was here, pretending to be someone else, and she
didn't say anything."

"Ever consider she may have had a reason?" Ryan
picked up a charred board and tossed it onto the growing
pile.

Sean shook his head, picked up the two-by-four at his
feet, and pitched it on top of the pile. What were they doing
there anyway, sifting through the charred remains of his
worst nightmare? Nothing would be salvaged. He gestured at
the mess of black and gray surrounding them. "There's no
reason good enough for *this*."

Except... maybe Mel had thought there was. He
couldn't stop replaying her voice in his head when she said
she'd do anything to make sure her daughter was okay.

"If you think she burned the stable down, you really
are an idiot."

"I know she didn't burn the freaking stable, Ry." Sean kicked another blackened board. "She was with me. The perfect alibi. You were there. You heard what Northrop — *DeVayne* said. She was in on her brother's scam, knew what he planned to do." He stopped to take a deep breath then continued through gritted teeth. "She was supposed to keep me busy and away from the stable last night."

"Well, she didn't do such a good job of that, did she?"

Sean's retort was interrupted by the beep of his cell. Turning his back on his brother, he activated the screen, quelling his disappointment when he saw the number for the sheriff's office.

"Some folks in here want to speak with you," said DC.

"Mel?"

"Nope. Far as I know, she's still in the hospital with bad burns to the hand," said the sheriff. "You got the state police, feds, and representatives from the California Racing Commission and California Thoroughbred Breeder's Association all wanting a statement from you about DeVayne. They want to inspect the horse in question, too. Thought I'd give you a heads-up they're heading your way."

Sean's lips twisted and he chuckled without feeling any humor. "Outstanding. Send 'em on."

* * *

Nick DeVayne had never led a particularly healthy lifestyle. Even when Mel had been with him, there had been nothing robust or fit-appearing about him. But her memories of the chain-smoking, booze-drinking, too-skinny man who was her biological father did nothing to prepare her for the wheezing, wasted human wreck lying in the hospital bed.

Dark veins showed through pasty yellow-white skin which draped over prominently pointed bones. An oxygen tube was clamped to his nose. Even lying very still seemed to take too much energy. The room stank of vomit and urine. It was a room filled with death and decay; a room where no hope could possibly survive.

And yet... Mel was desperately in need of just a glimmer of that commodity.

Trembling so hard she staggered when she walked, Mel stepped through the door and stood at the foot of the bed. The man lying before her barely resembled the father who'd tormented her. If she hadn't been told he was Nick DeVayne, she'd have passed by without recognizing him.

"Nick?" She spoke softly, though she wanted to scream at him, force him to wake up and give her the information she needed.

"Huh? Who's that?" He opened his eyes and squinted at her. The sclerae were deep yellow and muddy appearing. "Who're you?" His voice sounded rough, like he'd just come off a month of hard drinking and four-pack-a-day smoking. His words were slurred but Mel couldn't tell if that was because of his current mental status or because he was missing most of his teeth.

"It's Melanie," she said, keeping her voice quiet.

"Melanie, huh? I need more ice chips."

Joe picked up the white cup sitting on the bed tray and walked out.

"Do you know who I am, Nick? I'm Melanie, your daughter."

"Yep, I had a daughter named Melanie once. Ran out on me like her no-good mother did." He punched a button and the bed began to move up into a reclining position. He peered more closely. "So you're her?"

"Do you remember you came to Orson's Folly to get me when I was just a little girl?" Melanie swallowed hard as the memories assaulted her.

"Yeah, I remember you. Should have left you where you were. Always more damn trouble than you were worth."

Joe re-entered the room and placed the cup of ice chips on the tray in front of DeVayne. The sick man popped one into his mouth and sucked on it like hard candy.

"Do you remember the things that happened when I was with you, Nick? The things you made me do to make other men like me?"

"I remember you were no good at any of it." A wheeze that might have been a half-assed laugh squeaked from between his chapped lips. "And that you let one of the marks get you knocked up."

Mel gritted her teeth. No point in arguing with him. She'd let Nick believe that to protect Glenn and saw no need to disabuse him of the idea. No need to confront her past drove her. She had sought her father out for only one reason: to find out what he'd done with her baby. "Nick, when I had the baby, you took her away. You were going to sell her. Do you remember who you sold her to?"

His mad chortles sounded even more insane than Denny's had. "I didn't sell the brat. You were so useless, you couldn't even birth a baby right. Thing stopped breathing and turned blue. No way I could sell *that*."

Breath backed up in her lungs, and Mel grabbed the end of the bed to keep from falling. Then Justin was at her side, his arm around her waist, helping her steady herself.

"What's this?" DeVayne pointed a bony finger at Justin. "He your latest mark? He's old enough to be your father."

"And he makes a better one than you ever did to either me or Denny." Drawing strength from Justin, Mel squared her shoulders. "I want to know where my daughter is. What did you do with her?"

DeVayne laughed again. "That's what I'm saying. You don't *have* a daughter, girlie. You even screwed up a simple thing like having a baby. We were on the way to the man who was going to buy her when she stopped breathing. We left your *dead baby* in the trash at a rest area outside Oklahoma City." Laughter and wheezing merged once again, and he started coughing. "All these years you thought you had a little piece of yourself out in the world?" More laughter and coughing echoed after her as she stumbled from the room. "Hey, you see my boy, you tell him to stop in."

In a flash of vindictive rage, Mel whirled and stepped back across the threshold. "Your *boy* won't be coming to see you. He's been arrested. And whatever he's charged with... I plan to make sure it sticks to his repulsive, selfish hide."

Squaring her shoulders, she turned and walked out, ignoring DeVayne's pleas for an explanation.

Flanked by Justin on one side, Ricky on the other, Mel walked out of the building knowing she would never return. Shock chilled her and her steps were automatic. She blinked in the harsh midmorning sun. Remnants of snow from the night before lay glistening where the gardens edged the sidewalk. Mel saw them and pictured the cold, lifeless body of her child.

"All these years," she said softly, to no one in particular, "I thought of her as happy and loved. And all this time, she was dead." Her stomach quivered with memories of feeling her baby girl moving within, and a sob slipped out. She looked at Joe. He was blurry through the tears in her eyes. "She wasn't even buried or mourned. He just dumped her in the trash."

As they got to Joe's four-door pickup, she dimly registered that her three protectors suddenly seemed uncomfortable. After a couple of tentative false starts, Justin placed a hand on her arm and pulled her into his embrace, cradling her head against his chest.

"Aw, girl, I'm sorry. None of us thought we'd find this at the end of the search."

It was just one more loss. And it hurt that it was Sean's father holding her and not her fiancé — if he *was* still her fiancé. It hurt that he'd listened to the things her brother had said the night before and apparently believed them. Believed she was capable of doing anything that would hurt him, especially something like keeping him distracted so her brother could burn a stable filled with horses. Believed such a vile thing without even considering the source of the accusations.

She couldn't deal with him now. If he got over it, figured out he'd been wrong... maybe. But he hadn't been able to hold her gaze the night before. The look in his eyes just before he'd turned away from her had been a combination of hurt and hatred, and Mel hadn't known where one left off and the other began.

"Take me home, please." Her brittle-sounding voice shattered the uneasy silence. "Take me to my place in town. I don't want to see Sean."

She curled up into a ball on the back seat of the truck. Ricky sat next to her, his eyes soft with caring.

When they reached her apartment, Mel thanked them automatically and climbed slowly from the truck.

Justin hugged her hard. "It doesn't feel right leaving you here, girl."

"I'll be okay. I promise. I just want to be alone to do some thinking." She kissed him on the cheek. "Thank you for everything."

As she started up the stairs, a car turned in to the parking lot. Charlie. Mel had nearly forgotten they would be opening soon. So much for her alone time. Charlie stopped to talk to Justin. As Mel watched, Justin said something that made Charlie laugh. She laid a hand on his arm and looked up at him, her eyes sparkling. Justin seemed to go seven shades of red at the contact.

Mel turned away, unwilling to let the bite of her tears interrupt such a sweet moment. She was just at the top of her steps when Ricky hailed her.

"I'm staying to work my shift. Miss Charlie and I will be in the kitchen if you need anything."

Mel waved and nodded. They wouldn't leave her completely alone, but they would let her have her privacy.

* * *

"You sending for the medical record on Devil's Advocate raised a few flags, Mr. McGee." Carlton Windsor was tall and slender, somewhere in his forties. He'd identified himself as being with the California Racing Commission, investigating possible fraud.

He seemed to be the spokesman for his two companions, Michael Martin, a sixty-something balding man with the California Breeder's Association and FBI agent Julia Bronson, a slender woman with wavy auburn hair that fell almost to her waist. She looked like she should still be in high school, not investigating a case of fraud for the FBI.

The mess Mel and her brother had started was passing headache status and heading strongly for a royal pain in the ass. Sean led the trio to where he'd stabled Devil's Advocate. How long had Mel known what was going on? How deep was she in the game? The horse had sure responded to her the times she'd been out visiting.

As though he'd known her.

Sean's brain kept replaying how Mel had taken pains to tell him some of the specifics about her life of grifting. She'd stressed more than once that she had been part of the DeVayne family unit.

"I haven't had a chance to read through his medical records," Sean explained as they walked past the burned wreckage. "They only came in yesterday, and we had the fire last night. Thing is, though, I can't imagine racing this horse at all, let alone seeing him with so many wins. He's got such a severe case of bench knee, it's a wonder he hasn't broken bones."

Devil's Advocate hated the racing officials on sight. Ears back, he reared and kicked, threatening with his teeth.

"Sorry." Sean pulled a lead from the wall and moved into the roomy box. "North— that is, DeVayne tranqed him to haul him here, and he never has had a good temper that I've seen. The only person he flat-out hated more than this was DeVayne himself."

After several tries, Sean was finally able to clip the lead in place. He calmed the horse enough for the officials to take pictures, check his conformation, and check his mouth tattoo.

"Tat's been altered. One of the threes has been changed to an eight." Windsor spoke softly, but whether he was trying to keep the horse in a calm frame of mind or if he cared about the animal's feelings, Sean couldn't have said. Windsor read the number off while Martin entered it into a hand-held electronic device.

"That the real number?" asked Martin.

"Yeah." Windsor stepped back and out of the paddock. Pulling a folder out of his briefcase, he opened it and showed Sean the top picture. "This is Devil's Advocate at his last win, the Santa Anita Derby last April."

It took Sean less than a minute to spot the differences. "Good conformation, well-aligned front legs. Deeper chest. Looks about the same height and he has the same shape to his head, though. Color's a bit lighter but that could be the lighting in the picture. Might be more even, too, but it's hard to tell with this guy's burns."

"Comes back as Dark Angel's Opportunity," said Martin. "Never-starter, different dam, same sire." He looked up and met Windsor's eyes with a pointed look. "Los Mirabelle Stables."

"That's the owners I've been dealing with," said Sean.

Chills ran down his spine in waves that settled in the small of his back. His profitable gig had just become a huge fraud and conspiracy case. How deeply in was Mel? Could he protect her if it came down to that?

Would he? He tapped his fingers against the side of his leg.

"I need to ask you some questions, Mr. McGee." FBI Agent Bronson finally spoke up.

Sean sighed. *This isn't going to be good.*

"Will you be filing an insurance claim?" asked Agent Bronson, opening a small black notebook.

Sean pulled in a long breath and puffed out his cheeks. "Yeah, I suppose we will. I'm only part owner of the Cross MC, though the horse rehabbing is solely my venture."

"You've had trouble here on the ranch before." It was a statement, not a question, and it raised Sean's hackles.

"That was a totally unrelated matter."

"Yes." She lifted her head from her notes and regarded him with a measuring stare. "I was just thinking that trouble does seem to find you."

"Not by choice, I assure you," said Sean dryly.

She looked at her notebook again. "Los Mirabelle Stables contacted you, Mr. McGee?"

"Yeah." Sean frowned, trying to remember the name of his contact. "A Mr. Hector, I think his name was. But I've been dealing with Enrique Chavez since. I gather they're partners."

"Do you know why they contacted you, Mr. McGee?"

"Me specifically?" Sean shook his head. "No. But there are only a handful of accredited horse rehabilitation facilities in the United States, and I've got a high percentage rate for psychological rehab."

Agent Bronson tilted her head back and stared him down. "You have no idea how much like a scam that sounds to me."

Sean stepped back and looked the tidy agent up and down. Everything about her screamed city. "Don't know much about horses, do you, Agent Bronson? You want to look through my records? Am I being accused of a crime here for taking on what I thought would be a simple paying job?"

"Actually, it's your relationship with Mr. DeVayne's sister that's raising my concern." The agent consulted her notebook again.

Sean breathed in sharply. His stomach flip-flopped like a beached fish. He instilled a necessary chill into his voice. "My fiancée has been estranged from her family for several years, which would include her brother."

"You're sure about that?" asked Bronson. "He says he's been in touch with his sister for several months now. We found letters to her saved in his computer files. Sheriff Cooper has corresponding letters to her in physical custody, which he stated he got from Ms. Mitchell."

Mel's explanation floated through Sean's memory. *This is a paper trail... deletes from the computer... ditches the computer...* Only Denny hadn't killed the trail. Why not? Had he kept it alive for insurance? And if so, insurance for what? To control Mel? Had he been concerned she'd double-cross him?

Agent Bronson's voice startled Sean back to the current conversation. "Mr. DeVayne claims your organization was chosen because of his sister's relationship with you, and he has implicated both Ms. Mitchell and you in this scheme."

"That's ridiculous. Mel would never get involved in anything like this." Even as he bit off the words, Sean wished he believed them.

"What about you, Mr. McGee?" Bronson turned another page in the notebook. "Did you really only request the medical record for Devil's Advocate because you suspected something was wrong? Or were you going to rehab this horse into his brother?"

"Well, now, that would have been impossible, Agent Bronson." Sean crossed his arms over his chest and met her accusing stare with a measure of defiance. "Because you just can't take a horse's benched knees and make 'em straight."

Her two colleagues exchanged pointed glances then Martin nodded. "He's right. Horse should have been put down as a foal if his knees are benched."

"I guess that would be the point of losing the horse in a fire, then, wouldn't it?" she fired back. "If you discovered you couldn't fix him."

Sean cocked his head and flipped her a half smile. "Except we didn't lose *any* horses in that fire, Agent Bronson. You're slinging horse shit in the wrong direction."

"Maybe." The FBI agent angled her head to mimic his. Her mouth thinned and her eyes hardened. "And maybe I'm only slinging back what's being tossed out there to hide the real story."

Chapter Nineteen

Saturday night, Mel succumbed to her partner's bullying and took the night off while Sandy worked the shift.

"I do miss Bethany," she'd said. "But Ryan and Justin are having fun with her, and I really miss the crowd."

So Mel had stayed in her apartment. Sean never called.

The sounds of the band playing the closing number two hours early again filtered into Mel's consciousness. She didn't know why she cared. More than likely she'd have to desert the partnership and leave town. No way could she live in Orson's Folly if Sean broke things off with her, let alone be in a partnership with his sister-in-law.

A soft knock on the door startled Mel out of her introspection. At midnight, she could only think of Sean. She opened the door quickly, ready to do anything to make amends.

"Sandy."

"Hey, Mel. I saw your light on and just wanted to check on you before Ricky and I took off for home." Sandy stepped inside and closed the door against the chill. The kitchen light reflected off the shiny gold blouse peeking from beneath her denim jacket. She must have sung that night. "I think Bertie makes a great waitress. Good call on hiring her. She has a friend we can interview next week."

"Oh. Okay."

Sandy sighed. "He didn't call?"

"I don't blame him," Mel said quickly. She moved into the kitchenette and opened the fridge. Seeing nothing appealing, she closed the door with a soft thunk. "He thinks I should have told him as soon as I knew Denny was pretending to be Northrop."

"Exactly when did you know?"

"Earlier last night. Sean saw me talking to Denny and mentioned he was Northrop. Before I could tell him that was my brother, I, ah... I passed out." Mel turned to meet Sandy's look. "I wasn't keeping it from him. I wouldn't do that. We kept getting interrupted. I was telling him as we pulled in to the ranch and noticed the stables were on fire."

Sandy nodded. "Give him some time. He'll figure things out."

"He thinks I was in on it with Denny, doesn't he?"

Sandy averted her gaze for just a moment. When she met Mel's stare again, her eyes reflected sadness. "He thinks you would have done anything to get a lead on finding your daughter."

The wound that probably never would heal gaped just a little more at Sandy's words. "I *would* have done anything. Anything *but* hurt Sean — hurt *anyone* else. It's killing me that he wouldn't let me explain." She cradled her injured hand, which had begun to ache without the pain meds. She plucked the prescription bottle from the counter and toyed with it, not really wanting to take one. "I should have known Denny didn't know anything about my baby. I didn't trust him. I was stupid. I guess you know how that all turned out, anyway."

Sandy nodded. "Justin told us. I'm so sorry, honey."

Mel thought she'd cried herself out, but to her mortification, more tears fell. "I just feel like I let her down."

"You were in a bad situation. The adults in your life failed *both of you*." Sandy paused, her hand on the door. "Are you going to be okay here alone? I can call Ryan and tell him I'm staying the night."

"I'm fine. Finding out about my baby hurts but—" Mel looked down, biting her lip. "I — we need to talk about the partnership. I can't stay if Sean— if we—"

Sandy dropped her hand from the door. "Have you talked to DC?"

Mel shook her head. "He called but I was asleep. He left a message to call him Monday at the latest."

"Denny is accusing you and Sean of being in on his insurance fraud scheme. The horse he brought to Sean isn't even Devil's Advocate. That horse died in the original fire."

Gasping in shock, Mel grabbed her kitchen table for support. "No! Anyone who knows Sean knows he'd never do anything like that."

Sandy leaned on the little table. "And you? Would you do something like that?"

Anger flared, replacing the despair Mel had been wallowing in. "Do *you* think I would use Sean like that?"

Sandy lifted a shoulder. "I'm telling you how it looks from the outside. Everyone tells me it's been you and Sean since you were kids. But then they mention the time you spent away. How you came back different."

"I *was* different. I was broken when I came back."

"If it makes you feel better, most people are giving you the benefit of the doubt, saying your brother forced you to help him."

"I love Sean. I always have. There is *nothing* that could force me to hurt him." She frowned. "Even the need to find my daughter."

"Are you still broken?"

"Are you asking me that as your partner? Because you don't trust me either?"

Sandy stepped back and sighed. "I'm asking you that as your friend... because you still feel broken to me."

Mel sighed, wiped her tears. "Maybe I am."

"Give yourself time to heal. You know, maybe you should talk to someone."

An uneasy suspicion took hold and bloomed. "You think I'm crazy?"

"I think you've been through a lot." Sandy shrugged and fiddled with one of the buttons on her jacket. "Just — please don't do anything too quickly. Sean's... you know how slow he takes things. Sometimes, when his heart's involved, he seems to need time to catch up."

"He hurt me." Mel rubbed her chest as the emotional pain surged anew. "I needed him to believe in me and trust me the way he needed me to trust him about my baby girl."

"Really..." Sandy raised an eyebrow. "Took you a bit of time to get there, too, didn't it?"

"But I didn't accuse him of doing something to hurt me."

A half-smile tugged at Sandy's lips as she tilted her head to the side and regarded Mel. "No, you didn't give him the chance. You didn't trust him with the information and didn't give him the choice of how he would react before you closed him out."

Unable to move, Mel simply stared. "You're right. Because I was afraid he wouldn't be able to accept the ugliness of my time with Nick. And look what happened. Sean's answer, whenever we have an argument or whenever he has doubts, is to run and hide."

"You know, his whole life has been about losing people he loves. Some, like Ryan... like you... came back. Some, like his mom, didn't. He's always been a giver. He gives so much of himself that sometimes there's nothing left for him."

The pain in her hand made it impossible to concentrate. She returned to the fridge and poured a glass of apple juice. The small brown prescription bottle seemed heavy in her hand. After only a slight hesitation, she twisted the top and shook one into her palm.

"I think we got off track here," murmured Sandy. "Bottom line is, your brother's trying to make you and Sean take the fall for something you say you're not involved in. You need to decide if you're going to do something about it."

Sandy pulled a large gold envelope out of her bag. "Did you put a copy of your will in the safe downstairs?"

Mel started. "Excuse me? That's a random question. And no. I have my will up here."

"Then you might want to give this to DC, since it's got all your information on it and lists Denny as your sole heir should you die." Sandy laid the envelope on the table.

Sandy's name was scrawled across the front in handwriting that looked like hers. But she hadn't written it.

When Mel reached for it, Sandy stopped her. "Don't touch it. Give it to DC the way it is. You know how he doesn't like his evidence contaminated. The thing is, I wonder if your brother put that in the safe when he broke in. And Mel, the tampering with your car... that makes me think he was planning to kill you."

Mel stared at Sandy in disbelief. "But I don't have anything."

Sandy's laugh was genuine. "Check out the net worth of this bar sometime. Oh, and it's really late, so I'm not going to argue with you about this. Stop putting half your salary back on the books unless you want me to treat it as an investment."

"Sean told you?"

Sandy laughed again. "No, but now that I know he knew about it, I own him." She pulled the door open. "If you're sure you don't need anything, I'll call you tomorrow."

Mel sat and stared at the wall for a long time after Sandy left. It cut to the bone that Sean believed she would hurt him for any reason. But it just plain enraged her that Denny was trying to make things worse for them. She couldn't figure out his angle. She'd have to talk to the sheriff tomorrow and make sure he knew Sean had nothing to do with any of this.

* * *

After a night of no sleep, Mel called DC and met him at the bar around midmorning.

"Thanks for coming here on your day off." Mel poured a cup of coffee, parking it on the bar in front of him.

"Aw, you know I'm never really off duty." He glanced around. "This place looks different without customers. Almost peaceful." He took a long drink. "That's good. Thanks."

"Sandy said Denny is implicating Sean in the fraud scheme."

The sheriff's eyebrows rose, and he sent Mel a considering glance. "He's implicating *both* you and Sean."

"Sean had nothing to do with it."

"Melanie..." Cocking his head to the side, he studied her with a critical gaze. "Do you realize you're implying that you *were* working with your brother?"

"Will that get Sean cleared?" she countered.

DC sat back on the barstool and crossed his arms in front of him. "What's going on, Mel? Come clean here. The real story. I can't help anyone if you don't tell me the truth."

"I'm telling you that Sean didn't even know the man pretending to be Dallas Northrop was really Denny DeVayne until I told him so right after the fire." Mel's hands shook. If she could do nothing else, she could make sure Sean's name was cleared. "Just before you showed up."

She slid the envelope Sandy had left with her across the bar. "We found this in the safe here. I haven't opened it but Sandy has. She says there's a will in here, supposedly my will, leaving everything to my brother in the event of my death." She leaned on the bar. "This isn't my will. I would never have made Denny my heir. I'm guessing Denny put it in the safe the night he broke in."

"I thought you said he hadn't gotten into the safe."

Mel shrugged. "I didn't think he had. Point is, whatever's in here, I didn't write it."

"You realize this means nothing in the context of whether you and Sean were helping your brother with his scheme." But DC set the envelope with his hat. He took another drink of coffee. "Tell me what he had on you, Mel. What was he holding over your head?"

"He hinted that he knew how I could find my daughter. I had a baby when I was fifteen, and Nick stole her from me right after she was born."

DC slumped on the stool and blew out a breath. "So you *were* the hypothetical person you asked me about."

She held his gaze without flinching. "Yes, I am."

The sheriff shook his head, his mouth tightening into a harsh line. "I was hoping it was just someone you knew."

Mel lifted her shoulders. "Turns out the baby died before Nick could sell her, and he left her in a trash can."

"That's — wow. I'm sorry, Mel." DC looked away, but not before she saw a flicker of pain. "Do you think DeVayne knew this?"

She shook her head. "I don't think so, but who knows? Either way, he knew I *didn't* know it. Look, DC, all I care about is making sure Sean's in the clear."

"As far as I'm concerned, Mel, I heard what Denny said to you, and some of it seemed like you knew about the whole scheme. And some of it sounded like you didn't. But none of what DeVayne said on the scene implicated Sean." He shrugged and pushed to his feet. "In any case, everything's in my report. The FBI will want to talk to you, so I'm sure they'll be in touch. I'm not really handling this investigation."

She walked him to the door. "Thanks again for coming to see me, DC."

"No problem. By the way, how's the hand?"

She held it up, smiling wryly, and wiggled her fingers. "Doing this hurts."

He laughed. "Then don't do that."

She closed the door behind DC and turned the lock. Silence fell in the darkened barroom. Mel looked around, remembering the first time she'd walked in, answering Sandy's ad for help. She'd been so scared. Not of whether or not she'd get the job, but of being back in Orson's Folly. And of seeing Sean again. He'd been dating someone when Mel had returned, but it hadn't lasted long after she was back. Even so, it had taken her and Sean years to get together, to find each other again.

And less than a week for Denny to wrench them apart.

Except... they'd both pretty much managed to screw things up themselves. They hadn't needed help from Denny at all.

Given how fleeting their happy moments had been, how elusive their relationship was proving... She sighed. *Maybe we just aren't meant to be together after all.*

Pain sliced through her heart, turned to rage. "Why?" She picked up DC's half-full coffee cup and carried it toward the kitchen, stopping at the end of the bar and hurling it at the wall instead. China shattered and fell in pieces to the floor. The liquid blossomed like an inkblot on the wall, little streams running downward to form tiny brown rivers.

"Mel?" Sean's voice came from behind her.

Breathing heavily with her pent-up emotion, Mel turned. He hung in the doorway, his brows pulled together in a frown of confusion.

"How did you get in here?" she demanded.

"I used the key on your ring with the car keys to unlock the back door. Ry helped me bring your Jeep back."

"Thank you."

"Can we talk?"

Is this it, then? Had he come to return her Jeep and break things off? She nodded. "Okay. Here? Or do you want to go someplace else?"

He looked like he didn't want to be anywhere with her. But he sat at the bar on his usual stool.

"Dad told me about your baby. I'm — sorry."

Mel shook her head slowly. It was a fresh wound every time someone said they were sorry. For Sean to mention it was like having her heart shredded. She began to tremble. "Please don't. I don't want to talk about it."

"Honey, you're grieving."

Mel held up a hand. "Just stop. You don't understand. You can't possibly, so please just don't."

"Mel, please," he whispered. "Please don't go back to shutting me out."

She blinked in surprise. A half laugh escaped. "You don't get it, do you? It's not me shutting you out. It's you shutting yourself out this time."

Shock painted itself all over his face, and he stared at her in stunned silence.

"You think I'd deliberately hurt you. You think I let my brother hurt you so I could find out about my baby, that I would make that choice." It was getting hard to talk around the lump in her throat. The more she reasoned it out, the more she realized that it had been easy for Sean to blame her, because he'd never really trusted her to choose him over everything and everyone else.

"I want you to know I understand. You were afraid for her. She was just a child. Denny used her like a carrot to lead you into helping him. You wouldn't have done it if not for your little girl." He stood and walked around the bar.

Mel backed away. "Is that what you think? That I helped Denny hurt you?"

Sean hesitated, then nodded twice, short and sharp. Each nod felt like a punch to the gut. "Mel, I understand."

Her heart pounded madly against her chest wall. "And... you forgive me?"

His response was instant. "Yes, of course."

Mel actually felt her soul being torn in half to match the pieces of her heart. Tears spilled over and she let them. He forgave her. But he had no doubt in his mind — or his heart — that she'd been guilty.

She held out her left hand. "I promised I wouldn't take this off. You'll have to do it."

Sean stared, first at the ring, then at her face. "I don't understand."

"I know you don't." Mel struggled to keep her voice even and businesslike. "Sean, *you* have been in my heart from the time we were kids and sat together on that big rock. *You* have been my world. Everything good, everything real I ever had in my life came from you. Even when I didn't have you in my life, I held on to what we had." She swallowed back the tears. "I survived because I thought of you."

He was beginning to look uncomfortable and she hated seeing her Sean so hurt and uncertain. "Mel?"

"I don't know what I'm going to do without you, Sean. But we don't work. I'm broken. *We're* broken. Maybe we've been broken since Nick took me away."

"Mel, don't do this." His voice was barely a whisper. His eyes filled with hurt. He was pleading. But he wasn't saying the words she needed him to say. He wasn't saying that he'd never doubted her — or that he realized he'd been wrong to doubt her.

"I made a mistake, Sean. But I didn't make the mistake you think I did." Her gaze held his, unwavering — she couldn't back down now. "I didn't know Denny was pretending to be Dallas Northrop until you gave me his name Friday night. I didn't know you were his mark. I was trying to figure out who he was after, what his game was. But I didn't know it was *you*. And I never hid from you that he'd contacted me, that he was around. I never would have helped him hurt anyone, but I would have died myself before I let him hurt you or anyone in your family." She shook her head. "It's knowing that you could believe I'd help him that hurts more than anything else. Please, Sean. Take your ring off my hand. I'm not going to marry you."

Slowly, he shook his head.

"You didn't trust me." Mel gripped the edge of the bar, praying for the strength to keep herself upright. "You still don't, not really. It doesn't matter how much I love you or you me. That distrust will always get in our way."

Sean swallowed. He stepped toward Mel, reached for her with a hand that shook. Holding just her fingertips, he brushed his thumb over the emerald of her ring. Then, leaving the ring in place, he folded her fingers closed. "No. I won't take it off you. We can get through this."

"I don't think so." She straightened her fingers in his grasp but didn't pull away. "Tell me you never doubted me, or you doubted me but you know now I'm telling you the truth. Tell me you believe me. Tell me *honestly* what you think happened, Sean."

He stared. "I love you. I don't want to lose you."

Her heart wanted to explode with all the love she held back. His touch was killing her resolve by inches. But they had to end the illusion. And one of them had to be strong enough to do it. "I can see the doubt in your eyes. Even after I told you what happened, I can see you're still wondering if I'm lying to save myself. You still think I played some role — willing or unwilling — in my brother's game. If you can't look at me and tell me honestly that you have no more doubts, then take your ring off my finger."

He met her eyes; his mouth worked silently. She held her breath. Then, slowly, he pulled his hand away.

As she felt the ring being slipped off her finger, she closed her eyes against the soul-wrenching pain of the loss. When she opened them again, he was staring at her, his eyes filled with so much emotion it was almost tangible in the room.

"Mel, if it — if you find out you're—"

Ah, yes, the pregnancy thing. She pulled in a deep breath and let it out again. "Don't worry, I won't sell another baby."

His face turned red with anger. "That's not why I asked. I'd want to know, Mel. I want to help. I'll be there for you."

She shook her head. "I'm sorry. I shouldn't have said that. But as it turns out, I'm not pregnant. You're off the hook."

"Oh." His face seemed to collapse in on itself, and he averted his gaze downward for a moment. When he raised his face, a muscle worked in his jaw. "How — how do you know?"

"They ran a blood test in the hospital so they could take X-rays of my leg and give me meds."

He stood still, just looking at her, deep sadness in his eyes.

Unable to resist, Mel leaned toward him and pressed a soft kiss against the corner of his lips. "Goodbye, Sean."

He stared at her, the pain in his eyes reaching out to her, filling her. He laid her keys on the bar. Then he turned and silently walked out the way he'd come in, through the kitchen.

"I love you," she whispered to the empty room.

Pulling the folded piece of paper from her pocket, Mel straightened it and reread the instructions on the discharge papers from the hospital. *Followup obstetrical appointment to confirm probable early pregnancy.*

As Mel picked up her keys, she saw it. The fire of green emerald, the ice of white diamonds.

He'd left the ring with her keys.

* * *

Sean walked slowly toward Ryan, where he waited in his vintage Corvette. Each step was one more step away from Mel, widening the gap of the fresh crack in his heart. As if knowing his brother needed the silence, Ryan drove without speaking. Sean watched the miles tick by, only by the sheer force of his will not telling Ryan to turn around so he could beg Mel to take him back. His eyes kept sliding to the side mirror, wishing he'd see the red Jeep chasing after them.

They hit the outskirts of town, and Ryan pulled over at the switchback where Mel had slid off the road. "She's not following us."

Cold settled over Sean like an ice blanket, but he met Ryan's look. "I didn't think she would."

"Yet you keep looking for her in the mirror."

So his brother had noticed how hopeless he was. "Is this where you give me the lecture?"

"No," said Ryan softly. "It's where I ask you why you look like she ripped your heart out and stomped all over it."

Sean's sigh was a shaky sound, even to his ears. He couldn't stop the tremors that originated deep inside and just kept rolling over him.

"I think we both pretty much did that to each other. We — she broke off the engagement."

"That's... surprising. Want to talk?"

"Not really." Sean continued to look at the place where Mel's car had gone off the road. "But I think I need to."

He opened the door and got out, walking to the black skid marks on the pavement. It was impossible not to imagine Mel in her car, skidding on the wet pavement, scared. Alone.

Ryan approached slowly.

"She's hurt because I didn't trust her." Sean drew a deep breath, released it. "I think… if I could have told her I had no more doubts, it would have been okay."

"What do you have doubts about?"

Sean sighed. "She didn't tell me she recognized her brother, that he was pretending his name was Northrop. She said she was trying but we kept getting interrupted."

He looked at the embankment Mel had nearly gone over. The scene in front of him darkened, morphed into leaping flames. The sound of the wind blowing through the pines became the blow of the fire through the center of the stable. Sean's mind added the screams he'd heard from inside the flames, some of which he knew were from the trapped horse and some from Mel, but he'd been unable to tell the difference. And each terrified scream had ripped his soul to shreds.

A light touch settled on his shoulder, a big brother's offer of comfort. "You okay?"

He brought himself back to the road. Slowly he shook his head. "No. I don't think so. Friday night, after we got the horses out and she attacked Denny, the things he said to her… it felt like they'd been working together."

"Yeah, I picked up that you thought that, but I never knew why. So it was all because of what DeVayne said?" Ryan gestured to the scar at the edge of the road. "That must have been a pretty bad accident. It took a lot of force to break the axle. She must have been going the full speed limit when her brakes failed."

"It could have killed her." Sean's heart squeezed in his chest.

"Doesn't really sound like the kind of thing a person would do to his partner in crime — at least not before the con was finished."

"Who knows?" Shaking his head, Sean spread his hands. "Maybe it was a way to keep her in line, warn her about something."

Incredulity flared in Ryan's eyes. "Are you *looking* for reasons not to trust her?"

"No!" The mere suggestion sent him reeling back a couple of steps.

Ryan tilted his head thoughtfully. "You should think on that a little. It feels to me like you are."

Irritation sparked. "Why would I do that?" And what would be the point now, anyway? Sean stalked back to the car.

Over the roof of the 'Vette, Ryan stared at him, his expression unreadable. "Only you would know," he murmured. Then he climbed into the car and started it.

Sean jerked on the handle, opened the door, and climbed in.

Chapter Twenty

Even if Mel hadn't heard about the female FBI agent through the grapevine, she'd have pegged her for a city cop the instant she walked into Valentine's one morning a few days after the fire. Teal silk shirt with only the top button undone, charcoal jacket and trousers, shiny shoes. No purse. Long hair pulled back into a simple ponytail.

"I'm Special Agent Julia Bronson." She slipped a leather case from an inner jacket pocket and held up her ID for Mel's inspection. "Looking for Melanie Mitchell."

You already know you've found her, Agent Bronson.

Asking was merely a formality; so was offering the badge and ID. Leaning forward, Mel squinted at the identification, mentally tracing the blue FBI, taking in the details of the black seal, the photo that wasn't all that recent from the shorter hair length. The track lighting overhead flashed off the gold-toned badge. She took her time studying every minute detail just to piss off the agent. A logging truck rattled the door as it lumbered by on the highway outside, probably going too fast as usual. Silence burgeoned between them again.

"I'm Melanie Mitchell," she drawled, looking up with a shrug.

The agent snapped her ID closed and replaced it in her pocket.

Never trust the law had been ingrained in her throughout her time with Nick DeVayne. Thankfully, it hadn't stuck. She smiled. "Can I offer you something? Coffee? Water? Soda?"

"Thank you. Water would be nice."

"I know you didn't stop in for a social call." Mel pulled a bottle of water from the mini-fridge and set it on a napkin with a glass.

"Mr. DeVayne is asking for a deal," said Bronson.

In the middle of reaching for the bar rag, Mel froze. "What does he have to deal with?"

"He's offered proof that you and Mr. McGee were working with him on this insurance scam."

"Whatever proof he has will turn out to be fabricated." Mel shrugged and grabbed the rag. "Sean didn't even know that Denny was posing as Northrop until the night of the fire. I know they weren't working together." She set her jaw. "I know because Sean's mad at me right now for not telling him Denny was pretending to be Dallas Northrop."

"Why didn't you? Were *you* working with your brother?"

Mel laid her uninjured hand flat on the bar. "If I admit to knowing some of what he was up to, will you find a way to give Sean a pass in your investigation?"

Bronson stared at Mel for a moment. Then she shook her head. "I can't offer a deal."

"Then I'm afraid I have no information you don't already know in this case. Excuse me a moment." Mel left the bar and walked into the kitchen. She stood inside the double doors, waiting a few beats, then grabbed a jar of bar nuts from the pantry and re-entered the main barroom.

Bronson was waiting patiently. "Ms. Mitchell, truthfully, we're after the people who changed the tattoo on the horse's lip. We don't know if your brother got involved during the setup for this scam or if he saw an opportunity and took it."

"How do you think I can help?"

"We want you to talk to your brother. We think you may know him enough to be able to read him."

Mel shook her head. "It's been a long time. I never knew him that well."

"Yet he sought you out to run this scam, didn't he?"

Mel stared at the FBI agent. "Unbelievable. Guilt by unfortunate breeding? I'm his sister so I must be working with him by default?"

Bronson consulted a small black notebook, taking her time leafing through the pages. Oh, she was good at the game.

Mel was better. Humming to herself, she opened the jar of nuts and began filling the stack of tiny black bowls.

After several page flips, Bronson looked up with an unapologetic shrug. "We have enough evidence to start the process of looking at you for conspiracy to commit fraud."

"You have nothing."

"We have DeVayne and whatever he gives us on you and McGee."

"You don't get it. You *have* nothing because there *is* nothing. Denny's playing you. Wait here a minute." Mel slipped down the hallway to the office. The lock on the desk still hadn't been fixed. She yanked open the top drawer, pulled out a well-used deck of cards, and returned to the bar.

While the agent watched, Mel carefully selected the king, queen, and jack of spades. She laid them out in a row then shuffled the rest of the deck and set aside.

"Pick a card, Agent Bronson.

The question earned her a raised eyebrow.

"Humor me." Mel waved her hand over the cards between them. "Please."

Bronson tapped the queen of spades.

The bandage made movement awkward, but she managed to find a bit of her old rhythm. Rearranging the cards as she flipped them over, she then slid them around a few times, moving slowly. Only someone who closed her eyes wouldn't be able to pick out the card.

"Okay, where is she?"

Bronson pointed to the card on the left, and Mel turned over the queen.

She shuffled the three cards, moved them about, and stopped, spreading her hands over them. "Now where is she?"

"That one." The agent pointed to the one in the middle, and Mel flipped it to reveal the queen.

Bronson shot her a triumphant grin.

On the third try, Mel added in some hand flourishes with her injured hand.

Seeming slightly distracted, it took Bronson longer, but she pointed to the card on the left again.

With a shrug, Mel showed her the queen.

Once again, she laid out the cards, added more elaborate hand flourishes, and then began talking. "Where's the queen? Which card bears your lucky lady? Only three cards, which one's your girl? Will you find the love of your life?"

Julia Bronson hesitated a bit longer then pointed at the middle card. Mel lifted the king of spades. Bronson's eyes went wide, and Mel revealed the queen on the left.

A frown crept across the agent's forehead. "Do that again."

Mel began shifting the cards around. "Where's the lucky lady? Only three cards to choose from. Everyone's a winner. Just find the lucky lady."

She stopped and Bronson pointed decisively to the card on the left. Mel lifted it to show the jack of clubs.

Bronson shook her head. "I was so sure." She chuckled but then centered her attention on the cards. "Okay, one more time."

Mel flipped over the jack, showed Bronson the queen, then laid the cards out and began mixing them up again. "Find the queen, you'll be a winner. The lucky queen's in here. Only three cards to choose from. Flip over the queen, you win the game."

Bronson pointed to the middle card. Mel lifted the king of clubs.

The FBI agent shook her head. "I can usually spot these." Confused, she reached out and flipped over all the cards. King of spades, jack of spades, and king of clubs. "What the *hell*?"

"Looking for this?" Mel turned her uninjured hand over and revealed the queen of spades, nestled against her palm. "She hasn't been in the running since you found the king of spades." Mel demonstrated by showing the queen then deftly sliding her out of the way to show a second card in her hand. "I can show her to you whenever I want to, but she hasn't been on the board for you to pick." She pushed the cards aside and met the other woman's gaze. "Like I said, Agent Bronson, just like in this little variation of the shell game, you have nothing. Denny took himself out of the running and threw his marks at you as a smokescreen."

"And his marks would be?"

"Me and Sean."

Julia nodded thoughtfully, apparently trying to digest what she was being told. "How do we find out what your brother knows?"

"Easy." Mel scooped up the king of clubs and replaced it with the queen of spades. "You make sure he stays in the game. He'll do anything to avoid being hurt or thrown in prison."

"Ms. Mitchell — Melanie." Bronson laid a hand on Mel's arm and pinned her eyes in a cool stare. "We need your help getting to your brother. Will you at least agree to talk to him?"

"I'll try on one condition. Sean is completely out of this and he knows he's out of it. He gets a pass and you tell him, so he can stop worrying." Mel angled her head, one eyebrow raised. She had nothing left to lose, but she could damn well make certain Sean had everything to gain. "And you don't tell Sean what I'm doing. As far as he's concerned, you cleared him. Period."

Bronson hesitated.

"Agent Bronson, you know he's innocent. He may have been chosen for his reputation, or because of his relationship with me. But he'd never do anything like that. He'd never put any horse at risk, and if a horse can be saved, he'll save it. He'd never allow one to be hurt."

Bronson smiled. "You help us get into DeVayne's head, McGee gets a pass." She tilted her head and surveyed Mel with a critical eye. "I'm wondering what it would be like to play poker with you."

"You'd lose." Mel kept her voice carefully empty of emotion. "And I wouldn't even have to cheat."

* * *

The Orson's Folly jail was in serious need of updating to bring it into the twenty-first century. Heck, just bringing it into the second half of the twentieth century would be an improvement.

The thought of seeing Denny again sickened Mel. It had been nearly three weeks since she'd last seen him as he was loaded into the back of DC's cruiser. If she didn't see him for another three hundred years it would be too soon. She'd wanted the confrontation over and done with, but it had taken some time for Agent Bronson to set it all up.

Sean... I'm doing this for Sean and for my baby girl. One way or the other, she would make good on her promise to Nick DeVayne to make the charges on *his boy* stick.

When she entered the one-cell holding area, Denny was on the cot, lounging against the wall, one leg up and one on the floor. His eyes were closed but his face was relaxed. He might have been resting beneath a tree on a sunny summer afternoon. The casual observer was supposed to see an innocent man with nothing to worry about. He'd gotten good at using the body language. But she was just as good at reading, and the two twitching fingers on his right hand told an entirely different story. He was waiting for something.

"You almost had this one, didn't you, Denny?" Mel crossed the room and grabbed the single metal folding chair against the wall. She opened it and sat down just outside the cell. "I don't know how you found out about my operation, but you know, it's rude to try and nudge your way in like you did."

The briefest flicker of surprise entered his eyes, leaving just as quickly, and he shrugged. "You could have invited me."

"Like I knew where you were? You sent me letters but never gave me a way to contact you." She stretched her legs out. "I could have used your input a couple of times."

"What exactly were you running?"

Mel rolled her eyes. "Like you don't know. It wasn't hard at all, getting Sandy to trust me to buy into the bar. The trick was for me to buy it using her money."

Denny snickered. "You spent a lot of time here. I thought you were putting down roots."

So he'd been keeping tabs on her. What a creepy thought. "I was alone. I wasn't sure what I was going to do. I figured why not start in a place where the people trusted me already."

"You love these people."

"You know the first rule is not to care about the marks." She smiled, slow and easy. "And everyone's a mark."

"How'd you get started with your little operation?"

Mel allowed her smile to dissolve. He was buying into it, pretending he knew all about her scam, when of course he couldn't, since there wasn't one.

She shrugged, flicked her eyes off his face, and jerked her head ever so slightly in the same direction, as if trying to stop herself from looking over her shoulder. "I ran into a few of the right people in Vegas. Sometimes the cleaning business gets a little hot there and they subcontract. I could do a little out here, small but busy bar and all." Mel studied her fingertips, counted to ten.

"I'm curious. How did you get her to partner you up?"

"That was part luck." She shrugged, striving for a reluctant manner. "I knew the right people. Sandy got abducted a couple of years back and I just made myself indispensable. She started talking partnership as a joke, and I took it a step further along by making her an offer." On a roll, Mel stood and paced the confines of the room. "Got my first stake from my partners in Vegas." Mel picked at a fingernail, refusing to meet Denny's questioning gaze. "Oh, I've paid them back with some high-level cleaning, so we have a positive balance again." She stopped digging at the nail, extended her fingers, and frowned at her hand. "At least we did until you came along. I had to cash out on a very lucrative deal because the feds gave me some attention."

Denny's face went white. A bead of sweat formed on his upper lip. "Who are your partners?"

"Well, originally just a small group out of the casino where I worked in Vegas, The Electric Light." She smiled. Pretending naïveté came so easily. It was almost as though she'd never left the family business. "But turns out they're part of a bigger group out of Detroit. They go by The Engineers."

Denny rubbed his jaw with a hand that shook. "Mellie, that's part of the Detroit Mob."

She shrugged. "So I'm finding out. But what can I do? I almost had everything covered, but now I can't finish the job because of this thing you got me into."

"What exactly were you doing?"

She slashed her eyes across him, allowed some irritation to show. "Same as you, I expect. Surviving at all costs."

"I could have cashed out of the game with this gig, Mel." Had he always sounded so whiny?

"Well, you didn't offer to share, did you?" She lifted a shoulder. "I had a good thing, Denny. A real good thing. Valentine's has a phenomenal crowd on Fridays and Saturdays. You've seen it. A lot of the regulars from the next county... well, they have friends in high places, and let's just say they pay for their drinks with very large bills. Then I put the evening's take into two separate accounts. One my partner knows about... and one she doesn't."

"So it's simple money laundering."

"It was." She lifted a shoulder, let it drop. "Now the feds are looking at me and I can't finish my payoff."

His eyes darted around the room like he expected the walls to pull guns on him. "That could get dangerous."

Mel smiled and offered another shrug. "That's not going to be my problem."

Denny snickered. "You're going to leave it on your partner?"

She brushed a hand over her hair like a preening cat. "Yep. But not the partner you're thinking of." She punched some sweetness into her smile. "You told the feds *I'm* your damn partner, and I'm certain by now that news has made headlines with my, um... employers. Since I can't finish out my run, The Engineers are going to be looking to my *partner* to deliver on my contract with them." She leaned forward and delivered the killing blow in a whisper. "And they don't play games... or make deals with rats."

Horror crept over Denny's face, and he seemed to have trouble breathing.

Oh, yes, he had lots to think on. Mel stood and finished in a breezy tone. "Anyway, I'm sure they'll find a place for you in their organization... somewhere."

"Mel! Are you going to leave things like this?"

She shrugged and winked. "Looks like. If you cut another deal, that's up to you."

Her cell phone chimed with an obnoxiously loud rock song. Mel looked at the caller ID. *Wireless caller* showed above a number with a 313 area code. *Right on schedule.*

She caught her breath, licked her lips.

The outer door popped open and Julia Bronson bustled in. "Is that a cell phone? I was very clear, Ms. Mitchell. No cell phones." She held out her hand. "I'll need to see that."

Deliberately, Mel fumbled the cell, dropping it. The phone landed on her foot, bounced onto the floor. When she bent to retrieve it, she nudged it with her toe and sent it skidding along the floor. It stopped in front of Denny.

"Give me the phone now, Mr. DeVayne." Agent Bronson's voice was frigid.

Denny checked the readout then touched a button. "Oh, sorry. I think I accidentally deleted your call, Mellie."

She smiled tightly and accepted the phone. "No doubt they'll call back."

"Okay, Ms. Mitchell, your visit is over." Bronson held the door open and shot Mel a glare. "If you ever want to visit your brother again, you're going to have to follow the rules. No more stunts like that."

"Wait." Denny stood at the bars, his face vaguely green. "One more minute. Please."

With a long-suffering sigh, Bronson finally shrugged. "You can have two. But I'll take the phone." She held out her hand and Mel handed over the phone with a show of reluctance. Agent Bronson slipped through the door, closing it behind her.

"Thanks for deleting that call for me," said Mel. "I hope he doesn't call back until I get out of here."

"Mellie, what are you into?"

"I told you. I'm — I *was* a cleaner."

"What was that area code? Three-one-three?"

She shrugged. "It's a Detroit number, probably Frankie or..." she allowed her voice to thin. "It could be Sal."

"Sal? Sal K? As in Sal Kowalski?"

She shuffled her feet, looked the other way.

"He's the number two guy in the Detroit Mob, Mellie." Denny ran an agitated hand up and down one of the bars. "Damn it, sis, he'll shoot you just to see if his gun works."

Mel looked up, startled. "How do you know him?"

"Nick dealt with him a couple of times in Florida and again in Vegas. He's the reason Nick mostly stayed out of the bigger cities."

Julia Bronson opened the door. "Time's up."

As she walked slowly toward the door, Mel stopped just short of the threshold. "Denny... I get why you messed with my cars — you wanted my attention. But why — why did you try to hurt Ricky?"

The soft laugh sounded truly evil. "It was never about either of you. It was to keep your boyfriend occupied with what was happening in your life and to keep his attention in town. At your bar."

Mel exaggerated a shiver. "Oh. For a while there I thought the car thing was... someone else. You know."

"Ms. Mitchell, I must insist you come with me." Bronson tapped a neatly trimmed fingernail against the heavy metal door.

With a shrug, Mel followed the FBI agent into the hallway.

Allowing the door to slam shut behind them, Bronson marched Mel to the front of the sheriff's department office and indicated she should take the seat next to DC's desk.

The world seemed to tilt and spin as Mel sank into the green vinyl chair, and she leaned over to put her head between her knees.

"You're okay, just breathe in deep and blow out." Agent Bronson laid a hand on Mel's shoulder.

"Do you think he bought it?" asked DC, glancing up from the mound of paperwork in front of him. The cell phone Mel had carried with her to visit Denny sat next to an identical one near the sheriff's right hand.

Releasing a deep sigh, Mel straightened in her seat and wobbled her hand in a so-so gesture. "He doesn't want to. Nick wouldn't have bought it. But Denny's on his own, and he's never been as good at the con as he wants to believe. He really doesn't have the nerve for it."

"You did good," said Bronson, handing Mel a bottle of water. "We'll let him stew and see where he goes with it. This might backfire if he decides to sell you out for what he thinks you have running here."

"Part of the grift is to get the mark running scared. I hope whoever he's tangled up with in the racing world is less scary to him than the Detroit Mob." Mel twisted the cap on the bottle and took a drink. It didn't come close to alleviating the dryness in her throat. "Otherwise, he won't budge." She angled a look up at Bronson. "Either way, Sean's out of it now, right? Our agreement was... I try to get Denny to roll over and Sean's in the clear."

The FBI agent smiled and lifted her own water bottle in a toast. "Mr. McGee's been in the clear for more than two weeks. Since you and I first talked." She watched Mel over the edge of the bottle as she sipped.

She'd been had. Mel acknowledged appreciation for the agent's gambit with a half smile and a nod. "Well played."

Julia shrugged. Then she smiled. "Not so much. You've already walked through fire for your man. I suspected you'd do anything you needed to for him."

"He's really clear? And he knows it?"

Bronson nodded.

"Make sure it stays that way. I've got a bar to open this evening."

* * *

Shadows from the fireplace danced over the oak paneling, a perfect match for the shadows in Sean's empty heart. The fire had died down and the frosty November air was sneaking back into the living room.

Not that he particularly cared if he froze, but Sean hauled himself from the leather chair in front of the hearth anyway. The screen in front of the fireplace opened with a raspy hiss when he pulled the chain. He stirred the embers, tossed on another log, and waited. Orange fingers sprang up around the edges, consuming the wood and chasing the chill from the room again, though the warmth never touched the coldness dwelling inside him. The fire stoked, he settled back in his chair.

The shot of Jack clawed its way down. How many was that? He'd lost count. Shrugging, he poured another. That one he held in his hand as he watched the logs blacken and succumb to their fate.

The cozy glow of the fire in the living room grew, changed shape. The comforting crackle became a hissing, spitting viper engulfing the outline of the stables with flames that reached high into the night sky, taunting him, daring him to enter, promising him kisses directly from the devil's own hell if he did, and eternal emotional torment if he didn't.

Three weeks had passed but the growl of the fire, the screams of alarmed horses, and Mel's cries were never far from his memory. As the log in the fireplace split in two and fell off the grate, he saw instead the center beam of the stable collapse just as he got Mel and Dev out of the furious firestorm.

He tossed back the shot. Poured another.

"Staying in again?" Ryan stood in the doorway to the foyer.

"Looks like it." Not like he had anywhere to go or anything.

"The insurance adjuster was out again today with more questions. Did she find you?"

"Yep. I answered her stupid questions and she went away again."

"Did she say what the holdup is?" Ryan moved like a cat across the carpet to the liquor cabinet and poured himself a brandy. "We're not going to be able to rebuild before spring if we don't get started in the next week."

"Nope. She didn't say."

"We're going to need the stall space in the cow barns for some of the younger calves."

"You'll have 'em." Sean stared into the yellow flames again. Why didn't Ryan just take the hint already and go the hell away?

But he didn't, choosing instead to sit in the matching chair on the other side of the fireplace. "You want to tell me what damn fool thing you've done now?"

"Racing Commission's coming to get Dev next week. Rest of my rehabbers are going to a stock auction week after next. All you'll have to do is find room for the working horses and Domingo." Sean belted back his shot and poured another. "Now, if you don't mind, I was sitting here getting pleasantly loose when you interrupted me."

"So you're just giving up?"

Sean looked at his brother and shrugged. "Sure looks like it, doesn't it? That ought to make you and Dad happy... me getting back into the cattle business."

His bait went disregarded. "I ran into DC at the bar today. Came in for lunch."

Sean downed his shot but held off on pouring another. Ryan would only give him shit for drinking too much. "He's gotta eat somewhere."

"DeVayne made a deal with the feds to hand them the stable that was screwing you over."

"*Was* screwing?" Sean snorted and waved a hand in the air. "Look around. Mission accomplished." He didn't give a flying whatever about DeVayne. He did wonder if Mel had been spared in the deal, but he wouldn't ask.

"I heard an interesting story from DC. Seems the FBI asked Mel to get into DeVayne's head and persuade him to come clean about the original fraud scheme." Ryan swirled the brandy in his snifter.

Crap. Now I have to ask. Sean drew a fortifying breath. "So, she made a deal, too?" *Please let her be okay, not in trouble.* Holding his breath, he stared at the fire again.

"She did." Ryan sipped, grunted in apparent appreciation. "A very interesting deal, as it turns out. She was never in trouble. They just wanted her help. She only agreed to help them turn Denny against his partners after she made sure they were going to give you a pass on any investigation. She didn't care what happened to her. She swore you were innocent and if they wanted her help, you were going to be officially cleared before she gave them anything."

Sean tore his gaze away from the dancing flames and stared at Ryan, not certain what to make of the information. His brother studied him in silence, one eyebrow cocked upward.

"Well, wasn't that nice of her? Seeing as I *am* innocent."

"Turns out she was innocent, too," said Ryan softly.

Sean lifted a shoulder. "So she's been saying." He contemplated pouring another drink in spite of his brother. He wasn't even close to drunk, and if the conversation was going to go any further, he really wanted to be smashed.

"So her brother's now saying. Apparently, every time she came out to visit you, he made himself scarce so she wouldn't see him. He tried to intimidate her with threats, but she threatened him back." Ryan finished his brandy. "He swears she had no idea he was using you to validate the fake identity of the horse."

"Doesn't much matter, does it?" Ignoring Ryan's pointed look, Sean poured the shot but didn't touch it. "You're trying to put me on board a ship that's already sailed. Mel wanted out, not me."

"Why?" One softly spoken word tore through the room like a gunshot.

"Some lame reason." Sean laughed, though he found no humor in the situation. "Because I didn't believe in her. I thought she was working with her brother in order to find her daughter."

"When did you figure out you were wrong?"

Definitely not drunk enough for this conversation. Sean tossed back the shot. He stared at the empty glass. "Since about two seconds after she kicked me to the curb. I let her down by listening to her brother, not trusting her. I wanted to apologize. But those words... we've both used them so much, I don't know if they have any meaning anymore." He shook his head. "She won't want to hear them from me."

* * *

Now that Sandy was putting in a few hours on their busiest evenings, some of the pressure was off Mel. Bertie's friend, Tara, turned out to have waitressing experience and was a hard worker. Things were moving in a good direction for Valentine's, so Mel decided it was time for a life-changing discussion with her partner.

Sandy looked up from the desk with her ready smile as Mel entered the office. "How's the hand therapy coming?"

Mel grimaced, holding up her right hand, still lightly wrapped in gauze. "Slow healing the one burn at the base of the thumb. That was the worst one. The rest are good but it still hurts to move the fingers too much." With a deep sigh, she set a folder on the desk in front of Sandy.

"What's this?"

"These are papers to dissolve the partnership."

Sandy's jaw dropped. She pushed away from the desk and stood. "What? Why?"

"I've loved working with you, Sandy. But it's time for me to leave Orson's Folly. I had Mr. Wilson draw up these papers because I'm not coming back."

"I'll buy you out." Sandy shoved the folder back across the desk.

"That doesn't make sense, since you gave me the partnership free and clear." Mel pushed the folder back in front of Sandy. "Really, you know this is the only fair thing to do."

Sandy smiled wryly. "You're really leaving?"

"I have to," Mel whispered. "I owe Sean money for the Jeep, but I'll have to send it to him."

"He won't want it," said Sandy flatly.

"Well, he'll have no choice. After he gets it, he can burn it for all I care." Mel slipped her hand into her pocket, touched Sean's ring, pulled her hand out again.

"Don't worry, it won't be burned," said Sandy. "The insurance is taking its time paying out. Money's going to be tight for him."

"I'm so sorry," said Mel. "If only I'd been more—"

Sandy made an impatient gesture. "It's not your fault, so stop going there."

Mel held up her hands in surrender.

"When do you think you'll be leaving?" Sandy flipped through the folder, her forehead knitted in concentration.

"Week after next."

"Thanksgiving?" Sandy shook her head. "I don't suppose you'd come out for..." She sighed. "I guess not. I'm going to miss you."

The first tear rolled down Mel's cheek. "Back atcha. You take care of that baby. And Ryan, Justin, and..." Her voice was beginning to warble. Any second the tears would fall. Again.

"I will." Sandy walked around the desk and came to a stop in front of Mel. "Please don't go."

"I have to," she whispered.

"Why?" Sandy took hold of Mel's upper arms. "I know I'm overstepping, but he's miserable, you're miserable. Why did you break it off?"

"Because Sean forgave me for something I didn't do... couldn't have done."

"Oh, Mel, can't you forgive him for being wrong?"

"Of course I can forgive him for that. I made a mistake and so did he." Mel sniffed and blinked back hot tears. "But after I explained what happened, he still thought I was lying. And he forgave me. That's when I realized we're broken, Sean and me. And it can't be fixed." Mel gave up fighting the tears and ended up sobbing uncontrollably.

"Oh, hon..." Sandy embraced Mel tightly. "You're not broken. You aren't! You two are just hurt — damaged. You can still fix things."

"I did my best to make sure Sean would be okay. That's all I can do." Mel pulled out of Sandy's arms. "I've got to get back on the floor." She reached in her pocket again and this time pulled out the emerald ring. "Please give this back to him. I tried and he left it on the bar. It was his mother's."

Sandy looked at the ring and shook her head slowly. "No. That's a line I can't cross. Won't cross. You're making another mistake and I won't be part of it."

Chapter Twenty-One

Packing was almost too easy. Most of the things in the apartment could be left behind. Mel always traveled better when she kept it light. She sat on her sofa, remembering how Sean had complained about the lumps and broken springs. The wooden box with her most precious possessions sat on the table in front of her. She ran her fingers over the top. It would be the last thing she would pack. It always was.

The nausea hit at the same time someone knocked on her door. She managed to quell the upset stomach long enough to open the door for Sandy and a stranger.

"Excuse me a second." Mel raced for the bathroom. Of all the inopportune times to lose her breakfast.

When she returned, Sandy was still standing in the doorway with the stranger. Perhaps in his late twenties or early thirties, he had a sort of rugged appeal. He wasn't exceptionally tall for a man but he looked very broad and muscular. His face was on the wrong side of a shave but his nut brown hair was military short. He had an easy smile, showing lots of even white teeth, but though it reached his eyes, they didn't quite light with the happiness equal to his smile.

"This is Luke Corbett," said Sandy.

Luke extended a hand and Mel took it for the introductory handshake. His grip was firm, his hands warm and dry.

"Hello." Curious, Mel glanced at Sandy.

"Mr. Corbett has made an offer for Valentine's." Sandy regarded Mel with a speculative gleam in her eyes.

An offer?

"Oh, so I guess you'll want to look around up here." Mel kicked a partially packed box aside. "Sorry about the mess. I'm in the middle of packing up."

"Actually, I brought Mr. Corbett up here to meet you. As one of the partners, you have to approve the sale."

Mel's eyes flashed to Sandy's in surprise. "But the papers I gave you—"

"I tore them up." Sandy shrugged. "This is the right move for me. I can spend time with Bethany and working around the ranch. I'm still making an amazing profit on my initial investment. Since we're selling, it didn't make sense to dissolve the partnership. It'll be gone automatically when we close."

Suspicion crowded into her thoughts. Was Sandy trying to delay her leaving? "When will we be closing?"

"Mr. Corbett is pre-approved at the bank, and he's waived the inspections." Sandy smiled at the quiet man. "So we're hoping for a fast sale, probably the day after tomorrow. You'll be around for that long, won't you?"

Mel surveyed Sandy in silence. She supposed it wouldn't matter if the partnership was dissolved before the sale or not. Once the sale was completed, she would simply hand the money back.

A knowing smile sparked in Sandy's eyes. "We'll discuss the particulars later, but trust me, you aren't walking away from here with less than your share."

Apparently she was becoming too easy to read. She'd have to work on that. "Fine, I'll mail that to Sean, too. He can invest it in his business."

Lips set in a firm line, Sandy shook her head. "Racing Commission's coming out to pick up Dev tomorrow afternoon. Next week, he's shipping his rehabbed horses to auction. He's done. And I don't think he's going to change his mind."

Mel's breath caught. "Lacey?"

"She's on the list to be sold." Sandy held Mel's gaze for several seconds. *Sending a message?*

Mr. Corbett cleared his throat, breaking Sandy's stare.

"I'm sorry, Mr. Corbett." Sandy turned back to him. "Let me show you around." She gestured toward the bathroom. "It's small but it has all the basics."

* * *

The more days that passed, the easier it became to watch the flames eat their way through the logs when he added them. The hiss of the fire no longer sounded evil. He didn't hear the shrieks of the horses. But if he closed his eyes, he still saw that collapsing roof falling behind him and Mel.

He poured a shot, noted the bottle was almost empty. *Damn it.* He wasn't nearly plowed enough to get through the rest of the night. He hated switching his liquor in mid-drunk-on.

"You can't hide out in the bottle the rest of your life." Justin stood in the doorway.

He must have drawn the short straw tonight. Why the hell couldn't his family just leave him to himself? He did his chores, made his contribution to the ranch.

"Not much of one left to hide in tonight, anyway." Sean held up the bottle and shook it. About another shot's worth sloshed against the sides.

"You worry me, boy." His father hovered near the liquor cabinet.

"Don't. It's not necessary."

Justin opened the humidor on the sidebar and pulled out a cigar. Closing his eyes, he gave a long, appreciative sniff along the length. "You're making some big decisions on the second half of a whiskey bottle."

"Nothing other people around here haven't done." Sean tipped the bottle up then down, watching the amber liquid roll from end to end. "Including you, after Mom died."

Justin inhaled sharply. His face was an impenetrable mask except for his eyes. They registered deep pain. *Great. Now you know for sure I'm a jackass, old man, so maybe you'll leave me alone.*

But Justin held his ground. "Not really the same thing, is it? Your girl's alive and well." He stuck the cigar in his mouth and lit it, raising a cloud of blue smoke as he took a couple of puffs. "Leaving town day after tomorrow, though."

"Good."

"Good, huh? So you're really just going to let her go."

Sean laughed. "You seem to be under the impression I have some way of keeping her here."

"You're a bullheaded mule. I guess you get that from me." Justin shook his head. "You know all she needs is for you to admit you were wrong about her." He locked his steely blue gaze on Sean. "And you *were* wrong. She's still under the impression you hate her because you think she burned down the stables."

Sean lifted a shoulder. "Welcome to your son's screwed up life." He raised his glass in a toast. "Enjoy the show or leave me in peace. It's up to you."

Justin's laugh was harsh, his voice even more so as he spat a graphic curse. "If you call this peace, boy, then you *are* all kinds of screwed up."

Sean stared open-mouthed at his father, startled by the words as much as the tone.

"What's the matter, boy? Think you're the only one who can get drunk and curse? Think you're the first man in the family to push those he loves away out of a twisted sense of pride? Think again. And get your head out of the bottle before you find yourself permanently at the bottom of one." He raked a look filled with disgust over Sean, then turned and left the room with a shake of his head.

Masculine voices suddenly filtered in from the kitchen, interrupting the normal evening quiet. Sean thought he heard his name. *Aw, damn.* They weren't planning some kind of intervention, were they?

When Joe stepped into the living room, Sean almost got up and left. But no one accompanied the other man, so he stayed put. Apparently they hadn't decided on an intervention, after all.

"Got some interesting news here from Ben Jamison." Joe set a thick manilla folder on the arm of Sean's chair. "About Mel's baby."

Sean looked at the folder like it had just grown fangs and a rattle. "That has nothing to do with me."

"Doesn't it?"

Barking out a laugh, Sean shook his head and raised his nearly empty bottle in a toast. "Breaking news, buddy. Sean and Mel are over."

Joe sent him a long, hard stare then shook his head. "Okay, guess not. Well, information's there. Up to you what you do with it, though I'd appreciate it if you'd find some way to pass it on to Mel."

While Sean was trying to think of a snappy comeback, Joe slipped wordlessly from the room.

"Yeah, that's right. Run away," muttered Sean under his breath instead.

He tossed back the shot and picked up the folder. The damn thing was heavy. Frowning, he tapped it against his other hand. The fire was low. Perfect. He pulled the screen and started to lay the file on the bed of embers. At the last minute, he pulled his hand away, cursing his weakness. He'd never be able to obliterate her from his life the way he needed to.

"Fine, I'll find a way to get it to Mel," he mumbled to the empty room. The warmth of the fire and the whiskey he'd already consumed made him drowsy. He stroked a thumb across the edge of the folder and sighed.

Mel...

* * *

Chills washed over him, leaving violent shivers in their wake. What the hell? Sean pushed his eyes open, but the room was deep in shadow. A rustling sound at his chest interrupted his thoughts and drew his attention downward. One hand clutched the damn file against his heart. He should have burned the friggin' things.

The mantel clock chimed four times. The fire had mostly gone out, leaving him cold and stiff from sitting nearly all night in the chair. He closed his eyes hard and rolled his head to work at the kinks in his neck. But with his eyes closed, his father's face floated at the front of his memory, and he opened them quickly. Too quickly. Pain stabbed behind his eyeballs.

Closer to hung over than drunk, he stared down at the folder. Calling himself all kinds of fool, he pushed the switch on the floor lamp behind his chair, opened the file, and pulled out a handful of newspaper clippings. As he read them by the soft light, he knew they would give Mel peace. She needed to see them.

But he wasn't going to deliver them. He'd send them in with Sandy.

* * *

"No." Sandy deftly taped Bethany's diaper then picked up the baby. She gave her a kiss and a cuddle before sitting her in the infant seat. "Joe gave it to you to deliver. This isn't some game of post office where you pass it to the first person willing to do your job."

Exasperated, Sean huffed out a breath. "Fine. Where's Ry?"

"Ryan isn't going to do it, either."

"You speaking for him now?"

"Not at all." Ryan's voice came from behind Sean. "Sandy was there when I told Joe I wouldn't do it last night."

"Then I'll give it back to Joe and he can deliver it himself."

Ryan rolled his eyes. "He probably would have, but he's on duty at the hospital for the next three nights. Get over your issues and deliver it." He shrugged. "Or don't."

Exhaustion caught up with Sean, and he slumped. "Ryan, do you know what's in here?"

Ryan shook his head. "Nope. Wasn't addressed to me."

"Joe's investigator found out what happened to the baby. She didn't just go to some landfill." Sean shook his head. "Don't you think Mel should know?"

"Yeah," Ryan said on a matter-of-fact shrug. "I do." He picked up the infant seat and followed Sandy from the room.

Alone, Sean ran a hand through hair that was in desperate need of a barber. Catching a whiff of himself, he made a face and tried to recall the last time he'd hit the shower. Since the memory was so dim, he decided that might be the appropriate place to start his day.

On his way to the bathroom, Sean dropped Mel's folder on the foot of his bed. He scowled at the tidy brown and blue plaid spread. When had he last slept there? The last time Ryan had brought him up when he was too drunk to stand? That was more than a week gone. Sandy must have made the bed, because he sure as hell hadn't. He'd been too pissed at having been put to bed like a toddler. No one had "helped" him since. They'd all apparently grown tired of nursing his sorry ass.

The hot water coursed over his tired and aching body, washing away the stench along with much of the anesthetic he'd coated his emotions with since leaving Mel. He toweled himself dry and pulled on clean clothes, frowning when he had to tighten his belt by a full notch.

Along with the release of emotions from his cocoon of numbness crept a deep sense of regret. His dad hadn't deserved the supper of crap Sean had served him the night before. Shame heated his face as he recalled some of his hurtful words. He needed to seek out Justin.

Finding his dad turned out to be dismayingly easy. Sean would have preferred a couple of extra moments of looking. But Justin sat behind the ancient desk that had served as the centerpiece of Cross MC ranch business for probably more than a hundred years. He perused a blue ledger, every once in a while turning to enter something into the computer.

"I didn't know you knew how to use the computer," Sean blurted. *Nice. Great way to open, slick.* That even sounded lame to *his* hungover ears.

Justin drew a deep breath, raised his head, and subjected Sean to a long, silent stare. Then he shrugged and looked back at the ledger. "Lotta things you don't know."

No, of course the old man couldn't possibly make his apology at all easy. "I... was... out of line last night."

His father snickered without lifting his eyes from the book in front of him. "Only last night?" He entered something else into the computer.

Sean grimaced, locked his jaw against flapping out an acerbic response, and concentrated on relaxing out of the irritation. "Yeah, a lot of nights, actually, but can we talk about last night first?" He sighed. "What I said... about you drinking, when Mom — died. That was—" Damn it, where was the strength he'd always had to make things right?

About to drive out of your life forever, jackass.

His father held his silence.

"I'm sorry, Dad. That's not — how I feel. It's never been how I felt."

Justin picked up a pen and made a note in the ledger before he shifted and looked up, rubbing his jaw. "Your mother was stolen away from all of us. She was there one minute and not there the next." He sighed heavily. "A lot of men might have found themselves in a place where they wanted another woman around the house. Someone to help with running the place, and with raising his children, maybe even having more children." He smiled at Sean, and his eyes warmed. "That wasn't me. I couldn't even stand the thought of hiring a woman to keep house and cook. Might be I..." He sighed again, a heavy and tired sound that tore through the wall around Sean's heart. "Maybe I shortchanged you and your brother somewhere in all that, not having a woman to balance my influence in your life."

"No, Dad. Ryan and I never felt like that. What I said last night — it was me being a mean drunk." Unable to meet his father's eyes, Sean dropped his gaze and mentally traced the jagged lines on the Southwestern-patterned rug.

"Now, that last statement I'll agree with." Justin chuckled. "But I think you're missing my point. Your mother was all I ever wanted. If I could have wished her back, I would have. But I wasn't in the market to replace her. Since you and Melanie were kids, you haven't looked seriously at another female unless she had four legs and wore a saddle. I couldn't get your mom back, not for me, not for you and your brother."

Justin stopped talking. After a long moment, Sean glanced up and found himself under his dad's steady regard.

Right. The moral of the story being, the ball was in Sean's court.

"You don't have much time to make a decision," said Justin, setting his pen down on the blotter. "You let the opportunity pass, you could spend the next seven years looking for her like your brother did Sandy." He angled his head. "Or never see her again."

"I have to get Dev ready to go with the Racing Commission."

Justin raised a friendly hand and went back to his task.

Right, good copout, Sean. Stellar.

The folder with Mel's name scribbled across the front was heavy — and not just physically. Sean grabbed it and stepped outside. The November chill bit at the exposed skin of his neck, and he raised his collar. It had snowed again overnight, leaving the landscape crystal white beneath the dull gray sky.

A tan pickup towing a small horse trailer crawled along the driveway toward the stable. Sean dumped Mel's file on the seat of his own pickup, then crossed the yard to the barn where Dev was housed. The charred skeleton of the stables mocked him as he passed.

Dev wasn't at all interested in cooperating. Ears back, feet slashing, he squealed and shrieked at anyone who came near, especially the elderly veterinarian who had been hired to haul the horse and the vet technician accompanying him. The assistant made the mistake of showing outright fear. He probably had no business working with animals larger than lab rats.

Mel hadn't had any problem with the horse. She'd clucked and shushed him until he was nearly eating out of her hand. Sean had no doubt that, given time, she would have tamed the troubled horse. And if it hadn't been for Mel risking her life, he never would have gotten Dev out of the stable.

A frown furrowed the vet's forehead as he threw out his hands in surrender. "I'll call Mr. Windsor and see if I can put the horse down here and haul him away, instead of waiting until I get him back to the clinic."

Sean brought his head up sharply, unable to believe what he'd just heard. "What did you say?" he asked softly.

"I'm not interested in killing myself just to haul him to the clinic and put him down, when it's obviously going to be easier to destroy him here and have him hauled away."

Put down and hauled away because it was more convenient that way? They weren't talking about a sack of spoiled feed. Dev had a few problems—

An angry shriek resonated from the paddock.

Sean pulled his lips tight to cover his wince. Okay, a lot of problems. But that horse was alive. A living, breathing, sentient being. He and Mel had saved Dev's life together. And now some jackass was going to kill him and haul him away like that life was worth nothing? The fuse on Sean's temper began to smolder.

"No." He shook his head. "You're not destroying that horse."

The veterinarian's frown was replaced by a carefully crafted smile. "Mr. McGee, that's the plan. Whether I do it here or at my clinic is the only thing in question at this point."

"People risked their lives — the woman I love risked her *life* rescuing this horse from a burning stable. She has second and third degree burns from saving this horse's life."

Sean put himself between the vet and the barn. "Trust me when I say you are *not* going to destroy this animal."

"With all due respect, Mr. McGee, that's not your call." But as Sean advanced, the vet retreated a few steps. Gone was the pasted-on smile, replaced by widened eyes with hints of apprehension in their depths.

"Problem here?" Ryan appeared in the doorway, a coiled rope dangling from his left hand.

Relief spread across the vet's face. The fake smile returned and he bobbed his head up and down. "The California Racing Commission has contracted with me to pick up this horse."

"They think they're going to put him down." The smoldering fuse heated. Driven by broiling emotions, Sean fixed the vet in a hard stare and took another step forward.

Ryan hung the rope on the nearest fence post and folded his arms across his chest, subjecting Sean to a long, contemplative look. Then something sparked in his eyes, and he glanced at the vet, one eyebrow raised. "That true?"

"Yes, but I'm thinking it would be less stressful to the animal if we put him down here and have him hauled off."

Both of Ryan's brows shot skyward. "Really, now?" He looked from Sean to the horse, then leveled the vet in a narrow-eyed stare. His voice slid into a slow drawl. "'Cause I'm sorta thinking here that getting dead is going to end up pretty freakin' stressful to the horse."

"Look, Mr. McGee isn't the owner here. The horse was confiscated, and now the plan is to put him down." The vet's hands flexed against his legs. "I'm sure Mr. McGee will be compensated for the housing and care he's provided since the fire."

Sean snorted. He could imagine the pittance he'd receive, but that was the least of his concerns. Dev didn't deserve to be chucked out like yesterday's trash. He'd been through enough. Mel had thought him worth saving. He'd been important enough for her to fight for, even—

—die for.

Widening his stance, Sean set his jaw and furled his hands into ready fists as he stepped between the horse and the vet.

"How about we agree to a compromise here?" Ryan sauntered over and stood shoulder to shoulder with Sean. "I'll give you two minutes to climb in your truck and get off my land before I have the sheriff out here, looking at trespassing charges."

"But the horse—"

Ryan shrugged. "If you can load him in the next two minutes, you're free to take him."

The harried veterinarian looked at Dev, who laid his ears back, showed his teeth, and squealed. The little man edged his way toward the pickup, where his assistant already waited behind the wheel.

"I'll be calling Mr. Windsor."

Sean took a step forward. "What a coincidence. I'll be speaking with him myself in the next few minutes, to make him an offer he can't refuse."

Tires spun, flinging chunks of dirty snow as the truck fishtailed out of the yard.

His eyes still on the departing vehicle, Ryan shook his head. "You are more than likely going to pay an exorbitant price for an unstable horse that's not *ever* going to be a hundred percent sound. I hope to high hell you know what you're doing here."

Easing out the breath he'd been holding, Sean sighed. "So do I."

Ryan laid a hand on Sean's shoulder. "Welcome back."

As he strode to his truck, Sean glanced over his shoulder. "I'm not back yet. There's someone I've got to see."

* * *

Mel eyed the pathetic pile of belongings. Her life, all packed up. Her eyes slid across the room to the wooden box on the table in front of the sofa. A pair of pink spiked heels sat on top. One more thing for her collection of important memories. They'd probably fit in a corner if she did some rearranging. One day, she'd end up needing a bigger box.

She sat on the sofa and pulled the box into her lap, lightly running her fingers over the top before she opened it. In an absent motion, she grabbed a cracker from the package sitting on her coffee table and munched as she removed everything. She didn't want to go through the stuff, but it was all part of her typical ritual, the last thing she did before she left. She'd look over her cherished items, take comfort in her memories one last time before she reorganized them.

The shoes went in first and took up most of the space. Next, she unwrapped the brass horse and caressed his forehead with the tip of her finger. Her eyes moistened as she rewrapped the figure and tucked it into one of the shoes.

Lost in her tears, Mel packed away the other items, one at a time, faltering at the heart-shaped stone. With a sob, she tucked that safely into the corner of the box. Her stomach began to protest and she reached for another cracker. Another sob escaped her throat when she found the picture of Glenn, her baby girl's father. He'd never looked back, just like she'd wanted. So he didn't know his daughter had been born and had died the same night. She shoved the picture and her pay stubs in with the rest of her things.

She paused at the envelope filled with photographs Justin McGee had handed her. She hadn't even opened it, but maybe one day. She squeezed it safely against one side.

The last thing to go into the box was the picture of the two innocently happy children playing on the swing. It would be the first thing she saw the next time she lifted the lid.

The cracker wasn't doing it. Bile rose. Having found out that it was far easier to make it to the bathroom to barf up the contents of her stomach if she walked slowly while taking deep breaths, she stood and tried to maintain her calm as she crossed the tiny apartment.

Moments later, she rinsed her mouth and splashed water on her face. Looking up, she caught sight of her reddened cheeks in the mirror. *Now for the complementary hot flash.* This crap was draining her and attacking her resolve. It would have been nice to have someone who would take care of her.

Time to pack the memory box away. She ambled back to the sofa and stood with her fingers on the lid. The picture of herself and Sean playing on the swing looked up at her, mocking her with its happiness. Mel sat back down, staring at the picture but no longer seeing it for the tears that flooded her eyes.

Who was she kidding? She couldn't do it. One baby had been stolen from her when she'd been just a teenager. She couldn't leave and do the same thing to Sean. Whether or not they were together, he and their child deserved to know each other.

Her decision made, she stood and crossed the tiny apartment. For the first time in weeks, she felt confident she was doing the right thing. At the door, she grabbed her coat and tugged it on, too impatient to zip it. Ricky had shoveled the snow from her steps and thrown down some salt, but she negotiated them carefully nonetheless then climbed into her already partially loaded Jeep.

At the main road, she stopped while another logging truck blew by. A vehicle rolling right on the truck's tail skidded to a halt in front of her.

With a scream of surprise, Mel jammed on her brakes to keep from running into the giant silver wall in front of her. In seconds her brain registered the familiar pickup.

"Sean?" Her heart jumped into her throat as she threw open her door and slid down to the gravel.

He stalked toward her from the other side of his truck like a man on a mission. Oh, no, had he somehow guessed? Was he angry? He had every right to be.

It didn't matter. She was going to get it out before he said anything to make her change her mind.

They stopped three feet apart. He obviously had something to say. But so did she, and if he knew about the baby, she wanted her say first.

"We're having a baby."

"Joe found your baby."

"What?" Mel shook her head. Had she heard him correctly? "How did Joe find out about our baby?"

"His investigator tracked her down and—" He stopped and stared. "Wait. *What* did you just say?"

"Which baby are you talking about?"

"The one you had when you were fifteen?" Sean's face screwed into a confused frown. "How many babies have you had?"

Mel felt a sense of inexplicable calm settling over her. "That one... and the one I'm going to have in a little over seven months."

Sean's mouth fell open. He staggered and clutched at the fender on her Jeep. "You said you had a blood test."

"It was inconclusive. The followup test was — um, positive."

"Our baby..." A weak smile tugged the corners of his mouth upward, and he took a step forward.

"I couldn't leave without telling you."

Sean's mask settled in place. "I see." He glanced at the back of her Jeep, his eyes roaming over the boxes, and he seemed to choose his next words with care. "I guess this doesn't change your plans, then."

"It... I—" She eased forward, about to wager her heart on what she had seen in his initial happy reaction. "I was going—"

Without effort, Sean closed the distance between them. He tugged her into his embrace, holding her so tightly that her feet left the ground. "No, you *aren't* going." He spoke against her lips, and his words rumbled in his chest under her hands. His kiss came hard and fast. And she had no doubt of the need driving him. "It's not over, Melanie. We're *not* over. I won't let it happen."

He captured her mouth again, angling his head and cupping her cheek with one hand, taking them both deep, deep into the realm on the other side of need.

He murmured words of love against her mouth, her neck. His low voice carried the warmth she'd craved over the past weeks and she went still, mesmerized at the sound. "I was wrong about you," he said. "I was afraid you were dead when you didn't come out of the fire, and I let all my emotions get away from me." He retreated from the embrace to stand just a few feet away from her and traced her jaw with a forefinger. "But mostly, I let my pride get the better of me. I knew you'd never be involved in anything as heinous as that. And I let you down when I didn't stand up for you — fight for you."

For the first time in her life, Mel literally threw herself at a man. With her arms around his neck, he easily lifted her, and her legs settled around his waist.

"I love you, Sean McGee." She kissed his jaw, his cheek, the corner of his mouth. At last, she met his lips.

"Can we go upstairs?" he asked after he ended the soul-completing kiss. "I really need to get us to a private place."

Mel's eyebrows rose. "Missed me that much?"

He nodded and winked.

Chapter Twenty-Two

Standing in the middle of her mostly packed-up living room, Mel was more beautiful than Sean had ever seen her. White gauze still covered the burns she'd sustained in the fire. *For me. She got hurt helping me.* It sliced into his heart, that bit of white stretched across her palm and wrapped around her wrist. He couldn't change the past, but the future was wide open. Their future.

Sean pointed to the sofa. "Sit there." When she did, he smiled, knowing he'd just witnessed one of the few times she would ever follow such a direct order. "First things first," he murmured. Kneeling in front of her, Sean took her uninjured hand in his. "I seem to be getting in the habit of asking you to marry me. So let's consider the first time was practice." He kissed her fingers. "This one's for real. Will you marry me, Mel, even though I'm moody and mean and a thorn in your very lovely rear end?"

Mel squirmed and tugged her hand out of his and shoved it into her pocket. Wearing a tentative smile, she pulled out his ring. When he would have taken it from her, she shook her head and closed her fingers around it. "I figure

I owe you this one." Carefully, she set the ring on her finger and slid it over the knuckle. "I should never have asked you to take it off me."

Sean slid up along Mel's body, reveling in the way her softness gave against his taut muscles. He paused to press his cheek against her belly.

"Hi, Baby McGee," he whispered, choking back tears. "I'm your daddy."

He pushed her back on the sofa and nuzzled her neck, kissing her long and deep, losing himself in her taste, her scent. When she opened her mouth and her tongue tangled with his, Sean felt his control slipping. Reluctantly, he leaned back.

* * *

Mel whimpered when Sean sat up. But he pulled her to sit as well, careful of her injured hand.

"I'm sorry you got hurt." Sean grazed his fingertips up and down the top of Mel's arm, his slightest touch raising instant goose bumps. "Sorrier still I was such a jerk that I let you go to the hospital without me."

She twisted the hand over and considered the white swathe of gauze. "It doesn't hurt so much any more."

Sean picked up the thick folder he'd brought in with him. "Listen — about your little girl."

Mel pushed back the sadness. It was something she would have to deal with or it would take over her life. But just for the moment, she wanted to absorb all the happiness Sean was offering without that cloud hanging over her. She shook her head, afraid her voice would fail if she tried to speak.

"I should have been there for you when you saw your father, and I wasn't." Sean lifted a strand of hair and settled it behind her ear. His hand lingered at her neck. "I can only imagine what you felt when he told you that he'd thrown your baby in the garbage."

Tears welled, spilled over. "Sean, please, I don't want to talk about it."

He squeezed her arm. "Someone found her, Mel. Someone found the baby in the trash." He laid a newspaper clipping in her hands.

She tried in vain to still her trembling as she read about the "I-40 Baby," a tiny infant girl found in the trashcan in the men's room of a rest stop along the I-40 corridor just outside of Oklahoma City.

"She was alive when he left her," Mel whispered. Her gaze slid to the picture of a newborn baby wrapped in newspapers. Her eyes were open and she was obviously crying.

"There's a lot more, but this is the most important one." Sean took the first clipping and set it aside, replacing it with one dated just the past summer.

"*From Abandoned Infant to Champion Barrel Racer,*" she read aloud. Mel's breath caught when she saw the accompanying picture. It was like looking in a mirror back through time.

A slim teenaged girl with pale blond hair and light blue eyes stood next to an Appaloosa gelding. "*Natalie Joy Carter, found abandoned in a rest area on I-40 near Oklahoma City, started life off hard, needing life-saving open heart surgery before she was twenty-four hours old. Now she rides hard for the wins she has accumulated in ladies barrel racing events.*" Tears soaked Mel's cheeks.

Sean wiped them with a soft tissue, but they were falling too fast.

She sniffed. "My baby's a rodeo star."

"Read the horse's name."

Skimming the article, Mel finally found it and laughed. "Aces High."

"Sweetness, Ben Jamison took the liberty of contacting the parents. They were shocked to find out that their daughter had been stolen from you." Sean brushed a hand over her hair. His caring meant the world to her always, but never more than in this moment. "They're a little afraid you'll want to have her come live with you."

Mel shook her head, unable to take her eyes off the little part of herself she'd never known, other than the kicks she'd felt in her womb. "No... I'd never take her from her parents."

"They sent you a letter. That's the only thing I didn't look at."

Mel dashed at her sopping wet eyes. "I can't see. Will you read it to me?"

His hands trembled as he unfolded the single blue sheet of paper.

Dear Melanie,

I hope it's okay for me to think of you as Melanie. My name is Vanessa Carter, and my husband and I adopted your baby girl. Mr. Jamison told us the story of how she was stolen from you before she was left at the rest stop. I'm so very sorry that happened to you, but when my husband found her in that trash can, it was like a prayer had been answered. I can't have children of my own, and it seemed like God had brought this little angel into our lives. She needed open heart surgery right away to switch around the main blood vessels in her heart. She had a rough start but as soon as her heart was repaired, she thrived. We were allowed to adopt her, and we couldn't love her more if we had given birth to her.

We have always been honest with her that she's adopted. We knew she'd hear the story of how she was found, so we didn't lie about anything. But we did tell her that we didn't know why her mother had to give her up. We only knew it must have been something very hard to do.

Natalie Joy would like to meet you someday, and we would like that, too, if you decide you want to. Hugh and I are very afraid that you will want custody of our little girl. The thought of saying goodbye to her isn't something we want to face. We only hope that if you decide this, we can get together and think about what is best for all of us.

Your representative knows how you can reach us. Thank you very much for our little angel. We've tried to take the very best care of her.

Blessings,
Vanessa and Hugh Carter

Mel wiped her eyes for the millionth time. "Stupid hormones."

Sean folded the letter and set it on top of the pile of newspaper clippings, his own eyes bright with unshed tears.

"Thank you for reading that to me. I don't think I would've gotten through it." Mel opened her memory box and set the letter and clippings inside. "I need to talk to Vanessa." She picked up her cell phone but paused before she dialed and turned to Sean. "I want you to know I'm very sure of my decision here. I know what it's like to be ripped from your family and taken away by strangers. Are you okay with my choice to let her stay with her parents?"

Sean nodded. "As long as you are, yes."

* * *

The phone sat heavy in her hand. It had been a very emotional conversation all the way around. The Carters had asked that Mel write to Natalie and tell her the rest of the story. They'd agreed with Mel that taking things slowly was the best course of action. And when Mel told them she was going to have legal papers drawn up, stating she had no intention of using her extenuating circumstances to seek custody of Natalie, Vanessa Carter had cried.

Emotions spent, Mel lay in Sean's arms on the sofa. She looked around at all her packed boxes. "You know, I seem to have just a little bitty problem." Mel pulled back to meet his eyes. "Since Sandy and I sold this place, I don't have anywhere to live."

"We can live at the homestead for a little while." Sean kissed her and nuzzled her neck. "But I guess we'd better get started on that dream house." He sat up. Grinning, he laid a hand on Mel's belly. "We need us a nursery, woman! And a swing set... a tree house..."

Mel had no need to question whether her man was happy. She covered his hand with her own. "Just so you know... this baby gets delivered in a hospital. With drugs. Lots and lots of drugs."

Sean's grin faded into a loving smile. "Just so *you* know, Sweetness... you won't be going through any of this alone."

Epilogue

Reaching across the table between them, Sean snagged a rolled-up slice of ham from the platter Mel was arranging and took a bite. Sighing, she rearranged the slices to cover the empty space. She shifted in her seat, seeking a more comfortable position.

At the soft knock on the front door, Mel's heart leapt into her throat. The Carters had arrived. A fluttering sensation rippled through her abdomen, followed by a strong push against her ribs. Apparently, even Baby Mustang — who Sean insisted was a boy he planned to name Mitchell Mustang McGee — was excited about meeting them.

"Hey..." murmured Sean. "You okay with this?"

Mel looked up to find her husband watching her with a smile playing at the corners of his very kissable lips. A breathy laugh snuck past her lips and she nodded. "Nervous, but very okay."

The trembling in her hands increased when she heard voices heading in their direction from the foyer. "We should move to the living room. The kitchen is so—"

"Perfect." Sandy added a plate of oatmeal cookies to the other dishes of informal finger food on the table. "It's perfect."

Ryan entered the room, leading a middle-aged couple. "Mel, this is Hugh and Vanessa Carter."

Mel stood rather awkwardly. In her seventh month of pregnancy, she'd given up all hope of ever being graceful again.

Vanessa Carter was a very pretty, fuller figured woman with curly blond hair. Her eyes were pale blue and gentle, and reminded Mel of her mother, Sylvia.

Vanessa smiled a little uncertainly at Mel. "Oh, my. I'd have recognized you anywhere. Just look at her, Hugh. Nattie looks just like her."

Hugh was about as opposite to his wife as it was possible to be. Tall and lean, with black hair and nearly black eyes, his smile was easy and strong. "It's like looking at our girl all grown up."

Mel tried not to be too obvious as she looked beyond Hugh and Vanessa, hoping to glimpse Natalie. But as Justin followed them into the room, Mel realized sadly that the girl wasn't with them.

"Nattie had some last minute butterflies," Vanessa explained. "She went off with a very nice young man with red hair to see the horses. I hope that's okay."

"Ricky's my brother-in-law." Mel moved toward the kitchen window and looked out. "She couldn't be in better—" Her breath caught in her throat.

They hadn't made it to the stables. Her wonderful seventeen-year-old brother-in-law was pushing the Carters' fourteen-year-old daughter on the tire swing.

Sean came and stood behind Mel. With his arms around her waist and resting on her belly, he looked over her shoulder out the window. "I recognize that captivated look on her face," he murmured for Mel's ears only.

"And I recognize that careful look on *his* face," she whispered back. "Well done, big brother."

About the Author

Kay Springsteen grew up in Michigan but transplanted to the south at the turn of the century and now resides in the shadow of the Blue Ridge Mountains, where she enjoys photography, gardening, hiking and camping, and of course spending time with her terrific family. She is a firm believer in happily-ever-after endings and believes there is one out there for everyone; it just may not be exactly what you expect or think you want.

Don't miss the wonderful sequel!

Abiding Echoes

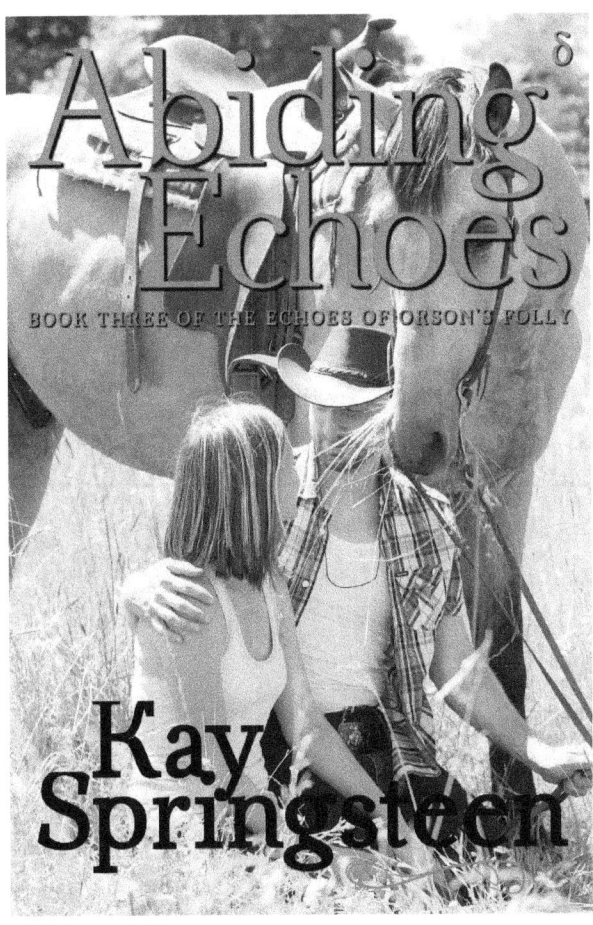

Did you read the first book in the series?

Lifeline Echoes

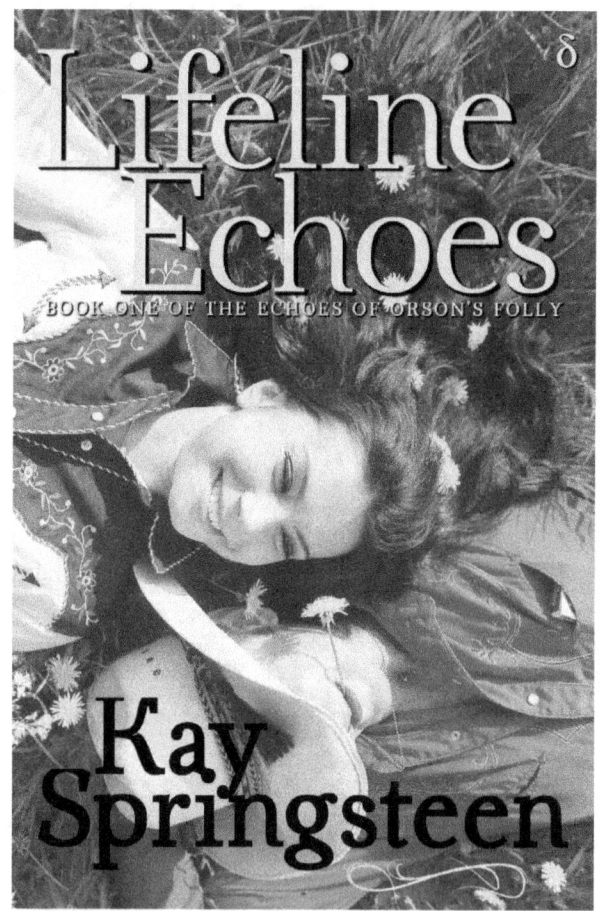

Prologue

There is no natural phenomenon which is held by all mankind in greater dread than earthquakes. Our ideas of permanence, solidity and strength are based upon the *condition of the earth, as we daily see it; so that when the firm ground shakes under us, there naturally comes over the mind a feeling of abject helplessness. ~New York Times, April 9, 1872*

Seven years earlier...

Splat.

"Son of a—"

Sandy glared down at her double chocolate iced mocha. Pale brown slush slid off the toe of one white shoe to form a sticky puddle on the blacktop.

A quick glance at her watch told her she'd have to hurry or she'd be late for her shift as a dispatcher for Los Angeles City Emergency Services. She kicked the melting mush from her shoe and stepped around the puddle of yuck and raced across the parking lot to the low brick building. Behind her, traffic on the packed freeway growled and honked.

Good morning, Los Angeles.

Sandy yanked on the heavy glass door and stepped into the coolness of the air conditioned building with a sigh.

"Morning, Alley Cat!" greeted Rose from behind the reception desk. "Lunch at Del Rio's today?"

"Hi, Rose. Yeah, lunch sounds great. Gotta run. I'm late." With a wave, Sandy hurried past the desk and into the ladies' restroom. She set her oversized purse on the counter and grabbed several paper towels. Crouching, she dabbed at the mush, noting with dismay that it had worked into the seams of her athletic shoes.

"Gross," she muttered. She'd be lucky if it didn't stink like sour milk at the end of her shift. After she mopped off the worst of it, she pushed to her feet and staggered sideways. Her hand hit the cool marble wall of the first stall as she fought to steady herself.

"What the hell?"

A low primeval rumble surrounded her, invaded her midsection and radiated up into her heart and throat. Sandy stumbled to the left then the right. The fluorescent light overhead became a flickering strobe.

Earthquake!

The word registered in the recesses of her mind, and spurred her toward the door. She had to get out of the enclosed space before the ceiling collapsed and buried her.

Sudden blackness swallowed her as the lights lost the battle to stay on. The grumble grew to a roar and then a scream. She lurched to the right, pushed off the wall, and careened through the bathroom door. The scream grew louder before she realized it came from her own mouth. The floor beneath her rolled and writhed as her cries were echoed by a half-dozen coworkers at their workstations. Shelves toppled, notebooks tumbled to the floor.

The roar dwindled to a dull grating, the heaving slowed and finally halted. Sandy lay on her side, her back jammed against the wall. Her insides still quivered and shook like jelly, the remnants of the quake continuing in her viscera. Chills washed over her as she sat up and took stock of the dispatch room. Her coworkers moved slowly, sitting and looking around, dazed expressions gracing their faces.

"Holy cow," murmured Rose, pushing to her feet and doing a three-sixty. "That felt like an eight or a nine."

Fluorescent lights overhead sputtered then half of them winked on. That would be the backup generator, running nonessentials at half power.

More operators pushed to their feet, their faces all wearing uniform dazed expressions. Jabbering filled the air as a dozen people seemed to find their voices at the same time. The cacophony crescendoed. Any second her head would explode. She closed her eyes and attempted to sort out what was being said.

"...my kids..."

"I think my arm's broken..."

"Maybe we should get..."

"Comm's down!" called out Albert Torres, IT wizard and technical problem solving guru. "Switching to backup."

Phones began ringing. Frowning, Sandy oriented herself and located her desk. Someone had to answer the calls. And there would be calls.

She located her station and placed the headset over her ear, then punched the button. "Emergency services—"

A shrill scream came over the line and assaulted her ear. Forcing herself to speak calm words of reassurance as she wrestled open her desk drawer and pulled out an empty notebook and a black pen, Sandy managed to discern that the caller was an elderly woman who was merely disoriented and frightened.

The phone lines began to flash as more calls came in. Around her, more dispatchers followed Sandy's lead and began answering.

"Backup comms are on line," announced Albert, emerging from the computer room.

The first report of a fire came ninety seconds after Sandy started answering calls. The gas line alongside the Convention Center had burst and somehow ignited. Hell had erupted in Central Los Angeles.

Sandy couldn't stop the tremors running along the inner fault lines of her own neural pathways. *I'm a professional. People are depending on me.* She studied the older system that had just been replaced by a two million dollar upgrade, only months earlier, and re-familiarized herself with the buttons and switches. Then, in a voice that only barely trembled, she dispatched Fire Station Number 9 to the L.A. Convention Center.

The first shift after Sandy's vacation was off to a very rocky start. Before that shift was over, she would learn two important things. First, she was getting the hell out of L.A. Second, it was possible to fall in love with someone, sight unseen, in twenty-three hours and fifty-seven minutes.

Chapter One

Present day

Sunny and warm, the perfect day for mourning lost love. Maybe this would be the year she'd finally be ready to move on. Even as the thought teased her, Sandy suspected it might take another cataclysmic event to let go of the man she'd given her heart to in less than a day.

Summer was a handful of days off, but the mountain air was clean and brisk, nothing like the heavy smog of L.A., where she'd first met *him*. She had no memories of the man in this place except for the ones he'd painted into her mind while they'd talked. Yet Wyoming was where she felt his presence.

Her red roan colt pranced beneath her, needing to run off his teenage-intensity energy. Dry dirt kicked up by Domingo muffled the sound of his hoof-falls to dull scuffling *plunks*, which he punctuated with occasional impatient snorts.

As they traveled, the dusty ground became more firmed and flattened. Gray rocky outcroppings thrust upward amid a tan landscape dotted by the washed-out green of desert grasses. More of the same lay between them and the scrub pines along the swell of foothills in the distance.

Sandy pointed Domingo toward those hills, finally allowing the exuberant colt to set his own pace. He catapulted them across the plain, brawny muscles alternately flexing and contracting beneath her, racing at a full gallop. The denim jacket she hadn't bothered to fasten caught the wind and billowed behind her. Chilly air worked icy fingers along the exposed skin of her neck, bringing with it a wonderful ache.

They topped a gentle rise and a sea of yellow and purple wildflowers surprised her, God's own casually sown garden. The sky overhead was deep blue and cloudless. With the prairie behind her and the snow-covered peaks ahead, Sandy pulled Domingo up inside a cathedral of Ponderosa pines, closed her eyes, and inhaled the pungent scent. It was exactly as he had described it, which made it the perfect place to remember him.

Seven years had passed, yet her pain was an exquisite, fresh wound, probably owing to the fact that she revisited the memory once a year on the anniversary of that horrific day. In the hills of Wyoming that he had loved and missed so much, in the place he had brought her to with just his words, Sandy picked the scab off the wound she never quite allowed to heal.

* * *

The job was all that mattered now. Sandy made herself disregard the toppled shelves and scattered books. She blocked out all thoughts about the likely state of her own home. As she listened to the chatter on the official channels, she kept meticulous handwritten notes regarding the status of each unit checking in.

"Battalion 9-Alpha, this is Engine Squad 9-Bravo, do you copy?" The connection was filled with static and the voice was muffled, hard to hear.

Sandy waited for the response of the battalion chief on scene. None came.

The callout was repeated, the voice sounding a bit more urgent. "This is L.A. Engine Squad 9-Bravo, dispatched to the Convention Center—" Again static broke the transmission.

Following protocol, after the second unanswered call, Sandy intervened. "Copy you, ES-9-Bravo. This is central dispatch. Your transmission is breaking up."

She checked her watch and jotted the time in her notes: 0724 hours.

The response was drowned out by a loud burst of static in the earpiece.

"9-Bravo, be advised you are breaking up," she repeated.

More harsh squawks of static burst from the receiver. Sandy winced. If that kept up, her head might explode — or at least an eardrum. Then, amid the static, she clearly heard the code every dispatcher dreaded. "9-Bravo is 10-60, this location. Code three, code three, code three... trapped..."

The code for firefighter down!

Static filled the airwaves again as Sandy punched buttons on her console, frantically trying to boost the signal.

"Dispatch, are you there?" The voice was screaming. "Central! This is 9-Bravo in need of assist. The building's coming down around us!"

Afraid to switch over to relay, with the risk of losing contact altogether, she motioned to Ellen, the dispatcher sitting next to her. Quickly, Sandy wrote on her notepad in bold black ink: UNIT IN TROUBLE.

At the next desk, Ellen nodded and switched channels to contact the Battalion 9 squad leader over the comm.

"9-Bravo, this is Central Dispatch," Sandy acknowledged. Stomach-wrenching fear threatened to leak into her voice, so she bit the inside of her cheek. Dread shot out little tentacles of hopelessness to curl around her lungs, squeezing the breath out of her. "I'm reading you, sending help your way. What's your location?"

"Civic Center parking garage — A level. The building's coming apart! We need extraction." The voice was still urgent but the panic had faded.

She had to get her own terror under control and keep it that way, Sandy reminded herself, *or she couldn't help anyone.*

"Copy you, 9-Bravo. Who am I speaking with?"

"Mick-" More static, then, "Mic-key."

Sandy scribbled everything she could make out into her handwritten notes. "Mickey, you're breaking up badly. How many do you number? How long have you been trapped?"

"Two confirmed, dispatch, possibly three. I can feel my partner. He's not moving. I heard someone else moaning down here earlier. I don't know how long it's been. I think I've been unconscious — I'm pinned — can't move. It's dark — can't see a thing."

Sandy passed off the information to Ellen so her coworker could convey it to the battalion chief. The sarcastic part of Sandy's mind registered the irony of having crossed into the twenty-first century and being reduced to the mockery of a child's game of telephone.

With a pointed shake of her head, Ellen caught Sandy's eye and handed her a message from the battalion chief. As she read, Sandy's heart fluttered in her chest before moving upward to stick in her throat. Her free hand rose of its own volition and covered her mouth, as if to prevent her from saying the words she was reading.

The Convention Center had collapsed with several men inside. Some of them were buried under four floors of rubble, while above them the fire from the gas main explosion burned fully involved and uncontained. Rescue efforts would be delayed and prospects for extraction were grim. A chaplain was en route.

God help them all! How could she tell the man on the other end of the comm that he wasn't going to be rescued? What could she say to someone when her words were likely to be the last he'd ever hear?

* * *

Ryan kicked in the clutch and rammed the gearshift into second to take yet another turn on the series of switchbacks through the mountains. The 1967 Corvette Sting Ray had been a mess when he'd bought her, but she'd been his mess. And a bargain at the price he'd wangled. It had taken almost every one of his days off over the past two years, but he had fully restored her from the engine up. The work had been a welcome distraction from other aspects of his life.

Currently, on his first long trip in her, he was enjoying the way she held fast to the road, caressing the pavement around the twists and turns through the mountains the way a woman caressed a lover.

The throaty growl of the engine wasn't quite drowned out by the whoosh of the wind over his face. It was early in the year to drive with the top down in the mountains, but Ryan didn't care. The bracing cold reminded him he was alive.

It had been too long, the guilty whisper nagged. He should never have let his life get so far out of hand. It shouldn't have taken an emergency letter from his baby brother for him to come home and make things right with the old man.

Tires squealed just a bit when he took the downward curve a little sharply. He was in the foothills now, only a few miles to go. He'd be able to open his baby up on the two-lane once the last hill was at his back. Soon the sun would drift down into the shadowy embrace of the mountains behind him, leaving him the stars for company. Damn, he'd missed the mountains of home.

Halfway through what he recognized as the last switchback, Ryan downshifted again and punched the gas. His mind registered the apparition blocking the road in front of him a bare second before reaction set in. He stood on the brake, sending the car into a slow sideways skid and stalling the engine.

"Holy hell!"

Darts of adrenaline screamed through his veins, sending his heart into a staccato rhythm as he stared at the horse and rider in the road.

Washed in the golden blush from the setting sun, the horse reared, angrily striking out at the air between them with menacing hooves, nearly unseating his rider. With a toss of his head, the startled horse reared again, baring his teeth and screaming defiance.

The red roan colt had excellent lines, but he was clearly too much for his rider. Though the horse responded to her steady touch, it was obvious any sense of control she had was an illusion. Ryan shoved the car door open and jumped to his feet, ready to pick up the pieces when the rider was thrown. But when she swung her gaze in his direction, fury blazed in eyes the color of chicory blossoms. Her face mirrored the horse's defiance.

Sparks of awareness replaced astonishment, and a grin pulled Ryan's lips upward as he lifted a hand in greeting.

"Jackass!" The rider shoved at the wild mass of dark hair falling across her face. The motion distracted her, giving her mount the opening to misbehave.

With a clatter of edgy hooves on asphalt, the big colt danced and circled, threatened to rear again, but she recovered quickly and held him down. Then she tugged on the reins, steering the agitated horse away from the road, and sidestepping him down the steep, gravel-covered incline. Upon reaching solid footing, the colt wheeled sharply around. The rider cast a scathing look over her shoulder as the horse erupted into a reckless gallop across the prairie.

Pain shot through Ryan's neck, and he realized he'd been clenching his jaw. Absently, he rubbed the back of one hand along his chin, but he kept his eyes on the horse and rider until they were no more than a speck in the distance.

"Well," he said to the early evening sky. "I've just been schooled."

He wasn't sure if he was going to shake things up with his return or get himself shaken up. But he sure as hell planned to find out who lived behind those haunting chicory blue eyes.

Shaking his head, he started to lower himself into the car when he froze. Why was it sitting at such an odd angle? He strode around to the passenger side and groaned at the sight of the front tire, rolled right off the rim from his sideways skid.

* * *

By the time she had encountered the stranger in the fast car, Sandy's earlier upbeat mood had degraded, thanks to the dull heartache she'd given herself from lancing her old wound. Ordinarily she would have laughed off the incident and introduced herself once she'd realized no one was hurt. But the moron had just sat in his car staring in disapproval, apparently waiting for her to move out of his all-important way.

Wherever the aggravating stranger was going, she sincerely hoped he didn't so much as make a pit stop in Orson's Folly. She was pretty sure another meeting of that sort would result in her doing more than yelling at him. Pictures of strangling the shit-eating grin off his face popped into her mind.

Her heart raced with the need to dispel her jitters, and Sandy let the colt have his head again. Domingo calmed them both by doing what he loved most, streaking at breakneck pace over the plains of western Wyoming.

By the time they slowed to a walk alongside the fence leading to the stable yard, her ire at the stranger on the road had mellowed to a mildly bad memory. Whoever he was, it was likely he'd already hit Orson's Folly and driven on through. The sun rested in the cradle between the peaks of two mountains, sending lingering shafts of red to cast long shadows against the blue and white buildings. Sandy closed her eyes, bracing against the little pinprick of pain, and allowed herself to remember the reason she'd first come to Wyoming.

* * *

"You hang on, do you hear me?" she ordered. "I won't go anywhere until they have you, I swear. But you have to stay with me. Promise!"

"Okay... promise." His words were slurred, his voice weary.

Sandy struggled to think of something to talk about — to keep him speaking and alert. "Do I hear an accent, Mick?"

His laugh was slow and soft. "Yep, I'm afraid so. I can't seem to get the Wyoming out of my voice."

That worked! "Tell me about Wyoming."

He sighed. "There's nothing like a wild gallop across the plains on a fast horse. If you can be up on that horse at daybreak, you feel like you're flying up to meet the day. And to be in the Red Desert at sundown's even better. If you time it right, just a split second before the sun's gone, you feel like you're inside all that red and orange glow. Then in your next breath you're standing in pitch black. When you look up, the stars are already popping out. So many stars they blend together. And there's always shooting stars for making wishes." He laughed softly. "I guess I sound a little pathetic."

"No." She wished she could touch him with more than her voice. "More like a homesick cowboy."

He was quiet for a time, then, "I guess maybe I am, Angel. I am homesick."

His quiet admission brought tears to Sandy's eyes, and she prayed he'd see those sunrises and sunsets and stars again. "So you lived in the desert plains?"

"I had the best of both worlds," he answered, his words filled with pride. "Our ranch is in the middle of a finger of desert that's nestled between two legs of mountains and forest."

"Why did you leave?"

"That's a story for another time," he said. "I'll tell you when we're on our first date."

"Are you asking me out?"

"Oh, we'll go out." His voice gave her visions of an easy cowboy grin. "I was just making the plans."

Her lips twitched at his audacity.

* * *

Cooled and brushed, Domingo nickered a soft goodbye as Sandy left the comfort of the stable and walked into the cold night air.

Stars twinkled into view overhead, millions of glistening pinpoint lights fusing into a lacy curtain of soft illumination against the darkness. A trail of shimmery light tracked across the sky.

For the first time in seven years, her automatic wish wasn't for something impossible. "I want to feel alive again."

Emotionally and physically exhausted, she tore her eyes from the stars with a heavy sigh and climbed into the rusty Chevy pickup. It was older than she was by several years, so she counted her blessings it still ran. Driving past the main homestead, Sandy tossed a wave to Justin McGee, sitting on the wide front porch of the ranch house puffing on his nightly cigar. With a smile and a nod, the old rancher politely touched a forefinger to the brim of his battered tan Stetson.

Just as Sandy reached the cedar fenceposts marking the entrance to the ranch, a pair of headlights swung in from the main road. So, the McGee men were about to receive a caller. Maybe Sean had finally convinced Melanie Mitchell to drop by after her shift at the bar.

The two sets of headlights collided, the bright beams briefly joining forces and splitting the darkness. Then the moment was gone, leaving Sandy with a vague impression of something low and fast before she was engulfed by the cloud of dust chasing behind.

Nope. She coughed against the sting in her throat. Definitely not Mel, who tended to drive her ancient economy car with the caution of a grandmother. Tough break for Sean.

* * *

Ryan braked in front of the old ranch house and killed the engine. He popped open the door but took some deep breaths before climbing out of the car.

Though the land slumbered beneath a blanket of darkness, the nighttime couldn't mask his memories. He knew just beyond the edge of the light lay open spaces, fields of green and gold dotted by brown-and-white cattle and rolls of cut hay, all in the protective embrace of the Rocky Mountains to the west.

Closing his eyes, Ryan inhaled deeply, intoxicating himself on the aromatic blend of cow manure, freshly mown hay, and mountain wildflowers that hung in the air. The sweet, somewhat earthy scent of home.

Overhead, a shooting star blazed a fiery arc through the myriad visible stars. Ryan thought of a time, so long ago, when he and Sean had lain next to their mother on a sleeping bag, watching the stars overhead. Every time she saw a shooting star, she had urged them to make a wish.

The memory faded as suddenly as it had come. What the heck was he doing, coming back to Wyoming?

"Not much call for such a fancy machine on a ranch," admonished a gravelly voice from the porch's shadows. "But you always did love speed, didn't you, boy?"

Ryan stiffened as Justin took a step forward into the light cast by the moon.

"Hello, Dad." Ryan kept his response respectful and reserved. Leave it to his father to act like this was just another homecoming after a night in town. "You look good."

Justin chuckled. "Still spreading it thick, I see." But fondness had crept into his voice. "What I look is old." He nodded in the direction of the huge barns that had been standing since before Ryan was born. "Your brother's out there locking up... if you want to go find him, let him know you're here."

The statement startled Ryan. "Since when do McGee barns need locking?"

The old man leaned against the porch railing and examined the tip of his cigar.

Ryan waited. It was maddening, but no amount of pushing would get his father to talk before he was ready.

Finally Justin shrugged, fixed Ryan with a pointed stare. "A boy goes away for sixteen years, he's bound to see some changes when he comes back a man."

Same old shit with you, isn't, Dad? But Ryan held his tongue and acknowledged the well-deserved punch straight to the heart with a nod and a wry smile. Then he turned and strode toward the barns.

Strong floodlights, mounted at the corners of each building, lit the yard. Sean was clearly visible as he slid the barn door closed and set the lock. He walked toward the stable, a black-and-white dog at his heels.

Ryan stood just outside the light's edge watching his brother, looking for a trace of the kid he'd left behind.

The skinny boy's frame had become lean and muscular. Glow-in-the-dark blond hair had toned down some, but Ryan noticed it still had a tendency to curl at the ends even though his brother kept it cut short. Sean had been thirteen when Ryan had left. He'd grown into a man.

When Sean emerged from the stable, he ordered the dog to stay inside. Then with a flexing of his muscles, he slid the door closed. Ryan raised an eyebrow. His little brother had developed some broad shoulders and strong arms. While setting the latch, Sean's hands stilled. He eased around, his body tense, ready for anything. It had always been uncanny, the way the kid had been so acutely aware of his surroundings; it still was.

Ryan stepped into the light. Green eyes identical to his own met and held his gaze. Ryan marshaled his expression and waited, unmoving.

Sean's tension visibly drained. His smile started slowly, in his eyes first, then spreading to his mouth, where it bloomed into a full grin.

"Ry!" In two long-legged strides, Sean was in front of him. "Oh, man, it's good to see you!"

In a move too sudden for Ryan to dodge, Sean folded him into a bear hug and lifted him off his feet, his carefree laughter driving out the last vestiges of Ryan's uncertainty.

Welcome home, Ryan McGee.

Also from Dingbat Publishing

AMANDA MOORE OR LESS

If Jason does have the itch, Amanda is after the tramp who's scratching it.

Scratching
the
Seven-Month
Itch

J.L. SALTER

δ

Chapter 1

Friday, May 22, 2009

Amanda Moore knew from the *Maneater* ringtone which friend was calling: the older, bossy, impetuous one. "Hello?"

"Not sure how to tell you this, but... he's cheating." It came out so easily that Christine Powers must have practiced. A rather startling announcement, considering she didn't even say hello.

"Okay, *who's* cheating?"

Christine's tense silence provided the answer.

"Jason? No way!"

"I wouldn't have said anything, but the evidence is overwhelming."

"That's insane! Jason?" Amanda's voice quavered. "Who the heck with?"

"Not certain... yet."

"Exactly how reliable is this evidence if you don't even know who she is?"

"Overwhelming." Christine always sounded certain.

"Well, spit it out! And quick. My *perfect* sister Kaye will be here any minute!"

"Oh. Maybe we should wait 'til you're not in such a rush."

"Yeah, well, thanks a bunch for getting me all riled up when I don't have time to talk." Amanda scanned her duplex as she struggled to process two domestic emergencies on top of a new crisis at work. "Look, I know Jason's not playing around. But this is very important — Kaye canNOT know ANYthing about this!"

"Mum's the word." Christine probably thought Mum was a deodorant. "Call me later and I'll give you the rest of my intel. Bye."

Amanda flicked her phone shut without reply. Her honey brown hair framed an attractive face which barely avoided being beautiful. Her bright blue eyes could make someone melt or cause them a chill, depending on the person and circumstances. Right now they were icy. Christine, Kaye... and Jason were all ganging up on her.

She checked the kitchen clock — about two minutes until Hurricane Kaye's arrival. Though distinctly skeptical of this sudden accusation, Amanda worried anyway. She knew Jason Stewart better than she'd known any other man, but significant gaps remained. In fact, maybe they didn't really know each other all that well. After getting comfortable within their relationship, Amanda had stopped trying so hard to "learn" him. And probably vice versa.

But even if Jason were taking her for granted, it didn't mean he was playing around. "Jason wouldn't cheat on me. Why would he?" *But if he IS boffing someone else, he's a dead man.* Amanda examined her short, unpainted fingernails. *Might need something else to claw that slut's eyeballs... whoever she is.*

Outside the apartment, a car door slammed — her elder sister was literally seconds away. Amanda sucked in a quick breath. *Remember, keep a hard shell so Kaye won't find any weak spot to probe. And not a word about this Jason mess, because she will immediately tell Mom and Dad that I've lost another one.*

Amanda glanced down at her work heels and smoothed her skirt. Her only ace in the sibling race — she had even prettier legs than perfect Kaye.

The doorbell rang. *She's ba-aacckk!*

Amanda's hand trembled slightly when she turned the knob. "Hi, Kaye!" There wasn't time to invite her inside because Kaye Moore-Smith was already lunging forward. They hugged awkwardly, with noticeable space between them. *No bags?* "I didn't have time to move much since you called yesterday, but there's still room to sleep and that single bed is pretty comfortable." Amanda pointed down the short hallway. It had been about two years since she'd seen Kaye and they didn't talk much on the phone, either. "Come have a look."

When Kaye had toured shortly after Amanda moved in, she'd acted like nobody could survive in less than 2,000 square feet. Now Kaye assessed everything as though she wore white gloves. With higher grades, fuller bosom, better hair (dyed blonde, of course), Kaye had always seemed the favorite daughter. Growing up, she'd been bossy and rather cold... and eight years older. She'd married right after college, moved to an upscale Indianapolis neighborhood, and quickly produced a child... a big plus. With her looks and ability to role play, Kaye could sell anything; currently she represented high-end office equipment. But their parents ignored the facts: Kaye was separated with a pending divorce and her thirteen-year-old daughter was a witchy brat.

And Kaye was finally developing a belly! Amanda hid her glee.

When Kaye peeked into the cluttered guestroom, which Amanda used as an ad hoc storage depot, she wrinkled her nose and delivered a short speech (which sounded rehearsed) about needing space to spread out, so she would find suitable lodgings in Nashville, about 25 miles west. She'd be in the area for most of four days, Kaye had said, so perhaps her company was covering the hotel costs.

"You hear anything much from Mom and Dad?" In their predictable e-mail-and-Facebook sibling conversations, this was Kaye's opening move.

Amanda sighed. "Mom forwards nearly every e-mail she gets, especially the ones telling you to send it to ten people in the next minute so you'll have good luck."

Kaye nodded without replying. Evidently she received the same.

"But she rarely sends anything about herself."

"And Dad?" Kaye asked.

"He still won't use a computer." Amanda smiled, rather tentatively.

"Well, he doesn't use phones much either, as I recall. Unless Mom slaps it to his ear."

They laughed together — the first time in many years. Amanda thawed a bit. Perhaps this visit would be different; maybe they could be more than estranged sisters. Probably not friends, but it would be nice to share something more than coolish civility.

Funny, how Kaye always seemed to be looking for something better. *Must have been tough on her soon-to-be-ex-husband.*

"So, how are things with your, uh... legal proceedings?" Amanda didn't know if her sister wanted to discuss this.

"The divorce? Oh, it's dragging out, but the lawyers prefer it that way. Tom and I had mostly agreed on all the big issues, but they keep finding wrinkles that supposedly have to be documented up the ying-yang." Kaye frowned. "More fees for them, of course." Without warning, she blurted out, "He cheated on me." Then she clamped her lips shut and looked away.

Amanda felt her jaw dropping. That was the first divorce detail Kaye had volunteered. "Oh, Kaye, I'm sorry…"

"Son of a gun was diddling somebody at work." Kaye's eyes reddened. "You want to know how I found out?"

Amanda *did* want to know… intensely. But — unlike celebrity breakups — with her perfect sister being the topic, it felt like prying. "No, you don't have to…"

"She left her nasty panties in Tom's glove compartment!"

They'd used his expensive BMW? *Shocking.* Her sibling was on the verge of tears and normally such pain would give Amanda a tiny bit of pleasure. But she just felt compassion, possibly for the first time since she'd been ten and Kaye had finally left for college eighteen years ago. "Your daughter… how's she adjusting?"

Kaye held her hand vertically. *Don't go there.* She and her witchy daughter had been at odds since Chelsea was nine, almost four years ago. Obviously the trip to Nashville was also an excuse for a beleaguered mom to just get away. Kaye shook her head. "I should leave. My reservation…"

Since she'd never intended to stay, why hadn't Kaye said so last night when she'd called? Nearly two hours of cleaning and straightening… Amanda shrugged. *Same old disapproving, resentful, competitive Kaye.* Maybe that was normal between sisters. *But it shouldn't be.*

By the time Kaye had used the bathroom and emerged with her nose wrinkled, only about twenty minutes had elapsed since her arrival. It was their longest visit in Amanda couldn't remember how long.

Amanda watched her depart. Kaye's home metropolis was much larger and finer — better stores, more culture, and supposedly fewer hicks. But Amanda would rather live with hicks than pretentious snobs. Besides, small town friendliness — underrated by most big city dwellers — was dependable and comforting.

"So Kaye is too refined to stay here overnight." *Fine.* Kaye's presence would have complicated the newly-launched crisis management effort... in case Jason the creep *was* playing around. Amanda inhaled deeply and put on her game face — she had a dinner date with Jason the cheater.

* * *

Thanks for reading! Dingbat Publishing strives to bring you quality entertainment that doesn't take itself too seriously. I mean honestly, with a name like that, our books have to be good or we're going to be laughed at. Or maybe both.

If you enjoyed this book, the best thing you can do is buy a million more copies and give them to all your friends... erm, leave a review on the readers' website of your preference. All authors love feedback and we take reviews from readers like you seriously.

Oh, and c'mon over to our website:
www.DingbatPublishing.Weebly.com

Who knows what other books you'll find there?

Cheers,

Gunnar Grey,
publisher, author, and Chief Dingbat

δ
Dingbat Publishing

www.ingramcontent.com/pod-product-compliance
Lightning Source LLC
Chambersburg PA
CBHW070733180626
46818CB00007B/2831